TO
TRUST
A
STRANGER

TO TRUST A STRANGER

KAREN ROBARDS

BOOKSPAN LARGE PRINT EDITION

POCKET BOOKS
New York   London   Toronto   Sydney   Singapore

This Large Print Edition, prepared especially for Bookspan, contains the complete, unabridged text of the original Publisher's Edition.

This book is a work of fiction. Names, characters, places and incidents are products of the author's imagination or are used fictitiously. Any resemblance to actual events or locales or persons, living or dead, is entirely coincidental.

 POCKET BOOKS, a division of Simon & Schuster, Inc.
1230 Avenue of the Americas, New York, NY 10020

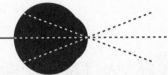

This Large Print Book carries the
Seal of Approval of N.A.V.H.

This book is dedicated to my new niece, Catherine Spicer, and my new nephew, Hunter Johnson. It is also dedicated to Samantha Spicer, Bradley, Blake, and Chase Johnson, Austin and Trevor Johnson, Jason Wearren, Justin Kennady and Rachel Rose. And of course, as always, it is dedicated to my husband, Doug, and my three sons, Peter, Christopher and Jack, with much love.

TO
TRUST
A
STRANGER

PROLOGUE

1987

"PLEASE. PLEASE DON'T DO THIS." Kelly Carlson's voice broke. Tears flowed as she looked beseechingly over her shoulder at the man prodding her forward. The wet tracks sliding down her pale cheeks shone silver in the moonlight.

"Walk down to the end of the car." The gun aimed at her back never wavered. The eyes of the man holding it were as cold and soulless as the dark waters of South Carolina's Lake Moultrie, which spread out like a black-tinted mirror before them, reflecting in its rippling surface the cold blue glitter of the stars overhead. The brand-new champagne-colored Cougar was parked on a twelve-foot-high wooded cliff overlooking the lake. It was a popular spot for family picnics in the summer. Tonight, with the temperature hovering at around forty degrees and the time well past two A.M., it was deserted except for the desperate little tableau being played out around the car.

"I'm begging you. Please." Kelly obediently stumbled forward, her gait unsteady, her boots crunching through drifts of fallen leaves. Her voice was high-pitched, near hysteria. Daniel McQuarry could have told her that begging for her life was a waste of time. He would have told her, if the duct tape covering his mouth had allowed him to say anything at all.

Woozy from the just-ended beating that had left him bruised and bloodied, sick at his stomach with the pain of what he judged to be roughly half a dozen cracked or broken ribs, he could barely keep her in focus as he leaned against the cool smooth curve of the driver's door, his hands cuffed behind his back, a gun grinding into his spine. Blinking the blood that poured from a cut on his forehead from his eyes, he watched her stumbling progress, mentally apologizing to her for not having recognized the danger earlier, in time to save them both from this. He'd been stupid, cocky, sure of his ability to follow the devil down to hell and come back out again smelling like a rose.

It was the story of his life, and now it was going to get him—and Kelly, pretty blond twenty-two-year-old Kelly, who'd made the mistake of trusting him with both the deadly secret she'd uncovered and her safety—killed.

Terror swamped the pain, causing his heart to race. He was twenty-five years old. He had a lot of living left to do. He didn't want to die.

Tough titty, as his grandma was fond of saying. Unless something went his way pretty damned fast, he was going to.

He moved, and the hideous stabbing pain cutting like hot knives through his chest drove out the terror. Nostrils shuddering with the effort of drawing in air through his battered nose, able to take only the shortest, shallowest breaths because of his damaged ribs, he fought to keep from passing out. If he did, they didn't have a chance.

Who was he trying to kid? They didn't have a chance anyway. All his highly specialized training not withstanding, there was no way that he could see out of this.

One of the four men—he knew them all, had worked and played with them as friends even while doing the job the government paid him to do—surrounding the vehicle popped the trunk. It rose, pale and ominous as Marley's ghost, above the black, gaping mouth that he realized with sudden icy certainty was intended to be his and Kelly's tomb.

He knew how they worked, and how they worked wasn't pretty. Violence came as naturally to them as breathing, and anyone who posed a threat to them ended up dead. They'd beaten the information they'd needed out of him—or at least, so they thought—and now that they had it, he was just so much garbage to be disposed of. Kelly too, despite the fact that she was the wife of the boss's son.

"Daniel, do something." Kelly's eyes were wide and terrified as she looked around at him. Her narrow shoulders in the black leather blazer she wore over jeans were visibly shaking. "Can't you *do* something? They're going to kill us. Please don't let them kill us." She started to sob, terrible wrenching sobs that hurt him to hear, and turned toward the man behind her. "Don't kill us. I'm so scared. Oh, God, I'll do anything. Anything. . . ."

"You shouldn't've done what you did." Her captor grabbed her shoulder to stop her, turn her back around. "Get in the trunk."

"No! Oh, please. . . ." Gasping and crying hysterically, Kelly shook free and bolted, taking everyone by surprise. She bounded away from the Cougar and fled toward the road, toward the empty ribbon of black asphalt some quarter of a mile away that would have offered her no succor even if she had had a prayer of reaching it, which she didn't. Her high, keening screams rent the darkness as she ran. Daniel's blood ran cold. A memory flashed into his mind of a pig he had heard once as it was being hung for slaughter.

"Get her!" They all, with the exception of the man behind him, raced after Kelly.

It was his last, best chance to make his move. Summoning superhuman strength, Daniel gritted his teeth against bodily weakness and the torture his ribs were inflicting on him and whirled, kicking out with his leg. The movement was slow and feeble compared with his usual highly trained ferocity, but it caught his captor by surprise.

He went down with an oath.

Daniel sprang away, heading for the beckoning line of trees some three hundred yards to the left. If he could reach the woods he had the merest sliver of a chance. But even as he frantically lurched forward, bent like an old crone and in agonizing pain that increased a thousandfold with every step, he knew that it was futile, knew that he wasn't going to make it.

In the distance he heard a shot and a gurgling scream: Kelly. His heart leaped, and tears—he hadn't cried since he was seven—began to ooze from his eyes.

When the bullet caught him, it was almost a relief. It hit him like a kick from a mule, knocking him forward, sending him sprawling on his face on the hard, cold ground. Instead of hurting, though, the explosion blasted away his pain. Senses dimming, he realized that his spinal cord had probably been severed, and that there was a great pumping hole in his chest. Blood was gushing out around him like water from a hose. Within seconds he was lying in a dark gleaming pool of it.

The good news was, he didn't feel pain any longer. He didn't feel afraid. What he felt was—cold.

The bad news was, he wasn't going to make it. He wasn't going to see his grandma or mother or brother or anyone or anything else he loved ever again in this life.

More tears leaked from his eyes at the thought.

But by the time they came for him, two of them, lifting him up by his armpits and his knees, carrying him back toward the car, he was able to look up at the star-studded sky with a little smile on his lips. When they shoved him into the trunk beside Kelly— poor dead Kelly, her eyes stared at him glassily—and shut the lid, closing him into darkness forever, he was able to hold that image in his mind.

He was still seeing that beautiful spangled sky as he died.

1

WAKE UP.

Julie Carlson's eyes blinked open. For a moment she lay still, heart racing, staring groggily into the darkness, not sure what had awakened her or why she felt so frightened. It took only a moment or so for her to realize that she was lying in her own bed, in her own bedroom, listening to the familiar hum of the air conditioner as it kept the sweltering heat of the July night at bay and smelling the comforting aroma of her own smooth clean sheets. Her potbellied teddy bear, a poignant memento of her late father, sat stolidly in its accustomed spot on the bedside table. She could just see the comforting shape of it by the faint glow of the alarm clock.

She must have had a nightmare. That would explain why she was curled up in a tight little ball under the bedclothes when she usually slept sprawled on her stomach; it would account for the now-slowing thud of her heart; it would explain her sense of— there was no other word for it—dread.

Something's wrong.

Although the words were distinct, the urgent whisper was in her head. She was all alone in her bedroom, all alone in the whole huge upstairs of her house. Sid, the dog, was obviously spending another night in the guest room.

At the thought, Julie felt her stomach knot. She had gone downstairs around eleven, to find her husband sitting on the couch in the den watching TV.

"I'll be up after the news," he'd said. Not wanting to start a fight—all they did lately was fight—she'd crossed her fingers and gone back upstairs to bed without uttering so much as a cross or demanding word. But here it was—she focused on the clock—at two minutes after midnight, and she was still alone in their bed.

Maybe—maybe he was still coming. Maybe he was watching Letterman. Maybe tonight Leno had an especially fascinating guest.

Get real, she told herself, uncurling her arms and legs as anger edged out fear. And maybe the Pope was a Protestant, too.

Listen.

Her attention immediately refocused. Trying not to be creeped out, Julie put out a hand, groping for the switch to the bed-side lamp.

Then she heard it, and froze.

The distant sound—vibration really—of the garage door going up made her eyes widen and her fists clench.

Her heart gave an odd little leap. Her stomach heaved. She forced herself to take a pair of deep, calming breaths.

Despite all her hopes, all her prayers, it was happening again.

Oh, God, what should she do?

Julie Carlson didn't know it, but she had less than an hour left to live.

Other than a single light in a downstairs room, her house was dark. It was a big house in an exclusive gated community just west of Charleston, and, if all went according to plan, in a few minutes she was going to be all alone in it.

Then he would emerge from the shadows beneath the rustling palmettos in her side yard, break in through her back door, and creep up the stairs to the first door on the left. That door opened into the master bedroom, where she should already—it was a few minutes after midnight—be sound asleep.

Surprise, surprise.

Roger Basta allowed himself a small smile. This was going to be fun. The thought of what he was going to do to Julie Carlson made his breathing quicken. He'd been watching her for weeks, getting the household schedule down, making his plans, anticipating. Tonight he got to enjoy the fruits of all that labor.

Sometimes, and this was one, he loved what he did for a living.

The light went out downstairs. The house was now totally dark.

Just a few minutes more.

He fingered the snapshot in his pocket. It was too dark for him to be able to see it, but he was nearly as familiar with the image on it as he was with his own face in the mirror. Julie Carlson in a white bikini, slim and tanned and laughing, poised to dive into the swimming pool in her own backyard.

He'd taken it himself three days before.

One of the quartet of garage doors that faced his position rose, and seconds later a big black Mercedes purred silently down the driveway. The husband was leaving, right on schedule.

The garage door closed again. The Mercedes turned left at the end of the driveway, and drove away toward the interstate some five miles distant. The house was once again dark and quiet.

Everything was going down as expected.

The burglar alarm would be off, which made his job just that much easier. He had a window of maybe three and a quarter hours to get in and out before the husband returned. He would need far less.

Although he might want to linger over this one. Remembering the picture, he smiled. He definitely wanted to linger over this one.

Julie Carlson was a babe.

His instructions had been to make the hit look like anything but the professional, targeted job it was.

His reply had been, Can do.

Crouching, Basta set the small black satchel he carried on the carpet of golf-course-quality grass that covered the lawn and unzipped it. The steamy July heat, complete with swarms of hungry mosquitoes and a faint fruity scent, wrapped uncomfortably around him. It reminded him that he was wearing long pants and a cotton turtleneck, both black, on a night that cried out for shorts and not much else. A quick rummage through the contents reassured him that everything he might need was in the bag: burglary tools, duct tape, a small flashlight, a thin nylon cord and a pencil to use as a garrote, a box of surgical gloves, another of condoms. He touched his knit cap, making sure it fit tightly around his head and over his eyebrows. He'd shaved his body completely so as not to leave telltale hairs at the scene, but shaving his head and eyebrows would, he feared, make him too memorable to those who might be questioned in the aftermath of the crime. The last thing he wanted was to be memorable.

Besides, his thinning gray hair gave him an innocuous look, he felt. Countless people usually saw him in the days before a hit—neighbors, passersby, convenience-store clerks, trash collectors—but nobody ever remembered him, because he looked like a fifty-something Joe Average. DNA notwithstanding, the cap worked. The first two hadn't had time to dislodge it before he'd had them duct-taped into immobility, and Julie Carlson wouldn't either.

He was that good.

Sliding the flashlight into his pocket, he rezipped the bag, picked up his pistol, stood up and headed around to the back of the house. The swimming pool sparkled in the moonlight. Lush pots of tropical flowers gave off a heady scent. Cicadas and crickets and tree frogs sang.

South Carolina would be one of his favorite states, he thought, if only it wasn't so damned hot and humid in the summer.

The back door, the sliding one opening

onto the stone patio and the swimming pool, was his target.

In a matter of minutes he'd be inside.

Piece of cake. The alarm was off, the locks were laughable, the woman was alone, and they didn't even own a dog. Might as well hang out a sign: *Come and get me.*

A light came on downstairs.

Basta froze in his tracks in the act of reaching for the doorknob, frowning at the window that was suddenly glowing warmly from within. This was unexpected. He retreated a few stealthy paces to the concealing shadow of an enormous magnolia, his senses on high alert. He'd been casing the house for three weeks, and she'd never once turned on a light after her husband was gone. Was she sick? Did they have company? No, he couldn't have missed that.

What gave?

The light went off as suddenly as it had come on, and the house was dark and still once more. He stared meditatively at the looming facade, the shiny black windows, the two doors that he could see, probing the darkness for her with every instinct he possessed. He was so attuned to her now as predator to victim that he fancied he could almost hear her breathing through the brick walls.

Where was she?

A sound made him turn his head sharply. It came from the side of the house where he'd waited until just moments before. Alert as a dog on the hunt, taking care to stay deep in the shadows, he retraced his steps until he once more stood beneath the palmettos. His eyes widened as he saw that another of the garage doors was open now.

His pistol came up, but there was no way he could use it.

He could do nothing but watch as Julie Carlson's silver Jaguar nosed out of the garage, gathered speed going down the driveway, then turned left at the street and vanished like a bat into the night.

Just as quick as that.

He was left to look blankly back at an empty house as, with a barely audible thump, the garage door closed again.

She was gone. It took a minute or so for that incontrovertible fact to sink in. When it did, he felt empty, cheated. A surging anger at having his careful plans disrupted threatened to swamp his previously good mood.

Could she have somehow known he was there? Basta looked quickly around, wary of a trap. Given the group he worked for, a double-cross was never beyond the realm of possibility.

Then good sense reasserted itself. There was no trap; he was too valuable to the organization for that. And she could not possibly have known he was there unless she was psychic.

The most logical explanation was that some sort of emergency had arisen. What, he didn't know, but then, he didn't need to know. The pertinent thing was that, sooner or later, she would be back.

And he would be waiting.

The certainty of that was calming. Glitches of this sort happened even to consummate professionals such as himself.

Acknowledging that, Basta felt better. Circling back around behind the house, he even began to hum. When he realized what the song was, he felt a spurt of amusement at the sheer appropriateness of it.

"Ti-i-ime is on my side. . . ."

2

"I DON'T WANT TO HURT YOUR FEELINGS or anything, McQuarry, but you sure are one ugly-ass woman."

Mac shot his partner a withering look. Hinkle, walking beside him, was snickering openly. It was a suffocatingly hot Friday night in July, and the two of them had just met up in the parking lot of the Pink Pussycat, one of Charleston's most notorious gay bars.

"Hey, I feel pretty, all right? Back off."

"*I* wouldn't date you, that's for sure."

"You are dating me, so shut the hell up." Mac's spike heel caught on a crack in the pavement and he stumbled, nearly twisting his ankle. Grabbing Hinkle's arm, he recovered his balance with no harm done beyond a warning twinge. "Shit. How women walk in these things beats the hell out of me. My feet hurt already. I'll be a cripple before the night's over."

Chortling, Hinkle pulled his arm free. "You better be keeping them hands to yourself, homes. Rawanda's the jealous type. She'll kick your ass, she catches you molesting me."

"You're just lucky the guy's fucking prejudiced. Otherwise your black ass'd be in this getup."

"I'd be lookin' good, too, unlike some people I could name. Hey, man, you can't go scratchin' yourself if you're gonna hang with me. It's not ladylike."

"I'm not scratching myself, I'm pulling up my fricking panty hose." Mac gave the waistband, which seemed more determined to head south than General William Tecumseh Sherman on his Civil War–era march to the sea, another savage tug. "Shut up, here we go."

They joined the throng on the sidewalk in front of the bar.

Located in the middle of a run-down area

taken over long since by girlie bars and porn shops, the Pink Pussycat was a three-story cinderblock building painted flaming flamingo with a giant, reclining neon cat swilling a martini affixed to the front wall. The small curtained windows were outfitted with black iron bars like a prison. A bouncer checking IDs stood just outside the door. It was near midnight, and there was a line. At least half the patrons, Mac was relieved to see, looked as freaky as he felt. He was six-one barefoot, maybe six-four or six-five in the damned spindly heeled shoes, which meant that at the moment he towered over the crowd. Oh, well, at least being able to see over everybody's head would make it easier to spot their target.

According to his sources, Clinton Edwards had a thing for buxom blond drag queens. And since Edwards' wife was paying through the nose so she could nail him good in their divorce, Mac was willing to turn himself into a buxom blond drag queen, wired for pictures and sound, to get the dirt. He hated domestic cases, hated them with a passion, and this one was even slimier than most, but McQuarry and

Hinkle, Private Investigators, were not successful enough to be particular about the jobs they took.

In other words, if it paid, he sashayed.

"That'll be ten bucks." The bald, multi-earringed bouncer looked them over without interest. In the spirit of getting into his role, Mac almost batted his heavily mascaraed eyelashes at him. But nah, the guy was shorter than he was but stocky, one of those weight-lifter types, and who knew, he might get into it. Fending off a two-hundred-pound-plus lovestruck fruit was not on tonight's agenda.

Well, it was, maybe, but in any case not this particular lovestruck fruit. Edwards weighed somewhere north of two-fifty, according to his bio, but he was sixty years old and all lard.

Yum-yum, Mac thought with an inward sigh. Just his type.

The things he did to earn a living.

Hinkle paid, and they walked inside. It was dark and smoky and smelled of beer and BO. Plastic palm trees adorned the corners, and the DJ was playing "Margaritaville." Couples, some male-male, some female-female, some who-knew-what, swayed on the tiny dance floor in the middle of the room. Up on the stage, a blonde with boobs the size of basketballs stripped in time to the music. She was peeling off her gold lamé panties before Mac realized to his horror that she wasn't a woman. Averting his gaze, he forced his mind back to business and scanned the room for their quarry.

Somebody grabbed his ass.

"Yow!" Mac was so surprised he jumped a foot straight up in the air. Landing on his spike heels, he wobbled, tottered, and nearly went down. Catching himself on a table, he got his ankles straightened out and turned around. It was all he could do to stop himself from reaching for his Glock, which was conveniently holstered in his eighteen-hour bra.

"Hey, now, don't you be grabbin' my bitch." Hinkle's grin as he warned the bespectacled accountant type who was looking Mac up and down with clearly lascivious intent made Mac long to pop him one.

"Sorry, man, I didn't realize she was with somebody." The accountant held up both hands in a gesture of peace, leaned back in his chair, and picked up his beer. Over the

mug's rim, his eyes met Mac's with an unmistakable message. Seeing that Hinkle's
attention was briefly elsewhere, his lips
pursed in a silent kiss.

Mac's eyes widened. Then he gritted his
teeth and managed a saccharine smile.

"See you around," the accountant said.

"Yeah, see ya." It was his best falsetto.
Careful to keep his assets out of reach,
Mac turned and minced toward the bar.
Christ, now both ankles were giving him
trouble. He had to remind himself again
just how much Mrs. Edwards was paying
them. If he hadn't, he would have turned
tail there and then and gotten the hell out
of Dodge.

"From now on, you watch my back," he
growled over his shoulder at Hinkle. But
Hinkle wasn't looking at him. He was staring across the room, an arrested expression on his face.

"Shit, there he is."

"Where?" Alert now too, Mac followed
his gaze. Sure enough, Edwards was
seated with a gorgeous-looking blonde—
Mac had to remind himself that the babe
was a *guy*—at a little round table in the corner. As he watched, the blonde stood

up, smiled flirtatiously at Edwards, then headed across the room. She disappeared inside a door adorned with a neon sign that read LADIES.

Jesus.

"Looks like you're on, boss," Hinkle said under his breath.

Mac looked at that door, looked back at Hinkle, and resigned himself to the inevitable. Sometimes a man had to do what a man had to do.

"You know," he said in his creaky falsetto, "I think I have to go tinkle."

With Hinkle laughing like a juiced-up hyena behind him, Mac teetered off to make a girlfriend of the blonde. If she could be persuaded to invite him and Hinkle to join her and Edwards at their table, his life was suddenly made a whole lot easier. If not, he was going to have to go to Plan B. He didn't even want to think about Plan B. It involved getting friendlier with Edwards than he ever wanted to be with someone who didn't have two X chromosomes.

Either way, he thought as he pushed through the door into the soft pink lighting of the little girls' room, it was going to be a long night.

He should have listened to his grandma and become a lawyer.

Julie turned another corner, took a quick look around, and, for the third time in five minutes, pressed the button that secured all four car doors just to make sure they really were locked. All right, so driving a shiny silver Jaguar deep into Charleston's bustling red-light district in the middle of a Friday night was probably not the smartest thing she had ever done. But then, when she'd left the house, she hadn't known where she was headed, so she really couldn't be convicted of total stupidity. Lying in bed listening to the distant hum of the garage door closing, she'd made up her mind, and lit out after Sid. She'd followed him blindly, desperate to know where he went when he snuck out of their house after he thought she was asleep, and she'd ended up here. Not exactly a positive reflection on their marriage, was it?

All up and down the street, neon signs blinked GIRLS! LIVE! ONSTAGE! and ADULT MOVIES and XXX. Acknowledging their import, Julie felt the knot that seemed to have lodged permanently in the pit of her stomach twist itself several degrees tighter.

Sid was forty years old and healthy as a horse as far as she knew. She was twenty-nine, with a slim curvaceous figure she worked hard to keep, great legs if she did say so herself, long black hair that waved naturally in the sauna-like heat, and a face that had taken her far from her wrong-side-of-the-track roots. She was clean, sweet-smelling, bought her lingerie at Victoria's Secret. In other words, there was absolutely nothing about her that might turn a husband off.

She and Sid hadn't had sex in more than eight months. And it certainly wasn't from lack of interest or effort on her part. But trying to entice her own husband into bed without success was ego-busting, to say the least.

Especially for someone who had once been called the prettiest girl in South Carolina.

Sid's excuse, when she confronted him about their dead sex life, was that he was under a lot of stress at work, so he'd appreciate it if she would just let him the hell alone. He was a contractor who, in partnership with his now-retired father, owned a very successful business, All-American Builders, which made tons of money developing subdivisions and building luxury homes across the state. She had no doubt that he *was* under a significant amount of stress.

But enough stress to keep him from having sex? Uh-uh. No way.

It had taken a while for the other shoe to drop, but finally it did when she'd found diamond-shaped blue Viagra pills mixed in with some vitamins in his medicine cabinet. At first hope had flared, and she waited with anticipation, sure he'd decided to see a doctor to fix their little problem. But nothing had happened. There'd been eight pills when she'd discovered the cache on Monday. By this evening—Friday—when she'd checked again, only six were left.

So she'd dressed for the night in her sexy best, even going downstairs to make sure he saw her in it, then lay in bed waiting for the jackass to come to her.

The rest, as they say, was history. What was going on became suddenly clear.

Sid was having sex, all right—just not with her.

At least he'd apparently been telling the truth about stress impairing his sexual functioning.

Ever since she'd awakened to the sound of the garage door going up, she'd been sick to her stomach. It was hard to admit that her Cinderella, rags-to-riches, fairy-tale marriage had about as much life left in it as yesterday's roadkill. To make matters worse, her whole family was now dependent on Sid: her mother and stepfather lived in a house he owned; her sister's husband worked as a vice-president at his company, a job that paid Kenny perhaps three times what he was worth, enough for Becky to stay home with their two girls.

Divorce was such an ugly word. But Julie had a sinking feeling that she was looking it right in the face.

Until just a little while ago, when she'd finally had enough sense to add two and two and get four, she hadn't allowed herself to seriously consider ending her marriage. Maybe, she kept telling herself, things would get better. Maybe work stress really was the reason Sid wasn't interested in her sexually anymore. Maybe there was also a perfectly reasonable explanation for why he was so cold and brusque to her most of the time, and why he slept in the spare bedroom, and why he snuck out at night after she had gone upstairs to bed.

Yeah, and maybe there was an Easter bunny, too.

She'd asked him about all those things, nicely and at the top of her lungs and every other way in between. His response had been that the stress of keeping her in the style to which she was definitely not accustomed had both robbed him of his manhood and given him insomnia, he slept in the spare bedroom because he didn't want his insomnia to keep her awake, and when he couldn't sleep, he sometimes went out driving around his subdivisions. Looking at houses he'd built relaxed him.

Her response was, Uh-*huh.*

But still, coward that she was, she had wanted to believe. A stable home, a stable marriage, were precious to her. As a child, she and her mother and sister Becky had been so poor they'd sometimes lived in homeless shelters. Hunger wasn't some abstract concept involving starving children in Africa—from experience, she knew exactly how it felt. Her looks had gotten her and her family out of that hell and had won her Sid, the handsome millionaire ultimate prize she'd been dreaming of all her life. She'd fallen wildly in love with him when she was barely twenty, and he, in turn, had seemed to adore her. But somehow, over the course of eight years of marriage, it had all gone wrong.

The love had disappeared from their marriage like air escaping from a tiny hole in a balloon: the loss was so gradual no one noticed until the thing went flat.

So here she was, at quarter to one, caught in a snarl of traffic on this X-rated street just around the corner from the Citadel, spying on her husband. Who had certainly not built a home anywhere in the vicinity that she knew of.

She should just turn around and go home, Julie told herself. Sid would kill her if he caught her following him—and she'd lost him anyway. She'd seen his big black Mercedes turn onto this street and that was it.

When she had turned the same corner just a few minutes later, nothing. At least, no Sid.

Plenty of people who made her think that

driving the Jaguar had been a bad idea, though. Like the promenading hookers eyeing her wheels from the sidewalk with dollar signs in their eyes. And the sleazy john-types who cast furtive glances her way before disappearing into the XXX doorways. And the shirtless, tattooed bald guy who crossed the street right in front of her, thumping a fist on the hood and waggling his metal-studded tongue suggestively at her as he passed.

That was it. Abort mission. She was going home. She who turns and runs away lives to follow her husband another day.

Julie hung a right into the nearest parking lot, swung the Jag around—and frowned to find her exit blocked by a beat-up blue pickup that pulled in behind her.

Her frown deepened when the doors opened and a pair of muscle-bound skinheads in sagging jeans and wife-beater undershirts got out. As they approached the Jag, Julie's eyes widened. A quick glance around told her that there was no place to go. Parked cars ringed the lot on all sides. There was only one exit—and the pickup loomed between her and it.

Instinctively she punched the lock button

again. It clicked vainly. The doors were already locked. The windows were up. The punks kept coming. What else could she do? Her cell phone was in her purse. Julie grabbed her shoulder bag, ripped open the zipper, thrust her hand inside, and rooted frantically around. A hairbrush—makeup—a jumble of miscellaneous junk—where oh where was that phone?

Just as her fingers closed around it, knuckles rapped on her window. Julie looked up to find an Eminem clone grinning through the glass at her.

"Hey, open up."

His tone was almost friendly, but the gun in his hand was not.

Julie's heart began to pound. Oh, God, she was about to be mugged, or carjacked, or worse. What was she going to do? What *could* she do? He was armed with a gun. She was armed with a cell phone.

If it came down to a duel, she was willing to bet that he could shoot her before she could punch in 911.

Whichever way it worked out, there would be no keeping this a secret. Sid was bound to find out. And if her husband discovered that she'd followed him into Charleston, he would kill her.

Always assuming that she was still alive to be killed, of course. The thought of Sid knowing what she'd done was scary, but the delinquent at her window was a more immediate threat.

"I said open the god-damned door, bitch."

Her assailant didn't sound friendly at all this time. He'd just been kind of holding the gun at waist level before. Now he was leveling it at her.

Julie imagined a bullet shattering the glass and tearing into her flesh.

Her heart sped up until it could have run a four-minute mile. Her mouth went dry. Her fight-or-flight impulse kicked in, and it didn't come down on the side of fighting. Slamming the transmission into reverse, she stomped the gas and rammed the heel of her hand down on the horn at the same time. The Jag shot backward. The horn blared. The thugs cursed and gave chase.

And the Jag crashed into the side of a black Chevy Blazer that was just at that moment backing out of a parking space.

The impact threw her forward, and

brought the Jag to a shuddering stop. At about the same time her window shattered, showering her with glass. Her head whipped around in time to see the punk who had knocked on her window thrust his arm into the car and pull up the lock. Before she could do anything but gasp, her door swung open, the punk leaned across her cool as a Popsicle to unfasten her seat belt, and she was yanked from her seat.

Her butt and elbows hit the pavement hard and she cried out. The punks jumped into the car. She barely had time to roll out of the way before her Jag and the pickup that had blocked it peeled rubber out of the parking lot.

The bad news was, her Jag had been stolen. The good news was, she was relatively unharmed.

The plaintive lament of a slide guitar and voices, both reaching her ears from a little distance, brought her out of her first shocked immobility. Her phone, she discovered, making a quick inventory, was still in her hand. She'd lost her car, but she still had her phone. Frantically she punched in 9, then paused, recovering enough wit to think the situation through. She was sprawled out in the parking lot of some girlie joint deep in the heart of Charleston, lying on pavement that was hot enough to toast bread even so long after sundown, wearing nothing but her hubby-come-hither sleeping attire of hot pink satin tap pants and a skimpy matching top, along with a pair of Nikes. Her butt was bruised, her elbows stung—and her car was gone. How was she ever going to explain this to Sid?

Oh, God, what if it hit the papers?

Maybe calling 911 was not the best idea, she thought with her finger poised above the button. But what else was she going to do?

"Have a fight with your boyfriend?"

The voice was masculine. The vision that filled her eyes as she glanced up in response was anything but. Pointy-toed black patent stilettos big enough to swim in. Muscular calves in opaque black panty hose. A red sequined skirt that stopped several inches above a pair of athletic-looking knees. A shiny black blouse with a deep décolletage that was filled in with a red and black polka-dot scarf. Breasts the size and shape of traffic cones. Long platinum blond hair. A lean hard chin and manly features whose gender was given the lie by garish makeup ladled on thick. All this on a broad-shouldered, narrow-hipped frame that stood easily six and a half feet tall. The overall effect was Dolly Parton morphed with the Terminator.

She must have been gaping, because the question was repeated with a hint of impatience. It recalled her to the full dimensions of her dilemma, and the oddity of her questioner was forgotten.

"They stole my car! Those two punks—they stole my car."

Julie peeled herself off the pavement and scrambled to her feet. Stabs of pain from her butt and elbows were ignored as she stared helplessly in the direction in which her car had disappeared. The street and sidewalks were still clogged with traffic, vehicular and otherwise, but her car was no longer in sight. Neither was the pickup. There was an intersection just half a block away. They could have turned left—or right.

Her legs went rubbery, and she swayed a little before she could lock her knees into place. A surprisingly masculine-feeling hand closed around her upper arm, steadying her.

"Are you drunk?" The voice was surprisingly masculine, too, given the appearance of its owner, and faintly disapproving. Glancing up, Julie confronted the full glory of twin arches of sky blue eye shadow above sea blue eyes and gleaming scarlet lips above a strong chin with the faintest hint of five-o'clock shadow, and knew despair. There was no help to be had here.

"No!" Impatient, she jerked her arm free, raised the phone, and added a 1 to the 9. Then she paused. Sid . . .

"You know, you banged into my car pretty good. You have a license? Insurance?"

"What?" She was so busy performing a fast mental search through the pros and cons of a variety of actions that she had pretty much blocked out everything else.

"License? Insurance? You know, the kind of information most people exchange when they've had a wreck?"

Julie took a deep breath, and tried to focus on what was being said to her. One problem at a time. Arnold and Dolly's bastard offspring was obviously afraid that he—she—oh, whatever—was going to be stuck for the damage to his car. A glance beyond him told her that it was pretty substantial. The dent extended from the middle of the right rear door to past the wheel well.

"Yes. Yes, of course I have a license and insurance. Oh, my purse is in the car. *They stole my car.* I have to get it back." Her finger shot to the final 1 and then she paused again, glancing despairingly toward the intersection. No doubt about it: the Jag was long gone. There was no way to keep this secret from Sid. She might as well go on and bite the bullet and call the police and be done with it.

Still she hesitated, racking her brain to come up with an—any—alternative. She glanced up appealingly, only to find that he was giving her the once-over. Julie was almost sure of it. She had been on the receiving end of enough of those looks to recognize it for what it was.

A bubble of near-hysterical laughter rose in her throat. How much worse could this night get? Her probably cheating husband had snuck out of their home after she'd gone up to bed. She'd chased him onto a block that looked like vice cops should be swarming all over it. There she'd had a wreck and been assaulted and her Jaguar had been stolen. Now she was standing in her skimpy satin husband-bait in the parking lot of some sort of sex bar with a drag queen checking her out.

About to call the cops.

Life didn't get much better than that.

He finished his perusal of her body, glanced up, and their gazes met and held. Hers was indignant, challenging. She was *not* in the mood to be sexually harassed by what looked like the humongous hooker from hell. His had something she thought she recognized as being very male in it. After the briefest of pregnant moments he broke off eye contact, and his gaze dropped down her body again. Blatantly this time.

Julie bristled and opened her mouth to slay him with a few choice words.

He beat her to it.

"Girlfriend, you really should be wearing heels with an outfit like that," he said in a slow, faintly disapproving drawl.

He'd been checking out her *shoes?* Julie felt insane laughter bubbling up her throat.

She swallowed it along with the blast she'd been getting ready to flatten him with, took a deep, calming breath, and glanced around.

People had entered the parking lot since she'd jumped to her feet: an entwined couple and an extravagantly dressed woman, walking separately, heading for their cars. It said a lot for the standards of the area that they didn't even give her in her sexy pj's and Amazonia in all her jaw-dropping glory a second glance.

Not that it mattered. The only thing that mattered was getting her car back and getting home before Sid. The problem was, how was she supposed to do that?

"Damn Sid anyway," she muttered aloud. This entire disaster was every bit his fault.

"Miz Carlson?" Amazonia asked then, on a faintly disbelieving note. Julie's eyes widened and shot to his face. Her previous conviction to the contrary, the night had suddenly gotten much, much worse. Whoever or whatever this—this person was, he knew her name.

Julie's heart began to slam against her breastbone. She met his gaze wide-eyed. A denial trembled on her lips, but she realized almost at once that it would only make her look foolish, and the situation even more questionable. There was no hope of concealing anything now. Might as well just punch in the final 1 and get it over with.

"Y—yes."

There was the tiniest pause as the heavily made-up eyes narrowed and the bright red lips thinned."Well, now," he said as his gaze ran over her once more, with an entirely different expression. "If that just don't absolutely beat all."

Julie wasn't sure what he meant by that, but she was sure she didn't like the sound of it.

"Hey, Deb-*bie,*" a slurred voice interrupted. Julie glanced around. The couple— an overweight, obviously drunken man in a rumpled suit and a beautiful blonde in an elegant black cocktail dress who clung possessively to his arm—came up behind them and paused, the woman obviously supporting the man, who was a little unsteady on his feet. The scent of booze emanating from the man was unpleasantly strong. Wrinkling her nose in instinctive protest, Julie realized that the greeting, uttered by the man, had been addressed to

Amazonia. Debbie? Julie shot him a glance. The name seemed far too ordinary for such an extraordinary individual.

"You still got the address? It's gonna be a hell of a good time." The man's gaze shifted from Debbie to Julie, and moved over her in a way that creeped her out. "Your pretty friend here's welcome, too."

"Oh, Clint, you know I wouldn't miss it for the world." Debbie smiled and spoke in a mincing falsetto that in no way resembled the growling masculine tone he'd used with her. "You and Lana go on ahead, sugar. I'll be along shortly."

"Remember, we've got lots of blow. All you need to bring is maybe your little friend, and we'll party all night. There's plenty of fun to be had by all." Clint gave Julie a leering smile. Julie recoiled. As Lana pulled Clint away, she glanced back over her shoulder at Julie.

"You stay away, bitch," she mouthed. Then, waggling her fingers at Debbie, she added aloud, "See you later, sweet cheeks."

Sweet cheeks? Debbie? It hit Julie with the force of a blow: Lana was a man. She gaped after the pair as they resumed their unsteady journey toward the far end of the parking lot. The beautiful, shapely blonde swaying so sexily in four-inch heels was a *man.*

"She thinks *I'm* a man!" Julie exclaimed as revelation struck.

She caught Debbie's eye just then, and discovered that he was grinning.

"Close your mouth, Miz Carlson, you'll catch flies," he chided in his masculine voice, and gently tapped her slack jaw with a forefinger. Her teeth clamped together with an audible click. "You should feel flattered. You made Lana jealous. You notice she's not jealous of *me.*"

For a moment Julie felt something like Alice after she fell down the rabbit hole. This was definitely a parallel universe. Then she remembered the mess she was in, and everything else was wiped from her mind.

"My car," she groaned, and started to punch in the final 1 before hesitating once more.

"You gonna call the police or not? I got places to go and things to do here. And we're going to need that police report for the insurance."

When a six-and-a-half-foot-tall transvestite crosses his arms over his eye-popping chest, gives you an impatient look, and starts tapping his pointed patent-leather toe, the effect is galvanizing, Julie discovered. She clutched the phone tighter, but could not quite bring herself to punch in that last 1.

If she did, all hell would break loose the minute she got home.

"Look, I've got a problem, okay? I don't want my husband to find out I was out tonight," she confessed, her shoulders slumping in defeat as she lowered the phone. Debbie knew who she was and therefore almost certainly knew Sid in some way or another, although her mind boggled at picturing mucho macho Sid having an acquaintance with a drag queen. But Debbie was such a bizarre figure that it seemed all right to confide, a little, in him. He would have his share of secrets, too. Besides, she'd wrecked his car, he wanted to call the police, and she was just now fully beginning to comprehend what a really bad idea that was. She was willing to bet good money that every cop in South Carolina knew or knew of her husband, and once she called them she might just as well take out an ad in the paper describing the night's debacle and be done with. If telling Debbie a little of the truth would win her enough sympathy to give her time to think, Julie was all for that.

"Oh, yeah?" Debbie sounded interested rather than sympathetic, but interested worked too. More people were coming into the parking lot now, and a candy-red Corvette drove past them on the way to the exit. It honked, and a manicured hand tipped in long, bright red nails waved gaily out the driver's window. Lana and Clint.

"If you know who I am, then you must know I'm good for the damages to your car," Julie said. "But I really don't want to call the police."

"Is that right?" Debbie was looking at her speculatively. "Suppose we get in my car where we can have a little bit of privacy and you tell me all about it. Maybe I can help you out here."

Debbie's very masculine-feeling hand curled around her upper arm again before Julie could answer, urging her toward his damaged vehicle. Julie glanced up, registered once again the mind-boggling dichotomy of platinum curls bouncing against breasts roughly the size of the Himalayas on a linebacker's broad-shouldered frame, then allowed herself to be persuaded. Turning to a flamboyant, gender-bending stranger for help was probably only a little less stupid than chasing after Sid in the first place, but under the circumstances none of the other options she could think of were any more appealing.

Debbie opened the Blazer door for her, and Julie slid into the black leather seat. It was only as he shut the door behind her and walked around the hood to get in himself that it occurred to her that maybe getting into a car with a strange man in women's clothes might not be the smartest thing she had ever done.

3

JULIE CARLSON WAS EVERY BIT AS HOT as Mac remembered. Great tits, great ass, great legs, skin the color of honey, long, tousled black hair that would look fantastic spread out over a man's pillow, kissable lips, big brown eyes. He'd first seen her at her wedding. At the time he'd been a cop, hired for the occasion to provide security, and while he'd been full of admiration for the sexy young bride he'd been busy thinking about other things, and she had never so much as glanced his way. Her eyes had been all for her groom: John Sidney Carlson IV, born with a silver spoon in his mouth that Mac had never stopped wanting to cram up his ass instead. Back then Sid made a splash with everything he did, and his wedding—his second wedding—was no exception. There'd been a thousand guests, including the governor and more big names than you could shake a stick at, TV and newspaper coverage, and Julie Ann Williams, one month out of her reign as Miss South Carolina, for a bride.

That was eight years ago. A lot of water had gone under the bridge since then, including his own firing from the Charleston PD, which Sid, the corrupt bastard, had almost certainly orchestrated. But that was just a tiny part of his beef with Sid. The major part, the part that Mac could never forget, concerned his brother. Daniel, who had been eight years his senior, had vanished some fifteen years before. And Mac had grown increasingly convinced that Sid, Daniel's friend from childhood, at the very least knew what had happened to him.

At first, they—his mother, his grandmother, and himself, Daniel's family—thought Daniel had simply taken off somewhere. He'd been twenty-five years old at the time, after all, and a free spirit if there ever was one. Then, when months passed without a word, they began to wonder if perhaps he'd gotten in some kind of a jam and was lying low. As months turned into years, they had entertained theories ranging from a foreign prison to amnesia. Mac's mother had died ten years ago, still uncertain about her older son's fate and grieving at his absence. Mac had promised her on her deathbed that he would find his brother. So far he hadn't been able to make good on that promise.

The last time he had talked to Daniel had been during a hurried telephone call. His brother had begged out of a basketball game he'd promised to take then seventeen-year-old Mac to because of a job he had to do for Richie. Richie—as in Richie Rich—was their private nickname for Sid, because Sid lived a life that seemed dazzlingly opulent to two working-class sons of a dead-in-the-line-of-duty cop. Something in Daniel's tone had made Mac think that whatever the "job" was, it was not the nine-to-five variety, but Mac hadn't asked and Daniel hadn't been any more specific than that. Once he'd become a cop himself, Mac had, quietly and on his own time, started searching for his brother, and checking Sid out had been right there at the top of his to-do list. He hadn't really expected to find much on Richie Rich, but what he'd turned up had surprised him. Sid's first wife, for example, had walked out on their marriage at about the same time that Daniel had disappeared. Interestingly enough, she couldn't be found. And word on the street was that Sid was involved in the drug trade. Given Daniel's apparently comfortable finances, his lack of a steady job after leaving the military, and his renewed involvement with childhood friend Sid, Mac had come to suspect that Daniel's "job" for Sid and his subsequent disappearance could both be linked to a drug operation Sid was running. But he couldn't prove it. Nobody in authority seemed at all interested in taking up the investigation. The Carlsons were VIPs in South Carolina, after all, with friends in high places, and nobody wanted to call the wrath of the powers that be down upon his own head. The consensus had been shut up, get over your brother, and find something else to do. It didn't help that Daniel had spent years flirting with the wrong side of the law. It also didn't help that the ex-wife was from California, that home of all things degenerate, where she'd presumably returned before dropping out of sight.

In the end, as was none too gently pointed out to him, all he had on Sid was basically gossip. When he'd persevered, trying to get proof of illegal activity, he'd ended up getting his ass kicked off the force.

Now, through the kind of twist of fate that Mac had almost quit believing in, he was being given a second chance to get at some answers: Sid's beauty-queen bride was sitting in his car with him, looking sexy as hell in an itty-bitty pink satin getup that played up all her best points, in a jam and scared of her husband and turning to him for help.

Suddenly the gods were smiling on him.

He fished his cell phone out of his cleavage—it was lodged in there right along with the wad of athletic socks that served as his right tit, while his Glock nestled securely under the wad on the left—punched a button, and started the car, all at approximately the same time. The AC blasted out hot air. He turned it down and rolled down the windows until the interior could reach a decent temperature. Street sounds formed a steady background noise not unlike the buzz of a giant insect.

"Uh, wait a minute." Julie Carlson sounded uneasy. The look she sent him was wary. God, she was a pretty thing. Sid had always been about a million times luckier than he deserved, and his wife was no exception.

"Sit tight," he said to her with a quick, meant-to-be-reassuring smile that he had no idea struck its recipient as downright scary, framed as it was in scarlet lipstick and platinum curls. He put the Blazer in reverse before she could say anything else and then spoke into the phone as Hinkle answered. "Yo. Change of plan. Get over to 85 Dumesnil Street and get some pictures. Edwards is having a party and I want an album."

"Me?" Hinkle squawked, his disembodied voice making his displeasure clear. "What about you? You seemed to be getting along with him real good. You turnin' tail now that the going's getting tough, you chicken shit?"

"Somebody hit my car, and I've got to sort it out. It's going to take a while. Get those pictures." He drove toward the exit. Now that they were moving, there was a breeze, which made the temperature inside the car almost bearable. Beside him, his passenger was looking more uneasy than ever. Mac smiled at her again. Sid's wife falling into his lap like this was the most promising thing that had happened to him in a long time, and he meant to make the most of it.

"Edwards doesn't know me from crap," Hinkle said. "How'm I supposed to get in?"

"Take a pizza. Pretend you're delivering. Hell, just walk in. Nobody'll notice. Edwards is drunk off his ass, and apparently there's going to be quite a crowd." There was a break in the traffic. Mac pulled out behind a big white Caddy and headed south. If the thieves were pros—and they almost certainly were—the Jaguar was long gone. But it was always possible she'd been robbed by a couple of kids out for a joyride, in which case the car might have been abandoned somewhere nearby.

"I don't think this is such a good idea," Julie Carlson said. "Would you take me back to the parking lot, please?"

Mac caught her eye, held up one finger—

wait a minute—and gave her another of those reassuring smiles. He watched her glance down at the cell phone in her hand and hesitate, and then he tracked her other hand as it crept up the door toward the handle. Was she thinking about jumping out? Not unless she had a death wish. The street was jammed with cars, and at this time of night it was a good bet that most of the drivers were feeling no pain. If he'd still been a cop, he could have done a month's worth of busts right here, knocking on windows and hauling the over-the-limit ones in.

"Yeah, like nobody's gonna notice a straight black man taking pictures at a gay white guy's orgy. I'm gonna get my ass kicked." Hinkle's gloomy-sounding voice spoke in his ear. "Shit. This always happens. Every damned time."

"Got to go," Mac said as he stopped at a traffic light, saw Julie Carlson's fingers curl around the door handle, and broke the connection.

"What was that all about?" She was looking at him apprehensively.

"I was supposed to take some pictures at a party, and now, thanks to you, I can't make it. A friend's going instead." Mac shot her a quick, assessing glance as he folded the phone and dropped it back down inside his blouse. There wasn't much positive he could say about the size-42DD Maidenform that was even now threatening to cut him in two, except that it made a hell of a holster for phone and pistol alike. That elastic was strong stuff. If NASA hadn't discovered it, somebody should clue them in.

He looked pointedly at her hand on the door handle. "You planning on getting out?"

"N-no." She looked guilty as hell. Her hand dropped back down into her lap.

"Because if you did, it could be dangerous."

She blanched.

Frowning, he spelled it out. "You could get hit by a car."

The light changed, and Mac went through the intersection, heading down toward the Battery, which in his estimation was the most likely place to discover an abandoned car. The air coming out of the vents now was cool, and Mac rolled the windows up with a touch of a button. She sucked in her breath.

"Um, where are we going?" she asked, real polite. Her hands were in her lap now, clasped around the cell phone, and she was chewing on her lower lip. She looked sexy as hell doing that. Mac noticed, and wished he hadn't. Getting turned on by Sid's sex-kitten wife was no part of his plan.

"You worried you're being kidnapped?" Realization dawned. There was amusement in his tone.

She stopped chewing on her lip, thank God, and her eyes shot to his face.

"Maybe. Am I?"

He had to give her this: she was no shrinking violet. There was challenge in the question, and in the look she gave him. His estimation of Sid's wife scooted a notch higher, even though it meant awarding Sid points for good taste.

"Nah. You're as safe with me as you would be with your own mama, I promise," he said soothingly, and turned right, onto an even more run-down street than the one they had left. Drunks and whores and people looking for trouble roamed the sidewalks here, ducking into seedy bars, keeping to the shadows away from the streetlights. Like cockroaches, most of these folks did their scuttling at night. Unlike cockroaches, some of them could be deadly. Fortunately, Mac knew the score.

"Look, Debbie, now that I've had time to think it over I think I'll just call the police." She lifted her cell phone ostentatiously; her forefinger hovered over the keypad without touching the buttons.

Debbie? For a moment Mac was at a loss. Then he remembered his new persona, and grinned. Debbie—his ex-wife's name, conjured up out of the blue when he'd glanced into the mirror in the ladies' room at the Pink Pussycat and noticed that, except for the height and shoulders, he kind of resembled her—definitely was not a normal-looking person. No wonder she was nervous.

"I thought you didn't want your husband to know you're out."

She started chewing her lower lip again. Mac, noticing, forced himself to concentrate on scanning the street for her stolen car. The hand holding the cell phone wavered.

"I don't." Her voice was low. "But . . ."

"So how about if we see if we can't find your car?"

She sucked in her breath, and her gaze flew to his face. "Do you think that's even remotely possible?"

Mac felt a stab of compunction. Being married to Sid was obviously no picnic, and she was looking to him for help. But he *was* going to help her, he quieted his nascent knight-in-shining-armor, even if there was an ulterior motive to his assistance. At least, he was going to do what he could to get her car back for her. After that, he made no promises.

He'd been gunning for Sid for too long to let a little thing like a flare of sympathy for his wife hold him back.

"Maybe. Sounds like somebody put in an order for a Jaguar of the same make and model as yours. Either for parts, or somebody wants to acquire one on the cheap. I'm betting on parts, though."

"Somebody put in an order?" Her tone was disbelieving, but she dropped the cell phone back to her lap.

He turned onto Bay Street and sped up to pass one of the horse-drawn carriages that took tourists on sight-seeing rides at all hours of the day and night and were a menace to traffic all over the city. In the distance, the bay looked black as oil except for an occasional string of lights that signified a boat. A foghorn gave its lonely call.

"Happens all the time, especially with a high-end car like yours."

Her thighs were pressed tightly together, he noticed, her long, slim, and shapely thighs that were bare beneath the crotch-high hem of the pink satin shorts she wore. Glancing down at them—he couldn't help himself—he found himself wondering if her skin tasted as much like honey as it looked. Annoyed at the direction his thoughts were taking, he shifted his gaze back out to the street where it belonged and picked up his phone.

"License-plate number?" he asked crisply, confining his gaze to her face now as he punched in some numbers. She told him, and he nodded.

"Yeah?" The grumpy-sounding voice on the other end of the phone belonged to Mother Jones. Mother was the go-to man for all the local car thieves; as a gung-ho rookie police officer Mac had arrested him twice in his first two months on the job, been first infuriated and then chagrined to discover that Mother was back on the streets within twenty-four hours each time, and then got clued in to the program before any real harm was done to Mother's operation or his own career. Fortunately, Mother was not one to bear grudges, and what with one thing and another, they'd ended up developing a mutual respect that had turned into almost a friendship over the years. If anybody could get information on a just-pinched Jaguar in south Charleston, Mother was the man.

"What you interested in it for?" Mother asked cautiously, when Mac gave him the particulars. At times like this, Mother tended to remember that Mac had once been on the other side.

"Lady who owns it is a friend of mine. Her husband's gonna go ape-shit when he finds out she let it get stolen, and she's sitting here beside me right now crying her eyes out, afraid she's gonna get beat up when she goes home."

Julie Carlson stiffened and looked at him indignantly. Mac shook his head at her, warning her to silence.

"Shee-it." Mother tut-tutted under his

breath, and Mac knew he had punched the right buttons. Mother was a devoted family man with six daughters. "Ain't no call for that kind of shit, you know? Man who'd rough up his woman, he ought to have his ass kicked."

"Yeah," Mac said, agreeing. "Can you help us out here?"

There was a pause. "If I can, you know it gonna cost you."

"No problem." He figured Julie Carlson was good for it. Hell, Sid was rich enough.

A grunt. "I'll make some calls, see what I can do. I'll let you know. What's the number?"

Mac gave him his cell-phone number, disconnected, and glanced at his frowning passenger.

"It's going to cost you to get your car back. Probably about a couple of thousand. If it can be done."

"I heard." She sounded disgusted. "I can't believe I have to pay to get my own car back."

"You don't want to, I'll call Mother back and tell him to forget it."

"No." There was a sudden note of panic

in her voice, and her hands tightened on her phone. "No, I want it."

Mac's lips compressed. She was definitely afraid of Sid. Under the circumstances, feeling sorry for her was a mistake, but feel sorry for her he did.

"Mother's going to want the money on delivery. If we're lucky, and he can find your car."

She looked worried. "I can write him a check. That is, if he brings back my purse, too. It was in the car."

A check. Mac sighed. "Darlin', he's going to want cash."

Now she was looking really worried. "I only have about fifty dollars in my purse. I can go to an ATM machine when I get it back, but I think the limit for withdrawals is two hundred dollars."

Mac thought of the cash advance Elizabeth Edwards had given him only hours earlier. It was stashed in the safe at his house, ready to be deposited in the bank bright and early in the morning. He pictured Hinkle's reaction if he knew what Mac was about to do, made up his mind, and mentally flipped Hinkle the bird. "I got it covered. As long as you're good for it. You are good for it, right?"

Sid's wife was definitely not a credit risk, and obviously she had an urgent reason to keep Sid from finding out what she had been up to tonight. The satin thingy she was wearing told its own story. She wouldn't stiff him.

"Yes. Oh, yes. Thank you."

"You're welcome." His voice was dry. The idea of Julie Carlson cavorting with a boyfriend was cheering, considering who she was married to, but unfortunately it got his thoughts going where they shouldn't again. She was hot stuff, no doubt about it—but, he reminded himself sternly, she wasn't bed material. Not for him.

What she was, if the gods continued in their current good mood, might just be the inside source he needed to finally get the goods on Sid. He would help her out of her present difficulty, and in the process pump her for all the information he could get.

Mac smiled as he turned down his street, a quiet row of small, single-story, tile-roofed homes that were reasonably well maintained but had seen better days, and parked at the curb. A motley collection of other cars had done likewise all up and down the street.

"Where are we?" She was sounding nervous again."

"My house. I happen to have some cash on hand. Besides, Mother finds your car, we're going to have to meet with him to get it back. It'd be better for my reputation if he doesn't see me like this." He made a gesture encompassing his finery.

"Oh." She looked him up and down, and her expression turned faintly sympathetic as her gaze met his. "He doesn't—know?"

"No," Mac said, refusing to acknowledge how sweet she sounded. He shut off the ignition. "He doesn't know. You coming in? You can wait in the car if it makes you feel safer."

She took another look around at the dark street, which was deserted except for old Mr. Leiferman down at the corner waiting under the streetlight for his Boston terrier to do his business, and shook her head.

"I'll come in with you, if you don't mind," she said, just as he'd been pretty sure she would.

She opened the door and slid out. He pulled the wig off, tossed it into the backseat, and scratched his head vigorously. Then he got out himself, locked the car, and headed for his front door. He could hear the delicate swish of her satin shorts as she walked beside him, and tried to shut his ears to the sound.

Reaching the porch, he unlocked the door and stood back to let her precede him inside.

As she stepped over the threshold into the pitch-dark house, a wry smile curved his lips.

Something Daniel used to delight in saying to him on the few occasions when little brother was invited into his room popped into Mac's head. It was so appropriate it was downright eerie.

Come into my parlor, said the spider to the fly. . . .

4

THE TINY WHITE POODLE that greeted their arrival with a series of ecstatic yaps and jumps reassured Julie *almost* completely. The dog was adorable, right down to her pink, rhinestone-studded collar and the small pink bow tied over each ear.

No straight man, much less a homicidal sex fiend, had ever possessed a dog like that.

"Hi, sweetheart." Julie crouched down, offering her fingers for the excited poodle's approval while Debbie flipped on a lamp. A quick sniff, and then the dog had both front paws on Julie's bare knee, begging for attention and wagging her tail so hard her whole body shook as she tried to lick Julie's face. It was a puffball of doggy lovableness that immediately sent Julie's opinion of Debbie skyrocketing. The clothes might be over the top, the wig might be too kitschy for words, but the poodle was perfect.

"Is she yours?" Just so there was no mistake.

"Yep. Meet Josephine." There was a dryness to Debbie's voice that caused Julie to glance up at him. He'd lost the wig, she registered with surprise, and his hair stood up all over his head in sweaty-looking dark blond spikes. Which, given his heavy makeup, made him look just as bizarre as before, only in a different way: Debbie as Boy George. The narrow-eyed look he gave his pet distracted her from his appearance. From it, Julie surmised that Josephine must be in the doghouse, figuratively speaking. Well, as Sid was always pointing out to her, that was the trouble with dogs: they barked, they had fleas, and they messed the floor. But, Debbie's tone notwithstanding, it was clear that he loved the animal: Josephine was exquisitely groomed, right down to her gyrating pom-

pom of a tail and little pink-painted toe-nails, and displayed the kind of innocent exuberance that was only ever seen in a cherished pet.

"She's a doll," Julie said sincerely.

"Yeah, well. This morning she ate one of my shoes." Debbie gave the poodle a dark look, and gestured at the living room in which they stood. "Make yourself at home. I'll be right back."

He clumped off toward the back of the house in his enormous high heels, turning lights on as he went. Julie was left to stand up and look around her.

It was a narrow, one-story, shotgun-style house, like many of the older dwellings in the eclectic mix of single-family homes, apartments, condo complexes, and cheap hotels that had been shoehorned into the area known as North of Broad. The room she was in, the living room, had white plaster walls, bare wooden floors, gold drapes pulled tight across the large single window that looked out onto the street, an enormous gold tweed couch with a rectangular oak coffee table in front of it, and a brown velour recliner. The TV took pride of place against one wall. Magazines and newspapers lay in a haphazard pile beside the recliner. Various nondescript prints of landscapes adorned the walls.

Debbie was clearly not an inspired decorator. It was kind of disappointing, given his flamboyant taste in clothes.

Julie sat down on the couch. Josephine jumped up beside her, her small head edging beneath Julie's arm. Patting the wiry tuft on top of Josephine's head, Julie realized that the dog smelled faintly of some floral perfume. How cute, she thought, charmed, and with relief dismissed the last vestiges of a lurking suspicion that she might have fallen into the hands of a rapist-murderer. Well, almost the last vestiges. He could still be a really kinky rapist-murderer, but the poodle made her far more inclined than before to give him the benefit of the doubt.

With her mind all but relieved of that particular worry, Julie immediately focused on another and looked around for a clock. As the saying went, time was of the essence.

Sid was usually home no later than three-fifteen. She had stayed awake enough nights listening for him to know. Which meant, if her spy project was to go undetected, she had to be home by three, complete with Jaguar.

What were the chances?

There was no clock anywhere that she could see. Too nervous to sit any longer, Julie stood and moved toward the kitchen, which was next to the living room. Josephine followed, trotting daintily at her heels, her nails clicking on the floor. The narrow, L-shaped kitchen was as aesthetically uninspired as the living room. The end of the L, obviously intended as an eating area, had been converted into a small home office. There was a metal desk with a computer on it, a chair, a pair of file cabinets—and a clock on the wall.

1:58. She had just over an hour to retrieve her car and get home before her absence was discovered.

Nibbling anxiously at a fingernail, she stepped back into the hall and glanced toward the back room, the bedroom, where her host had disappeared. At that moment Debbie himself stepped into view, emerging into the bedroom from an adjoining room, a bathroom presumably, because he was holding a towel to his head with both hands, rubbing briskly.

He was wearing jeans, but his chest was bare.

It was a very masculine-looking chest: wide beneath broad shoulders, tanned, muscular, adorned with a thick wedge of dark brown hair. His biceps were tanned too, and thick with muscle, and his forearms were sinewy and appropriately hairy. The jeans were old, hanging low on his hipbones to reveal a washboard stomach and part of an innie naval before hugging long, powerful-looking legs.

Anyone who looked less like a Debbie would have been difficult to imagine. Julie blinked at him in surprise.

He must have felt her gaze on him, because at that moment he lowered the towel and their eyes met. The makeup was gone. His hair no longer stood up from his scalp in sweaty spikes. Looking as if it had been just washed and towel-dried, it was sandy blond now and slightly tousled. His face was lean, hard-jawed, handsome. Without the distorting effect of the eye shadow, his eyes, which were a light, almost translucent blue beneath thick brown brows, were to die for. His nose was straight, his mouth long and firm and well cut, his chin square.

In short, in his masculine incarnation, Debbie was gorgeous.

Julie stared at him for a moment while all kinds of inappropriate thoughts chased themselves around her brain.

"You *are* gay, right?" The question just popped out, and she could have bitten off her tongue the moment it did. His gaze held hers for a long, uncomfortable moment as his jaw tightened and his eyes narrowed.

"Does it matter?" The look he gave her was cool, shuttered, a little wary. Had she committed some unforgivable faux pas by asking? Probably. Her knowledge of drag-queen etiquette was admittedly a bit rusty.

"No. No, of course it doesn't," she assured him hurriedly. "I think that all people should have the right to be exactly who they are. Free to be you and me, and all that."

She truly *didn't* care if he was gay, except that, from a purely female point of view, it seemed such a waste. In fact, though, now that she thought about it, it was probably better that he was. Otherwise he was too mouthwatering for her peace of mind, especially given her hanging-by-a-thread marriage and her sexually deprived state. Anyway, she felt more at ease with him if she thought of him as a girlfriend. She could admire his physical attributes without the smallest risk of succumbing to them, which was kind of nice.

Her girlfriend the hunk. The thought made her smile.

"Whatever." He gave her a narrow-eyed glance as if to assess her sincerity, then stepped out of her line of vision, moving on into the bedroom. Moments later he reappeared, pulling a faded, faintly ragged-looking black T-shirt over his head.

Coors, it said on the front.

What your well-dressed drag queen wore on his downtime this season? Her brow wrinkled. She wouldn't have guessed it, but then, what did she know?

As she was lately learning, not much about not much.

"I really need to get home," she said, her surprise at the new Debbie ebbing in the face of the urgency of the situation. "How long do you think this is going to take?"

His expression relaxed.

"Not long. Mother will call when he has

something. You want me to go ahead and take you home, and then call you about your car?"

"No. No." Julie chewed her lower lip, thinking aloud. "Sid will notice the Jaguar is gone as soon as he pulls in. I've got to have the car. And I've got to be home by three."

"You're scared of this guy, aren't you?" There was a faintly harsh note to his voice. Julie looked at him in surprise.

"Sid? No!" She recovered, and shook her head vigorously. Too vigorously? she asked herself, then answered: Yeah. The lady doth protest too much.

"Not usually," she amended with a grimace. "It's just—Sid's not going to like it if he gets home and finds me gone."

And that was the understatement of the year.

"Miz Carlson, you out running around on your husband?" The question was gentle. The glance that slid over her was speculative, and at the same time more masculine than she would have expected, given that it came from Debbie. Of course, the last time he had given her one of those looks, he'd been checking out her shoes. Still, it made Julie remember all over again what she was wearing—or, rather, what she was not wearing, like panties or a bra. Or any semblance of normal clothes. She was suddenly acutely conscious that her nipples were plainly visible through the slithery camisole and that her long tanned legs were bare to the very tops of her thighs.

Now that Debbie had morphed into a hot-looking guy it didn't seem right somehow to be wearing part of her collection of man-bait in his presence. But of course, she reminded herself, he was *Debbie,* and they were fast becoming girlfriends, sort of, and anyway the outfit covered her better than a bathing suit, even a one-piece. She certainly had never expected it to be seen by anyone, because she'd never meant to put so much as a toe outside her car. So if he was giving her that look because he thought she was some kind of an exhibitionist, he could just quit. Anyway, speaking of sartorial deficiencies, until just a few minutes ago *he* had looked like Steroid Barbie, all tarted up and headed downtown.

So there.

"Wearing this?" She glanced down at herself derisively. "I don't think so."

"You look pretty good to me."

Her eyes flew to his, and for a moment their gazes held. That masculine look was back in his eyes—wasn't it? Or was it her imagination? Before she could quite sort the matter out, his expression changed, and he shook his head at her. "What you look like, girlfriend, is a woman who just rolled out of somebody's bed."

Her spine stiffened and her chin came up. "I did. Mine. I rolled out of bed, shoved my feet into my shoes, and jumped into my car. Where I stayed until it got stolen."

"If you say so." He sounded politely skeptical.

"I do."

"Fine by me." He shrugged. "Want something to drink? I got water, orange juice, beer. . . ."

He moved toward the kitchen, which brought him close—too close. Having him invade her personal space was unsettling—he was a surprisingly big man, and he *looked* so very male—so Julie felt compelled to move too, backward out of his path, and nearly tripped over Josephine in the process. Josephine yelped and shot toward the living room and safety, Julie stumbled, and Debbie grabbed her arm to steady her. Julie was just recovering her balance when Debbie let go suddenly and looked down at his hand.

"You're bleeding."

Julie's brow knit. There were, indeed, smears of blood on his palm. Twisting her arm around and craning her neck, she looked down and discovered a nasty skinned place about the size of a half dollar on her elbow. Blood oozed to the surface even as she watched. Until that moment she hadn't even been aware of the injury. Now that she was, she could feel it burning.

"Let me see." His hand encircled her wrist, and he shifted her arm so that he could look at her elbow.

"It's no big deal. Just a little scrape."

"Tough guy, huh?" He glanced up, met her gaze, and grinned. At close quarters, Julie reflected, those blue eyes could be quite dazzling. "Well, you're going to have to humor me. I get all light-headed at the sight of blood, see, so we're going to have to fix it. Come on."

She had to smile at the sheer absurdity of it. "Wuss."

But she didn't resist as, his hand still gripping her wrist, he pulled her after him toward the bathroom. Passing through, Julie caught just a glimpse of an untidy bedroom—chest against one wall, unmade queen-sized bed, Debbie's discarded clothing flung over a bentwood rocker in the corner so that one stretched-out black panty-hose leg trailed from the pile toward the barge-sized pumps on the floor—before she found herself in a small, green-tiled bathroom that had obviously not been updated in decades. The toilet and tub/shower combination were, like the sink, white and strictly utilitarian. The room smelled of soap. Droplets of water still clung to the clear plastic shower curtain. A jar of cold cream with the lid off was on the counter; a big scoop was missing from its shiny white contents. Obviously Debbie had just used the cold cream as a makeup remover.

"Let's get you cleaned up."

He turned on the sink taps, pumped liquid soap onto his fingers from a dispenser beside the sink, then rubbed it, none too gently in her opinion, into the open wound on her elbow.

"Ow! That stings!" Julie jumped as the soap hit her raw flesh, and would have jerked her arm free, but he held on. He was behind her in the confined space, his body keeping her in place as he maneuvered her elbow under the gushing water.

"Thought you were a tough guy." He met her gaze through the mirror. A teasing smile just turned up the corners of his mouth as the water did its work and vanquished the soap. Unfortunately, having the soap flushed away by a stream so strong it could have come out of a fire hose didn't feel much better than having the injury assaulted with soap. She wrinkled her nose at him through the mirror. His expression changed. The smile vanished, and his eyes were suddenly unreadable.

"How old are you, anyway?" The question was abrupt.

"Twenty-nine. What about you?" She pushed back against him in a vain attempt to win free of his ministrations, then suddenly stopped. His body felt hard and masculine, and having it pressed so close to hers sent currents of electricity shooting along her nerve endings. Whatever he was or wasn't, he *felt* like a guy. Her instantaneous physical reaction to that fact both unnerved her and reminded her far too forcefully of the sorry state of her love life.

It was, she reflected wryly, a sad day when she found herself getting turned on by someone named Debbie.

"Thirty-two. There, I'm done."

He stepped to the side, suddenly no longer touching her anywhere at all, which, she told herself, was a relief. She watched his face through the mirror while he directed his attention to the faucets, turning them off with quick twists of his wrists. If he was aware of the effect he was having on her, he gave no indication of it. Of course, he probably had no idea that he'd given her a thrill. Under the circumstances, she could hardly expect that she would float his boat.

"How old's your husband?"

Instead of making a move on her, which in her confused state she might even have welcomed, he handed her a towel.

"Forty." She patted her elbow dry.

"A little old for you, isn't he? You must be the second wife."

She put down the towel. He passed her

a tube of ointment and laid a Band-Aid on the sink in front of her.

"Yes, I am. So what?" She gave him a quick want-to-make-something-of-it look, then started to apply the ointment because the scrape was really beginning to sting.

"So what happened to wifey number one? Did he dump her for you?" He tore open the Band-Aid and handed it to her.

"They were divorced years ago." She accepted the Band-Aid, positioning it carefully over the scrape.

"Have you ever met her? Or talked to her, or anything?"

"No, I haven't. She's been completely out of the picture since long before I came into it." Having finished with the Band-Aid, she lowered her arm and looked up at him with a sudden frown. "What is this, twenty questions?"

He shrugged. "Just curious about how the other half conducts their love lives."

"Oh." That made sense, in a way. "Thanks for the Band-Aid."

"No problem."

Julie met his gaze, made a mental note of her own sudden vulnerability to sheer masculine good looks, and turned and headed toward the living room again.

He followed her. Josephine, who'd been an interested observer all this time, trotted on ahead and beat Julie to the couch. Julie sank down beside the poodle and was rewarded by a cold nose prodding her arm. Gathering Josephine onto her lap, she gave her a hug.

Debbie stopped a few feet away, folding his arms over his chest and regarding her with a thoughtful expression.

"Okay, let me see if I've got this straight: You rolled out of bed, stuck your feet in your shoes, jumped in your car, and drove into Charleston. In the middle of the night. Care to explain why?" He took up the conversation—or was it an interrogation?—where they had left off earlier without missing a beat.

Josephine licked her arm. Julie accepted the only affection on offer and cuddled her close. Just having the dog near was comforting. She had always wanted a pet of her own. Maybe, she thought with a glimmer of gallows humor, she should try to think of what was happening less as a catastrophic marriage breakdown and more as a golden opportunity to trade Sid in for her very own dog.

At the moment, she was about ready to go with the dog.

"Maybe I just felt like going for a midnight drive."

His expression said *yeah, right,* and Julie sighed.

"Look, I'm sorry about your car, I'm grateful for all your help, and if you can somehow get my car back for me I'll kiss the ground you walk on, but I really don't want to go into every little detail of my personal life, okay?"

"So you *are* cheating on your husband."

"No, I am *not.*"

At the outrage in her tone, he lifted his hands, palms up, in a placating gesture. "Okay, okay. Hey, if you don't want to tell me what's going on, fine. It just seems to me like if you're rolling out of bed in the middle of the night to drive downtown in your underwear, then are scared to death your husband is going to find out, something is wrong in your life and—maybe you need a friend."

His voice gentled on that last, and the smile he gave her was disarmingly charming. So charming, in fact, that it caused a pang in the region of her heart. God, he was good-looking—and she wanted to trust him, she really did. He was right, at the moment she could use a friend.

"I'm wearing pajamas, not underwear," she said for the record.

"My mistake."

"How do you know my name?" There was a wary note to that, because she was busy reminding herself that it was better to be safe than sorry. Impossible as it seemed, he *might* have some sort of connection with Sid. Of course, she realized with a sick feeling in the pit of her stomach, in that case the trick would be to keep him quiet about what he already knew.

Debbie shrugged, and stuck his hands into the front pockets of his jeans. "I've seen you around. You own a dress shop out in Summerville, don't you? Flashy evening gowns, sequins, feathers, that kind of thing?" He grinned. "Nothing in my size, though. You might want to rethink that. Us larger gals like to look pretty, too."

Julie smiled involuntarily at the idea of him trying to squeeze into one of her gorgeous gowns, none of which came in a size larger than 8. If he did somehow manage to get one on, and then actually wore it out, he would ruin her reputation forever.

"I'll keep it in mind," she said. Actually, she designed and made gowns and other wardrobe essentials for beauty pageants, and her shop was strictly for contestants and their handlers, but there was no point in going into all that.

The clock was still ticking. That thought left her unable to sit still a moment longer.

"Oh, God, what time is it?"

She put Josephine on the floor and stood up, moving toward the kitchen to check. Debbie stopped her with a hand on her arm. Too nervous now to be more than peripherally conscious of the hard warmth of that hand as it curled around her upper arm, Julie glanced up at him.

"Two-twelve." He was looking past her shoulder at the VCR atop the TV. Following his gaze, Julie realized that there'd been a little digital time readout in the room with her all along.

"I've got to get home." She pulled free of his hand to pace the long wall that separated the living room from the kitchen.

"I'm no friend of your husband's, you

know," he said, watching her. "Nothing you tell me will get back to him, I promise. And you never know, maybe I can help you get whatever this is sorted out."

The ensuing pause as she stopped pacing and their gazes met lasted perhaps a couple of heartbeats.

"I think Sid is cheating on me." Julie blurted it out. She hadn't really made a conscious decision to confide in Debbie, the words had just sort of come out on their own, but the minute they left her lips she experienced an overwhelming sense of relief. She had needed to tell someone, she realized. Needed someone to listen to her suspicions and tell her that she was being an idiot—or not.

"Ah," Debbie said, the single syllable drawn out. "And what makes you think that?"

"He's been sneaking out at night after I've gone to bed," she said. "Tonight I followed him. I heard him leave the house and I jumped out of bed and followed him. I lost him on the street where I hit your car. I was turning around in the parking lot when those punks stole the Jag."

Julie took a deep, shaken breath and

folded her arms over her chest. It felt—cleansing, somehow, to utter her suspicions aloud. No more pretending that Sid was the perfect husband, or that hers was the perfect marriage. Telling the truth was cathartic.

"Let me get this straight," Debbie said after the briefest of pauses, rocking back on his heels and giving her a severe look. "You were tailing your husband in your own car? A *Jaguar?* You ever think he might just possibly have glanced in his rearview mirror and noticed you behind him?"

Julie's eyes widened as the terrible possibility sank in.

"I never thought about that. I just jumped in my car and took off after him." Coming close to panicking at the idea, she mentally reviewed the drive.

"Girl, you're not safe to be let out." He shook his head in disgust.

Julie ignored that, reached the end of her cogitations, and felt relieved. "If he'd seen me, I would have known it. Sid's not subtle. Believe me, I would have known it."

Debbie looked thoughtful.

"It ever occur to you that maybe he's just

going out for a late-night snack or something?"

Julie grimaced. "And winding up on a street with triple-X bars and strip joints? I wish I could think so, but I don't. Besides, we—I have other reasons to think he's having an affair."

"Oh, yeah?" He eyed her with interest. "Like what?"

"On Monday I found eight Viagra pills in his medicine cabinet," she confessed. "By tonight there were only six. And . . . and . . ."

"You weren't the lucky beneficiary, hmm?" Her expression must have told the tale, because he grinned. "Okay, I get the picture. So hubby's been sneaking out at night, has he? Every night? About what time?"

"Two or three nights a week for the last month. A weekend night, usually, and one or two others. It varies. I usually go to bed around eleven, and he's out by midnight."

"You ever followed him before?"

"No."

"So . . ."

He was interrupted by a muffled ringing sound. Digging his cell phone out of the front pocket of his jeans, he opened it and spoke into it. "Yeah?"

Julie held her breath as the voice on the other end said something she could not quite hear. Then Debbie grimaced. "Shit."

The expletive scared her. He wouldn't say that if things were going according to plan, would he?

"Okay, you do that. Yeah. Catch you later."

He broke the connection, then returned the phone to his pocket. His gaze as it met hers was rueful.

"What?" she asked faintly.

"Well, the good news is they found your car."

"They did?" Hope springs eternal.

"Too late. It's been stripped. Engine, tires, even the stereo. All gone."

5

"OH, NO." JULIE FELT LIMP SUDDENLY, as though all the rigidity had suddenly evaporated from her bones. Her knees threatened to give way, and she swayed as the room did a slow revolution around her.

"Whoa!" Debbie reached out and snagged her elbows, stopping her spineless wilt before she ended up in a puddle on the floor. Mindlessly she tilted toward him, and he pulled her against his chest. He felt very strong, very solid, very safe—a rock to lean on. She snagged handfuls of his T-shirt for support and breathed.

"Okay, don't panic. We can still figure out something to get you off the hook." He rubbed her back reassuringly. Julie allowed herself the pure luxury of being comforted. He was warm, and strong, and he smelled faintly of soap and cold cream, and his wide, well-muscled chest was the perfect pillow for her head. It felt so good to be in a man's arms again that she snuggled close. Her cheek rested on a firm pec, and she could hear the slow, steady beat of his heart beneath her ear. He must have sensed her need for comfort, because his arms wrapped around her, holding her close.

She'd missed this: being held by a man. Even in this nonsexual context, it felt so amazingly good.

"Like what?" Her voice sounded despairing to her own ears. She closed her eyes, and tightened her grip on his T-shirt. Her next words were tragicomic. "I might as well just go ahead and kill myself and save Sid the trouble."

"That might be a little drastic, don't you think?"

From his voice, it sounded like he was smiling. Her eyes opened, and a swift upward glance confirmed it: he *was* smiling.

Well, she supposed she was glad someone could.

"Not really." Her voice was glum.

"You know, most people in your situation would probably just get a divorce."

Debbie's dry observation so exactly meshed with her thoughts that Julie glanced up again, startled.

"I'm thinking about it," she admitted. To actually express the thought aloud was liberating somehow. "But, to me, divorce is kind of a big deal."

Just watching her mother change marriage partners had probably traumatized her for life. As a little girl, she'd promised herself that when *she* got married, it would be forever.

"People do it every day."

"*I* don't." She took a deep breath and, much as she hated to do it, pulled herself out of Debbie's arms. Wonderful as it felt to be cuddled and comforted, it was over. Time to face the music. "I suppose I might as well go ahead and call the police. I'm going to have to report the Jaguar stolen now. Sid's going to have to know."

The thought made her stomach churn.

With fear? She didn't know how else to describe what she was feeling.

Oh, God, when had she become afraid of Sid?

Debbie frowned at her.

"How about if I take you home, and you go on upstairs to bed just like you've never been out at all, and then I break into your garage? When your husband gets home, he'll discover your car missing and call the police. They'll find signs of a break-in and assume the Jaguar was stolen right out of your garage. Doesn't make any difference where the car goes missing from, you know."

Julie stared at him as hope did its eternal thing again.

"Isn't lying to the police a crime?"

He shrugged. "Hey, crime happens. Spitting on the sidewalk's a crime. So is murder. It's all a matter of degree. This particular one won't cause so much as a ripple. The question is, would you rather tell the police you've been in bed asleep all night or tell your husband exactly how you came to lose your Jaguar?"

Julie shuddered. It wasn't even close. "Okay, so I'll lie to the police."

He grinned at her. "Attagirl."

Another problem reared its thorny head. "My purse was stolen too. Oh, I guess I can say I left it in the Jaguar. Which is true. I *did* leave it in the Jaguar, so that part won't be a lie. Exactly."

"Don't think of it as lying. Think of it as telling carefully selected facts." His grin broadened. "Welcome to the dark side, Luke Skywalker."

She made a face, then stiffened as a hideous possibility occurred to her. "What if the police find the punks who stole my car and they tell where they got it?"

"They won't find them."

"How can you be so sure?"

"I just am. Believe me. Mother and his pals run a tight ship, no violence, not hurting anybody, and the cops mostly look the other way."

Julie took a deep breath, and glanced over her shoulder. The clock read 2:15. She was out of time. And, she realized, despite countless objections raised by her basically cautious, law-abiding nature, out of options. The decision had been made: she was going to go with his suggestion.

"I need to get home. Sid's usually back by three."

"No problem. Let's go. Let me grab some gloves."

"Gloves?"

"I don't want to leave fingerprints all over your garage when I break in." He was already heading toward the bedroom again.

"Oh." Her voice was small. She couldn't believe that she was actually going to take part in a crime. The thought was scary. She'd never even so much as filched a quarter from the collection plate at church before.

He was back in a moment, stuffing a pair of black knit gloves into the pocket of his jeans. "All set?"

Julie nodded and turned toward the door. As she did, she saw Josephine, almost hidden behind the recliner, happily worrying a magazine that she held between her front paws. That corner of the room was strewn with shredded strips of newsprint and glossy magazine pages. Julie remembered the pile of reading material that had earlier waited beside the chair, and her eyes widened. There was nothing left but confetti.

Apparently following her gaze, Debbie saw the same thing.

"Damn it, Josephine!"

Josephine looked up at that, bright-eyed, tail wagging, the picture of innocence—if it hadn't been for the strips of shredded magazine dangling from her mouth.

"Hold on a minute," he said with a sigh, and swooped down on the offender. Josephine was scooped up without protest, and borne off toward the back of the house, her adorable pom-pom of a tail still wagging furiously.

"What did you do with her?" Julie asked with some trepidation when Debbie returned, minus the poodle.

"Locked her in the bathroom. There's not much she can get into in there, I don't think." He opened the door, then stood back to let her precede him outside.

The steamy heat felt good, Julie thought, and realized that she had been cold, from nerves or his air-conditioning, she couldn't be sure which. The jasmine-laden night air wrapped around her like a lover's caress, and she welcomed it.

"Even if she did chew up your magazines, you're lucky to have her. I've wanted a dog for years. Sid won't hear of it," she told him over her shoulder as she walked down the short front sidewalk toward his car. The street was deserted now, except for the insects that fluttered around the streetlight on the corner. Lights were on in the upstairs windows of two of the houses; a few night owls were apparently still up. Overhead, a pale sickle moon and thousands of pinprick stars gleamed ghostly white. All in all, and in spite of the fact that she was sick with some weird combination of betrayal and fear, it was a beautiful night.

"Sid's smart." There was a sour note to Debbie's voice that made Julie frown reproachfully at him.

"How can you say that? Josephine is adorable."

A grunt was the only reply. He walked around the car to unlock her door for her, opened it, then waited for her to get settled inside before closing it again. Julie made a face as it occurred to her that, had the slight impediment of his sexual preference not stood in the way, Debbie would have been the kind of guy that women drooled over.

Herself included.

"I am so incredibly nervous about this," she said as he got in beside her.

"About what? Deceiving your husband or lying to the police?" His sideways glance was teasing as he started the car and pulled away from the curb.

She frowned at him. "You're not helping."

He drove to the corner and then turned right. "As long as you stick to the story that you went to bed at the usual time, heard nothing, and have no idea what happened to your car, you'll be fine. With your husband and the police."

Julie grimaced. "Easy for you to say. You don't have to do it."

"You can always change your mind."

Julie thought about that, considered the consequences, and shuddered. "No. I'll lie."

"That's the spirit. Hang tough."

He turned up the ramp onto the expressway, heading northwest. The streetlights glared yellow, completely outshining the moon. A few cars whizzed past, but not many. It was too late—or early, depending upon one's point of view—for the kind of heavy traffic that usually poured into and around Charleston in the summer, courtesy of clueless tourists who didn't know that summer was the worst possible time to visit, thanks to the humidity and swarms of biting insects.

A thought occurred to Julie. "Hey, wait a minute. How did you know which way to go? You don't know where I live. Do you?"

The glance he gave her was unreadable in the shadowy interior of the car. "I assumed you lived out in Summerville near your shop. Am I wrong?"

"No-o, you're right. We live in Summerville." She eyed him doubtfully. His reply had been just a shade too casual—hadn't it? Or was she being paranoid again?

It's not paranoid if they're really after you. The saying popped into her head uninvited. Under the circumstances, it seemed appropriate.

But Debbie had fallen into her life purely by chance, and since then he had put himself out to help her. More, he had proved to be kind and caring, a friend.

And she badly needed a friend.

"Just tell me where to turn off." He sounded cheerfully unconcerned, and, because she really had no basis for them, she let her suspicions go.

"The first Summerville exit."

"Same as the shop. What's it called?"

"Carolina Belle."

"Maybe I'll stop in again sometime. If you start carrying larger sizes, that is." A crooked smile accompanied his sideways glance.

"Actually, I only sell to the trade." Julie smiled too at the sudden irresistible picture of Debbie in one of her gowns, and was grateful for the resulting easing of the tension that had her hands curled into fists in her lap. "Pageant contestants, that is. And their handlers."

"Are you telling me that you've got to be in a beauty contest to buy clothes at your shop?"

He sounded so affronted that Julie's smile broadened. "Basically."

As a former Miss South Carolina, a veteran of pageants from the age of two on, and the wife of a rich and prominent businessman, her credentials for running a shop that sold custom-designed and fitted evening gowns, swimsuits, and costumes for use on the state and national pageant circuit were impeccable. Carolina Belle was, in fact, quite successful, and she made a decent little income from it. Divorcing Sid would be bad for business, she thought, and with that gloomy reflection felt her muscles start to tense all over again. Every other girl in South Carolina entered beauty pageants; it was almost a sport, like football or something. All the ones she took on liked to think that if they faithfully dieted and exercised and waxed and tanned and bleached and curled, they would end up just like Julie: Cinderella after the ball and the wedding to the prince. An acrimonious divorce wasn't part of that dream.

Glancing down, she saw that her hands were once again curled into fists in her lap.

"Life's a bitch," Debbie said.

Julie suddenly, totally agreed. "Amen."

There was a pause as he sped up to pass a lumbering semi. Then he glanced at her.

"Listen, next time you feel like following your husband on one of his nocturnal adventures, don't. You want him followed, call a professional."

If he was trying to distract her from her own gloomy thoughts, he succeeded.

"A professional?" She almost hooted. "A professional what? Husband follower?"

"Private investigator. You hire one, he gets the goods on your husband for you. It's a lot less messy than doing it yourself, believe me. And a lot less dangerous for you."

"A private investigator?" Julie wrinkled up her nose doubtfully. "I wouldn't know how to go about finding one. It seems kind of risky just to look one up in the yellow pages. And—well, you know how things are around here. Everybody's related to everybody, or knows everybody, or something. Word would get out. There'd be gossip. Sid would find out." Julie shuddered.

"Not if you got somebody you could trust."

"There's nobody I trust. Not when it comes to Sid." It was so true that there was a tinge of bitterness in her voice. Sid was a Carlson, and a Sidney, and in South Carolina the Carlsons and the Sidneys, along with the Pughs and the Pettigrews and the Hughleys, were God. He was related, by blood or marriage, to half the population. The other half, like her own less-than-pedigreed family, just didn't count.

"You can trust me."

"You?" She glanced at him in surprise.

"I'm the McQuarry half of McQuarry and Hinkle, Private Investigators." He said it almost apologetically. Julie's eyes widened.

"You're a private investigator? Are you serious?"

"Serious as a grave."

"I never would have guessed." Julie realized she still sounded incredulous. Debbie—a private investigator? Turning the notion over in her mind, Julie realized that it was no more mind-boggling than picturing him as a bank clerk. In fact, less. Everybody had to have a job. "Do people actually hire you to spy on their husbands?"

"All the time." The skin around his eyes crinkled as he smiled. "Wives, too. You'd be amazed at how many spouses cheat. Sometimes I think most of 'em do. What you're going through isn't anything out of the ordinary, believe me."

That was so depressing that Julie was momentarily silenced. She didn't say anything more until a big green sign just a few hundred yards ahead jolted her back to reality.

"This is the exit!"

She thought he was going to miss it—she'd given the warning way too late—but he was already pulling into the appropriate lane as she spoke. Of course, she'd told him the first Summerville exit. Good thing he'd remembered.

The Blazer rolled down the ramp, paused at the red light at the bottom, then headed into the sleepy bedroom community of Summerville.

The tiny, picturesque town had an old-resort feel to it. The streets were wide and perpetually shady, lined with huge bearded live oaks and masses of azaleas. The historic district consisted of gracious antebellum structures complete with soaring Greek columns, some of which had been converted into shops and hotels and others of which remained private residences, nestled cozily side by side. Carolina Belle was located in an area of newer development a little to the north. At Julie's direction they turned the other way, heading toward the Ashley River, where some of the finest new houses in the area had been built, many of them by All-American Builders. As they drove along the deserted streets, she checked the time again: 2:50. They were going to be cutting it close.

Butterflies took wing in her stomach. Returning to her house suddenly seemed about as appealing as a convict might find returning to prison. She was going to have to face Sid and lie, face the police and lie. . . .

She really, truly, positively didn't want to go home. She had to struggle with herself not to ask him to turn the car around and floor it in the opposite direction.

"How long is it going to take you to break into the garage, do you think?" she asked, careful to keep her voice even.

"Not long. A couple of minutes."

"Is that all?" It seemed a ridiculously short amount of time to circumvent metal garage doors and deadbolt locks. "The house is new, you know. The locks are pretty sturdy. Oh, and what about the alarm system?"

If it went off, the police would come right away. He could be caught in the act.

"Was the alarm set? Did Sid set it when he left? Did you?"

Julie thought. She'd been in such a hurry not to lose Sid. . . .

"Sid usually sets it before he goes to sleep. But it wasn't set when I left—it would have gone off—and I never touched it. So it's off."

If Sid had set it before he left, he would have had to turn it off when he got back home. And whenever it was turned off, the alarm beeped a loud warning in their bedroom.

If she'd been asleep, she would almost certainly have woken up. And Sid, knowing that, would have taken the safer route of not turning the alarm on at all. After all, there was no real risk. Crime in Summerville was practically nonexistent.

"Then we're in business."

Julie pointed out her house, an eight-thousand-square-foot Greek Revival mansion that Sid had designed and built himself, and the Blazer stopped in front of it. The tall iron gates were still open—they stayed that way most of the time because it was a pain to wait for them to open electronically—but he didn't pull up the driveway.

"It'd be better if we walk up. That way, the neighbors won't see a strange car pulling into your driveway in the middle of the night," he said, answering her unspoken question.

"Good idea." Although the neighbors were in all likelihood sound asleep. At least the other houses—she could see only three from where she stood, the Macalasters', the DeForests', and the Cranes'—were all dark. Like her house, they had been designed and built by Sid's company to similarly tasteful specifications, although of course the facades were all different. Sutherland Estates was Sid's showcase development, which was why they had a house in it. Whichever development was his baby of the moment was where they lived.

Since their marriage, they'd had no permanent home. Sid's father—his mother had died when Sid was young—was living with his girlfriend in the family's moldy Civil War–era mansion in Charleston's historic district, which Sid, as the only child, expected to inherit one day. Given that circumstance, he'd seen no compelling reason to establish a real, true home of his own. At first, when Julie had hoped to fill the many rooms of the various big houses with children, she'd planned to go to the mat with Sid about settling down permanently as soon as she got pregnant. But Sid basically felt about children the way he felt about dogs, and he'd kept putting her off about having any of their own. She'd let the matter slide, and now she guessed that she wouldn't be going to the mat about living in this house permanently, either.

It was starting to look like she wouldn't be living in any house permanently. At least, not with Sid.

She and Debbie were both out of the vehicle now, and Julie was walking around it to join him. He was wearing the gloves, she saw as she reached him, and carrying a crowbar in one hand. Her stomach turned over at the thought of what they were about to do, but there was no help for it. She was just going to have to lie as convincingly as she could and hope for the best.

Too nervous to talk, she walked silently beside him up the driveway. It was paved in brick, and pink and white creeping petunias bloomed in bright profusion along the edges. Night reduced their colors to no more than shadowy patches of dark and light, but their perfume scented the air. Julie reached under a loose stone and grabbed the spare house key. The katydids were busy, adding their distinctive chorus to the soft chirp of the crickets and the piping of the tree frogs. The strategic stand of palmettos that, along with a brick privacy fence, provided protection from the Macalasters next door rustled faintly as some nocturnal animal moved about among the branches. The sound certainly didn't result from a breeze. There wasn't any. The air could only be described as sultry.

They reached the garage, a long, single-story brick rectangle angled away from the street with a quartet of identical white car doors set into it, and paused.

"Which one?" he asked.

Julie indicated the second door from the left.

He glanced at it. "Piece of cake."

"You've been great," she said, the words

heartfelt, looking up at him through the shadowy darkness. "I don't know what I would have done without you tonight."

"I try." He smiled at her, a slow, charmingly crooked smile that did something funny to her insides. Reaching into his rear pocket, he pulled out his wallet, thumbed through the contents, and withdrew a white business card, which he handed to her. "My number's on this. Next time you get the urge to go chasing after your husband in the middle of the night, call me instead."

"Will do." She glanced down at the card. It was impossible to read anything in the darkness. "And I'll call you tomorrow about the damage to your car."

"Sounds good."

She needed to make a move. Seconds were ticking swiftly past, and seconds added up to minutes, and minutes were all she had. Still, she hated to walk away.

She didn't want to go in. She wanted to stay out here in this heavy perfumed darkness forever with this stranger who had somehow morphed into her new best friend.

So he happened to be a guy named Debbie: it didn't matter. It occurred to her that whoever he was, whatever he was, she felt safe with him. She'd gotten more comfort from him tonight than she had from her own husband in years. Once she walked away from him, she was on her own. Her problems were strictly hers to deal with.

"I've got to go in now."

"Yeah." He was hefting the crowbar in his gloved hands, his expression unreadable in the darkness.

She summoned a smile. "If you hear about me being arrested on the morning news, you'll know just how bad a liar I am," she said. Then she impulsively laid a hand on his arm, and rose up to press a quick kiss on his warm, sandpapery cheek.

"Thank you," she said. "You were right: Tonight I really needed a friend."

"No problem."

She gave him one last smile, turned her back, and walked away.

Even before she rounded the corner of the garage, she could hear the grating of iron on metal.

He was doing his part by breaking in. Now all she had to do was go to bed, wait, and lie through her teeth when Sid started screaming.

Mac watched her go, and realized that he felt like the biggest criminal left unhanged. She was sweet, unbelievably sweet considering who she was married to, and more vulnerable than she knew. It had become obvious to him over the course of the last hour or so that, when it came to Sid, she didn't have a clue.

But even if he told her, even if he shared all he knew with her, she almost certainly wouldn't believe him. Besides, whether she did or not, knowing so much might put her in a bad situation. He wasn't one hundred percent sure Sid was dangerous, at least as far as she was concerned, but he strongly suspected that he could be.

The best course of action was probably just to keep his mouth shut and let the situation play itself out. Hang loose and wait to see what developed. As long as she stayed clueless, she was probably perfectly safe. She could get her divorce and get off the stage before anything bad happened to anyone.

Thus there was really no reason at all for

him to feel like he was crouched on a deer stand waiting to take potshots at Bambi. But, Mac realized as he wedged the end of the crowbar beneath the metal door and gave a mighty heave, telling himself that wasn't much help. He could rationalize all he wanted. He still felt guilty as hell.

6

BASTA HAD JUST REACHED the foot of the wide, curving front staircase when he heard the unmistakable sounds of someone entering the house.

He froze, his senses on high alert, then clicked off his small Mag-lite and slipped silently into the nearest room: the den. Earlier he'd prowled through it, just like he'd gone through the rest of the house. Getting the lay of the land, so to speak, so tonight wouldn't be a dead loss.

Just in case his quarry didn't return before he had to leave. But, it seemed, she had. Who else could this be?

Waiting just inside the den's doorway,

careful to stand to the side so, should someone decide to flip on the chandelier in the cavernous entry hall, he wouldn't be caught in its light, he kept his eyes trained on the darkness beyond the door and listened intently. Soft footsteps were heading his way, barely audible at first as they came through the kitchen but a little louder as they reached the cool black and white marble of the hall. Whoever it was was in a hurry, and feeling secretive, too—so far, no light had been turned on anywhere in the house.

Basta inhaled, then smiled. After so many years in this business his senses were nearly as acute as a dog's. And what he smelled was—the soft, sweet scent of a woman.

It was Julie Carlson all right.

A moment later she stepped into view. Moonlight from the glass sidelights on either side of the front door bathed the hall in twin shafts of soft silvery light. They glinted on the shiny pink thing she was almost wearing: nice, was his verdict. She passed out of his line of vision, and he moved to keep her in view, visually catching up with her again as she began to climb the stairs.

She was moving quickly, and her long, slim legs flashing in the moonlight were even nicer than her outfit.

Watching her, he smiled. They were all alone, the house was dark and quiet, and she was his for the taking. There wasn't much time left—it had been nearly three when he'd started down the steps—but then he didn't need much. Five minutes, if that was all he had, would be enough. Although it seemed a shame to rush, he was professional enough to do it if circumstances dictated.

And right now it seemed they did.

Silently he stepped out of the den and began to follow her up the stairs, keeping a tight grip on his bag. She wouldn't have time to make a phone call and there was no gun anywhere in the house, so it didn't matter if she heard him. Might even add to the fun if they had to play chase, although he couldn't toy with her for long because they were out of time.

He didn't want to cut it too close. It was his nature to be careful.

She didn't hear him. He was certain of that. She reached the top of the stairs and disappeared into the enveloping blackness of the upstairs hall. Heading for her bed-room, no doubt: a big, fancy affair with a marble Jacuzzi in each of the two adjoining bathrooms and a leopard-print throw on the enormous bed. His hand tightened on the cool wrought-iron railing as he regret-ted that he was not going to have time to do everything he wanted to her on that bed.

In just a minute or so he would have her bound and helpless. Then he would strip her naked and do her fast and squeeze the life out of her.

Tomorrow he would collect what was still owing on his fee and get back to his regu-lar life. For starters, there was a fishing boat out there with his name on it.

As he neared the top of the stairs, he fan-cied he could hear her getting into bed: a soft rustle of bedclothes and a creak as she settled down, and over all the surpris-ingly hurried in and out of her breathing.

He smiled. He'd soon have her breathing faster yet.

Behind him, his sharpened senses picked up something less pleasing: sounds coming from the garage.

He frowned, pausing with one foot on the

top step as he listened. Yes, he could definitely hear something he wished he could not.

The husband must be home. Some five, ten minutes early.

For a moment Basta hesitated, irresolute. Julie Carlson lay tantalizingly defenseless maybe thirty feet from where he stood. He could hear her breathing, smell her scent, practically taste her. She was his. He vibrated with longing to do what he'd come here to do.

He would do it, he promised himself. But not tonight.

His lips pursed as he faced the inevitability of that. With the sounds from the garage, the window of opportunity had just slammed shut.

He had to get out of the house.

Turning, he ran silently down the stairs, then with long swift strides headed for the door he had entered by.

Julie Carlson didn't know how lucky she was, he reflected as he let himself out the door, then slipped away through the shadows.

She got to live for one more day.

7

SID WAS CHEATING ON HER. Julie knew it as well as she knew her own name, and the knowledge hurt more than she had ever imagined it would. It felt like a boa constrictor curled around her chest, crushing it so that she could hardly breathe.

Last night he had come running up the stairs at seventeen minutes past three, according to the bedside clock. The mere fact that he was coming upstairs at all at such an hour—to say nothing of the hurry he'd been in at the time—told her that he'd missed the Jaguar as soon as he had arrived home, just as she had known he would. She'd pretended to be asleep, although it was hard to keep her breathing slow and rhythmic when her heart was racing like a NASCAR winner's engine. She'd been curled on her side, the covers pulled high over her shoulders, her eyes shut, when he'd reached the bedroom door. For a moment he'd loomed there, both hands resting on opposite sides of the jamb, breathing hard and just staring at her as she lay in bed. He was wearing a dark suit—Sid always wore a dark suit, even in the dead of summer, because he didn't believe in relaxing standards even in the heat—and his wire-rimmed glasses had been askew, which they never were, because Sid was nothing if not meticulous. He was a hair shy of six feet tall and thin— Sid watched his diet religiously—but even so he had looked almost . . . *menacing* standing there.

Which was ridiculous. Sid was many things—Julie could think of more than a few choice epithets now that she turned her mind to it—but menacing wasn't one of them.

At least, it never had been.

She'd held her breath, waiting for the inevitable explosion, waiting for Sid to totally lose it like he did more and more often when he was mad, until she remembered that she was supposed to be asleep.

Breathe, baby, breathe.

So she breathed, in and out, real rhythmic—and after a minute or two Sid had exhaled slowly through his teeth and gone away.

Just like that.

Without uttering a word about her missing car. In fact, he'd said nothing whatsoever to her until this morning, shortly before nine A.M., the time when he usually left for work and she was usually just getting back from her morning run, which she had skipped this morning because she didn't want to be the one to notice the car was gone. He'd "discovered" the Jaguar was missing when he started to leave for work. He came roaring into the house and dragged her downstairs to view the broken door and empty garage bay and stomped and cursed and carried on just like she'd known he would—only about four hours too late.

Give the man an Oscar, she thought with a cynicism that was new to her.

And give her one, too. Because she pretended to be surprised and bewildered and absolutely without a clue as to what could have become of her car. In fact, she'd been so disingenuous about it she'd reminded herself of the *Home Alone* kid clapping his hands to the sides of his face.

My car's been stolen, oh, my!

And all the while she had professed ignorance and tried to calm Sid down she had been dealing with the fact that her marriage was dead. Because if his little midnight excursion had been innocent, he would have had his hissy fit the minute he got home at seventeen after three.

Gotcha, she thought, gazing steadily at Sid, but the knowledge gave her no satisfaction. She didn't want to *get* Sid. She wanted to live happily ever after with him, just like they'd been doing for the past eight years.

Only apparently he hadn't been so happy. And neither, she realized, had she.

All the while he ranted and raved, she watched him as objectively as she might have a strange animal in a zoo. Who was this man, with his thinning dark hair, his cold gray eyes, his narrow, clever face?

Julie realized that she didn't know him anymore.

Maybe she never had. Maybe, with her infinite capacity for mentally spinning straw into gold, she'd made him into the man she wanted him to be, and he'd never really been that man at all.

To add insult to injury, he threw temper tantrums like a thwarted two-year-old. A grown man beating walls with his fists and stomping his Italian-shod feet on the kitchen floor was not a pretty sight.

Her reaction to his histrionics must not have been all he'd hoped for, because he turned on her as they waited in the kitchen for the police to arrive.

"You seem pretty damned unconcerned about the whole thing," he snarled at her as she sliced a banana into the blender to complete the healthy shake he liked for a pick-me-up. He was dressed in a fresh dark suit, and she was wrapped in a robe.

"It's only a car, Sid." Icy calm, she pressed the blender button and looked at him. As he digested her reply, his face, she noticed with the detached interest that seemed to be the only emotion she could summon at the moment, turned almost the color of the trio of bright red tomatoes ripening on the windowsill behind him.

"Only a car! Only a car! It's a fucking Jaguar, you stupid . . . ! Of course you don't appreciate it. You don't appreciate any damned thing I've done for you. You don't appreciate your fifty-thousand-dollar car, or your million-dollar house, or this whole lifestyle I've given you that is light-years beyond anything you ever had in your life, you with your trailer-trash family!"

Two police officers arrived just then, which was probably a good thing because she was on the verge of abandoning her icy calm in favor of braining him with the blender. The good news was, she was so furious by that time that lying to the cop was much easier than she had antici- pated—*no, officer, I didn't hear anything*— because she was thinking about how much she wanted to kill Sid all the while. The bad news was, she no longer even much wanted to try to save her marriage.

On second thought, maybe that was good news, too.

Sid and the cops ended up leaving at the same time, which meant that she'd been left home alone with a whole bellyful of nasty things to say and no one to say them to.

Which was probably just as well. Before she took a baseball bat to Sid's head, as she badly wanted to do, she needed to take a deep breath and *think,* she told herself sternly. There was still a chance, no matter how remote, that she was wrong about what Sid had been up to the night before. So he'd lied about cruising his houses. Maybe he was doing something totally innocent that he didn't want her to know anything about.

Like planning a marvelous surprise for her thirtieth birthday? Gee, that wasn't until November. Volunteering to work the twelve-to-three shift in a homeless shelter? She'd had no idea Sid was so altruistic. Screwing some babe whose husband worked the night shift? Bingo! Give the lady a cigar.

In any case, she told herself, breathing deeply again, there was a right and a wrong way to end a marriage, or a smart and a dumb way, however you wanted to look at it. If hers had to end, she was going to do it the right, smart way.

Which meant no going off the deep end.

She ordered herself to chill, then got dressed and headed out for the shop. If her life was disintegrating around her she was going to have to deal with it later. She had an appointment with a client at ten-thirty, which meant she was pushing it, time-wise. And she still had to deal with the fall-out of having her purse stolen: canceling her credit cards, replacing her driver's license. . . .

It was only as she reached the garage that Julie remembered about her missing Jaguar. Her life was going to hell on a greased slide, and she didn't even have a car. Gritting her teeth, she turned on her elegant stacked heel, marched back into the house, and called a cab.

It was just like Sid not to remember, or care, that she would need a ride to work.

Sid was all about Sid. He always had been, but she hadn't realized it until just recently because for a long time she'd been all about Sid, too.

No more. Julie was important, too.

Whatever happened, she was going to face it with dignity. She was going to hold her head up and smile.

Evidently her smile was less than a success, though, because when she pushed through the glass-and-steel front door of her shop and stepped into the pristine white showroom, Meredith Haney, one of her two assistants, turned from the rack of competition gowns she was straightening to greet her and broke off in mid-hello.

"What's up with you?" Meredith asked, her hand falling away from the sparkly blue gown she'd been rehanging. A short, perky twenty-four-year-old blonde, Meredith was a former Miss Marion County.

Clearly there was no point in trying to pretend nothing was amiss. Best go for the obvious cause.

"My car was stolen last night," Julie said as she headed toward her elegantly appointed office. Then, over her shoulder, "Is the ten-thirty here yet?"

"The *Jaguar?*" Meredith breathed, ignoring her question even as she abandoned her task to follow Julie into the back. "Oh, my God, were you *car-jacked?* Or . . ."

"It was stolen out of my garage." Julie tucked her purse—a cream-colored straw that felt strangely light because there was so little in it—under her desk in her private office and opened the top left-hand drawer of the desk. There it was, right where she always kept it in case of emergencies. . . .

"Oh, my God!" Meredith said again, stopping in the doorway and staring at her wide-eyed. The sleeveless denim jumpsuit she was wearing—out of *Carolina Belle*'s daywear stock—was, Julie noted absently, both chic and becoming. "Are you just *sick?*"

"Yes. I'm sick. Absolutely sick." She had never said anything more true in her life. Abruptly she changed the subject. "Is everything ready for the ten-thirty? And where's Amber?"

Amber O'Connell was her other assistant, a twenty-year-old brunette former Miss Angel of Beauty. Julie's tone was brusque because she so badly needed to get rid of Meredith. All she required was about two minutes alone to get her fix, and she'd feel a hundred percent better.

"She called to say she's running a little late. She had a problem with her car." Meredith paused, and grinned. "Nothing like yours, though. Hers just had a flat tire. Anyway, everything's set for the ten-thirty. It's Carlene Squabb, by the way."

Carlene Squabb. Of course, it would be.

Her day just kept getting better and better. Now she *really* needed Meredith to go away.

"Why don't you . . ." she began, only to be interrupted by the tinkling little bell that announced that someone had entered the premises.

"That'll be Carlene," Meredith said, sounding as cheered by the prospect as Julie felt. She turned and headed toward the showroom, and at long last Julie was left alone. She snatched the Hershey bar out of the drawer, unwrapped it, broke off a piece, and popped it into her mouth.

As it melted, bathing her tongue in chocolate, she closed her eyes in the closest she'd come lately to ecstasy.

"Julie Ann Williams, are you eating *candy?*" Her mother's scandalized voice caused Julie's eyes to pop open. For an instant she stared guiltily at the comfortably plump, shockingly redheaded woman in the doorway. Then she swallowed.

"Yes, Mama, I am," she said, and defiantly popped another of the succulent rectangles into her mouth right where her mother could see. Her mother didn't really resemble her in looks even if you didn't count the red hair, which you couldn't because it was dyed. Her jaw was wider, her features were less regular, and her artfully made-up eyes were hazel. Julie, as her mother always said wistfully, looked like her father. For all his faults—and they were numerous—Mike Williams had been one good-looking man.

"A moment on the lips, forever on the hips."

"Mama, my hips are a size six."

"See what I mean."

"Mo-*ther.*"

"They were a size two when you won the title."

"That was eight years ago!"

"So are you planning to go up two sizes every eight years? I'm just asking because that's exactly what happened to me, you know. A little here, a little there, and bingo, I'm a size twelve."

Her mother, as Julie well knew, was actually more of a size sixteen. Dixie Clay lied about everything from her weight to her age to her shoe size to how many times she'd been married. It didn't matter. Julie could feel the sugar hitting her bloodstream at about the same time the guilt hit her brain. Her mother, blast her, was right. The cost of wallowing in chocolate was high, especially for a woman who might soon be single again. Julie slid the drawer shut—discreetly—and narrowed her eyes at her sole surviving parent.

"Did you want something?"

"I heard your car got stolen." Her mother came on into the office and stopped in front of the desk, planting hands tipped with bright tangerine nails on the black acrylic surface, looking Julie over with a critical eye. Julie braced herself for criticism of her simple white linen sheath: her mother preferred bright colors. Whatever else might have changed over the years, Dixie's taste in fashion had remained exactly the same: bold and eye-catching, just like Dixie herself. She was dressed today in snug white capri pants, a vividly patterned purple, orange, and white tunic-length silk blouse, and high-heeled white mules. With her fire-engine red hair in an Ivana-style upsweep, bejeweled sunglasses dangling from a gold chain around her neck, and beaded earrings the size of chandeliers just brushing her shoulders, she was a sight to turn heads.

Just like she'd always been. Ever since she was a little girl, Julie could remember people staring at her mother. Dixie might never have been a conventional beauty, as she would be the first to admit, but she'd certainly had something that made people want to look at her.

Sid said she was tacky, tacky, tacky. Which, Julie reflected with a quick stab of angry pain, was just one more reason to get rid of Sid.

"Last night." Julie nodded in wry confirmation, relieved not to have to defend her clothing choice. The urge to tell her mother everything was suddenly strong, but if she did there would be no putting the genie back in the bottle. Her mother would be horrified. She would dissect the subject to death, then call Becky and dissect the subject to death with her, and then, as there was not a subtle bone in her body, probably be all for confronting Sid.

Which was something Julie wasn't ready for. Not yet. Not until she had some answers herself.

Instead Julie asked, "How did you find out? It's only been about an hour since I reported it to the police."

"Kenny told Becky, and she called me."

"Oh." Kenny was Becky's husband. Most days, as one of the company's two vice-presidents, he worked directly with Sid. Sid would have arrived at work livid about the stolen car. Kenny would have called Becky pronto, and her mother, the next to be alerted, would have instantly been on her way to check on her younger daughter for herself. That was how the family's jungle-drum system worked.

"They stole it right out of your *garage*? You didn't see anything?"

Julie repressed a sigh. "I was asleep."

"I hear Sid had a cow." There was concern in Dixie's voice. Julie met her mother's frowning gaze, and wavered. Again the urge to confide in her was strong.

The little tinkle that announced some-one's arrival sounded again. Saved by the bell, Julie thought.

"I've got to get to work."

Meredith appeared in the doorway. "Carlene Squabb, Julie."

It was all Julie could do to suppress a gri-mace. The urge for chocolate was sud-denly strong again. She was having a really bad day, it was only ten-thirty, and one more little bite wouldn't condemn her to a lifetime of plus sizes—would it?

"Take her on in, Meredith. I'll be right there."

Meredith nodded and disappeared. Her voice mingled with Carlene's in the distance. Julie stood up. Her fingers inched toward the drawer, and she clenched them into a fist as she looked at her mother. "Mama . . ."

"Don't forget you're supposed to be at Becky's at two," Dixie said. "Did you remember to get a gift?"

"Malibu Barbie." It was Kelly's birthday. Kelly, age four today, was Becky's baby. Becky was having a party for her, the little girl's first real birthday party, and Julie had volunteered to help out.

"She'll like that. Is Sid coming?"

Julie shook her head. The mere mention of Sid made her stomach twist into a knot. Oh, God, if she divorced Sid, Sid would fire Kenny, and Becky and Kelly and six-year-old Erin would have their comfortable lives ruined. "I don't think so. He's busy."

"Seems like he's always busy these days." Her mother looked her up and down, frowning, then held out her hand imperiously. "Julie."

Julie met her unyielding gaze, and realized she was busted. Which was probably just as well. Swallowing hard, she opened the desk drawer, picked up the candy bar, and reluctantly handed it over.

"See you at two," Dixie said, satisfied, tucking the candy bar into her purse, and turned to leave. "Oh, and by the way, you should add a scarf or some beads or something to that dress. It needs a little color."

"Yes, Mama." Julie had long since learned the futility of arguing with her mother. As a general rule, she pretty much agreed with whatever Dixie said, then she did as she pleased. She walked her to the door, said good-bye, then after she was gone just stood staring for a moment out at the bright and busy street. With the world ablaze with heat and light outside, how was it possible that her glass-fronted shop could feel so cold and dark? Julie closed her eyes, then determinedly opened them again. Enough of that. She refused to wallow. Wallowing was for sissies.

Pushing all thoughts of Sid and corollary

images of chocolate from her mind, Julie headed for the largest of the fitting rooms, where she knew she would find Meredith and Carlene. Sure enough, as she entered, Meredith was in the act of easing a glittering scarlet ball dress over Carlene's raven head.

"God, I need a cigarette! Could you please hurry up?" Carlene said as her head popped out of the dress. All four walls were mirrored, and as a result about eight images of Carlene stared at Julie as she entered.

Julie greeted Carlene, nodded wordlessly at Meredith, and took over. The dress was her own design, lovingly conceived and executed because Carlene, however trying Julie might personally find her, was a strong candidate to win the Miss Southern Beauty pageant to be held the following Saturday night. If Carlene won Miss Southern Beauty, then she would go on to the Miss American Beauty contest. If she was victorious there—and Carlene, if she kept her mouth shut and her bitchy tendencies in check, was lovely enough to make it a possibility—she would compete for Miss World Beauty. All providing wonderful exposure for Carolina Belle, of course. And exposure for Carolina Belle took on a whole new level of importance if she was contemplating divorcing Sid.

"This will just take a minute," Julie said, carefully zipping up the back of the gown. It was a truly gorgeous creation, if she did say so herself. One of her most inspired. Both Carlene and Mabel Purcell, Carlene's handler, had gone gaga over it when they'd seen the sketches. "I don't anticipate having to make any changes. It . . ."

Julie's voice broke off as the zipper stopped halfway up Carlene's back. Frowning, she looked more closely at the elegant folded edges of scarlet silk concealing the zipper and the inches of smooth tanned back that still remained between them.

It was clear at a glance: the dress, custom made to Carlene's measure, was not going to zip.

Julie stared disbelievingly at the gap in the back, then looked at the dress—and Carlene in the dress—through the mirror. Everything was just as it should have been—full skirt aswirl with hand beading, boned, lined, fitted to the millimeter, strapless bodice, breasts round and firm as oranges swelling coyly over the top. . . . Julie's gaze fixed on those breasts. Instead of oranges, she was looking at cantaloupes.

"You got implants!" Julie couldn't help it. She was aghast, and sounded it.

Carlene nodded complacently. "I had it done last Friday. Don't they look great?"

She turned this way and that, thrusting her newly eye-popping chest out as she surveyed herself with satisfaction in the mirror.

"The pageant starts on Thursday. That's only four days." It wasn't just the gown. There was the swimsuit, too, and the conservative black suit for the interview with the judges and the kicky little sundress for the opening breakfast with the press. . . . "Your whole wardrobe will have to be refitted!"

"Is that a problem?" Carlene asked with a little frown, meeting Julie's gaze through the mirror. Julie thought of the size of the order, of Carlene's chances of winning, of the small pageant world that would hear within the hour if Julie totally lost it and wrapped her fingers around her most promising client's neck. She thought briefly, fleetingly, longingly, of the calming effects of the confiscated bar of chocolate. Then she summoned up her most professional manner, and even managed to smile. Admittedly, it was a rather grim smile, but it was a smile nonetheless.

"Well, it certainly can be done, but it's going to take some doing. To begin with, you need to try everything on again and . . ."

"Julie, you're wanted on the phone. Mr. Carlson." Amber, now well over an hour and a half late, appeared in the dressing-room doorway with the message. It was an indication of how badly the day was going that Amber's lateness was the least of Julie's concerns.

"Thank you, Amber." She massaged her temple discreetly. "Meredith, remeasure Carlene's bust, would you, and mark the gown? Then let's go to the swimsuit. Amber will help you."

"How long is this going to take?" Carlene reached for her cigarettes, which were lying atop her purse on a nearby chair.

"I'm sorry, but Carolina Belle has a no-smoking policy, remember? Because the smoke makes the gowns smell, and the judges don't like that," Julie said, as Meredith took over with a quick, discreet roll of her eyes.

"Fuck," Carlene said, straightening away from the chair.

With that elegant reply echoing in her ears, Julie escaped to her office with a soothing "I'll be right back."

Oh, God, she didn't want to talk to Sid now, she thought, staring at the phone as if it were a snake coiled to strike. In fact, she didn't want to talk to him at all, ever again in her life. But there was no help for it. The glowing yellow light that signified a caller on line one would not be denied. Picking up the receiver, Julie punched the button and said hello.

"You remember to get my cleaning?" Sid asked. She knew his voice so well, and yet today it was almost like listening to a stranger. A lying, cheating, louse of a stranger.

" 'Fraid not. It's kind of hard to stop by the cleaner's when I don't have a car." Her voice was brittle. He didn't seem to notice.

"Well, try to get it before you come home, would you? We've got that charity auction at the country club tonight, remember. Dad and Pamela will be there."

Julie remembered, and groaned. The last thing she needed at the moment was to have to act the part of Sid's loving wife before his father and his father's girlfriend.

"I called the insurance company about your car, by the way. They'll be sending a loaner over to the shop before noon." Sid's tone was suddenly friendlier. Julie suspected, from certain background sounds, that he was no longer alone. Then Sid said "Thanks, Heidi,"—Heidi Benton was his administrative assistant—as he was apparently handed something, and her suspicion was confirmed.

"Fantastic." Her reply was flat.

"You're mad, aren't you?" He sighed. Julie could still hear Heidi moving around in the background. "Because of this morning. I yelled at you, and I shouldn't have."

"No, you certainly shouldn't have," Julie agreed, giving him a big crocodile smile that he couldn't see. He was being nice for Heidi's benefit, she knew. "And thanks for giving me a ride to work, by the way."

"I'm sorry, okay? I was upset about the car." His voice dropped. "I love you, Julie."

Julie's eyes widened. The remark was so totally out of character for Sid that she could only assume that either he wanted Heidi to hear it or he was trying to ease his own guilt about cheating by throwing a little verbal affection her way. Before she could reply, Sid hung up. Which was a good thing, Julie thought. She wouldn't have known what to say. Sid hadn't said he loved her for so long she couldn't remember the last time, and he *never* apologized.

Maybe she was totally paranoid, totally unhinged, but this was almost more suspicious than the missing Viagra.

Julie realized that she had to know, one way or another, finally and for sure and without any doubt, what Sid was up to. If he was a true and faithful husband with nothing more than anger issues, sexual dysfunction, and a bad case of insomnia— well, she could work with that. She would kick herself for her suspicions and invest in even more sexy lingerie and try her best to make her marriage work.

But if he wasn't, he was marital toast.

With her stomach twisting itself into a pretzel at what she was about to do, she dragged her purse out from under the desk and dug for the business card she had dropped inside it that morning. This time she would let a professional do the spying for her.

Punching in the number on the card, she listened to the phone ring once, twice.

"McQuarry and Hinkle, Private Investigators." It was a woman's voice.

Julie took a deep breath. "May I speak to Debbie, please?"

8

"DEBBIE?" RAWANDA ASKED, SOUNDING BLANK.

Mac had been standing in front of his desk shuffling through the papers on top hunting for receipts when Rawanda, sitting behind the desk and engaged in the same task, answered the phone. He glanced up, alerted by the name she uttered. Rawanda was short and round in all the right places and pretty, with face-framing black curls and eyes the color of caramels. She'd been working for McQuarry and Hinkle for almost a year, answering the phone and filing and doing word processing, hired because they'd gotten a subsidy to cover her salary through a state program that paid to put former convicts to work. Rawanda had done six months for check kiting, but insisted she was now completely reformed. During the time she'd worked for them she'd managed to get her well-manicured nails firmly into Hinkle's vulnerable hide. Now the subsidy was just about up, and they were going to have to scrounge up the money to keep her on at their own expense, because, as Hinkle put it, *I ain't lettin' this bitch go.* Mac pretty much agreed with that, although for a different reason: Rawanda was flat-out good at her job. At the moment she was frowning into the phone, her head shaking from side to side.

"Ain't no Debbie here, ma'am. You must've dialed the wrong number."

Even as Mac realized who must be on the other end of the line, Rawanda was looking at him with widening eyes.

"Debbie *McQuarry?*" She blinked at Mac. "You sure?"

"Give that to me," Mac said, and took the phone away from Rawanda before she dropped it. All too conscious of two curious pairs of eyes and ears suddenly focused on him with all the subtlety of a pair of Rottweilers spotting a kitten—Hinkle was sitting on the couch at the far side of the room, where he had been going through some pictures from the night before—Mac spoke into the receiver.

"McQuarry here."

"Debbie?" Julie Carlson's voice sounded a little uncertain. But he would have recognized it anywhere, regardless.

"Out here in the workaday world, I generally go by Mac."

"Oh." There was a tiny pause. "I hope I didn't say the wrong thing to whoever answered the phone. I mean, I didn't mean to cause you any trouble or anything. I never thought—it never occurred to me that you wouldn't go by Debbie at work as well."

Mac couldn't help himself. Even with Rawanda and Hinkle watching avidly, he had to smile. "Don't worry about it. You haven't exactly outed me. What can I do for you?"

"Well, I need to make arrangements to pay for the damage to your car—" There was another of those tiny pauses—he could almost picture her chewing her lower lip—and then the rest of the words came out in a rush. "And—and I want to hire you to follow my husband."

Her voice had dropped so low as to be almost inaudible as she finished. But Mac heard, and understood.

"Smart call." His tone was brisk. If this was as difficult for her as it seemed to be, he wanted to make it sound like business as usual for him. He'd been expecting her to call this morning about the damages to his car if nothing else, but for her to hire him to tail Sid was on the order of life handing him a little present. Now that he'd been put on the scent, he'd had every intention of tailing Sid anyway. If the scumbag was merely cheating on his wife, that was one thing; but if he was up to something else, Mac meant to move heaven and earth to find out what it was. Getting paid for his efforts was pure gravy.

Paybacks are a bitch, he said to his mental image of Sid, then returned his attention to Sid's wife, who was still talking.

"I don't have any idea how to go about this. What do I need to do? Is there somebody in your office I need to make arrangements with or—you understand I want to keep this completely confidential."

She sounded nervous, skittish, as though she was ready to abandon the whole idea at the least hint of a problem. Mac blocked out of his mind a sudden vivid image of the way she had kissed his cheek the night before—no need to get the guilt thing going again—and set himself to reassuring her.

"I'll handle it myself, don't worry. And nobody else has to know. I'll need a little more information, though. Could we meet? Where are you now?" If the idea of seeing Julie Carlson again had a certain appeal above and beyond his desire to learn everything she knew about her husband, he wasn't admitting it even to himself.

"At my shop." He got the impression she was growing increasingly nervous. "I can't come to you. I don't have a car, remember? And you can't come here. Sid might find out. I . . ."

"Okay," Mac interrupted soothingly, before she could spook herself into canceling the whole thing. "I understand. Isn't there a Kroger across the street from you? How about if I drive over there and wait for you in the parking lot? You won't have any trouble recognizing the Blazer"—his voice took on a humorous note meant to reassure her—"it's the one with the big dent in the side, remember? All you have to do is hop in. I'll be parked in the row right behind the Taco Bell. Just give me a time."

He heard her sucking in air. His muscles tensed in anticipation of a hang-up. But she didn't.

"It's Saturday, so Carolina Belle closes at noon. I suppose I could meet you at about a quarter after. Oh, gosh, I can't believe I'm doing this. If Sid finds out . . ."

"He won't," Mac said. "Not unless you want him to, that is. You're doing the smart thing here. Just keep reminding yourself of that, and try not to worry. I'll see you in the Kroger parking lot at quarter past twelve. Okay?"

Not for nothing had he worked selling yellow page ads to pay the bills during his freshman year at USC. If nothing else, he knew how to close a sale.

"Okay."

Asking for the order still worked. But she didn't sound happy.

"I'll be there waiting. Twelve-fifteen in the Kroger parking lot."

"Okay," she said again. He heard someone calling her—another woman—and she drew in her breath.

"I've got to go," she said into the phone, and hung up.

Mac hung up too, slowly, lost for the moment in thought. She had sounded scared to death, not that he was particularly surprised. Taking on Sid Carlson was scary work, as he knew himself to his cost. The consequences of losing could be devastating. Sid cornered was a scorched-earth kind of guy.

Grimacing at the memories that reflection brought with it, Mac looked up to find both Hinkle and Rawanda staring at him.

"Debbie?" Rawanda's questioning gaze slid over as much of him as she could see with his big oak desk standing between them.

"Who was that?" Hinkle demanded at almost exactly the same moment.

Mac shrugged, and returned to rifling through the remaining papers as though the call had been nothing more or less than business as usual. Somewhere in the pile there had to be a receipt for a hundred twenty-three dollars for new tires, to replace two of his that had been slashed on a stakeout at the beginning of the month, and eighty-nine dollars for the motel room required to listen in on the adulterous tryst taking place on the other side of the wall. No receipts, no reimbursement. He had instituted the rule himself, but that didn't help when Rawanda, who now handled petty cash, applied it to him.

"A new client. I promised her total confidentiality. So don't ask." This case he didn't mean to share with anyone. Even if Julie Carlson hadn't insisted on confidentiality, he would have kept quiet about it. Hinkle, who, having gotten busted out of the police force right along with Mac and having subsequently been let in on the whole thing about Daniel, was now as wary of Sid as a bird was of a snake. He would have tried his damndest to talk Mac out of getting involved with the Carlsons in any way, shape, or form.

Actually, Hinkle probably would have had a point, but with this tantalizing new opportunity falling into his lap like a gift from the gods, Mac wouldn't have listened. No way in hell was he walking away from this thing now.

"Debbie?" Rawanda sounded even more incredulous than before. She glanced at Hinkle. "That woman on the phone was asking for *Debbie* McQuarry. I didn't know the boss here sometimes went by Debbie."

Mac sent her an aren't-you-funny glance, but otherwise ignored her as he continued to shuffle through the papers. Hinkle grinned at Rawanda, then looked at Mac.

"This is someone you met last night, right? At the Pink Pussycat?" In response to Rawanda's increasingly agog expression, Hinkle added for her benefit: "Mac was in drag for the Edwards case. He was calling himself Debbie." A grin split his face. "He was looking pretty hot, too."

"Damn, and I missed it!" Rawanda met Mac's gaze, looked him up and down with exaggerated lasciviousness, hooted with laughter, and stood up. Her black spandex mini hugged her butt and made a virtue of plump but curvaceous legs lengthened by her platform pumps. Her low-cut white tee revealed a great deal of her other ample assets. "I just love this detecting business. How come you guys never take me along on none of your cases? I bet I could detect real good."

" 'Cause you're way too fine to go poking your nose into trouble." Hinkle stood up, slid the photos he'd been looking at back into a manila envelope, and crossed the well-worn linoleum floor to hand the envelope to Mac. The three of them shared a basic two-room suite outfitted with a single telephone line, a black vinyl couch, and a trio of ancient wooden desks, one of which was positioned in the small reception area and belonged to Rawanda. It was located on the second floor of a World War II–era office building not far from Mac's house. The building wasn't exactly Trump Tower, but it was affordable even when private-eye pickings were slim, as they usually were in the summer, when all sensible residents left Charleston for cooler environs and the city was aswarm with tourists. Considering the uncertain nature of the business, affordable, in Mac's opinion, was key.

"You going to take these over to Mrs. Edwards today?" Hinkle asked, nodding at the envelope.

Rawanda came around the desk to slip her arms around Hinkle's waist, and he reciprocated. They made a good-looking pair, Mac observed absently, with Hinkle tall and slim and dapper in a pale seersucker suit and Rawanda all curvy and sexy in her poured-on clothes, but their association, which he had not foreseen when he had hired Rawanda, was probably not going to be good for business in the long term. When the breakup came, as it inevitably would—he was readier to believe in the tooth fairy than in the long-term success of male-female couplings—the fallout was going to be bad. Rawanda, he had already learned, did not do things by halves.

Ah, well, that was a worry to be saved for another day, along with a host of others.

"Monday. Mrs. Edwards is out of town for the weekend."

Mac walked around his desk and stowed the envelope in the bottom drawer, which he locked, pocketing the key. Josephine, who'd been stretched out in the knee space beneath the desk, turned onto her back, waving her tiny paws at him. He eyed her askance. He had already learned that Josephine, like most females, tended to smile the sweetest right before she bit him in the ass. Figuratively speaking, of course.

"She should be real happy. We got the goods on Edwards. Big time." Hinkle was smiling down at Rawanda as he spoke.

Rawanda batted her eyelashes at him.

"You-all ever thought about trying to sell them pictures back to Mr. Edwards? If I were him, I'd sure-nuff pay to keep anyone from seeing me down on my hands and knees with . . ."

"That's called blackmail, sugar," Hinkle interrupted. "It's a crime."

"Oh." Rawanda batted her lashes some more. "We sure don't want to commit no crime."

Mac, mentally rolling his eyes, interrupted before the billing and cooing made him lose the doughnut he'd eaten for breakfast.

"Okay, gang, I'm out of here. Hinkle, don't forget you're on the third shift at that Hanes warehouse down in the Battery tonight. You be sure and keep your eye out for anybody pilfering panties."

Hinkle groaned. "Like I said before: How come *I* get all the shitty jobs?"

"Hey, last night I was the one who got my ass grabbed, remember? Rawanda, as of right now you're on doggy duty. Actually, I'll probably need you to keep Josephine all night."

Rawanda pulled away from Hinkle to

plant both fists on her hips, shaking her head vigorously at Mac.

"Uh-uh! I ain't keepin' that dog for you no more. Last time you left her with me, here at the office, she went crazy. Attacked my purse like one of them pit bulls and wouldn't let go for nothin'. My cell phone was in there, ringing like there was no to-morrow, and she wouldn't even let me get to it. I missed a call from my parole officer, which ain't no good thing, let me tell you. She chewed the strap clean off it before I managed to pull it away. I already took the money out of petty cash to pay for my purse—thirty-two bucks, which I cannot afford—but I ain't takin' no chances with her going crazy on me again. And I sure ain't takin' her home with me. Anyway, this is Saturday. After twelve o'clock, I am *o-fic-ially* off duty for the weekend. You're the one whose granny sweet-talked him into taking her dog. In my book, that makes her your problem."

"I'm meeting a client this afternoon. Tonight I'll probably be on stakeout."

"Well, boo-hoo, sing me another sad song."

Hinkle was grinning. He loved Rawanda's

sass. Mac glared at Rawanda, opened his mouth to continue the discussion, and gave it up. He could tell by looking at Rawanda that there was going to be no winning this one short of firing her, which he wasn't going to do. And they both knew it.

"Fine. I'll take her with me. Josephine." Mac snapped his fingers authoritatively. Nothing happened. He tried again. Still nothing.

In the sudden silence he became aware of an ominous grinding sound.

He looked under his desk. Josephine the ever-obedient was going after the right front leg like a beaver in a building frenzy.

"Josephine." He would have cursed if he'd been alone. Josephine never even glanced around.

"Hey, boss, looks like your dog's eating your desk." Rawanda was chortling as she looked under the desk with him. "Must be hungry. Whole leg's just about gone."

Shit.

"I needed a new one anyway," Mac said with as much equanimity as he could muster, and hauled the culprit out, brushing the crumbs of his admittedly old but perfectly serviceable desk from around her mouth as he straightened with her in his arms. Her tail went wild, and she gave him a look of pure doggy devotion and licked his cheek. Mac tucked the dog under his arm football-style without succumbing to the now-familiar urge to wring her neck, waved, and got the hell out of his office before his guffawing companions drove him to murder. He loved Grandma Henderson devotedly, but why he had let her talk him into taking her dog when she moved into a retirement home was beyond him.

But he had, and now he was stuck. His grandma loved the thrice-damned animal, and he loved his grandma. He even took the pooch to visit her once a week, which entailed a visit to the doggy beauty parlor beforehand so Grandma would see Josephine looking nice. You couldn't get much more devoted than that.

But so far—and he'd been the proud possessor of the purebred toy poodle for approximately three weeks—Josephine had been the canine equivalent of the bad seed. Despite her deceptively angelic looks, she had chewed up an armchair, a briefcase, a plastic trash can, a lamp cord, a bed pillow, a rug, and enough wood products to qualify for the termite hall of fame. When he'd walked back into his house last night after driving Julie Carlson home, he'd found his shower curtain in shreds, which was why Josephine was at the office with him today: he was scared to leave her alone in his house. Now she'd started in on his desk. He was starting to wonder if the dog was part devil. The bad part.

"Bad dog," he said dispiritedly. He'd already learned that those words were not, apparently, part of her doggy lexicon. Sure enough, she licked his hand in response.

"No lick," he said. She apparently didn't understand that either, because she did it again.

Shit. Tromping down the stairs—the ancient elevator had been broken for a week, and given its recent history he felt safer with the stairs anyway—Mac headed toward where his car was parked behind the building. He was a low-country boy born and bred, and the truly oppressive heat didn't bother him. In fact, he kind of liked it.

What he didn't like was truly oppressive

heat coupled with perfumed dog frizz. The combination made him itch.

He dropped Josephine into the back-seat—which was useless, as she jumped into the front before he was even all the way inside—and started the car, thinking longingly of doggy shelters all the while.

The air conditioner shot out a blast of air hotter than anything ever produced by any furnace. The radio blared. Even as he offed the radio with a savage forefinger jab, Josephine planted her front paws on his shoulder and licked his ear.

"No lick," he said, jerking his head away, then gave it up. He had already discovered that there was just no reasoning with Josephine. Popping open the glove box, he fished a dog biscuit out of the bag he had learned to keep in there and handed it to her, then peeled rubber out of the parking lot as, satisfied, she settled herself down on the passenger seat for a quick snack. As he headed out toward Summerville to the sound of crunching and the certainty of crumbs, he forced himself to mentally tally the poodle's good points before the idea of doggy shelters took unshakable possession of his mind.

The problem was, the only good point he could attribute to Josephine at the moment was that merely being in possession of her made him look gay.

Which, as far as he was concerned, was only a good point when Julie Carlson was around.

Probably letting her think he was gay was not exactly ethical, Mac reflected as he blew past most of the light traffic headed away from the beaches. But twice, once after he'd just kind of instinctively checked her out there in the parking lot of the Pink Pussycat and again after he'd shed his Debbie regalia, he'd seen a look on her face that warned him that if she realized he was straight her comfort level with him was going to go way down.

And he wanted her to be comfortable with him. She represented a tantalizing new link to Sid. What with being fired, getting divorced, and all the hassles involved with establishing a new business, his hunt for Daniel had been kind of on the back burner for the past five years. But he hadn't forgotten. He would never forget.

Anyway, if, between the dress and the wig and the poodle, she had chosen to assume he was gay, he could not really be blamed, he told himself. After all, he had not actually lied.

When she'd asked him if he was gay, he'd asked if it mattered. And *that* was not lying.

Exactly.

But it occurred to him, as he took the Summerville exit and then drove the few blocks to the Kroger, that he did not particularly like the idea that Julie Carlson thought he was gay.

And even less did he like the idea that he did not like the idea.

The whys and wherefores of that did not become clear to him until he had been parked behind the Taco Bell for some minutes and at last saw Julie Carlson herself come walking across the steaming asphalt toward him.

Even through the rising veil of heat she looked cool and tempting as vanilla ice cream in a slim white dress that somehow managed to be both classy and sexy at the same time. Her hair was pulled back from her face to hang in a shining black waterfall down her back. She was frowning slightly, one hand raised to block the sun from her eyes, as she scanned the parked cars. Her long tanned legs flashed beneath the hem of her dress as she moved. He was willing to bet dollars to doughnuts that they were bare, and to his dismay just thinking about Julie Carlson's bare legs made him hotter than the asphalt.

Unbidden, lightning snapshots from the night before flashed through his mind: the sweet-smelling suppleness of her in his arms; her breasts, firm and round as oranges with pert little nipples that seemed to beg for attention, pressing into his chest; her truly world-class ass all slithery in satin as it rubbed up against his definitely noticing crotch; the silky texture of her hair; the creamy smoothness of her skin; the soft warmth of her lips as she kissed his cheek.

The truth hit him like a hammer over the head: He had a galloping case of the hots for his newest client, who was not incidentally his oldest enemy's wife.

He was walking into quicksand here, and if he had the sense God gave a gnat he'd turn around and walk back out again before he wound up floundering over his head.

9

DEBBIE—NO, THAT WASN'T RIGHT, hadn't he told her that he went by Mac on the job?—didn't look particularly happy to see her, Julie thought as she slid into the Blazer beside him. Which made them even, because she wasn't all that thrilled to see him, either. Having made up her mind that hiring a private investigator was the smartest thing she could do, she was now suffering a major attack of buyer's remorse. If he hadn't shown up, she wouldn't have been altogether sorry.

But she would have been on her own. And the thought of that made her shiver despite the heat.

"Hi," she offered as she closed the door, then smiled with genuine delight as Josephine jumped into her lap from the back seat. "Hi, Josephine."

"Hey." He sounded about as glad to see her as he looked. Scratching an ecstatic Josephine behind the ears, Julie frowned at him. "Careful, she'll lick you to death."

"I don't mind." Her frown deepened as Josephine licked her chin. There was something about his expression . . . "Is something wrong?"

Their gazes met and held for the space of a couple of heartbeats. Then one corner of his mouth quirked up wryly.

"What could be wrong?" He reached past her, opened the glove compartment, and extracted what looked like a dried-up brownie from a paper bag. "Josephine." When the poodle looked at him, he tossed the brownie into the backseat. "Go get it."

With an eager yap, Josephine leaped into the back. He put the Blazer into reverse, and pulled out of the parking space. Julie absently watched the play of light and shadow over his classic profile and then, as he turned his head, the chiseled planes and angles of his face. As she'd lain awake into the dawn, his had been one of the many images that had chased themselves endlessly through her mind. Remembering her physical response to him in his male incarnation had both stimulated her sex-deprived senses and, by extension, depressed her even more than she was already. He was, she was less than delighted to discover, just as attractive by the glaring light of day. He was wearing jeans, sneakers, and a white T-shirt with a blindingly bright Hawaiian shirt open over it, and he looked good enough to eat.

Good thing there was no chance of him being on the menu. Her life was messed up enough right now without adding another potentially explosive element to the mix.

"Where are we going?" Unlike last night, she didn't feel particularly nervous about the answer, Julie realized. Whatever her feelings might be about hiring a private investigator—and they were so tangled that it would probably take years if she tried to sort them out—she no longer had any qualms about the man beside her. He was, quite simply, a friend.

"We'll attract less attention if we drive around as we talk. Put your seat belt on."

He pulled out onto the street as she complied, and turned left, heading away from the business district. Traffic was fairly heavy, and there was a good possibility that she had at least a passing acquaintance with most of the people in the surrounding cars. Flipping her visor down to provide some degree of cover, she sought to make herself as invisible as possible.

"You can quit trying to hide. The windows are tinted." He glanced at her. "So how's your elbow?"

"Fine. Nobody even noticed the Band-Aid."

"What happened after you went in last night?"

Julie grimaced. "Sid came in at the same time he always does—and didn't say anything about the car being missing until nine this morning."

"Oh, yeah?" Clearly he understood the implication of that.

"Yeah." Her tone was glum.

"Actually, I saw him go into the house. I decided to hang around for a while in case . . ." The words trailed off.

"In case what?"

He glanced at her again, his expression

unreadable. "In case you needed me. In case your husband lost it when he found out the Jaguar was gone, and started roughing you up or something."

Touched, Julie smiled at him. "That was sweet. Thank you."

His eyes held hers for the space of a heartbeat, and his mouth did its wry thing again. "Sweet's my middle name."

His attention returned to the road.

"For your information, Sid doesn't rough me up. He's not the violent type. Anyway, I don't see how you would have known if he did."

He grinned, and the atmosphere lightened. "Hey, I'm a professional. I have ways. So what happened at nine this morning when he supposedly made the big discovery?"

"He threw a tantrum. And called the police."

"Oh, yeah? You have any trouble there?"

"By the time they got to the house I was so mad at Sid I didn't even care if I *was* lying to the police."

He laughed. "That works."

Turning down East Doty, where Civil War–era relics were crammed doric-columned porch to doric-columned porch, he turned serious again. "Calling me was a smart thing to do. Following your husband around yourself would only have gotten you into trouble."

"I found that out last night."

"There are worse things than getting your car stolen." The Blazer stopped at a light, and his gaze met hers. "Look, I've got to tell you: I've never worked on one of these cheating-spouse cases where the party who hired me was wrong about what was going on."

Julie took a deep breath, and her hands clenched in her lap. "I'm prepared for that. And I don't think I'm wrong. But I have to be sure."

"You will be. Either way."

Josephine jumped back into the front seat and landed in Julie's lap.

"Good girl, Josephine." Julie hugged the little dog.

"I think she likes you."

"What's not to like?" Julie sent a teasing glance his way as Josephine curled up in her lap like a cat.

"Nothing that I can see." His response was barely audible. But the tone of it seemed so infused with purely heterosexual meaning that Julie frowned. He met her eyes for the briefest of pregnant moments, then slid his gaze along the bare length of her legs, his expression openly covetous. Julie's eyes widened. Then he added: "I have to tell you, girlfriend, those are absolutely to-die-for shoes. Are they Manolos?"

So much for her sudden suspicion that he was behaving in a very *male* way. She should have remembered: Debbie had a thing for shoes. He'd recommended heels with last night's lingerie, after all.

"Jimmy Choo."

"Ah." He nodded. "Nice. Too bad they don't make 'em in a size twelve."

Julie grinned. "I doubt there's much market for Jimmy Choo sandals in a man's size twelve."

"You'd be surprised, Miz Carlson. You'd be surprised."

"Julie, please."

"Julie, then. And I'm Mac. It's kind of hard to get taken seriously in a business setting when you're a man and then someone goes and calls you Debbie." He braked at a traffic light.

"Did I cause a problem for you at work? I'm sorry."

"Lucky I own sixty percent of the business. With a more conservative boss, you could have gotten me fired."

Julie laughed. Then she sobered as she got down to business. "You'll have to tell me how this private-investigator thing works, because I don't have a clue. Do you have a daily rate or something? Do you take checks? Credit cards?"

"In your situation you're better off paying me cash." He was suddenly all business, too. "That way nothing can be traced back to you if your husband should somehow get suspicious and start looking into things. You should know that can happen. Domestic cases have a way of getting real nasty sometimes."

Julie had no doubt of that. As soon as Sid found out she was thinking divorce the proverbial excrement was going to hit the proverbial fan.

"I'll bill you for my hours," he added. "It'll probably end up being two or three thousand dollars by the time everything's said and done. If I think it's going to go over that, I'll get your approval first."

Julie nodded. "Okay. And you'll let me know how much your car is to fix, won't you?"

"I'll add it to the tab. If you're not careful, you're going to wind up owing me your firstborn child."

The words were meant to be humorous, but they caused a tiny pang in the region of Julie's heart. If the divorce happened, the children she wanted and that Sid had resisted would never become reality. And at twenty-nine, her biological clock was already starting to tick loud and clear.

"So tell me about your marriage. For example, when did you and your husband first meet?"

Julie was glad to be distracted. "I met Sid the night after I was crowned Miss South Carolina. There was a big reception at the governor's mansion and he was there. I was talking to the governor, so thrilled to be there that I was pretty much on cloud nine anyway, and then Sid came up and that was that. He swept me off my feet. We dated for the year of my reign, and then married a month after it was over."

Instead of being moved by her story, Mac frowned as he listened. Which, considering how her marriage looked like it was turning out, was probably a more appropriate response anyway.

"What were you, twenty when you met him? Didn't your family have any objections to you getting involved with a man so much older?"

"Eleven years isn't that much," Julie said. "And no, my family didn't object. Are you kidding? There were just the three of us—my mother and my sister Becky and me—and we were so poor that eating at McDonald's was like going to a fancy restaurant. Sid was rich. He was handsome. He was charming. And I was in love with him. My family—my mother especially—was over the moon."

His lips tightened. "What happened to your father?"

Julie hesitated a moment before replying. Talking about the father who had never been there was still, after all these years, a little painful.

"He and my mother divorced when I was little. I used to see him periodically—a couple of times a year. Then he went away somewhere. I just saw him once more, and then he drowned a couple of weeks later."

A lump—stupid, stupid lump—rose in her throat, and she swallowed hard to get rid of it.

"Sounds like you had a tough life." There was a certain rough sympathy to his tone. His gaze slid in her direction, and Julie saw that he was looking—what?—a little annoyed? Or maybe that was just how he looked when he felt sorry for someone.

Julie's chin came up. She wasn't much into sympathy, at least not when it was directed at her. All her sympathy went to people who were in the same boat she had once been in. She did her best to reach out a hand to them, teaching a regular class on makeup and grooming to the ever-changing residents of the local women's shelter, donating clothes and fittings to poor women who had nothing to wear to job interviews, and generally doing what she could to help others along the path. But she no longer wanted or needed sympathy for herself. She had pulled herself out of poverty by her bootstraps—or, to be more accurate, by her high heels. And if she had to, she could do it again.

Her response was, therefore, deliberately light. "It was interesting."

At that moment Josephine stood up on her lap and gave an imperious-sounding yap. All attention immediately focused on her.

"What?" Mac said to Josephine, sounding exasperated. Her tail wagged madly, and she yapped again.

"She's got to go to the bathroom," he translated for Julie's benefit, and glanced around. They were approaching the Azalea Park and Bird Sanctuary, which was a magnet for tourists, although the locals, being blasé about so familiar a site, rarely visited. Pushcarts offering all manner of foodstuffs, vendors hawking balloons, and a juggler tossing china plates in the air prowled the area in front of the gates. Visitors streamed along the footpaths leading into the park.

Mac found a parking place near the gates and pulled in. Julie looked around nervously. She really didn't want to be spotted in his company—she could hear the questions about her companion's identity now—but that didn't seem very likely. The chance of someone she knew being at this particular tourist trap at just past noon on a steamy Saturday in July was so slim as to be negligible.

He reached into the backseat and came up with a leash. It was pink leather and rhinestones, like Josephine's collar.

Josephine wriggled excitedly when she saw it. His expression was something less than excited as he clipped it to her collar.

"Want to walk for a few minutes, or would you rather wait in the car?" His gaze met hers.

"I'll walk."

He turned off the engine, pocketed the keys, and got out of the car. Julie got out, too, and waited on the sidewalk for him to come around. The sun blazed down, the heat was oppressive, and the tourists were, for the most part, elderly folk decked out in plaid Bermuda shorts and crushable hats. Still, Julie felt happier than she had all day. Josephine squatted and relieved herself the moment she hit grass. Then Mac, his expression faintly martyred, and Josephine, wreathed in doggy smiles, headed toward her. Looking from one to the other—the tall, broad-shouldered, athletically built man with his surfer-god looks and the prancing white puffball of a very feminine poodle, linked by a rhinestone studded pink leash—brought a smile to her face. Julie was suddenly very glad that she was not facing this situation with Sid alone. Debbie and dog might be unlikely allies, but they were allies nonetheless.

"Still feel like walking?" He smiled wryly at her. Josephine wagged her tail.

"Sure." Julie turned toward the gates. Mac and Josephine fell into step beside her. Josephine, being adorable, attracted her fair share of glances. Those glances inevitably shifted from the tiny prancing dog to Mac at the other end of the leash and tended to end with surprised expressions. Mac smiled in answer to the smiles directed at him, but Julie noticed that he didn't look particularly happy to be the focus of so much attention.

Just before they stepped inside the park, Mac signaled to one of the ice-cream vendors, who responded by pushing his cart their way. A pair of elderly women walked by, birding glasses in hand, casting covert glances at Mac and Josephine as they passed.

"Tell you what, I'll buy you an ice cream if you hold the leash," Mac said.

Julie laughed and took the proffered leash as the ice-cream vendor reached them. Mac ordered a DoveBar, then glanced inquiringly at Julie.

"None for me, thanks."

"You sure?"

She nodded, and he shrugged and paid. The ice-cream vendor moved on, and they headed inside the park. Now that Julie held the leash, the attention Josephine attracted was unambiguously positive.

"You don't like ice cream?" Mac took a bite out of one corner. Julie watched enviously as he crunched through the crisp chocolate shell to expose the creamy white goodness within.

"I love ice cream. I just don't eat it."

"Why not?"

"A moment on the lips, forever on the hips." God, she sounded like her mother.

His gaze ran over her body. "You don't look like you need to worry."

"If I didn't worry, I *would* need to. Just eat your ice cream, okay? It's not like I'm starving or anything."

Her stomach growled just then, giving the lie to her words. Julie's eyes widened, then flew to meet his. He grinned at her.

"It's lunchtime, and I haven't eaten yet." She felt compelled to explain away her body's embarrassing gaffe.

"So take a bite of ice cream." He held the DoveBar out to her. Julie eyed the unbitten corner covetously. She *loved* DoveBars. They were right up there with Hershey bars on her forbidden list. "One bite won't make you fat."

One bite. One piece of chocolate. It was a slippery slope, as her mother had pointed out earlier, and Julie knew it. But still—she surrendered to temptation, and sank her teeth into the treat held so tantalizingly close.

Oh, it was good. It was *so-o* good. Smooth milk chocolate wrapped around sweet vanilla ice cream—she could just die.

"Thank you," she said, when the treat had left her mouth in search of her hips and she was able to talk.

"My pleasure." He held the DoveBar out to her again, but this time she shook her head. Firmly. He shrugged, took another bite, then passed the rest to Josephine, who, apparently unconcerned with her girlish figure, downed it greedily. When she was finished she looked up, clearly hoping for more. She had a ring of chocolate around her mouth and looked so comically expectant that Julie had to chuckle.

"Don't laugh. You're not in much better shape." Mac grinned at her. They had stopped in the shade of an enormous magnolia while Josephine wolfed her treat, and the scent of the waxy white blossoms wafted around them. The path underfoot was crunchy gravel, and birdsong filled the air. The only tourists in sight were busy exclaiming about a yellow-throated bullfinch or some such creature apparently perched high in a bearded oak some twenty yards away.

"I have chocolate on my mouth?" Julie's fingers rose to her mouth self-consciously. Tracing the perimeter, she shook her head at him. "I do not."

"Yes you do. Just there." Still grinning, he touched the center of her lower lip with his forefinger, then rubbed his finger back and forth along the line where her lips joined. Her response to the playful gesture shocked her. Her lips parted, and heat shot from where his finger touched clear down to her toes, awakening every single nerve ending in between. She had to stop herself from touching that hard warm finger with her tongue, or drawing it into her mouth and biting down, or . . .

Oh, God, was she pathetic or what? Even as she gritted her teeth and pressed her lips together to stave off the impulse, her gaze flew to his face. Surely he must be experiencing this surge of mind-blowing electricity too? It was impossible that such sizzling heat could be affecting her alone.

But if he was battling a sudden fierce attack of sexual desire, he showed no sign of it. He was looking down at Josephine, his expression perfectly peaceful, and his hand was already dropping away from her mouth. The dismal truth hit her like a splash of cold water in the face: her body was at full boil, and his hadn't even hit simmer.

Of course it hadn't. He wasn't interested in her that way. Good thing, too.

Grimly reminding herself of all the reasons *why* that was a good thing, Julie took a deep and, she hoped, unnoticed breath.

"Do you need anything else from me? I have to be getting back." Her voice sounded perfectly normal, she was pleased to discover.

"Numbers where you can be reached, including cell phone. As much as you know about your husband's daily schedule and usual associates. The kind of car he drives, including license-plate number. Anything else I can get later." He glanced up, met her gaze, and smiled. Those beautiful blue eyes, she was both chagrined and relieved to discover, showed no awareness of her as a woman. "And one dollar."

"One dollar?" Julie asked, surprised. Then, realizing that she had left her purse in the car, she shook her head. "I don't have any money on me."

Mac sighed, pulled out his wallet, extracted a dollar bill, and handed it to her.

"Now give it back to me."

"What?" Julie was smiling at the sheer silliness of it as she obeyed. "Why?"

"Retainer. Congratulations, ma'am: You've just officially hired yourself a private investigator."

And that was *all*, Julie told herself sternly as they retraced their steps to the Blazer, and tried to feel happy about it.

"From here on out you want to be care-

ful. When you're with your husband, be-
have as normally as possible. Whatever
you do, don't get in a fight with him and tell
him you're having him investigated. You
could wind up getting hurt," he warned
some ten minutes later, as, with the information Julie had scribbled in a notepad for
him tucked safely away in the glove compartment, he stopped in the Kroger parking
lot.

"I told you, Sid isn't violent." Julie
opened the door and got out. The bright
heat of the parking lot was almost disorienting after the air-conditioned protection
of the Blazer. Josephine, dislodged from
her comfortable perch on Julie's lap, stood
on the seat wagging her tail in doggy
good-bye. Mac gave Julie a skeptical look.

"Emotions tend to run high in this kind of
case. People do all sorts of unlikely things.
So you mind what I say." His tone was cau-
tionary.

Julie smiled. "I will."

Promising that was easy. Whether Sid
was apt to turn violent or not, she wasn't
about to tell him what she had done. He
would be livid if he found out. She started

to shut the door, then hesitated, glancing in at him again. "When will you start?"

"Right now. There's some preliminary work I can do, and tonight I'll be parked out in front of your house, waiting for the midnight ride of Paul Revere Carlson."

"Funny." It was lame, but it made her smile again, and smiling, as she had discovered earlier, boosted her spirits. Actually, *he* boosted her spirits. He and Josephine.

"Mac. Thanks."

Their gazes met, and the skin around his eyes crinkled as he returned her smile with, she thought, a touch of ruefulness.

"You're welcome. Julie."

10

"AUNT JULIE! AUNT JULIE!"

Erin and Kelly both came tearing into the hall as Julie stepped through the door of her sister's house. Although it was nowhere near as big and fine as Julie's, it was a comfortable, two-story brick house in a nice neighborhood. Becky and Kenny had moved in when the former construction worker had been offered a job by Sid shortly before Erin was born, and they seemed prepared to spend the rest of their lives there.

If Kenny didn't lose his job as collateral damage in her possible divorce, that is.

"Erin. Kelly." Echoing the girls' boisterous

greeting, Julie set her packages down on the blue slate floor and opened her arms to them. They reached her at the same time, and she was giving them both a big hug when her sister walked into the hall, looking harried.

"Hey, Jules. You're just in the nick of time. In five minutes we'll be knee-deep in preschoolers and Mama's decided that this is the moment to start drawing smiley faces on four dozen balloons." Becky rolled her eyes. "What I need is someone to finish filling the party bags. That means you."

"Hey, Beck." Julie grinned at her sister over the girls' heads. Becky was three years her senior, and was in appearance pretty much a younger version of their mother, minus about thirty pounds and the red hair, of course. She had mink brown hair cut sensibly short, and a round, cheerful face. Her body was sturdy rather than slender, and she looked very much the suburban mom in belted khaki shorts and a white camp shirt.

"Julie, is that you?" Dixie yelled from the kitchen. "Get in here. I need help."

"Hi, Mama," Julie hollered back. Then, to

Becky, "My car got stolen last night," as Kelly, the birthday girl, began jumping up and down with excitement, loudly begging to know if the gaily wrapped packages on the floor were for her.

"I know *that,*" Becky said, turning a well-practiced deaf ear to her daughter. "What I want to know is, how mad was Sid?"

"Mad." Julie switched her gaze to her not-to-be-denied niece. "One for you, and one for Erin."

She handed a package to each girl. Kelly immediately began tearing at the wrapping paper on hers, eager to get at the gift.

"But it's not my birthday," Erin objected, hesitating even as she accepted hers. Erin looked much like Becky, although she had her father's gray eyes. She was a sweet, earnest child and Julie loved her dearly.

"Ith *my* birthday, Aunt Julie," Kelly lisped importantly, looking up from her struggle to tug the ribbon off. Kelly's build was far more delicate than her sister's, and her hair was darker, mahogany rather than mink, and wildly curly. She was a pretty, lively child, and Julie loved her dearly, too. "I'm five now."

"Wow, five. That's a big girl." Julie smiled

at Kelly, and then at Erin. "I thought you needed a present to help celebrate your sister turning five."

"Was he mad at *you?*" There was concern in Becky's voice. Julie wondered, as she had once or twice before, if perhaps Becky suspected that all was not shining in Camelot, but she shook her head and said, "He was just mad," as Erin, reassured, started unwrapping her gift, carefully separating the edges of the paper instead of ripping it off with abandon as Kelly was doing. Telling Becky the truth was even less an option than confiding in her mother. Becky would worry, and if she was worried, Kenny would know and badger her until he found out why, and then Kenny would run immediately to Sid. Kenny was fine as a brother-in-law, he loved her sister and the kids, but he knew which side his bread was buttered on. And in this case, Sid was the man with the butter.

"Barbie!" Kelly shrieked gleefully, having finally succeeded in getting the wrappings off, and headed at a dead run for the kitchen, brandishing her gift. "Nana, look, Aunt Julie got me Barbie!"

"I got Barbie too!" Erin yelled after her

sister, having unwrapped enough of the present to identify the contents, and took off in hot pursuit.

"What do you *say?*" Becky called after her daughters as she and Julie trailed them into the kitchen, which was a big square space decorated in cheery yellow. A taped-up HAPPY BIRTHDAY banner formed a swag over the top of the window that looked out into the neat backyard.

Dozens of brightly colored balloons with a rainbow of ribbons attached bobbed against the ceiling. Dixie, holding a balloon with two circle eyes but no mouth drawn on it in one hand and a permanent marker in the other, bent over her granddaughters, admiring their gifts.

"Thank you, Aunt Julie," the girls chorused as their mother prompted them again. Then, still clutching the dolls, they tore off in the direction of their bedrooms.

"Here, Jules, finish filling these. They each get a Fruit Roll-Up, a package of SweeTarts, three stickers, a barrette, and a pencil." Looking harassed again, Becky pushed Julie toward the kitchen table, which was cluttered with Powerpuff Girl–decorated party bags, about two-thirds of which were filled, and a jumble of the aforementioned goodies. Julie went to work as Becky turned to the birthday cake on the counter and started sticking small blue candles into the white icing.

"Kelly and Erin remind me so much of you two at their age," Dixie said with a hint of nostalgia as she drew a smiling mouth to complete the balloon, then reached for another one. "If Becky weren't so silly about entering the girls in pageants, I bet Kelly could win as many titles as you did, Julie."

"No," Becky responded sharply. Dixie pursed her lips at her older daughter, but before she could argue the doorbell pealed. With a quelling look at her mother, Becky went to answer it to the accompaniment of wild whoops from her daughters, who skidded past in an effort to beat her to the door.

"Can you believe she's that way? You winning all those pageants was the best thing that ever happened to us, her included." Dixie's gaze shifted to Julie in a transparent appeal for support. From as far back as Julie could remember, Dixie had entered her in every beauty contest that came along, worrying over her hair and makeup and strategizing over how to come up with eye-catching costumes on their dollar-store budget, which had actually been a good thing, because Julie had learned how to design and make the most beautiful clothes out of nothing, which in turn had led to Carolina Belle. Julie's looks would be their ticket, Dixie had prophesied time and time again, and so it had proved.

"Sometimes I think Becky's downright ashamed of where she came from," Dixie continued in a hurt tone that she was careful to keep low so that Becky would not overhear.

In her mind, Julie heard Sid calling them *trailer trash,* and could not find it in her heart to blame her sister, although she would never say as much to their mother. Much as she hated to admit it, *trailer trash* was putting a positive spin on their childhood. Lots of times, between Dixie's tumultuous love life and complete lack of marketable skills, they hadn't even had so much as a trailer to live in. When Dixie was in between husbands and boyfriends, there'd been cheap motel rooms and women's shelters and even a memorable month spent living in a tent in a campground just like Girl Scouts, as Dixie had bracingly described the demoralizing regimen of public showers and toilets and sleeping on blankets on the ground, while Julie and Becky tried to go to school and pretend their lives were just like everyone else's. Always, for Julie, there'd been beauty pageants, the winning of which was often accompanied by a little prize money or some gift certificates or something to buoy them along. When she'd turned thirteen and Becky was sixteen, they'd ganged up together to put their dual feet down about their mother's love life, absolutely refusing to move in with her boyfriend du jour and insisting they get a place of their own. That's when they'd become trailer trash, which had been a wonderful thing because that rented double-wide was the first permanent home she and Becky had ever known. After that, Dixie had forsworn men, and all three of them had waited tables and cleaned houses and weeded flower beds and babysat and did whatever else they could find to do just to afford to eat and pay rent on their treasured new home. Then Julie had won a big one, Miss Teenage South

Carolina Peach, when she was fifteen, and modeling gigs had started coming her way, and what with those and some local television commercials and a few more titles that came with scholarships attached, their lives had become almost normal and she'd even been able to go to college. Becky, with whom she had shared her winnings as much as she could, had opted for a job at a rent-a-car place, and Dixie had met and fallen in love with Hiram Clay. Then Becky met Kenny, Dixie married Hiram, and Julie won Miss South Carolina and met Sid, all in the same year.

And so here the three of them were, eight years later, living out their happily-ever-afters. Each of them had gotten what she'd always wanted, and each dream had a flaw. Dixie's husband had been disabled in a car crash four years after the wedding; Becky's wholehearted embrace of her role as the Perfect Suburban Mom had a kind of compulsive quality to it that Julie suspected was the result of their tumultuous childhood; and in her own case, the sad truth was that the stable home and loving marriage that she'd craved all her life— were not.

So much for the idea of happily-ever-after. Julie was pretty sure that, in reality, happily-ever-after simply didn't exist.

"I don't think it's so much that Becky's ashamed," Julie said. "But that was then and this is now, Mama. I can see why she thinks that putting Kelly in beauty pageants probably isn't a good idea. For one thing, it might make Erin feel bad."

Dixie said, *"Julie,"* as though Julie had deeply wounded her. Then, bristling slightly, she added, "Are you saying that you think Becky felt bad when you were winning all those pageants?"

Julie suppressed a sigh. "I don't know, Mama. But . . ."

Erin and Kelly came running back into the kitchen with two of their friends at their heels just then, and any thought of continuing the conversation was forgotten. The birthday party was under way.

When it was over, Julie just had time to pick up the cleaning and get home before Sid did. Julie was in the shower when he came upstairs to get his clothes out of his part of the huge his-and-her walk-in closets, dressing areas, and bathrooms that adjoined the master suite on either side, so she missed seeing him. By the time she came downstairs, dressed and ready to go, he was already standing in the living room waiting for her.

He was wearing a classic black tux, which became him. With his dark hair brushed back to hide the bald spot at his crown and his wire-rimmed glasses firmly in place on the bridge of his long, thin nose he looked both elegant and distinguished. Looking at him as she paused in the arched doorway, Julie was reminded of why she had married him in the first place, and her heart ached.

How could he do this to her? To them? The questions quivered on the tip of her tongue. It was all she could do not to ask Sid outright, but she remembered Mac's warning in time to bite the words back. Sid would only deny everything anyway, so what was the point?

"You're not going to wear *that,* are you?" Sid asked, snapping the cell phone on which he'd been talking closed and looking her over with a critical eye. Feeling immediately defensive, Julie glanced down at herself. Her cocktail dress was fuchsia silk, short and sleeveless, with a flirty ruffle around the hem. Until that moment, she'd thought that it looked great. That *she* looked great.

"What's wrong with it?" Her throat felt tight.

"It makes you look hippy. Every bit of the weight you've gained lately seems to have gone right to your butt, have you noticed? Well, too late now. We'll be late if you go change." His gaze ran over her again, mildly disdainful as only Sid could be, and then he took her arm and practically propelled her out the door in front of him. Moments later Julie was buckled into the front seat of the Mercedes, where she rode in tight-lipped silence to the country club. Once there, she plastered a big smile on her face and settled in for an evening spent hiding her mega-butt and pretending her marriage was wonderful while guilty visions of Hershey squares and DoveBars molding themselves to her rear danced through her head.

"Here's the big guy." Wreathed in smiles, Sid stood up as his father, John Sidney Carlson III, known as John, threaded his way through the crowded room toward them. He was heavier than Sid, obviously decades older, and bald except for a white fringe above his ears, but there could be no doubt that the two were father and son. They exchanged a back-clapping embrace as Julie greeted his girlfriend du jour with a smile and an air kiss. Pamela Tipton was a couple of years younger than she was—John was seventy-one—and lovely. She had a short, silvery-blond pixie cut, enormous blue eyes, and a size-two body. Complete with a very small, very toned tush.

"And how's my favorite daughter-in-law?" John asked, turning to her. Smiling gamely at this old joke—she was his only daughter-in-law—Julie lifted her cheek for his kiss and then sat down again to feign interest in the ensuing conversation. Sipping at a glass of iced tea, she barely picked at a salad and concentrated on looking happy when she was feeling anything but.

If she had only herself to consider, she thought as she exchanged friendly chitchat with Mary Bishop, the lieutenant governor's wife—the couple shared their table along with Sid's partner Raymond Campbell and his wife Lisa and Circuit Court

Judge Jimmy Morris and his wife Tricia—maybe getting Sid out of her life might not be such a bad thing.

In fact, she was beginning to cotton to the idea of telling Sid to take a hike. A permanent hike. As in, take this marriage and shove it.

On the way home, Julie was surprised at how much she longed to fling both her suspicions and her private investigator in Sid's face. With the supreme density that she had come to expect from him, he seemed to have no idea that she was angry. Reminding herself that discretion was the better part of valor, she bit her tongue as he made a few general comments about the evening. Fortunately, his cell phone rang before she succumbed to the temptation to do more than nod in reply. He started talking to someone about some problem that had to do with the supply of bricks. Julie stopped listening, entertaining herself by looking out the window instead.

It was a beautiful starlit night like the one before, but its beauty merely served to underline her own unhappiness. After a few minutes in which her mind wandered hither and yon, she found herself thinking about

Mac, and as soon as she did, some of her inner turmoil eased. She'd had fun with him under the unlikeliest of circumstances, he was the hottest-looking guy she'd met in forever, his dog was an absolute darling, and—he was gay. Oh, well. In this case, three out of four was probably a good thing.

As the Mercedes drove up their street she oh-so-casually glanced around but saw no sign of Mac or his Blazer. Of course, he could be anywhere—or nowhere. As dark as it was under the overhanging oaks that lined the street, it was almost impossible to be sure that he was—or wasn't—there.

Once inside the house, Sid—naturally—headed for the den while she went directly upstairs and stripped off the fuchsia dress. She knew herself well enough to know that she would never wear it again.

She was as afraid of looking hippy as a little child might be of a monster hiding under the bed.

Which Sid knew, of course. He'd said that to make her feel bad. He was good at that, making little needling remarks that stung forever. She knew she should ignore them, but she couldn't.

He knew what buttons to push, and he pushed them with cruel glee.

Kicking off her shoes, Julie peeled off her panty hose, then headed into the bathroom in her bra and panties to turn on the taps. She would take a long, hot bath, put on the ugliest, most unsexy nightwear she could find, and go to sleep. No more humiliating trips to the den to see when—if—he was coming to bed. No more worrying about what there was about her person that turned him off. No more wondering if he was cheating.

Finding out what Sid was up to was Mac's problem now. The knowledge was a tremendous relief.

Still, while the water ran she could not help going into Sid's bathroom and just peeking in his medicine cabinet. There, on the third shelf, was the bottle of vitamins. Pouring the contents into her palm, she took a quick inventory: mixed in with the businesslike yellow-and-white capsules were six—count 'em, six—blue diamond-shaped pills.

Sid must be staying home tonight.

Lip curling at the thought, Julie returned to her bathroom, turned off the taps, and walked thoughtfully back into the bedroom. Flipping off the light so that the room was plunged into darkness, she crossed to the window and edged the heavy silk drape aside so that she could look out. Moonlight filtered across the lawn, overlaying the silvery velvet of the grass with black chiffon shadows from the trees that shifted and swayed as if to music she couldn't hear. Beyond the low brick wall that fronted the lawn, the street was a solid impenetrable black. Was Mac's Blazer parked down there somewhere? Maybe. He'd said he would be waiting. But she had no way of knowing for sure.

How long she stood there, lost in thought, she couldn't have said. What brought her out of her reverie was, from downstairs, the faint but unmistakable sound of the door between the kitchen and the garage opening and then closing again.

Sid had either left something in the car or, Viagra notwithstanding, he *was* going out.

Julie's whole body stiffened at the thought. All of a sudden she knew, *knew,* that she wasn't going to be able to bear just waiting around for Mac's report.

She certainly wasn't going to be able to calmly have her bath and go to sleep.

She wanted to see what Sid was up to with her own eyes. She *needed* to see what Sid was up to with her own eyes.

That would be closure. And for her to finally, once and for all, end her marriage in her own mind and heart, closure was what she needed.

She heard a low, vibrating hum. She knew that sound, too: the garage door was going up.

Galvanized, Julie ran for her closet, yanked on the first dress that came to hand—a red mini styled like a polo shirt—grabbed a reasonable pair of shoes—slides with tiny shaped heels—and, shoes in hand, sprinted barefoot for the stairs.

If Mac was out there, she was going with him. If he wasn't, she would follow Sid herself.

Flying through the hall, she yanked open the front door, leaped down the white stone steps, and sped across the soft, cushiony grass toward the small iron gate at the far corner of the yard.

Bright beacons lit the driveway, stretching toward the street like reaching arms. Sid's car rolled in near silence out of the garage, heading down the driveway. Would he see her? Julie's heart began to slam against her breastbone as she glanced over her shoulder at the moving car. No. She was far enough away that she was pretty sure he couldn't. But she was going to be too late. . . .

The Mercedes turned left at the street exactly as it had the night before. Julie was forced to hold up just as she reached the gate, ducking behind the brick wall, drawing in great gulps of air as she listened to chorusing katydids and caroling crickets and waited for the big car to pass. She heard the purr of the expensive engine, the swish of tires on pavement, and then Sid was gone.

Bursting through the gate, she bolted onto the still-warm pavement just as the Mercedes reached the corner. Its taillights glowed bright red as it paused at the stop sign.

Oh, God, where was Mac?

She looked wildly around. There, in front of the Cranes', a vehicle was parked. In the dark it was impossible to be certain, but it might be the Blazer.

Or it might not.

Taking a deep breath, she sprinted toward it just as its headlights came on, pinning her in their glare.

11

MAC COULDN'T BELIEVE HIS EYES when Julie darted into his headlight beams like a startled deer. Before he could do more than slam on his brakes—running over a client was not something that was generally conducive to repeat business—she was yanking open the passenger door and flinging herself into the seat beside him.

"Go, go, go," she said urgently, slamming her door. "You'll lose him."

Sid's Mercedes was, indeed, disappearing around the corner.

"Damn it . . ." Mac began, then gave it up as he realized he had a choice: he could sit there and reason with Julie or lose the man he wanted in the worst way to follow.

With one narrow-eyed look at her, he took his foot off the brake and headed out in pursuit. She fastened her seat belt and settled in.

"This was not part of the plan," he said as he reached the intersection.

"Screw the plan." Julie sounded breathless. "He's my husband, I'm paying to have him followed, and that means that I get to go along if I want to."

The Mercedes was perhaps three blocks away, easing through Summerville's side streets toward the expressway. Mac kept it in sight, but was careful to stay far enough back to not attract Sid's attention.

"Oh yeah? Just what surveillance handbook did you read?"

"He didn't notice me the last time. *And* I was in my Jaguar."

"You got lucky." His mouth was grim. She was wearing some kind of perfume—every time he breathed he got a whiff of it, soft and tantalizing. Her hair, black as the night, hung in loose waves around her face. Her eyes were huge with excitement, glinting at him in the faint light from the dash. Her lips—those lush, beautiful lips that he had been fool enough to touch earlier in the day; the warm, soft lips that had kissed his cheek—were parted as she breathed. The dress she was almost wearing stopped at approximately mid-thigh, and clung to every delectable curve on the way down. And he was willing to bet every dollar he possessed that her long tanned legs were bare again.

This he did not need. It was distracting, to say the least. *She* was distracting.

"I'll stay out of your way, I promise. You won't even know I'm here."

Mac almost laughed at the impossibility of that. Up ahead, Sid hit Summerville's main drag and turned, as expected, for the expressway. Mac followed, keeping well back.

"This is stupid." He turned up the long ramp onto the expressway in Sid's wake, and glanced at her. "This is not happening again. *I* follow your husband. *You* stay home. *I* bring you a full report and pictures, if warranted. *You* pay me. Got it?"

"If I'm paying, I get to do it any way I want."

"Not if you're paying *me.*"

"If you don't like it, you can quit. Just turn around, take me back home, and quit. I can always follow Sid myself."

She had him there. No way in hell was he going to quit. He'd wanted to get the goods on Sid too badly for too long—and now there was Julie's well-being to consider, too.

Although thinking about Julie as anything other than Sid's wife was a truly dumb idea.

"You pull this again, and I will quit," he said, although he knew that by his not immediately turning around the threat lost most of its teeth.

A small smile curved her mouth as she realized she'd won.

"I won't be any trouble, you'll see," she said.

Mac had to fight not to roll his eyes.

"Where's Josephine?" She glanced into the backseat.

"The only creature that could possibly be more in the way than you on a job like this is Josephine. I left her at home." In the bathroom, actually. This time he'd taken care to tie the (new) shower curtain out of reach. With the rug stuffed into the cabinet under the sink along with the toilet paper, and all toiletries plus his razor stashed in the medicine cabinet, there was no possible damage she could do. He didn't think.

Julie leaned forward suddenly. "He's changing lanes. He must be getting ready to get off. There—see?"

They had reached Charleston, and the Mercedes was, indeed, pulling into the far right lane. Traffic was fairly heavy—it was a Saturday night in July, after all, and tourists were as ubiquitous as fire ants—so Mac didn't much worry about being spotted. Yet. It was when he had to get out of the Blazer and follow Sid with Sid's extremely noticeable wife in tow that the situation was going to deteriorate into farce.

"I see," he said, and pulled into that lane too. It was only as they passed into an area of figure-eight ramps lit up bright as day by the huge overhead lights that he noticed the color of her dress. "Did you *have* to wear red? Why not just stick a flashing light on your head and be done with it?"

She glanced down at herself. "It wasn't intentional. I just grabbed the first thing I could reach and pulled it on."

"I guess I should thank my lucky stars that tonight you bothered to get dressed."

"Don't be bitchy, Mac." She smiled at him, a sweet and coaxing smile that made his blood heat. God help him, but he was a sucker for her kind of smile, for her kind of dark, sultry looks—oh, face the facts, a sucker for her.

Also just a sucker in general, he told himself sourly, for letting what should have been a fairly simple thing—get more information on Sid, check it out, see if it led anywhere he might be interested in following—get so involved. If he had an ounce of sense, he'd turn around right this minute, take her back home, give her the name of a couple of other private investigators she could contact, and wash his hands of her.

But even as he had the thought Mac knew he wasn't going to do it, so he gave up thinking for the moment and concentrated on keeping the Mercedes in sight as they left the expressway and made their way through Charleston's crowded warren of streets.

"He's going to the same place. I knew it." Julie leaned forward again.

"If he's meeting someone, they probably

have a regular place to be together." Mac glanced at her and sighed. "Look, why don't you let me take you home? I'll follow him—*alone*—the next time he goes out. One thing I don't need—and you don't need either, if you just had the sense to know it—is you creating some huge scene when we catch up to Sid and his cutie."

Julie looked at him then, and he was surprised at the sudden glint in her eyes.

"I'm not going to make a scene," she said. "I just have to know. Sid and I have been married eight years. That means something to me. I don't even think I love him anymore, but the fact that we are married *means* something to me. I just can't walk out without seeing with my own two eyes that he's cheating. Can you understand that?"

Meeting her gaze, Mac found a new reason to want to stick it to Sid. A man who could cheat on a wife like his didn't deserve to keep her—but then, that was Sid. He always had been sure he could have his cake and eat it, too.

"What I understand is that I'm nuts for not turning around right now and driving you home," he said shortly, and she made a face at him.

He turned a corner to find himself on the street where he had met Julie the night before. The Pink Pussycat was three blocks down on the left. Would Clinton Edwards be there again, blissfully ignorant that he had been busted by his wife? Probably. It had been his experience that people stayed true to their patterns. There were approximately four dozen bars, strip joints, massage parlors, and porn shops crowded into a six-block square. When he had been a cop, this area had been known as no-man's-land. Robberies, rapes, shootings, assaults, and various other crimes happened down here in multiple numbers every single weekend night when the weather was good. And in Charleston the weather was almost always good.

"I can't see him." Julie had one leg beneath her now, peering through the windshield at the press of cars. The street was congested with traffic; the sidewalks were thick with pedestrians looking for a walk on the wild side as part of their vacation.

"I can." No need to add that, if he lost sight of the Mercedes, he could always follow its progress on the handy-dandy little device stored at the moment in the console between the seats. That, plus the tiny transmitter he'd had the forethought to slip under the Mercedes' bumper not long after he'd dropped Julie off at her store earlier, made this particular part of tonight's surveillance not a problem.

"What's he doing?" Julie's voice was urgent.

"Parking. Sit tight. I would pull in right behind him, but no point in letting him spot us first thing."

That bit of sarcasm earned him a withering look. Mac finally allowed himself to smile as he drove on past the lot where the Mercedes had turned in.

Truth was, he'd made up his mind: as far as keeping Sid under surveillance was concerned, tonight he was going to have to write off as a dead loss. The situation, if it played out the way it very well could, had the potential to get explosive, and nobody needed that, least of all his wrongheaded client. The thing to do was to take Julie on a nice tour of some of the area's establishments—not the hole-in-the-wall dives where perversions of almost unimaginable varieties gave the term "performance art" a whole new meaning, but the more mainstream bars—proclaim Sid lost, and return her home again safe and sound with the clear understanding that he would do the job on his own another day.

Or else.

An alley up the street led to an out-of-the-way parking lot that was used mainly by clients of the rent-a-room-by-the-hour hookers that worked over the adult bookstore on the building's main floor. The lot was dark, its patrons were as bent on secrecy as he was, and the chances of encountering Sid in it were, he calculated, near zero.

"He'll be long gone by the time we get back to where he parked," Julie said, throwing him an impatient look that said *some private eye you are.* Mac didn't grin, but didn't miss it by much. Now that the evening's agenda had changed, he was starting to enjoy himself.

"I have an idea where he's headed." Actually, he didn't—this whole area seemed out of character for Sid—but he did have a good idea of where Sid *wasn't* headed, and under the circumstances that worked just as well.

"You do?" She sounded impressed, he noted as he parked the car.

"Ma'am, that's what us PIs do." His voice was suitably modest.

Clearly she was in no mood to appreciate subtle humor. She was already reaching for the door handle as he turned off the ignition. He grabbed her arm—and in the process registered that it was slender, firm, with warm silky skin—before she could bolt off in pursuit of Sid. "Whoa. Slow down a minute."

"What?" She glanced around at him. Impatience came through loud and clear.

"We're going to have to make some adjustments here. Unless your husband's a blind man." There was always the possibility, however remote, that they might encounter Sid in the street.

"What kind of adjustments?"

Mac let go of her arm and reached into the back. He groped around the footwell behind her seat, and came up with the prize he sought: his Debbie wig, right where it had landed the night before. He handed it to her.

"What . . . ?" She looked down at the hunk of hair in her hand as if she thought it might bite her.

"Don't you want to find out for yourself if blondes really do have more fun?" He grinned. She didn't.

Her eyes met his. "You're kidding, right?"

"Nope. Put it on."

Julie looked revolted, but after one more glance at the wig she flipped down the visor and did as she was told, twisting her own hair around her head and smoothing the long platinum strands down over it.

"I look like Jennifer Lopez disguised as Britney Spears." She sounded appalled.

"Just as long as you don't look like Julie Carlson, we're in business." He flipped her visor closed, and leaned across her to open her door. "Let's go."

The temperature had cooled off considerably from the steam-room conditions that had existed that afternoon, but it was still hot and humid, he noted as he got out of the car. Street noises, indistinguishable voices, and throbbing strains of music provided a background for the closer sounds of Julie shutting her door and walking around the Blazer toward him. Actually, he thought, appraising her almost unwillingly as she rounded his front bumper, she looked pretty good as a blonde. Then he permitted himself a wry inner smile. Might as well face the truth: With that killer bod and those yard-long legs, she could dye her hair neon green and still knock men dead at forty paces.

"Yo, man, it cost you twenty dollah to park here." A hulking kid in a wifebeater and homeboy jeans appeared out of the shadows, walking forward with his hand out and an insolent swagger that told Mac he'd gotten lucky with this scam before.

"You collecting for Fitch now?" He turned to face the kid, keeping his posture re-laxed—he wasn't expecting trouble, but you never knew—and Julie came up on his left side. Her hand curled around his arm just above the elbow as she stepped close, facing the kid too, pressing against his side as if for protection, and her perfume wafted up to his nostrils. The whole I-didn't-inhale thing was crapola in this case, there was no way he could resist it, and the scent of her plus the gentle slide of her fingers against his skin sent his libido into overdrive. He gritted his teeth in sheer self-defense.

"You know Fitch?" Luckily—with Julie disordering his senses, he wasn't in any shape for the situation to get aggressive—this gave the kid pause.

"Yeah."

"Oh. Sorry, man." Easy as that, the kid melted back into the shadows. Beside him, he heard Julie let out a sigh of relief. Her hand slid down his arm and over his wrist, trailing fire every millimeter of the way, to nestle into his. His fingers closed around hers automatically. Still holding her hand, because he found that he was absolutely incapable of not holding it once presented with the temptation, he started walking down the alley toward the main drag with her tap-tapping on those sexy little heels right beside him.

"The punks who stole my car looked just like that." She was sticking close. He could feel her arm brushing his, generating a heat that radiated throughout his body.

"They all look just like that."

He was feeling tense, and it had absolutely nothing to do with the thought that the kid or others even worse might be lurking in the shadows waiting to pounce.

"Is Fitch the owner of the parking lot? And do you really know him?"

"Yes. To both." His replies were terse. He realized that, but bending his mind around more eloquent conversation was beyond him at the moment. The mind-over-body thing he prided himself on was taking a couple of minutes to work.

"You know some interesting people."

They reached the street before he had to reply. Stepping onto the sidewalk, they were immediately caught up in a river of people sweeping along porn central. Having Julie go up on tiptoe and crane her neck both ways brought them a great deal of unwelcome attention as the current was forced to part around them.

"I don't see Sid anywhere." She was keeping her balance by resting the hand that wasn't clutching his flat in the center of his chest. He could almost feel the outline of her fingers like a brand through his shirt.

"I know where to look." The reminder that she was not free was timely. This was not some hot little honey that he would be getting better acquainted with between the sheets later. This was Julie Carlson, his client, Sid's wife.

Too bad the part of him that most needed to know that didn't seem to have much of a brain.

"Come on." He removed her hand from his chest and started walking. Her fingers were entwined with his now, and, short of wresting his hand free, which with the best will in the world he couldn't seem to discover within himself an inclination to do, he appeared to be stuck with that. Not even bothering to look for Sid—if they ran across him it would be pure bad luck—he headed toward Sweetwater's, one of the more mainstream of the girlie bars on the strip.

Everybody and his daddy ended up at Sweetwater's sooner or later. If Sid was meeting a lady on the sly, Sweetwater's was the one place he wouldn't go. It was both too raunchy and too public for a lying, cheating, fornicating pseudo family man and pillar of the community like Sid.

"You really think he's here?" Julie asked after Mac had paid their cover and they were ushered inside. The question, which should have been hushed, had to be almost shouted to be heard over the pounding music.

"Maybe."

The warehouse-sized front room was aglow with a disorienting purple light. The reflecting walls were the silver of aluminum foil. Pairs of women, naked except for swirls of glitter paint decorating their already decorative bodies, danced back to back in Plexiglas cages about seven feet above the floor. Couples—basically fully dressed men and half-naked women, except for the few female tourists who were as easy to spot as skunks on snow—shook their booties with enthusiasm. The hostess, a fine-looking redhead in a silver thong and glow-in-the-dark pasties, met them at the door and led them toward a purple leather banquette that stretched most of the length of one wall. Small rectangular tables stood in front of the banquette at approximately four-foot intervals, leaving just enough room for a couple behind each table. There were about half a dozen couples sitting there now like ducks in a row. Mac took a closer look at some of the action going on behind those tables and amended that to, like depraved ducks in a row.

Two lap dances, one spanking, one woman busy beneath the table, and one titty grope were in progress as they approached. The hostess indicated their table—a lap dance to the left, the titty grope to the right—and he stood back to let Julie slide in before him. Her eyes were as big as saucers as she glanced around, and he felt a momentary stab of compunction at exposing such an obvious neophyte to the seamier side of Charleston's nightlife.

He appeased it with the reflection that, given the area, this was one of the more mainstream places he could have taken her.

"What can I get you?" When they were both seated a silver-thonged waitress appeared, smiled at him rather than Julie, and bent deliberately close as she waited for his answer. The resulting view was well worth looking at, but considering his company he refrained. Fortunately, this far from the car-sized speakers it was possible to hear and be heard without being right in the waitress's—uh—face.

"Heineken." He glanced at Julie.

"White wine."

The waitress smirked, gave Julie a pitying glance, and turned on her heel. And yes, she was wearing heels. Spikes. Silver. And they and the minuscule silver strip snaking between her cheeks were it. Whatever other faults Sweetwater's had, he mused as he reflexively eyeballed her retreating form, at least the scenery was good.

"Oh my God, there's Sid!"

What? Mac didn't say it aloud, but his head whipped around in the direction Julie was looking so fast he was surprised his neck didn't snap.

There was Sid all right, dark suit, slicked-back hair, wire-rimmed glasses, the ultimate preppy sleazeball, headed straight toward them with the redheaded hostess all smiles as she said something to him over her shoulder and two women, both lookers in thongs just like the redhead, hanging one on either arm.

It was all Mac could do to keep his jaw from dropping in amazement. Christ, had the prescient SOB somehow gotten the drop on *them?*

"Oh my God," Julie said again, a hand flying to her mouth.

Shit.

But Sid didn't appear to have any idea that anybody who shouldn't be was present—and Mac meant to keep it that way. He reached for Julie—her eyes were now big as *flying* saucers and locked on Sid—and slid both arms around her waist. Time for damage control. Fast.

Clearly startled, she met his gaze.

"Climb up on my lap."

He blocked her view of Sid—and Sid's of the pair of them—with his back as he spoke. Julie's face was just inches away now, so close he could see the creamy texture of her skin, the little veins of gold in her eyes, each separate velvety black eyelash. Her eyes were wide and shocked and her lips were soft and curved, and to make bad worse she felt warm and supple and sexy as hell in his arms. He willed himself to ignore his body's immediate response, to cool out, to respond to this unforeseen emergency like the professional he was.

Then Julie did as he told her and climbed onto his lap, straddling him in a remarkably good imitation of the base position of the undulating lap dancer on her left. Her slim, tanned legs pressed tight on either side of his—and yes, he discovered as he automatically grasped warm, taut-muscled, satin-skinned thighs to settle her into position, her legs were bare.

His self-control did a kamikaze dive as suddenly Sid's presence became the least of his problems. He had to instantly remind himself of just what had happened to those suicidal Japanese pilots and pull up while he still could.

Saved from fiery self-immolation by the narrowest of margins, he took a deep breath and assessed the situation.

She was facing him now, instead of Sid, which was good.

And her sweet little twat in the silky black panties that he'd gotten just a glimpse of as she'd swung astride was nestled against the big, dumb part of him which had already proved conclusively that it lacked a brain.

Which was bad.

12

HANGING ON TO MAC'S SHOULDERS for balance, Julie perched atop his lap and glared at Sid through the reflecting silver wall. Her suspicions were right on, she realized, and felt her stomach clench. She'd known it, of course, all along. Sid was with a woman—two women. Two nearly naked women who were on him like white on paper and seemed to know him pretty damned well.

Although the pounding music made it impossible to be sure, she was almost positive she'd heard one call him *Sid* in a squeaky baby voice that sounded like Marilyn Monroe on helium.

Her cheating husband was no more than

ten feet behind her now, and if it hadn't been for Mac's restraining hands on her legs she would have dismounted and walked over to him and punched the no-good dirty rotten lying cheater right in the nose.

Can you spell "history," Sid? she thought, watching him pull one of the Minnie Mouse–voiced silicone queens close to his side and nuzzle her neck. 'Cause that's what you're getting ready to be.

Sid must have sensed something, or maybe felt the force of her gaze, because just then he glanced her way. To her horror, his eyes fixed on her as she sat astride Mac's lap, sliding down her back in an appraising kind of way, then glancing into the mirror-like wall in an attempt to see her face. Julie panicked, then realized that her image, like his, was faintly distorted by the silver panel, and the blond wig was probably enough to throw him off. Still . . .

She dived for cover. Figuratively speaking, of course.

Pulse racing, she ducked without, she hoped, seeming to do so, by the simple method of bending her head and pressing her mouth to Mac's. Desperate situations called for desperate measures, after all. She wasn't ready to confront Sid yet: she wanted to sort this out in her head *and* with a really hardball-playing lawyer before Sid realized she was on to him. Plus, she was still just a little afraid of Sid's reaction if he should discover that she was following him, although what he might actually do, she didn't quite know. Keeping quiet was the result of a gut feeling, not justified by anything except a kind of sixth sense.

But that sixth sense was giving her as shrill and urgent a warning as a smoke alarm in a house on fire.

So she shook her false hair forward to hide her face and kissed Mac, knowing that, as her partner in this emergency, he would understand why she was doing it and play along.

His lips were dry, warm, and firm, and, she discovered, she quite liked kissing them, his sexual orientation notwithstanding. He didn't seem to have any problems with the kiss either. At least, he did not push her away or recoil in disgust. In fact, after one pregnant instant in which their gazes met, he even seemed to get into it.

His lids closed and his hands slid up her thighs with a carnality that made her still-open eyes widen.

He took over the kiss, handling it like a pro, slanting his mouth over hers and licking between her lips until, just from instinct, her eyes closed and her lips parted to let his tongue inside. Then his tongue filled her mouth, and he was kissing her so expertly and so thoroughly that it was clear he'd had some experience somewhere. His arms went around her, hard and strong as steel bands, and his hands splayed over her back, so hot they burned her skin even through her dress. He pulled her close against him, flattening her breasts against the solid wall of his chest.

She loved it.

The same sizzle of electricity that had afflicted her when he'd touched her mouth at the bird sanctuary shot through her again times about a trillion, and she went all soft and shivery inside.

The warm, wet invasion of her mouth thrilled her clear down to her toes. Which, she discovered as they curled in ecstatic response, were now bare, her shoes having apparently slid unnoticed from her feet

sometime within the last couple of seconds. Totally swept away, she wrapped her
arms around Mac's neck and put her
tongue in his mouth and kissed him back.

"That'll be ten dollars," the waitress said.

What could have been seconds or life-
times later, Julie registered the words and
their meaning and pulled her mouth from
his. The way she felt gave dazed and confused a whole new meaning, she thought
as she lifted her lids to stare at him in dazzled surprise. His eyes met hers. Julie saw
that his pupils had dilated to the point
where his irises looked almost black. A
dark flush rode high on his cheekbones,
and his lips were still parted from their kiss.
He was breathing hard. She could feel the
rapid rise and fall of his chest against her
breasts.

"Mac," she said, alerting him to the waitress's presence. His mouth tightened, and
his eyes as they met hers had a hot, sexy
gleam in them that made her catch her
breath. Oh God, he was gorgeous, she
thought, her gaze drinking him in.

"Got it." His gaze flicked to the waitress.
One hand dropped away from her back to
dig in the rear pocket of his jeans for his

wallet. The other joined it seconds later as, his arms still around her but loosely now, he opened his wallet and extracted a bill. He handed the bill to the waitress, of whom Julie was now only peripherally aware. All her senses were suddenly too full of Mac again to allow anything else to really register. His crotch was pushing into hers, and there was a hard and urgent mound beneath his jeans. It felt so incredibly good pressing against her that she sucked in her breath and pressed back.

"Keep the change." Mac was speaking to the waitress, but his voice was thick and his eyes were on Julie again. The waitress said something—probably *thanks,* although Julie couldn't be sure—and disappeared. Mac shoved the wallet back into his pocket, shifting beneath her in the process. Julie felt the nudge of that jeans-covered bulge against the most sensitive part of her and suddenly knew what it meant to truly crave something.

Forget chocolate: what she wanted with every greedy nerve ending was sex. With Mac.

Her throat went dry, her loins tightened and began to radiate heat. She shivered, conscious of an almost overwhelming urge to rip off her panties and have her way with him there and then.

Then it hit her like a baseball bat over the head that this was Debbie—*Debbie*—and he had a giant—really, truly, enormous—hard-on. For her.

She blinked in befuddled, passion-clouded surprise. What was the deal with that?

"Do you—do you go both ways?" Her voice was soft and faintly unsteady. Puzzled, she frowned into his eyes, but even as she tried to make sense of the whole thing she snuggled closer against him, her arms tightening around his neck, loving the hot prickly feel of her nipples as they pressed against the solid warmth of his chest, loving the silky slide of her panties over the hardness in his jeans, particularly loving the throbbing deep inside her panties, too turned on at the moment to do more than wonder vaguely about the fine points of his sexual wiring.

He stared at her, seemingly uncomprehending, for the space of a couple of heartbeats. Then she saw a flicker in his eyes as comprehension dawned, and he grimaced.

"No," he said, and slid a hand around her nape beneath the heavy flow of artificial hair, pulling her mouth back down to his. Then he kissed her again.

Oh, God, if she had ever been so hot for someone in her life she didn't remember it. His kiss was hard and hungry and yet gentle at the same time, and she was completely bowled over by the warm wet urgency of it. He explored her mouth with an expertise that made her dizzy while she kissed him back and pressed her breasts against his chest and moved sensuously against the tangible evidence that he was experiencing at least this one heterosexual urge. His hands were under her dress now, both of them, cupping her bottom, squeezing her cheeks through the silky panties, and she melted inside like microwaved plastic.

Oh, God, a little more of this and she was going to come. . . .

Somebody lurched into their table. There was a tinkling crash, and Julie felt a cool rain of liquid on her bare instep even as she dragged her mouth from Mac's and glanced around.

"Sorry." The man who'd been enjoying

the lap dancer was on his feet trying to get out between the tables. Obviously drunk, his attention focused on the near-naked woman who was pulling him by the hand, he'd stumbled into their table, causing her wineglass to topple onto its side, break, and disgorge its contents. Wine trickled over the edge of the table onto her foot. With no more than an impatient look at the cause of the distraction, Julie shifted positions to escape the stream and turned back to Mac.

What they were doing felt too good to interrupt for a spilled glass of wine.

"No problem," Mac said to the man, looking past her.

"Can I get you some more wine?" The waitress appeared with a handful of napkins and started mopping. Julie, impatient, leaned forward to nibble Mac's ear, just to keep him from losing focus until they could get back to business. The lobe was soft and tender and tasted faintly salty. But she was starting to sense some resistance from Mac.

"No thanks," Mac said to the waitress, sounding as if he was talking through clenched teeth. He was still turned on, she could tell—among other obvious signs, his instant stiffening when she twirled her tongue in his ear was a dead giveaway—but distraction was taking its toll. Then, not particularly to Julie's surprise, his hands closed over her hipbones and he lifted her bodily off him.

"Mac!" She wanted to weep.

Despite her plaintive protest and clinging hands he managed to slide out from under her, slippery as a fish wriggling off the hook, and as her bottom hit leather his hands were busy tugging her arms from around his neck. The waitress, finished with her mopping, loaded the broken glass onto her tray and moved away. Defeated, Julie slumped down onto the banquette, Mac's hands gripping her wrists.

"Sid's gone into the back room. We need to get out of here while we can."

Sid. Glancing around, Julie realized that Mac was right: Sid was nowhere in sight. She also realized that, in the heat of the last few steamy minutes, she had completely forgotten about her cheating spouse. Un-believable—but the cause was leaning toward her, looking a million times better than chocolate ever had as he held her wrists in an unbreakable grip, and the situation was extreme when even the size and warmth of his hands keeping her away from him struck her as sexy.

Meeting his gaze, she realized that while his eyes still held a trace of that superheated gleam, his lips were set in an obstinate line and his jaw was hard. Clearly, Romeo had left the building. Meanwhile, she felt as if she'd been poleaxed. The intensity of the voltage that had leaped between her and Mac had robbed her of any outside awareness as thoroughly as if she'd been unwary enough to press her lips to a stun gun.

"Come on, move it."

Apparently not subject to extended postmortem ruminations of his own, Mac slid out from behind the table, picked up his beer and took a quick swig, then pulled her out after him, one hand wrapped around her wrist as if he was afraid she'd try to escape. Still feeling vaguely dazed, Julie fell in with the program. At the same time she tried to figure out what, exactly, had just happened. Her mind reeled as she considered. She'd caught Sid with his hand in the cookie jar, and kissed and been kissed by

Mac cum Debbie, all within the space of maybe ten minutes. The unsettling thing was, the events seemed to be assuming almost equal importance in her mind. When she stumbled, glanced down to see what had tripped her up, and discovered that the offending object was one of her own tan leather slides, she wasn't even surprised to find that she had been on the verge of leaving in her bare feet without even realizing it.

Now that was dazed and confused.

"What's the holdup?"

As she stopped, Mac looked around at her with a frown.

"My shoes."

She tried to right her shoe with her toes so that she could slide her foot inside, but she couldn't do it because, she thought, all her blood was still busy rushing somewhere more interesting than her brain. Watching, Mac made an impatient sound and swooped on the shoes, scooping them both up in his free hand. Hanging on to them, he headed purposefully toward the door, towing her barefoot behind him.

Stepping out of the chilly purple gloom of Sweetwater's into the dark, crowded bustle of the street was disorienting. The heat enfolded her, welcome as a blanket on a winter's night, and Julie realized that the nightclub had been downright cold. She simply hadn't noticed after the first few minutes because she had been wrapped in Mac's arms.

Which in spite of the overenthusiastic air-conditioning had made her hot enough to want to get naked. Right there. Right then.

With Mac.

The realization was mind-boggling.

"Here."

Mac stopped just past the line waiting to get in, handing her her shoes. She leaned against the smooth painted brick of Sweetwater's outer wall to slip them on while what seemed to be the entire population of several states went by around them and he created a jostle-free zone for her with his body. As she stood on first one foot and then the other, he watched without saying a word. When she straightened, shoes in place, his gaze met hers.

The sizzle in his eyes was as tangible as the heat in the bricks she leaned against.

Hmm. Something here was not right.

Mac broke off eye contact then and started walking, hauling her after him, plowing through the throng on the sidewalk like a wide receiver with the football tucked under his arm and the goalposts in sight. Julie followed in the wake he created, entertaining a variety of thoughts in quick succession as, with dispassionate assessment, she eyed his retreating back.

He had nice shoulders, broad and muscular in a navy tee that equally showed off equally nice arms. He had a nice butt, small and tight and sexy in well-worn jeans. He was tall, athletically built, handsome.

Any woman would salivate.

So it wasn't surprising that she wanted him. In fact, it would have been surprising if she didn't. She was a normal, red-blooded American female, after all, and he was a hunky guy. To say nothing of the fact that she was in a marriage so dead rigor mortis was about to set in and, to clench matters, was extremely sexually deprived.

But he wanted her, too. She wasn't mistaken about that, and that was where the question lay. Her thoughts curled around boat-sized high heels and blond wigs and mountainous boobs and pink leashes and Josephine. And she tried to recall just what he'd said when she'd asked him point-blank if he was gay.

She couldn't remember exactly. But the short answer, as recorded by her brain, had been *yes.*

Just a little while ago, when she'd asked him if he went both ways, he'd said no. And punctuated that by kissing her until her brain was practically fried.

So where did that leave her? Julie wasn't sure, but "frustrated" came to mind.

"Hold on just one minute," she said, digging in her heels.

They were in the alley now, headed toward the lot where the Blazer was parked. It was dark and shadowy and smelled of booze and garbage and should have been scary as all get-out, but Julie scarcely noticed. Her attention was all for the man pulling her along after him as if she'd been a recalcitrant Josephine.

No, probably he would have shown more consideration for the poodle.

When she balked, he stopped, turning to face her.

"What now?"

The various lights from the establishments they'd left behind created a reddish glow at the mouth of the alley that allowed her to see his expression. He looked almost—wary.

"What did you mean, no?" She narrowed her eyes at him. In the shadows along one wall, something stirred. Seeing the movement out of the corner of her eye, she jumped about a foot in the air and skittered toward Mac. He released her wrist to wrap an arm around her waist and pull her against his side, his gaze focused on the threat. They both watched as, not ten feet away, a man got to his feet and, with no more than a single glance at them, staggered toward the street.

The smell of booze was suddenly overpowering. Julie realized that they had disturbed a sleeping drunk.

"You want to have a conversation, wait till we get to the car."

With that curt response Mac was off again, pulling her behind him, not pausing until they reached the Blazer. With more haste than courtesy he bundled her inside, slammed the door behind her, and got in himself.

Then, without a word, without so much as a glance at her, he started the car. He was reaching for the button that controlled the lights when she turned off the ignition.

"What the . . ." As he glanced at her in surprise, she curled one leg beneath her, leaned across the console, and pressed her lips to his mouth.

13

His RESPONSE WAS INSTANTANEOUS and unmistakable. His lips molded themselves to hers and the blaze of heat that flared between them told Julie everything she needed to know. He tasted faintly of beer. His kiss was hungry, insistent, arousing. An instant memory of his hands, hot as they slid up under her dress, making her hot as they cupped and caressed her bottom, threatened to make her forget her purpose. She wanted him—*God,* she wanted him.

And he wanted her, too. No doubt at all remained about that.

Shaken but satisfied at the result of her impromptu research, Julie lifted her mouth from his before she could completely lose her head, breaking off the kiss even as he pulled her across the console and into his lap.

"You're not gay." If her voice was faintly breathless—all right, a lot breathless—it was also accusing. His hands still gripped her waist; hers rested on his shoulders. She was half lying, half sitting, with her back cradled by his arm and her breasts just brushing his chest. He curved over her, his wide shoulders blocking out her view of the rest of the front seat. Their faces were just inches apart. She could feel the warmth of his breath feathering across her lips. Unfortunately, it was too dark to read his expression. But she imagined it—he was no doubt looking guilty as hell.

"You—are—not—gay." She said it again, with emphasis, as if to drive the point home to herself as well as him.

That seemed to make an impression. He took a deep breath and straightened, pulling her up with him and then lifting her back over the console into her own seat. Once there, she gave a tug to her skirt to make sure she was decent, folded her arms over her chest, and glared at him.

"I never said I was." His voice was cool as a glass of lemonade.

To her annoyance, as he spoke, he restarted the car as though nothing at all out of the ordinary had happened. The lights came on, bouncing off the wall in front of them to reflect on his face. He did *not* look guilty, she noticed with increasing ire. He looked—he looked as calm if they were discussing the vagaries of the weather.

"You did too." Once again she searched her mind for his exact words. "When I asked you before you said . . . you said . . ."

"I asked you if it mattered." He pulled out of the parking lot and turned down the alley. The beams illuminated graffiti-adorned brick walls, a Dumpster with a partially open lid, piles of litter. He glanced her way. "If I remember correctly, you said it didn't."

Julie narrowed her eyes at him. "Well, *now,*" she said with more than a hint of bite, "it does."

"So I'm not gay." He slid her another of those so-calm-she-wanted-to-kill-him looks before edging out into the still heavy traffic. "Put on your seat belt."

Julie's lips compressed. Mentally counting to ten, she put on her seat belt. Her temper was heading toward slow boil, but she decided to suspend judgment until she was sure she had the full picture. Maybe there was something she was missing here.

"Are you a cross-dresser?"

He gave a grunt that might have been laughter. "Only when I have to be. As far as I'm concerned, panty hose could have been invented by the Spanish Inquisition. How women wear those things is beyond me. And bras are a bitch, too. But the shoes were killer. I was really starting to get into the shoes. Yours especially." He switched into his Debbie voice. "Girlfriend, I gotta tell you, those little heels you're wearing are the bomb."

He leered at her slides.

Julie glowered at him. "You'll notice I'm not laughing." In fact, she was starting to feel like a fool for ever believing he was gay in the first place. There had been so many signs—how could she have been so blind? "Let me make sure I understand this time: You're straight, right?"

"Yeah, pretty much."

"Pretty much?"

"Well, actually, about a hundred percent."

"You *lied* to me." There was a definite sizzle in her tone.

He threw a quick glance her way. "I didn't lie. You made assumptions, and I just didn't correct them."

"Oh, that makes it all better."

"Look, if you'd known from the beginning I was straight, would you have let me help you?"

Julie sneered. "Are you actually attempting to claim that you lied to me for my own good?"

"That's pretty much it in a nutshell." He sounded almost pleased at being presented with such a tidy summing-up.

"Yeah, right." Julie took a deep, calming breath. "So, you want to explain the whole Debbie thing to me?"

"I was working. Undercover, you might say. The guy I was tailing—you met him in the parking lot last night—is into drag queens. Ergo, Debbie." He shrugged, looking unrepentant, and his eyes twinkled at her infuriatingly. "Hey, babe, a PI's got to do what a PI's got to do."

"Maybe I should point out here that I am *so* not finding this amusing."

There was a pause as they reached the expressway and he pulled on and accelerated, quickly leaving the worst of the traffic behind. Julie used it to take a firm, two-handed grip on her temper before she could lose it completely.

"What about Josephine? Is she even yours? Or were you just using her as a prop?" Her voice was sharp with growing outrage.

"Until three weeks ago, Josephine belonged to my grandmother. Then Grandma moved into a retirement home and I inherited her dog, complete with collar, leash, and a weekly appointment with the groomer."

Julie looked at him suspiciously. Imagining him with a grandmother—a grandmother he cared enough about to adopt her tiny fluffball of a poodle—was a stretch. A big stretch.

"Is that the truth?"

"Yes." A smile touched his mouth as he glanced at her. "Cross my heart."

Julie snorted. "That certainly clenches it for me."

"I don't know why you're mad. You liked Debbie."

"Not to make out with!" As soon as she said it, she could have kicked herself. The dignified thing to have done would have been to ignore those breath-stealing kisses completely. Too late now.

"Ah. Good point."

He gave her a look that made her hot all over again—until she remembered that he had deliberately deceived her. Debbie, indeed.

Talk about your wolf in sheep's clothing—what she had here was a hound in poodle-wear.

She glared at him.

He continued in a semi-apologetic tone, "At the time, making out with you didn't seem to be an option."

"It's not an option now, either." Her voice was tart. She felt like a fool, and she didn't like the feeling—or, for that matter, at the moment at least, its cause. "What happened back there was strictly a one-time thing that was entirely dictated by unfortunate circumstances. So don't start thinking you're about to get lucky, because you're not."

"I swear, if you hadn't just now put the idea in my head, such a thought never would have crossed my mind." He shook his head virtuously. When Julie responded with a *yeah, right* look, he grinned. Julie realized that she was being teased. "But in the interests of full disclosure, I think I ought to mention that we have a strict company policy against 'getting lucky' with clients. Of course, being that I'm the boss, I guess I could make an exception if you asked me real nice."

"Not a chance." She gave him a smile that was scarcely more than a baring of her teeth. "I'll give you credit, though: pretending to be Debbie as a come-on technique is original, if nothing else. Although actually, from a woman's point of view, I have to tell you that being lied to about something like that pretty much sucks."

"Just for the record, I think I should point out here that you're the one who came on to me. You kissed me first back there, not the other way around, remember? And if I'd been trying to get you into bed, you'd have known it a whole hell of a lot sooner." A beat went by. "Besides, I never actually lied."

"Okay, that's it. You lied and you know it. And if you want my opinion, deceiving me like that was a pretty rotten thing to do."

"Darlin', you're losing sight of the big picture here. Who I choose to sleep with doesn't matter. What matters is that here in the down-and-dirty divorce wars I'm on your side."

"What matters is that you lied."

A swaying eighteen-wheeler whizzing around them so fast it made the car shake distracted their attention before the conversation could deteriorate further. Then they were at the Summerville exit and the Blazer was easing off the expressway into the dark, deserted hush of the town.

A glance at the dashboard clock told Julie that it was 1:43, and sent her thoughts careening back to her larger problem: Sid. Tonight she had plenty of time: a good hour and a half before her cheating husband snuck back in the house. Should she pack and leave before he even got home? Or wait with folded arms like a wife in a comic strip until he got in and let him have it with both barrels? Or should she bite her tongue, bide her time, and see a lawyer before she walked out?

The idea of even having to set eyes on Sid again, much less spend a few more nights under the same roof with him, made her sick to her stomach and almost made the decision for her. But she'd been cool so far and, she thought, had made all the right moves. She didn't want to lose what advantage knowledge gave her now.

Sid would be ruthless about finances, ruthless about everything. She'd seen him in operation on the golf course, the tennis court, and in business deals when things got sticky: always, he played to win.

He would play to win in their divorce, too.

Glancing at the man beside her, she pushed thoughts of Sid and their divorce to the back burner. All she could deal with was one problem at a time, and her personal private investigator was another one. Mac had deliberately deceived her over the Debbie thing, but he'd also been a strong shoulder for her to lean on when she'd needed one. He had made her laugh and made her hot at a time when she hadn't thought either was possible, and for that she was grateful. The idea that she wouldn't be seeing him again cost her a pang, much as she hated to admit it even to herself. Still, his job was done. Thanks to him, tonight she had seen what Sid was up to with her very own eyes. As for anything else—such as a quick hop in the sack, maybe, just because she wanted to more than she had wanted anything in forever— well, the cold hard truth was that she needed another man in her life right now like she needed a bad case of poison ivy.

Especially another *lying* man.

"Okay, you're right, I guess it doesn't really matter that you lied." Her voice had lost its angry edge; instead it was faintly frosty. "You did what you were hired to do, and I recognize that. Seeing as how this whole thing got resolved so quickly, I'll understand if you want to impose some kind of minimum charge for your time." Their gazes met as he glanced at her with a gathering frown. "Add the cost of fixing your car, of course. If you'll let me know how much it all is, I'll see that you get your money right away."

"Whoa, wait a minute. Not so fast, Miss America."

The tone of that made her frown at him. "What?"

"I don't think this whole thing *is* resolved.

A rich, prominent man like Sid doesn't cheat on his wife by going someplace like Sweetwater's and hooking up with the girls there. He was way, way too visible, almost like he wanted to be seen. A man cheating on his wife hides out in a hotel or an out-of-the-way apartment or meets his honey on a business trip. Trust me, I know. I investigate this kind of thing for a living."

Julie's frown deepened. "So what are you saying?"

"I'm saying something doesn't make sense. I don't know what Sid was doing in Sweetwater's, but I don't think he was hooking up with his honey."

A sudden memory made Julie's eyes widen.

"He didn't take any Viagra tonight. There were still six pills mixed in with his vitamins. I counted when we got home from the club, and he never came upstairs again."

A half-smile quirked up one corner of Mac's mouth. "Well, there you go. Proof positive."

"Do you think it's possible that Sid's *not* cheating?" Funny, the idea didn't bring any upsurge of happiness with it. Probably because she knew, deep down inside, that it just wasn't true. But also, she thought, because the marriage was over where it counted, in her heart. It had taken a combination of Sid's behavior tonight and her sizzling reaction to Mac's kiss to make her realize that. Her attraction to Mac might be a phase—in fact, it probably was, a rebound kind of thing as she came to terms with the end of her marriage—but still she wanted more in a personal sense than Sid could give her, had ever given her. She *deserved* more.

It was Julie time.

"Possible? Anything's possible. But I don't think so. If he's taking Viagra and you're not getting any, I'd say it's a pretty sure bet he's cheating. But you haven't caught him at it yet. He had another reason for going to Sweetwater's tonight. I just haven't figured out what it is." He sounded thoughtful.

Outside the Blazer, the whole world seemed to be asleep. They were driving along familiar residential streets now; the houses were dark and the streets themselves were deserted. Julie was still digesting his words when he glanced at her again.

"Why don't you let me keep looking into this for a few more days?"

If I did, I could keep seeing you for a few more days. The thought caught Julie unaware. Its implications annoyed her. He was a phase, she told herself. A *phase.* She watched *Oprah;* she knew. The death of a marriage, like any other death, brought on various psychological states as the individual tried to cope. Mindless promiscuity probably came right after discovering your husband was cheating for everybody. *She* was not going to fall into that trap. She was going to keep herself on an even keel, or die in the attempt.

She shook her head. "I don't think so. That would require being civil to Sid and acting as if everything between us is hunky-dory for a few more days, and I just don't think I can do that. Besides, you lied to me."

They had reached her street now. A glance told Julie that it was as dark and quiet as the rest of the town.

"You want me to apologize for Debbie? All right, I apologize. Next time I run across a beautiful damsel in distress while I'm dressed like one myself, I'll jump her bones immediately just so there's no mistake."

Julie glared at him. Then the sheer absurdity of the image he'd painted made her smile, albeit reluctantly. If he had come on to her while dressed as Debbie, she would have run screaming for miles.

Seeing her smile, he smiled too. "That's better." His smile turned coaxing. "Don't you want to know who the lucky recipient of all that Viagra is?"

Julie hadn't thought of that. Oh, God, did she want to know? The possibilities were endless, now that she considered them. Was it one of the women who worked for him? Heidi, his administrative assistant, came immediately to mind. She was young, pretty, and appeared to think Sid hung the moon. Or maybe it was one of their friends. In that category there were endless possibilities. Or a neighbor. Or—or anyone. It could be anyone at all. Just thinking about it made her feel sick, but Julie realized to her own surprise that she needed to know. If she didn't, she would wonder forever. The idea that a woman she *knew,* maybe even one she considered a friend, was having an affair with her husband behind her back was almost like a kind of mental poison. Unless she learned the truth, she would never be able to look at any of them in quite the same way again. She would always wonder, Was it you?

"How long do you think it would take?" Her smile had vanished, and her mouth was suddenly dry. She swallowed to try to wet it again.

"Probably no more than a week."

Oh, God, could she bear living with this burden—and Sid—for a week more? She'd been so in love with Sid once. Now she just wanted to walk away and never have to see him again—but of course nothing in life was ever that easy.

Nothing in her life, anyway.

"I could use that time to find a lawyer." She chewed on her lower lip. It was important that she think about Becky and her mother, as well as her own financial security. Knowing Sid, he would do his best to see that they all ended up back in the double-wide if he could. He would love that.

"Good idea." Mac pulled up in front of her house, doused the lights and engine, then looked at her. "You realize that once Sid finds out you're filing for divorce, he's going to play to win. You need to make sure your lawyer is someone you can trust."

Julie gave a ghost of a laugh as the near impossibility of that occurred to her. "All the lawyers I know are Sid's friends."

Mac grimaced. "That's a problem. Want me to check around, see if I can find somebody who's up to taking on Sid?"

"Would you?"

"With pleasure."

Julie felt the last of her hostility over the discovery that Debbie was a fraud waft away. Mac was still a shoulder to lean on, and she was glad, really, really, glad, that he wasn't walking out of her life just yet. Still, if he was going to be staying on for a while, she wasn't going to let him off the hook so easily.

She shot him a severe look which he didn't see. He was staring out through the windshield, apparently lost in thought.

"You did your best to deliberately deceive me. Admit it."

The look he shot her was almost startled. "I did?"

"About Debbie."

"Oh." A beat went by. "Maybe I was a little bit deceptive."

"Admit it. You lied."

"Fine. You want to hear me say it? I lied."

"That's better. Don't do it again."

He grinned at her. "But I wasn't kidding about the shoes. I've got a real thing for your shoes."

Julie shot him a withering look. Then she realized that at some point after he'd parked the car, he'd picked up her hand. Or maybe she'd picked up his. Since she couldn't remember them coming together, she couldn't be sure. But they were joined now, her smooth slender fingers laced with his long capable ones. She felt the strength of his hand clasping hers, felt the heat radiating from his palm to hers, and her pulse rate shot to double time. Which might feel nice, but probably wasn't a good thing. Her life was chock-full of man trouble already; more she definitely did not need.

She glanced up at him.

"I'm not going to sleep with you, you know," she said. Best to lay it on the line—for herself as well as for him—even if she did feel a little prickle of regret at turning her back on what she was pretty sure would be really phenomenal sex. By saying it aloud, she fixed the ban firmly in her own mind; also, he was put on notice that there was no quid pro quo beyond a reasonable sum of money for his efforts on her behalf.

His lips compressed. His hand tightened on hers. Their gazes met. His thoughts were impossible to read in the darkness, but the hard grip of his fingers said a lot.

"It's usually considered good manners to wait till you're asked."

"I just want to make sure we have everything clear."

"Clear as crystal."

He released her hand, but she could feel the lingering warmth of his grip even as she pulled her hand back to the neutral territory of her lap.

"Okay. Good. I'm going in now."

She opened the door. The interior light came on. A glance over her shoulder told her that he was watching her get out. His eyes were narrowed and his mouth was a thin firm line. His expression was hard to decipher, but it certainly couldn't have been described as warm and friendly. Or anything close.

"I'll be in touch. You've got my number if you need me," he said as he met her gaze.

His voice was definitely businesslike. Her warning had set the right, necessary tone.

To her own annoyance, Julie found herself regretting that she had ever opened her mouth on the subject as she headed inside.

14

SOMETHING WAS WRONG. Julie Carlson was off schedule. She was supposed to be at home, in bed, asleep. For the second night in a row, she was not. Where the hell was she? If he didn't get the job done tonight, there was going to be hell to pay.

The phone call from the Big Boss had made that clear.

"You get it done tonight, you understand? *No more screwups.* Do I make myself clear?"

So clear Basta broke out in a sweat just remembering the conversation. Now he was here to get the job done.

Basta had already prowled around inside

her house, looking for some kind of clue as to what was going on. There were no phone messages, he'd discovered as he disabled the phone. No notes on the refrigerator to let her hubby know where she had gone. The car the insurance company had provided her with was still in the garage; the only vehicle missing was the husband's Mercedes. That meant that either she was out walking around the streets—so unlikely at this hour that he didn't even bother to go looking—or somebody had picked her up.

Maybe all of a sudden she had something going on the side. Basta frowned as he pondered that. The thought did not bother him particularly. Except for its effect on his plans, he did not care if she slept with the entire male population of nearby Fort Jackson. But he was a businessman, and time was money. He was running out of time.

And the Big Boss was running out of patience. In his line of work, it was never a good idea to tee off the boss.

If he missed her again tonight—and it looked like he might well be going to—there was going to be a problem.

He'd looked in the closets, under the

beds, even in the damned refrigerator, on the off chance that she had somehow heard him come in and decided to hide. Nothing. Of course there was nothing.

She would never have heard him. She was not in the house.

He could almost smell the balmy breezes of Key West. That's where he should be right now, sitting out on a starlit hotel balcony, a rum and Coke in his hand, enjoying his reward for a job well done.

Not kicked back in a leather armchair in his intended victim's cave-dark den, playing Donkey Kong with the sound turned off on a Game Boy he'd found while searching the spare bedrooms, waiting with growing frustration for said victim to get home where she belonged.

This time, if she so much as stuck a toe in the door while he was still there, he was taking care of business regardless. It was getting to him, this waiting. Especially this waiting under the fulminating eye of the boss.

As it happened, he was so busy hammering the stupid little alligator things that were part of the game that he didn't even hear her come in.

A burst of light as the enormous chandelier in the front hall was flipped on nearly gave him a heart attack. For a split second, from pure astonishment, he sat as if turned to stone, his thumbs frozen on the game controls, his gaze snapping to the open doorway, trapped in a flood of illumination. Then instinct kicked in and he dove over the side of the chair, placing its bulk between himself and the door, sheltering behind it as he peered cautiously over the arm like a kid playing hide-and-seek.

Luckily he managed to hang on to the Game Boy. If he had dropped it, the sound might have been enough to alert his prey.

Because it was her. Even as his heart resumed its normal steady beat, he was reaching out into the hall with every sense he possessed.

Several light footsteps, a sigh, the merest flicker of a shadow across the square of light that was all he could see of the hall—it was enough. Julie Carlson was home. He knew it as well as if he'd gotten a full, 360-degree view of her.

A quick glance at his watch brought a smile to his face. Tonight there would be plenty of time.

The ensuing wave of relief left him feeling buoyant in its wake. As his mother had always told him, all things come to he who waits.

The light went out in the hall as suddenly as it had come on. Basta listened to her footsteps moving lightly up the stairs. When she reached the top, he stopped concentrating on her to carefully unzip his bag and place the Game Boy inside. He couldn't leave it. It had his fingerprints all over it, he'd had to take his gloves off to operate the tiny controls, and besides, he wasn't finished with the game. He waited for a little while, ten minutes or so, to give her enough time to get really settled in and comfy. Then he pulled on his gloves, rolled the ski mask down over his face, and fished his Sig Sauer semiautomatic out of the bottom of the bag. Time for the fun to begin.

Go back.

Julie listened to the little voice in her head and made a face at herself in her bathroom mirror.

"I'd love to," she answered it aloud. "But sleeping with him is a really dumb idea."

It occurred to her that when people started talking back to the little voices that they heard, that's when they knew they were really in trouble.

So she wasn't going to listen to the little voice anymore, much less talk to it. Even if she really, really wanted to do what it suggested. Her inner self obviously had no idea of how complicated things could get if she gave in to its urging.

That thing with Mac tonight was the closest she had come to having an orgasm in months, Julie thought as she turned her attention back to her own reflection and anxiously examined what looked to be a wrinkle forming between her eyebrows. Actually, years, now that she came to think about it. Sid's lovemaking had been perfunctory for some time before he'd finally given up the ghost altogether. Call her difficult, but she just wasn't able to get off in the five minutes tops it usually took Sid from the first peck on her lips until he rolled over and went to sleep.

Yet one more reason to get rid of Sid: He was lousy in bed. At least, she thought he was. She didn't really have much to compare him with—which brought her thoughts back full circle to Mac.

She would love a chance to compare Sid with Mac.

Julie glared at the tiny line between her brows as ferociously as if it were the source of her wayward thoughts, and scooped Mudd out of a jar, slapping some over the wrinkle before slathering it lavishly over the rest of her just-washed face.

Go back outside.

She was *not* going to let the fact that she was staring divorce in the face get her down, she told herself determinedly. She was not going to start hearing voices. She was not going to have a nervous break-down. She was not going to sleep with Mac. She was not going to crack a base-ball bat over Sid's head. And she was def-initely *not* going to gain a hundred pounds or so. Perish the thought.

Get thee behind me, chocolate, she thought, glancing over her shoulder in some regret as the last of the Hershey's Kisses she kept in her lingerie chest for emergencies swirled down the toilet, where just minutes ago she'd gathered the willpower to dump them. Then, in a hasty mental aside just in case some listening spirit took that too seriously, she amended that to *Get thee gone, chocolate.* She certainly didn't want the rejected calories ending up on her already substantial enough behind.

In any case, she was going to get her stress release in a less destructive way from now on.

And *no,* not from a Mac-induced Big O. Although she was really starting to regret not having gone for it while she had the chance, she comforted herself with the knowledge that she had done the right thing.

Aromatherapy might not be as much fun, but it came with a lot fewer drawbacks. The most important of which was, a man wasn't involved. The smell of the chamomile bath salts was soothing, just as the printing on the packet had promised. Julie breathed deeply, filling her lungs with the aroma as steam filled the bathroom. As soon as the bath was ready, she would slide down into the hot water, immerse herself in the calming scent, and press the button that would activate the Jacuzzi.

Bliss. Or at least, as close to bliss as she could get under the circumstances.

Go outside now.

Take that, stress, she thought, pretending the little voice was not there as she inhaled again with grim determination. The steam was sweet smelling but—unsuccessful. So far, anyway. She resolutely refused even to think about checking out her lingerie chest just to make sure that no Hershey's Kisses had been left behind. Instead, she returned her attention to the task at hand. She was not going to lose her looks over this, and not losing her looks involved taking care of her skin. The last of the Mudd she slathered down the middle of her nose like peanut butter on bread.

Rinsing her fingers, she looked at herself in the mirror again. With her hair swept up into a ponytail high on the top of her head and the mask covering every bit of her face now except for white circles around her mouth and eyes, she looked like Pebbles Flintstone doing *The Creature from the Black Lagoon.*

It took a lot of ugly to make a woman beautiful. Good thing all anyone ever saw was the end result.

Was it Cindy Crawford who'd said looking good was the best revenge?

No matter. It was now her mantra. Every time she even started to think of Sid and his extracurricular activities she was going to do something positive for herself.

Like treat her skin to a mask. Or scrub her teeth with super-whitening paste. Or wax her legs.

Or take a really hot, relaxing bath foaming with calming herbs, and go to bed. Where she was going to go right to sleep and not, not, *not* dream of men.

Not Sid the Jerk. Or Mac the Hunk. Or anyone remotely male.

Give her a society that was man-free, and what a happy world it would be.

Go now.

She hadn't even heard that, she told herself with a final glance in the mirror. The mask was already starting to harden. It was crisping around the edges, and cracks were starting to appear in her cheeks. A few more minutes and she would rinse it off, slather on moisturizer, wax her legs, and get in the tub. After that, she would go to bed, and *sleep.*

She was not going to end up a withered,

embittered old woman with wrinkles and bad teeth and hairy legs and a rear end the size of a schoolbus just because she'd had the bad judgment to marry a cheating no-good asshole.

So there.

Upon entering her bedroom some ten minutes before, she'd flipped on the light, stripped off her clothes, and grabbed a nightgown out of the lingerie chest. The nightgown was more husband-bait, a short, silky leopard-print thing with black lace trim and spaghetti straps, but there was no help for it, so, beyond deciding that a shopping spree for oversized T-shirts and cotton panties was definitely in order, she had resolved not to obsess about it. Sliding the newly despised garment over her head, she had flipped off the light and crossed to the window, pulling the curtains apart to see if she could see Mac's car.

Too dark.

Just as well anyway, she told herself as memories of that steamy interlude at Sweetwater's intruded, making her loins ache and tighten in reflexive response. Julie watched her eyelids droop and her lips part in her fuzzy reflection in the window glass, recognized the look for the sexual yearning it was, and sighed. Clearly she was destined to stay chronically hungry in more ways than one.

A moment or two later she had shut the curtain, turned her back on the window, and retreated to her bathroom, scooping up the Hershey's Kisses on the way. Sex, as usual, remained tantalizingly out of reach. But tonight, chocolate was at hand.

Once inside the bathroom, with the help of her reflection in a three-way mirror, a critical look at her much-maligned butt, and a little hard-won self-control, she'd dredged up enough unexpected strength of character to flush the chocolate before it could add to the landmass that seemed to be following her around, and resolved there and then that even if her life went to hell, her looks weren't going with it.

GO NOW.

Don't shout, she almost answered aloud, but remembered that talking back to the voice was bad. A glance showed her that the tub was almost to the brim. In full Creature mode, Julie walked barefoot across the cool white tile, bent to turn off the taps, rescued the floating jar of leg wax that had been warming in the water, inhaled deeply of the aromatic steam that didn't seem to be doing crap about her stress as far as she could tell, straightened and turned back toward the sink, jar in hand. She would rinse the mask off her face, wax her legs, and get in the tub, where the stress-reducing part of the chamomile would surely kick in.

She took a single step and stopped dead.

A man was staring at her through the bathroom mirror.

A man with his back pressed flat against the bedroom wall outside her bathroom door. A man with a black ski mask pulled down over his face so that she could see nothing of him except for the dark glint of his eyes through the round holes. A man who was at that very moment watching her watch him.

Every tiny hair on her body catapulted upright as Julie met his gaze in horror.

The little voice screamed. Julie was too dumbstruck to follow suit.

Then he stepped into the doorway, filling it, blocking all hope of escape.

Her breath escaped from her body in an audible hiss.

"Hello, Julie," he said as she stood frozen to the spot. The caressing note in his voice and the gloating way he looked her over sent chills racing along her spine. In that split second she realized that she was facing every woman's worst nightmare come true: a rapist, maybe even a killer. At the same time she registered with the tiny part of her mind that was not absolutely numb with terror that he was big, not so much tall but burly, and dressed all in black and carrying a gun which he held negligently in one surgical-gloved hand.

Oh, God, a gun to use on her.

He started to lift it, to point it at her. Her heart freed itself from its state of shock-induced suspended animation to give a great leap in her chest. She sucked in a huge gulp of air, found her voice, and screamed like a siren, all in a single instant. Then, acting purely on instinct, she hurled the jar of leg wax at his head.

It was a heavy jar, dark blue glass filled with warmed wax, and it hit him square in the middle of the forehead with a sound like a cork popping out of a champagne bottle.

"Son of a *bitch!*" he yelled, staggering backward and clapping a hand to his forehead as the jar spun away to crash against the wall and drop to the tile with a clatter. He disappeared through the doorway. For a split second after he was no longer in sight, Julie remained frozen in place. She knew he was still there, heard breathing and cursing and movements that told her he was just beyond the door.

Run.

No duh, was her inner response to the little voice as, with terror giving wings to her feet, she flew toward the door, knowing that this was, very possibly, her only chance to get away.

Exploding from the bathroom like a sprinter on speed, she saw in a single petrified glance that he was only a couple of feet away, a big dark shape with one hand still clapped to his forehead as he bent over to pick up the gun he had apparently dropped. She leaped past him even as he looked up.

"Son of a bitch!" Abandoning the gun, he

lunged for her, trying to grab her with both arms.

"No!" Dodging, gasping for breath, her heart pounding so hard that she could hear nothing beyond the drumming of her own blood in her ears, she fled toward her bedroom door and the hall and the stairs and the outside door below, screaming her lungs out all the way.

Oh, God, oh, God, oh, God, he was chasing her, surprisingly nimble and fast on his feet considering his size. He was going to catch her. She knew he was; it was just a matter of minutes, seconds. . . .

Frantically she tried to recall some basics from the self-defense class she had taken once. Its mantra had been, if attacked, SING. S-I-N-G. The only problem was, now in her time of extremis she couldn't remember what the S stood for.

The only S word she could call to mind that seemed at all appropriate was *scream.*

And she was already screaming like a steam whistle and it didn't seem to be doing much good, unless deafening him as well as herself was part of the plan.

"Help! Help!"

He was right behind her as she reached

the top of the stairs, lunging and grabbing and *closing his fist over the flying banner of her hair.*

Julie shrieked loud enough to shatter glass in Columbia as her head was jerked backward so hard she was surprised her neck didn't snap. Then his arm wrapped around her waist, yanking her against him, and his gloved hand clamped down over her mouth and nose, silencing her, suffocating her. She was enveloped by the heat of his body and the smell of talc from the glove and sweat from the man.

"You shouldn't've hit me," he growled in her ear. She smelled onions on his breath.

Her stomach heaved. Lack of oxygen and terror made her head swim. Her heart pounded. Her skin crawled everywhere his rubberized fingers touched as if ants were running amok over her flesh. Still she fought as he dragged her back toward the bedroom, tearing at his gloved hand with her nails, kicking at his shins with her bare feet, twisting and writhing and struggling with every ounce of strength she possessed, with every atom of knowledge the streetwise little girl she had once been had had to learn to survive, knowing even as she fought that it was probably futile, that she was not going to be able to save herself, that, at maybe a hundred twenty pounds soaking wet, she was no match for a brute who was easily twice her weight.

He dragged her back over the threshold of her bedroom, back into the room with the tasteful white carpet and taupe walls and huge black-lacquered bed. Understated, all of it, right down to the white summer linens on the bed. A room for quiet contemplation and restful sleep, not unspeakable acts and violence and death.

Oh, please don't let him kill me.

The prayer shot skyward even as she managed to grab his mask and pull it off over his head, and he picked her up and threw her down on her back on the bed.

She landed with a bounce. He was on top of her before she could move, pinning her with his weight, forcing her deep into the mattress even as she tried and failed to knee him in the groin, tried and failed to roll free. Her nightgown was twisting toward her waist, she could feel the rough abrasion of his clothes against her tender skin, feel the heat and weight of him with a revulsion that was like nothing she had ever experienced in her life. She knew what he intended to do, knew it and screamed her terror into his face and thrashed and kicked and fought, all to no avail.

"Shut up, bitch." One hand wrapped around her throat, cutting her scream off in midblast, brutal in its intent to cause pain, squeezing so that she gagged and choked and squealed like a small animal caught in a trap. Her gaze caught on her teddy bear sitting Buddha-like on the bedside table, and she realized with a sense of horrified disbelief that it might be the last thing she saw before she died. He was crushing her throat, cutting off her voice, her air. Her blood seemed to spike in her ears. All she could do was claw frantically at his hand and wheeze.

"Shut up," he said again. She nodded jerkily, so grateful for the chance to live that she would do anything, and he loosened his grip enough so that she could once again breathe. He let go of her throat and grabbed her wrists, lifting them over her head as she lay unresisting, intent on drawing in blessed air. The weight of his body pinned her as he transferred both her captured wrists to one huge meaty hand.

Then, with a ripping noise more terrifying than anything she had ever heard, he began to bind her wrists together with a roll of duct tape that had somehow appeared in his hand.

The tape wrapping her wrists felt sticky and tight and full of doom. She struggled weakly, trying to pull free of it. She couldn't break it, couldn't free her hands.

One hand returned to grip her throat punishingly.

"Give me any more trouble, and I'll crush your throat and be done with it," he said, then used his teeth to tear the tape from the roll. As he patted the strip down, his face was so close his oniony breath made her gag. His body, huge and smothering and ripe with BO, lay over hers, effectively rendering her helpless. Her heart pounded so hard she was surprised it didn't burst through her chest. She panted with terror; her bruised throat was pulsing in and out like gills on a fish.

Except for the light streaming from the open bathroom door the bedroom was dark, and his features were lost in shadows. But she could see the gleam in the eyes just inches from her own, the flash of his teeth against parted lips, the dark jut of his nose. . . .

His nose.

Savage as a cornered animal, Julie lunged upward and fastened her teeth on his nose and clamped down.

She heard a crunch. Blood, warm and salty, spurted into her mouth.

He howled, punching her viciously in the temple and throwing himself off her as her teeth were jarred loose by the stunning blow. Her head was knocked sideways. The room spun and she saw stars.

It didn't matter. Her fight-or-flight response was operating at full throttle now, and this time it screamed flight. She felt his weight shift and, spinning room and stars and all, she was off that bed as if propelled by industrial-strength springs, off the bed and bounding toward the door, running like Death himself was after her as she very much feared he was. She flew over the carpet and across the hardwood floor of the hall and down the slippery marble steps so fast that her feet barely touched ground, breathing in great ragged gasps that hurt her throat, her heart beating like the wings of a trapped bird, screaming like a thousand lost souls on their way to hell.

"Bitch! Bitch! Bitch!"

Oh, God, please let him not have his gun.

Her shoulders scrunched in terrified expectation of a bullet in the back as she leaped down the last few stairs.

"Come back here!"

He was gaining on her, getting close, so close, grabbing for her, exuding so much fury and menace and evil that she could feel them like some huge trio of hounds snapping at her heels. Cold sweat poured from her body as it seemed to her that she was running in slow motion with the front door drawing ever farther away. The smell of him, oniony and rank, surrounded her. The rasp of his breathing filled her ears. The floor seemed to vibrate beneath her feet as he lumbered like some enormous, death-dealing monster in her wake.

"Julie!"

Mac's voice shouting her name was the most welcome sound Julie had ever heard. It came from the direction of the kitchen. Screaming, Julie veered that way, scant inches ahead of the man behind her, her bare feet slipping and sliding over the cool slick marble of the entry hall, her bound hands stretching out in front of her, her fingers clawing at the darkness as if it was something tangible she could grasp and pull. She bolted through the dining room's arched doorway, then raced across freshly waxed hardwood toward the kitchen.

"Julie!"

"Help! Help me!"

As her feet hit the cool stone of the kitchen floor, the overhead light came on, all but blinding her. Unable in that split second to see, she careened into the corner of the glass-topped kitchen table and bounced off and kept going, not even feeling the pain as the sharp corner thrust into her tender abdomen.

Then—thank God, thank God—she saw Mac, standing in the doorway between the kitchen and the family room, one hand on the light switch. Her first glimpse of him seemed to catch him in midmotion, and then he saw her, too, and stopped dead, looking tall and strong and out of breath and nearly as terrified as she felt.

"Mac!"

She launched herself at him from maybe six feet away, sobbing and gasping and trying to warn him of the monster coming behind her in a hysterical screech that was all but incomprehensible to her own ears. Two things registered in the same instant: one, Mac—Mac!—was holding a gun; and two, she couldn't hear the monster behind her anymore.

Oh, God, where was he?

"What the hell . . ."

Mac caught her as she landed against him, wrapping a hard arm around her waist, pulling her close to his chest as she screamed her warning. He held her one-armed while he shifted in a quick dance step that brought his back up against the nearest wall. His grip on the gun stayed firm and sure, and he aimed it toward the door through which she had come.

"Julie. Julie. It's okay, I've got you safe." He spoke over the noise she made, and she collapsed gasping and shuddering against his chest. His body was tense, ready for action; she got the sense that he was balanced on the balls of his feet. Clearly he knew his way around a gun. He exuded controlled power, and she was suddenly possessed of absolute faith in his ability to protect her. Accordingly, she clung to him as to a rock in a murderous sea. "Stay right here, and I'll . . ."

"No!" She clutched his shirt front with both her bound hands, her hold a death grip that she never meant to release. "He's got a gun."

Then her ears started to ring, and the world was once again spinning madly. Her knees gave way and the floor seemed to rise up to meet her. If he hadn't caught her, she would have slithered right down the front of his body to expire in a quivering puddle of spineless terror on the floor.

15

"JULIE! CHRIST, JULIE!"

She had fainted in his arms.

At least, he hoped it was a faint. Any other possibility scared the hell out of him.

Mac supported her dead weight with one arm, running a quick, anxious glance over her at the same time as he tried to keep an eye on both doors that opened into the huge, gleaming, stainless-steel and white kitchen. The silky thing she was almost wearing made it hard to keep his grip on her. The brown crust that covered most of her face appeared, at closer glance, to be some kind of cosmetic rather than any of the more horrific possibilities, like blood or burns, that had flashed into his mind when he had first spotted her flying toward him. Her wrists were bound tightly together with silver duct tape. Her throat was a deep, ugly red that gave promise of turning purple later. But there was no blood that he could see, and no other obvious sign of injury.

Had she been raped?

Fear for her joined forces with a deep, atavistic fury that made him want to go after whoever had done this to her and rip him apart with his bare hands, or, at the very least, empty a magazine into him.

The perp was still in the house. Mac knew it with the kind of sixth sense that had, long ago, made him such an effective cop.

He could not leave Julie alone to go after the bastard.

That much coolheadedness he retained. If the perp by some unlucky chance managed to get him first, the way would be clear for the sick bastard to finish what he'd started with Julie.

The graphic mental images that accompanied the thought made him feel murderous all over again.

Cool out, he warned himself. His first objective had to be to get Julie to safety.

With a low growl of frustration he bent and heaved her over his shoulder. Her arms and head hung sack-of-potatoes-style down his back. The silky animal-print stuff of her nightgown was cool against his ear and cheek. The lace that hemmed it tickled his jaw whenever he moved his head. She was not heavy but she was awkward to carry, to no small degree because her slithery gown made her deadweight keep wanting to slide off his shoulder. He had to hold her tight, with his arm locked across her thighs. Her position might very well have left her something less than decently covered, but he was too preoccupied with getting them both out of there to register the occasional glimpse of a sweetly curved cheek more than peripherally. He did notice, because he couldn't help it, that the backs of her thighs felt smooth and firm and silky—as well as surprisingly cold to the touch. From shock or the air-conditioning, he couldn't be sure, but he was betting on shock.

She'd said her attacker had a gun. The chances were good that the guy would run for it, but criminals were not known for their reliability and Mac wasn't taking any chances. What he was doing was hauling ass.

A single set of keys dangling from a hook near the door caught his eye. Thinking fast, juggling Julie and his pistol and praying that he wasn't about to be jumped from behind, he snagged them, fairly sure that they were the keys to the white Infiniti in the garage. It was a loaner from her insurance company; that much he knew. That made it, in effect, her car.

He was taking her straight to the nearest hospital. Sid would get home sooner or later, the police would do their thing, and what had happened in the Carlson house tonight would be the talk of Summerville tomorrow. In the interests of keeping Julie's retention of a private investigator confidential, it would be better if he took her in her car. After he made sure she was safe and in good hands he could fade into the scenery, and, when the time came for her to give a statement, she could claim that she had escaped on her own and driven herself in.

Always provided that she was conscious and talking by then.

Mac dismissed the thought as useless and distracting, and backed warily out through the heavy panel door leading into the garage.

Except for the light from the open kitchen door, it was dark in the garage. It was far warmer than the air-conditioned house, and smelled faintly of freshly cut grass and 10-W-40. Mac was jumpy as a squirrel in a cat's backyard and moving fast as he rounded the Infiniti's hood and tried its rear door, knowing that they could come under fire at any second. To put her in the car required both hands. Cursing a blue streak under his breath, he placed the Glock on the roof. Unarmed now and feeling hideously vulnerable, he did a clumsy juggling maneuver with her inert body that by the grace of God somehow ended with her lying, knees bent, on her side in the backseat.

Good enough. Mac shoved her feet all the way inside, closed the door, grabbed the Glock, and leaped for the garage door that he had broken into on his previous visit to the house. It had not yet been fixed; he knew, because he'd entered through it. Keeping a wary eye on the bright rectangle of light, he heaved the door up, wincing at the telltale rattle it made, then jumped behind the wheel of the car, placing the Glock within easy reach on the front passenger seat. The key fit, the engine turned over, Mac slammed the car into drive, and they were out of there.

Thank God. Until he hung a left at the end of the driveway and felt the tension leave his shoulders, Mac didn't realize just how scared he'd been.

He had left the Blazer parked across the street. Pulling up behind it, he stopped, sprinted to the driver's-side door, opened it, retrieved his cell phone, and locked the door again. Jumping back in the Infiniti, he saw that Julie had not stirred. She was still breathing; her breasts rose and fell rhythmically beneath the flimsy nightgown, and her truly world-class legs shifted restlessly as he watched.

Alarm at her state made his movements jerky and his foot heavier than usual on the accelerator. Peeling out around the Blazer, he dialed 911 and reported a break-in in progress at Julie's address. At least that would get some uniforms on the scene, though he doubted that it would do much good.

Unless the intruder had shit for brains, he was already long gone. Mac gritted his teeth at the thought. It went way against the grain with him to just let the son of a bitch escape, but under the circumstances there seemed to be no help for it.

It occurred to him then that the degree of his fear and anger was way out of proportion, considering Julie Carlson's role in his life. He should be feeling a decent amount of concern, a little chagrin that the attack had happened right under his nose, but nothing like the combination of grinding fear and murderous rage that was at that very moment churning through his guts.

Mac didn't think he'd ever been so petrified in his entire adult life as he had been when he'd first heard Julie scream.

Speeding through the stop sign at the corner with scarcely more than a pause and a glance, he went cold all over again as he remembered.

After she had left him, he had settled down in the Blazer to wait for Sid to get home, turning his spy ears on so that he could listen to what was going on in the house but not hearing anything because there was nothing to hear. Julie was alone. The time to really listen was after Sid was inside the house. If anything was going to happen, it would happen then.

Julie had said Sid wasn't violent, but Mac had his own reasons for knowing better than that. The thing was, Sid apparently wasn't violent to Julie. Of course, that could be because she'd never given him cause.

Having him followed as a prelude to divorcing him might well, in Sid's book, constitute cause.

In any case, Mac wasn't inclined to bet the farm that it wouldn't. If Sid had made them at Sweetwater's—and he didn't think Sid had, but it never paid to take things like that for granted—Julie might just discover a whole new side to her husband that she apparently had no idea existed.

If that were to happen, Mac meant to be on hand. Over the last twenty-four hours, watching out for Julie seemed to have become his mission in life.

Besides, knowing what time Sid got home and what he did after he got there could be important in figuring out exactly what was going down. Maybe Sid would make a phone call. Maybe he'd go out for a walk. Maybe he'd simply go to bed.

Although not, Mac was glad to remember, with Julie. Mac didn't think he could listen to that. No, he knew he couldn't listen to that and stay sane.

Which was a bad sign. A really bad sign. Julie Carlson was his client, for God's sake, and his link to Sid, and that was all. He had no interest in her beyond that.

Yeah, and his real name was Debbie, too.

Mac grimaced as he realized that the situation was starting to get way out of hand.

She kissed him like she was dying to take him to bed, then twenty minutes later told him she wasn't going to sleep with him. Well, that was fine by him, because he wasn't planning to sleep with her either. Sleeping with her would be the equivalent of a last fatal step into quicksand.

Unfortunately, he couldn't help recalling some saying about what happened to even the best-laid plans of—was it mice and men? He couldn't remember how it went exactly, but the upshot was that the plans went to hell, and the mice and men that made them pretty much wound up being roadkill.

Under the circumstances, though, keeping his eye on the ball wasn't all that easy. When he'd been sitting in the Blazer in the dark, growing old waiting for Sid's Mercedes to pull up the driveway, pretty much all he had found to do was breathe and think about Julie. He had tried not thinking about her, but that didn't work, so at last he gave up and allowed his memory—and his fantasies—free rein.

Having to take a leak was almost a welcome interruption.

He'd gotten out, taken care of business, then set off on a leisurely stroll around the Carlson McMansion just for something to do. Standing at the edge of the stone patio, looking at the moonlight glinting off the kidney-shaped swimming pool, he had acknowledged that there just might be a real solid reason why Julie wanted to hang on to her marriage.

Yo, little bro, big bucks buy babes.

He could almost hear Daniel saying it, all those years ago, and a wry, faintly tender smile touched his mouth at the memory. As a cocky sixteen-year-old he'd confronted his big brother, who at the time had no steady employment that he knew of, about the illegality of his newest money-making venture, demanding to know how he could have done something so damned stupid as to fly a buttload of marijuana into the country from Mexico in the small plane he'd somehow managed to buy.

Daniel had grinned that big, shit-eating grin that had driven girls wild and made his more serious-minded little brother increasingly want to pop him in the nose, and said he did it because there were big bucks in it, and yo, little bro, big bucks buy babes.

Julie Carlson was definitely a babe. Had big bucks bought her? Looking around ye olde McMansion, there didn't seem to be much doubt.

"Mac?" Julie's voice was faint, but it snapped Mac's attention back to the present as effectively as a shout. Glancing over his shoulder as the Infiniti scooted through yet another stop sign, he saw that her beautiful brown eyes were open at last and she was struggling to sit up.

"Yeah," he said. "Don't move. We're on our way to the hospital."

"Oh, God, Mac, he—I . . ." Her reply ended in a wordless quaver.

That quaver went through him like a knife.

"It's okay," he said, his voice gruffer than usual because he wasn't sure he was ready to hear the details of what had happened. He figured, while he was driving, it might be better that he not know. If the answers were bad, talking about it might further traumatize her, too. "You're safe now."

"I—must have blacked out." She sounded faintly woozy still, and she kept trying to sit up, although her bound wrists seemed to be making sitting up more diffi- cult than it should be. Or maybe she had some injury he hadn't spotted, and it was hindering her. The thought turned him cold.

"No shit," he said. Then, with another glance at her over his shoulder that nearly caused him to sideswipe a mailbox, he added, in the hard, cop voice he hadn't used in years, "Did you recognize him? Was it someone you know?"

"No. I don't know. I don't think so. God, he—he knew my name." She shuddered, and he cursed under his breath. Easy, he reminded himself, take it easy.

He deliberately gentled his tone. "Can you describe him? What did he look like?"

She shook her head, and took a deep, shaking breath. "He was wearing a mask, at first. And then—I didn't get that good of a look."

"Are you hurt anywhere? Any pain or anything like that?"

"My head hurts," she said after letting a beat pass in which Mac realized his palms were starting to sweat. "He punched me in the head. And my neck. He was going to strangle me, I think. After—after . . ."

Her voice broke. Mac ground his teeth. He took the safer tack of glancing at her through the mirror. She was sitting up now. Her head rested limply back against the tan leather upholstery. Her hair in that ridiculous cascading ponytail still nearly reached her shoulders. Her face was covered with a cracked and flaking layer of something brown.

"And my hands are numb," she continued more strongly, as if rallying.

Mac sucked a calming breath in through his teeth. The idea that some bastard had wrapped her wrists with duct tape made him want to start breaking faces. To say nothing of the rest of what had been done to her.

"I'll get the tape off for you when we get to the hospital. Just a few more minutes." His tone was soothing.

"The hospital?"

"That's where we're going." Clearly she hadn't registered what he'd said the first time. That worried him. Just how hard had she been hit? He stepped on the accelerator, glanced in the mirror again—and went straight through a stop sign. Jesus. He hadn't even seen it. Good thing the traffic in Summerville at three in the morning was so light as to be almost nonexistent.

"Mac. Pull over." There was a sudden urgency to her voice.

"What? Why?" He glanced in the mirror again.

"I think I'm going to throw up."

Mac groaned, and pulled the Infiniti over to the side of the road.

Julie was already fumbling at the handle when he got her door open.

"Hold still." He had his pocketknife out and ready. Hooking his fingers beneath the edge of the tape, he sliced through the sticky layers with relative ease, then pulled the tape off with one quick yank and felt a twinge of guilt as she winced. He imagined the sensation was something akin to having a mega-Band-Aid removed the quick way. In short, not pleasant.

"Mac, *move.*" The order was urgent, and then she pressed her lips tightly together as if she was afraid of what might follow the words. Even as she flexed her fingers and shook out her hands, she swung her legs out of the car and scooted forward. Her bare feet were pale against the dark bristle of the grass as she tried to stand. Her legs were long and slim and luscious beneath the hem of that unbelievably sexy nightgown. From the neck down, she was every teenage boy's wet dream; from the neck up, she was every grown man's fear of what he would end up sleeping with for the next fifty years once the honeymoon was over.

The bad part was, even with a silly pony-tail and a face full of muck, she still looked beautiful. And with that thought, Mac realized to his dismay that he was already smack in the middle of the quicksand, and it was closing over his head.

She was about halfway out the door

when she swayed and sank back. Mac, standing a little to one side to give her room, saw that she needed help and bravely put himself directly in the line of fire. Grabbing her by both elbows, he hauled her out. With an arm wrapped around her waist he supported her as she stumbled about six feet away from the car.

He then stood over her feeling helpless while she dropped to her knees at the side of the road.

16

HER HEAD SWAM, HER STOMACH HEAVED, but in the end she managed to keep herself from vomiting by sheer force of will. After a moment in which the issue hung in the balance, Julie sank back on her heels and flopped forward so that her head rested on her thighs and her arms lay limply on the grass beside her folded legs, too dizzy and exhausted to even sit up. Her stomach settled, but her head throbbed mercilessly, her throat ached, and her newly freed hands tingled and burned. Julie looked at the marks the tape had made on her wrists and shuddered.

"Julie?" Mac crouched beside her and

put a hand, warm and large, on her back. For once the muggy heat was welcome; she felt cold to the bone. The scent of fresh-cut grass was all around her. The grass itself felt cool and faintly damp beneath her.

Julie turned her head toward him, registered the gilt-edged outline of his head against the star-dusted sky, registered the broad-shouldered power of his build, registered his sheer masculine beauty, and felt comforted. No matter if he had deceived her in the matter of Debbie, Mac could be counted on to keep her safe.

"I'm glad you're not gay," she said.

"Me too." His voice was dry. He was looking her over carefully. She smiled at him. If it hadn't been for Mac—well, she wasn't going to think about that. Not now. If she thought about what might have happened, she feared she would totally lose it, which would not help the situation in any way that she could see.

"How are you feeling?"

"I'm okay," she said.

"I can tell." The dryness took on a grim edge. She watched as he glanced away from her, then back. "There's a water fountain over there. Feel like a drink?"

It was only then that she realized they were at the edge of Sawyer Park, a children's play area consisting of a grassy acre chock-full of swings and slides and sandboxes and other assorted kiddie paraphernalia. She knew it well, thanks to countless afternoons spent playing in it with Erin and Kelly.

"Sounds good."

Before she could make more than a feeble attempt to rise, he made a sound under his breath and scooped her up in his arms. He straightened as easily as if she weighed nothing at all, and started walking with her toward the small silver monolith of a drinking fountain that gleamed in the moonlight some hundred yards away.

Julie didn't even think about protesting, but curled close against his chest and looped her arms around his neck, content to be right where she was. Her knees felt rubbery, her head swam, and she had a funny feeling that she wasn't quite hitting on all her usual mental cylinders. She wasn't sure she could have walked to the water fountain even if she'd wanted to. But she didn't want to. She loved being in Mac's arms. They were hard and strong beneath her knees and around her back. His chest was firm and solid, and his whole body was so *warm.* She realized that what she was experiencing was probably a trauma-induced primitive female reaction to his superior male strength, mentally deplored the retro-ness of her own response, and settled down to savor it anyway. She let her head rest on his wide shoulder, closed her eyes, and tightened her hold on his neck.

"Okay, I'll bite," Mac said a beat or so later, sounding slightly grumpy. She opened her eyes to find that they were closing on their goal fast: his long strides were eating up the ground. "Want to tell me what the heck that stuff is on your face?"

For a moment Julie couldn't think what he was talking about. Then she remembered the Mudd, and surprised herself by smiling. Here she was, enjoying a little escapist romantic fantasy about being borne away into the darkness by a truly hot guy, and all the while she looked like a refugee from an *I Love Lucy* episode. Was that the way life worked or what? At least, her life.

"Mudd."

"You usually sleep with mud on your face?" He sounded politely interested.

"Mudd. M-U-double dee. It's a mask. For your skin. I was going to take a bath before I went to bed, and I put Mudd on my face first. Then I saw *him* in the mirror before I could get in the tub."

She shuddered, and his grip tightened. The instant when she had seen her attacker in the mirror was vivid—too horribly vivid to be borne. She tried to dismiss it from her mind; it was impossible. Out of nowhere came the memory of her little voice. Goose bumps prickled to life all over her as she realized that the voice had been warning her. It must have been some kind of sixth sense. On some level, she must have realized that there was someone in the house.

That thought was scary, too. She didn't much like the idea that she knew things she didn't know she knew.

"How did you know I was in trouble?" Maybe he'd had a sixth sense experience, too.

"Darlin', you have a scream like a banshee. I was standing outside by your pool when you let loose. Hearing you took about twenty years off my life, by the way." He took a deep breath. "Then I saw that someone had already broken in. It wasn't the best moment I've ever had, let me tell you."

For a moment neither of them said anything more. His feet moving over the grass and the chirping chorus of the usual insects were the only sounds. Moonlight bathed the playground in a ghostly glow. The playthings took on a whole different ambience in the dead of night, Julie discovered. A sinister ambience.

She felt a chill race down her spine and realized that the sheer terror of being attacked in her own home was still with her, hiding deep within her body's cells to reemerge at will like a particularly nasty virus. Never again, she feared, would she feel totally safe. If it could happen there, it could happen anywhere, even in this innocuous little playground. "Assume the worst" seemed to be her body's new rule of thumb, and she was correspondingly anxious. Thank God Mac was with her. She would have been spooked out of her mind otherwise.

No, if Mac hadn't been with her, she

wouldn't have been here in this cheerful-by-day, eerie-by-night playground to be creeped out by ghostly toys.

Maybe she wouldn't have been any-where. The thought sent a whole series of chills chasing after the first. He must have felt her shiver, because his arms tightened around her, cuddling her closer.

"Mac. Thank you."

"For?" He slanted a glance down at her. His face was very close.

"I think you probably saved my life."

He grunted. "Not a problem."

"What if he comes after us here?" Her voice was low. The terror was bubbling up again, sparked by their isolation, by the darkness, by the sense that anything could lurk in the shadows. She glanced fearfully around.

"I'll keep you safe whatever happens, I promise. But you don't need to worry: he won't come. He's long gone, believe me."

"You have a gun, don't you?"

"Yup."

"You know how to use it, right?"

His mouth twitched. "I used to be a cop. Before that, Navy SEAL. That make you feel better?"

"A little. No, actually, a lot." She felt dizzy, and rested her head against his shoulder again. He looked down at her.

"You okay?"

"Yes. Why aren't you a cop anymore?"

His jaw tightened. She felt a sudden tension in his body. For a moment she thought he wasn't going to answer, and she lifted her head and looked at him inquiringly. His gaze met hers and held for the briefest of moments. Then he glanced away.

"I got fired."

"You got *fired?*" Getting fired from the police force was the last thing she would ever expect to happen to Mac, Julie realized with some surprise. The Debbie thing notwithstanding, he was just about the most solidly reliable person she had ever met in her life. "Why?"

He sighed. "Because drugs went missing from the evidence room and were found in my possession. A boatload of people were willing to swear I'd been dealing. I got fired. I would have been prosecuted, but the department didn't want the publicity."

"You were innocent." It wasn't a question.

"Yeah, I was. The guy I was investigating

at the time got to me before I could get him."

They reached the fountain then and he set her on her feet, keeping both hands on her waist and standing behind her, bracing her body with his. Julie rinsed her mouth several times then sluiced her face and throat, which felt bruised on the outside but didn't hurt particularly when she swallowed. No internal damage then, she judged, and felt thankful. The water was more lukewarm than cold, but it rinsed the Mudd away and made her feel better nonetheless. After several splashes she felt almost normal. When she was finished, she looked around at Mac, blinking as she wiped the water from her cheeks with her fingers.

"Here." He turned her around with his hands on her hipbones and wiped her face dry with the hem of his shirt.

"Now your shirt's wet." She steadied herself by grabbing onto his waist. It was narrow and hard beneath his T-shirt. His muscles flexed beneath her fingers as he moved.

"I'll survive."

He reached out and tugged at the

scrunchie that held her hair up. Her hair was falling out of its high ponytail anyway, with tendrils straggling around her ears and down the back of her neck and tickling her cheeks. The bulk of it tumbled around her face as he pulled the scrunchie free. Julie instinctively shook her head to restore what order she could to her errant locks, then winced at the resultant stab of pain. He handed her the scrunchie and she slid it onto her arm.

"Better," he said, looking her over. "Not that you didn't look good with that mud stuff all over your face and your hair done up like a mop, of course."

Julie smiled. "Lying's going to get you in big trouble one of these days."

For a moment he simply looked down at her without saying anything. His hands rested on her upper arms. Their heat burned her skin. He was standing very close. Her breasts were just inches from his chest, her pelvis just inches from the zippered front of his jeans. A sudden, sensual hunger sprang to life inside her. She shivered a little, remembering the way he had kissed her earlier, welcoming the memory because it crowded out all the horrible memories that had come later. He made a slight, restive movement and she glanced up. Her gaze collided with his. He was frowning down at her, and the air between them was suddenly charged. Her lips parted. Her breathing quickened. His fingers tightened on her arms.

She felt positively light-headed—and she didn't think it was because of the blow to her head.

"We need to get going. You up to walking, do you think?" His abrupt words belied the heat in his eyes.

She smiled dreamily up at him. The alternative, of course, was for him to sweep her up in his arms again and carry her away into the night. Every atom of her being practically drooled at the prospect. In some small part of her mind, Julie recognized that weakness and fear had rendered her vulnerable, and mentally girded her loins. She *wanted* to be in his arms, but, she reminded herself sternly, a little wanting of that nature could be a dangerous thing.

"I can walk." Her voice sounded far more robust than she felt.

He let go of her arms, and she was both

glad and sorry to be taken at her word. Instead of sweeping her up, he slid a hand around her elbow with all the decorousness he might have shown a maiden aunt, and urged her forward. Setting her jaw determinedly, Julie started walking, breathing deep of the heavy night air that was, she discovered, the opposite of revivifying. She made it about half a dozen paces. Then her knees dissolved from rubbery straight to pure liquid, and she folded like an accordion. Mac grabbed her around the waist in the nick of time, barely saving her from ending up flat on her face in the grass.

"To hell with it," he said, sounding angry, and scooped her up again. Try though she might, Julie couldn't summon up so much as a smidgen of regret. Her head swam and her limbs felt as limp as cooked noodles—but not limp enough to prevent her from wrapping her arms around his neck. It was then that she faced the awful truth: Dangerous or not, Mac's arms felt like home to her now.

For the length of a couple of strides neither of them said anything. Julie breathed in the slightly beery, slightly musky scent of him and snuggled as close as she could get. He basically walked and breathed.

Then Mac gave a disgusted grunt. His hands—one on her bare thigh just above her knee, one just below her right breast—tightened.

"Just for the record, are you wearing anything at all under that nightgown?"

Julie looked up at him, admiring the clean, classical lines of his jaw and chin and noting with some interest that blond men were perfectly capable of sprouting a considerable amount of five-o'clock shadow given the right circumstances.

"No. Not a thing."

"That's what I thought."

He was sweating, she noticed, observing small beads of moisture on his forehead with interest, although she didn't think it was from effort. After all, he had carried her from the car to the drinking fountain without any trouble. And, hippy or no, she didn't weigh all that much.

"So what's your point?" she prodded when he didn't say anything else.

"No point."

They reached the car. Keeping a steadying arm around her waist, Mac set her on her feet to open the front passenger door. Tugging the hem of her nightgown down— it had ridden up to the point of indecency as she slid down his body—she leaned contentedly against him, her bare shoulder butting into his chest, her silk-clad hipbone nudging his abdomen. She shifted position a little and her hip brushed the front of his jeans. There was a palpable hardness there. Julie registered it, and her lips curved into a small, purely feminine smile.

"Don't you like my nightgown?" There, she was flirting with him, openly, unmistakably flirting, pounding head, bruised throat and all. Julie realized that she hadn't flirted in years; flirting, she rediscovered, was fun.

Mac looked down at her with a considering expression. The now-open door waited beside her like an eager mouth, but she wasn't ready to be swallowed up by it just yet.

"That depends." He sounded cautious as he studied her face. Then he seemed to make up his mind about something. His jaw tightened, his lips compressed, and he added in a firmer tone, "Now be a good girl and get in."

When she didn't move but just stood

there smiling beatifically at him, he grimaced and bundled her inside with ruthless efficiency, lifting her legs in when she
was slow to do so, pulling her seat belt
down and leaning across her to fasten it.

"Depends on what?" Voice sultry, she
slid her hand up inside his T-shirt as he
leaned across her, enjoying the feel of his
warm, satiny skin, the hard smoothness of
his stomach, the brawny width of his chest.
He froze at her touch, and as her fingers
traveled upward, burrowing into the soft
mat of hair she discovered, his gaze met
hers. Their faces were so close she could
feel the warmth of his breath on her skin.

His eyes were hot; his mouth was—sexy
as hell. She couldn't stop looking at it. Her
hand stilled on his chest, palm flattening,
fingers spreading luxuriantly in the silky
hair. She could feel the steady beat of his
heart against her palm.

"On whether you meant what you said
earlier about not sleeping with me."

There was a huskiness to his voice that
made her breathing quicken. Her lips
parted. Instinctively she lifted them toward
his.

His eyes narrowed; his lips compressed;

his head pulled back. Then his hand caught hers and pulled it out from under his shirt despite her sound of protest.

"Mac!"

He hesitated, his hand tightening on hers, and their eyes met again. Electricity leaped between them, so strong it practically ignited the air. Then he muttered something that sounded like *damn* under his breath, leaned forward and kissed her, his mouth slanting across hers with a hungry urgency that made her dizzier than she already was. Julie's eyes closed. Her lips parted. His kiss was hot, and fierce, and tasted faintly of beer, and she responded to it with mindless pleasure. Her loins tightened and began to throb. Her breasts swelled greedily toward his chest. Her fingers curled around his, claiming his hand for her own. Head reeling, she licked into his mouth and pressed the hand that was joined to hers palm-down over her breast. It rested there, radiating heat through the thin layer of silk, hard and heavy and crazy-making on the soft fullness of her. His hand on her breast felt so wonderfully, unbelievably good. . . .

For a moment, as she held his hand to

her breast and her nipple pebbled against his palm, she thought he wasn't going to respond. Then he made a sound deep in his throat, the kiss seemed to burst into flame, and his hand got with the program, tightening and squeezing with an almost compulsive need. Her heart pounded; her loins throbbed; her toes curled. His kiss drove her wild. His hand caressed her breast, cupped it; his thumb ran knowingly back and forth across her nipple. She moved enticingly, straining upward against the constraint of her seat belt, her hand sliding behind his neck to pull him closer yet; a delicious tightening sensation began deep inside her body. She moaned, arching her back—and then he was pulling away, lifting his mouth from hers, removing his hand from her breast, putting inches of space between them when all she wanted to do was get closer to him than his own underwear.

She opened her eyes and gave him a look that said *do me right now or die* as clearly as if she'd shouted it. Although, of course, verbally she would never be that crude. Instead she fluttered her lashes and gave him a sexy little murmur of encouragement.

"Mac . . ."

His eyes narrowed at her.

"Don't mess with me, Julie, or I'm liable to forget you're operating with a bad case of scrambled brains here."

And with that he pulled his hand from hers and withdrew, just like that, shutting her door and walking around the hood to get in himself.

"I do not," she said with what dignity she could muster, crossing her arms over her still tingly chest and scowling at him as he put the key in the ignition, "have scrambled brains."

"Tell me that after a doctor's looked at you." He started the car.

"Maybe I'm just rethinking my position." She uncrossed her arms, and trailed a teasing finger down the sinewy arm closest to her. "After all, why shouldn't I sleep with you?"

"Because it's a bad idea." He dodged to escape her touch. Julie let her hand drop.

They were moving now. The car slid through the night with a whisper of tires, leaving the playground behind. In seconds they were once again cruising past dark houses with sleeping families tucked cozily inside.

"Why is it a bad idea? Don't you want to sleep with me?" She hunched her shoulders petulantly, casting him a sidelong look.

He laughed. They were moving into the commercial district now, and by the light of 7-Elevens and Dunkin' Donuts and street-lamps she was able to see him quite clearly. He looked—better than a choc-olate-glazed. And also faintly rueful.

"Does that mean yes or no?" There was an edge to her voice.

"I'd say definitely yes."

She rested her head on the seat back and glared at him, exasperated. "So what's your problem?"

His eyes cut to her. "My problem is that we need to have this conversation when you're not a couple of french fries short of a Happy Meal." He sounded way too pa-tient for her liking.

"That's ridiculous."

He shrugged. "Maybe."

She made a face at him. "Chicken."

"Damn right," he said, and made clucking sounds. "And here we are."

To her annoyance, he sounded relieved.

He parked in the lot to the left of the emergency-room entrance and turned off the car. Then he sat for a moment with his hands resting on the steering wheel, staring out through the windshield at the nearly full lot with a gathering frown on his face. The yellowish glow of the tall lamps that illuminated the area allowed her to see him clearly. His mouth and jaw were taut; his eyes were hard.

"What?" Julie asked when he didn't say anything.

"Okay." The word was abrupt. His gaze slashed toward her. "I need to know. Were you raped?" His fingers curled around the steering wheel as he spoke, then tightened so that his knuckles showed white.

"No. *No.*" Julie swallowed as the brutality of the attack came back to her in a sudden sickening wave. "He—I think that's what he had in mind, but it didn't happen."

"Why not?" He looked fully at her then, and his tone was milder. The tension in his body eased. Even his grip on the steering wheel relaxed to a degree.

"I bit his nose. Then I ran."

A beat passed. *"You bit his nose?"*

Julie nodded.

"Hard," she said with relish, remembering. "It was bleeding. I heard it crunch. Then he screamed and rolled off me, and I jumped up and ran downstairs."

He stared at her for a moment as if he couldn't believe his ears. Then his face relaxed and a hint of a smile turned up one corner of his mouth. "That would work." The smile widened into a grin. "You're something, you know that? Really something."

"So sleep with me." Julie's tone was deliberately, flirtatiously seductive. Her gaze locked with his.

"Later," he said. "Maybe."

He pulled the keys from the ignition and got out of the car. Julie watched as he came around to open her door. She was starting to feel really bad again, she realized, light-headed and sick at her stomach, and it occurred to her that maybe Mac was right—maybe she was short a few vital french fries. Or maybe she felt so ill because talking about it so graphically had brought the reality of the attack back to her with a vengeance. Before, when she'd been flirting with Mac, the whole nightmarish sequence of events had seemed far away, long ago, and almost as if it had happened to someone else.

That kind of distancing was, she realized, probably some sort of defense mechanism kicking in. Whatever, its protective effect was gone now, and she felt *bad.*

Mac opened her door and reached across her to unfasten her belt. This time she didn't move, just lay limply back against the seat with her hands in her lap, battling a renewed urge to heave. When the latch released, he eased the seat belt away from her and took a quick, assessing look at her face.

"Hang on a few more minutes, tough guy," he said, his voice both rough and surprisingly tender at the same time, and slid his arms around her to scoop her out.

Julie didn't answer. She was too busy trying to keep all her cookies on board. Instead, she curled her arms around his neck and burrowed her head into the hollow between his neck and shoulder and closed her eyes, trusting him to take care of everything, to take care of her.

It was amazing to consider how much, in such a short span of time, she had grown to trust Mac.

"When we get inside," he said, striding toward the emergency room doors with her in his arms, "here's what I need you to do. . . ."

Later, after the police had arrived along with a frantic-seeming Sid and, some ten minutes after that, Julie's even more frantic-seeming mother and sister, Mac slid out from behind the potted ficus and the newspapers that had served as his cover and left the hospital. The circus was in full swing inside. He didn't want any part of that. And Julie didn't need him anymore. At least, not at this end.

Dawn was just beginning to outline the eastern horizon in glowing orange. Not that the early hour made any difference to his plans. He slid into the taxi that waited, and made a second phone call as it pulled away from the curb.

When Mother answered, clearly peeved at having his beauty sleep disturbed, Mac cut him off with a few well-chosen words.

"I need some information."

17

BY TUESDAY MORNING Julie was back at work. She'd spent Sunday night in the hospital for observation and Monday night at her mother's. Although to everyone else she insisted that she was fine, to herself she acknowledged that she was still not mentally over the attack. Or physically over it either, for that matter. As Mac had suspected, she had suffered a slight concussion—or, as he'd so descriptively put it, scrambled brains. She had a baseball-sized bruise on her temple, three more in the approximate shape of ladyfingers on her throat, and one small crescent-shaped one just to the left of her belly button. All were an ugly shade of purple, and the ones on her face and throat were all but impervious to attempts to hide them with makeup. In their honor, she wore a petal-pink sleeveless sweater dress with a high, concealing turtleneck that she would have ordinarily deemed too hot for the weather, and accessorized it with a narrow purple belt and a pair of sinfully expensive purple sandals.

At least, she thought with a glimmer of humor, eyeing herself in one of the mirrored walls of her shop, no one could say she wasn't color-coordinated.

They could say plenty of other things, though. She was starting to feel like a one-woman sideshow. She'd been badgered for details by everyone from the police to Sid to her mother and Becky to friends and neighbors to people she didn't remember ever meeting in her life. Only Sid's combined cajoling and threatening of the publisher had kept the story out of the local newspaper. The consensus was that the attack was probably related to the theft of her car: either the thief had come across her picture in her purse—on her driver's license, maybe—and been moved by it to attack, or the attack had been part of the original plan, which had been aborted for some reason, and the criminal had come back to finish the job.

After all, what were the chances of two unconnected crimes occurring at the same address within two days?

Not to worry, though: The police assured her that (a) they would solve the case; and (b) it was unlikely that the criminal would return.

Given what they knew, Julie supposed that both were reasonable assumptions. She was not convinced of either point, however: look how easy they were to fool. She *was* sure that the man who had attacked her was not one of the punks who had stolen her car. No way, no how. Number one, the punks who stole her car had her keys, a fact of which the police were not aware and which she could find no way of letting them in on that did not involve admitting her lie; they would not have needed to jimmy the back door, which her attacker had done. For obvious reasons, she discussed that small glitch in the official theory with no one but Mac. He had called her twice, once at the hospital and once at her mother's, and they'd spoken briefly and guardedly, but she had not seen him since he'd left her in the emergency room.

To her own dismay, she caught herself missing him. A lot.

It was an unusually busy morning, both because Monday's appointments had been blended with Tuesday's and because of the looming start of the Miss Southern Beauty pageant. Besides Carlene, Julie was dressing seven other contestants. All had come in for final fittings, and finding herself knee deep in adjusting built-in padded bras and waist-whittling spandex dress liners was cathartic. Life was, more or less, back to normal, and Julie was grateful for that. She never in her life wanted to go through another weekend like the one she had just spent.

When the phone rang around one, Julie was on her knees putting the last few stitches in a client's competition evening gown. Her mouth was full of the pins she had removed from the aqua silk-satin creation as she worked her way around the hem, tacking it up.

"Julie, you have a phone call," Meredith said, entering the dressing room and looking down at her. "Someone named Debbie."

Julie almost swallowed the pins. In the interests of personal health and safety, she spit them out in her hand.

"Thanks." She motioned Meredith over to continue the task, and stood up, smiling at her red-haired client through the mirror. "Excuse me. I'll be right back."

This one—Tara Lumley—was sweet, as most of them were. Her handler sat quietly in a corner thumbing through a magazine. Absolute dolls, both of them. Too bad that, in Julie's expert opinion, Tara didn't have a prayer of defeating Carlene. Julie was all for someone, anyone, defeating Carlene.

Julie deposited the pins in a crystal container on her desk, and picked up the phone.

"Hi," she said, her voice far huskier and more intimate than it would have been if she truly had been addressing a Debbie whose name and gender matched.

"Hi, yourself." The sound of Mac's voice made her heartbeat quicken and her hand tighten on the receiver. Julie recognized her response as a bad thing, and enjoyed it anyway. "You got any plans for lunch?"

"I've already eaten." Two carrots and some crackers, just before noon. Oh, God, she wanted to see him. So much it scared her.

"Me too. So's how about you heading across the street to the Taco Bell anyway? I need to talk to you."

"About what?"

"Tell you when you get here."

Julie hesitated, thinking of Tara. Amber had gone to lunch, which meant that Meredith would have to handle everything alone. But Amber would be back within the hour, and Meredith was perfectly capable of dealing with anything that came up, as long as Julie was back by three. That's when Carlene was scheduled for her next fitting. Thinking of Carlene, Julie groaned inwardly and made up her mind. She deserved a break today.

"Be right there," she said, and put down the phone. Catching a glimpse of herself in the mirrored wall across the room, Julie frowned. Suddenly pink and purple to match her bruises didn't seem like such a good idea—and the clingy skirt seemed to make her butt look enormous. Frowning, she walked into the showroom and rifled through the racks until she found the square-necked lilac sundress she sought. It was short, slim-cut, and far more chic than the pink sweater dress, and had the added advantage of working well with her sandals. Hurrying back into her office, she changed, hanging her discarded dress on the rack with some of the newly arrived stock that had yet to be put on display. With the addition of a four-strand pearl choker to hide the worst of the bruises on her throat, and pearl earrings, also from stock, she was ready. Observing herself in another of the ubiquitous mirrors as she left, she smiled. With her black hair and tanned skin providing a nice contrast to the lilac linen and pearls, she looked good. Very Jackie O, but good.

Butterflies took flight in her stomach at the idea that Mac was waiting for her right across the street, and she shook her head at herself. She was reacting like a teenager in the throes of her first crush. And over Debbie! The thought made her smile.

After calling Meredith aside and telling her that she had to run a quick errand, Julie walked across the street to the Taco Bell. She said a cheery *good afternoon* to one of the clerks from the candle shop next door, who was outside smoking a cigarette and stared at the still faintly visible, despite her best efforts with makeup, bruise on her temple with unabashed curiosity. The sun was blinding as it bounced off the pavement, the heat hung like a translucent veil in the air, and the passing cars were no more than shooting flashes of color and carbon monoxide.

Traffic was heavy as usual at midday as shoppers patronized both the strip mall where Carolina Belle was located and the larger shopping center directly across the street. Julie was careful as she hurried across the road, shielding her eyes with her hand and looking both ways. Jaywalking was officially illegal, but everyone did it, including the tourists. Summerville was that kind of town.

The Taco Bell was busy. A line of cars crept toward the drive-through window, and through the plate glass Julie could see that the restaurant was full. She was just about to head inside when a short, sharp whistle drew her attention. Glancing around, she spotted Mac, and her pulse rate immediately increased. He was near the back of the parking lot, leaning against the Blazer with his arms crossed over his chest, dressed in jeans and a white T-shirt under a Hawaiian shirt so bright it rivaled the sun. A pair of Oakleys were wrapped around his face. It was clear from the smile just touching the corners of his mouth that he was watching her, but the sunglasses kept her from seeing his eyes.

God, he was gorgeous, was the thought that immediately sprang into her mind. Then, with an inner groan: Why did he have to be gorgeous?

Even as the thought hit her, Julie felt an answering smile curve her lips quite of its own volition. Gorgeous or not, she was glad to see him. Really, *really* glad to see him.

And a little embarrassed, too, she realized, which wasn't surprising when she thought about it. After all, this was the man she had kissed shamelessly the last time she'd set eyes on him. The man whose lap she had straddled and whose hand she had boldly pressed to her breast. The man she had all but begged to make love to her.

The man who had said no.

She didn't know whether to be mad at him or grateful for that.

"Yo," Mac said by way of a greeting as she got closer. His arms uncrossed, his hands dropped, and Julie realized that he was holding one end of a leash. A black leather leash. Eyes widening, she followed it down past the front of the Blazer just in time to see Josephine emerge from behind one of the small, scruffy bushes that grew in the grassy strip that separated the Taco Bell parking lot from the Kroger parking lot next door: Josephine, minus her pink hair bows and nail polish, sporting a black leather collar with silver studs.

Spotting Julie in turn, Josephine gave a sharp little yap of recognition and danced to meet her.

"Hi, Josephine." Julie squatted to pet her. Josephine waxed ecstatic, wagging her tail so hard her whole body shook, licking Julie's chin and her hand and in every doggy way possible giving Julie to understand that she was delighted to see her.

"What did you *do?*" Julie glanced up at Mac accusingly. He had straightened away from the car, she saw as her gaze traveled up the lean, hard length of him with appreciation, and was at that moment in the act of removing his sunglasses.

"What? Oh, you mean the collar? I got her a new one. The pink was doing bad things to my self-esteem."

"She looks like dominatrix poodle." Julie gurgled with laughter as she stood up.

"She does not." Tucking the Oakleys away in his shirt pocket, he looked at Josephine, who was balanced on her haunches in front of Julie with her front paws waving in the air in an obvious bid for more attention. "Damn, she does."

"Yes, I know. He has *no* taste," Julie said to Josephine in a commiserating tone as she picked the poodle up. "You can tell from his shirts. But don't worry, I'll talk to him about getting your collar back, I promise."

"You got a problem with my shirts?" Mac sounded affronted. He was also grinning.

"Not at all. Except that a person needs sunglasses to look at them."

"They make me look like a tourist. I'm trying to blend in."

"I'm sorry to be the one to break the news, but I don't think it's working."

Julie was smiling as she glanced up from

petting Josephine. Her eyes met Mac's and held. The memory of the last time they were together quivered in the air between them, as intangible but indisputably there as the heat, and Julie felt her body quicken in instinctive response. Then, from the security of Julie's arms, Josephine wriggled and whined, drawing Julie's attention away from Mac to her doggy self, as was, no doubt, her intent. Which was probably a good thing, Julie thought as, acting as Josephine's surrogate, she unfastened the offending collar and handed it, leash still attached, to Mac with an audible sniff, while Josephine shook her head in obvious pleasure at being liberated. She was still a married woman in the first throes of a divorce, after all, and Mac was still, hard as it was to accept the *Oprah*-certified truth, probably no more and no less than a predictable phase she was going through.

A hunky predictable phase.

A hunky predictable phase who had saved her life.

A hunky predictable phase who had saved her life and whose mere presence made her day.

"Just like two females to stick together.

For your information, Mr. Blackwell, she's lucky to be alive to get a new collar," Mac said, shooting Josephine a dark look as he unlocked the passenger door. "While you and I were out having fun the other night, she ate my bathroom wall. Chewed a hole in it the size of a basketball."

"Oh, dear." Julie couldn't help it. She laughed. "She must have been bored."

"She must have been something. Like suicidal." Mac opened the door and waited for Julie to get in. As she passed him, his gaze touched on her bruised temple and the corners of his eyes tightened in obvious concern. "How are you feeling?"

His tone had gentled.

"Better than I look."

"Not possible," he said, and closed the door before she could reply.

Julie sat there with her arms around Josephine and her heart skipping like a little lamb in springtime while he came around the front of the car to slide in behind the wheel. He's a phase, she reminded herself sternly once again as he tossed the collar and leash in the back and she got a good look at an athlete's muscled arms and torso in motion. Just a phase.

"So what do you want to talk to me about?" she asked in as businesslike a tone as she could muster as he started the car. Josephine wriggled out of her hold, then stretched her length across her lap and closed her eyes. The warm weight of the little dog was soothing. Absently, Julie stroked Josephine's frizzy coat.

"Word on the street is that nobody local did this." His gaze touched meaningfully on the bruise on her temple. The Blazer headed for the street. "At least, if it's someone local, he's not one of the usual cast of criminals and perverts."

Julie felt her stomach tense as she tried to ward off memories of the attack.

"What does that mean?"

"It could mean a lot of things. A burglar escalating things to a whole new level. Somebody just moved in from out of town, whose MO's still off the radar. I'm not sure yet. Which is one reason I wanted to talk to you. I want permission to search your house."

Julie stared at him. A blue Corvette just outside her window kept pace with the

Blazer, and Julie realized that they had reached the street and were moving with the flow of traffic. The wizened little man driving it, natty in a linen sport coat and striped shirt, had to be at least eighty. You go, guy, she thought with a tiny inner smile, and returned her attention with some difficulty to the topic at hand.

"The police have already searched the house." Her voice was constricted. She did better if she just flatly refused to think about the attack.

Something in Mac's expression made Julie feel like there was a drop of ice water trickling slowly down her spine. Looking at him, she gave an involuntary little shiver. Josephine, apparently feeling the movement, looked up from her nap with big, questioning eyes. Julie rubbed her ears, and found some relief in doing so.

"I know," Mac said. Julie was starting to recognize that impassive face. It meant there was something he wasn't sharing with her. "But you've got to understand that the police are busy. They've got lots of crimes to investigate—and your husband made it clear to the powers that be that he wants to minimize this one. Any clue why he'd want to brush a brutal assault on his wife under the rug?"

Julie gave a bitter little laugh, and burrowed her fingers deep in Josephine's coat. "That's easy. The subdivision. Sid's company developed it, you know. It might hurt property values if people started thinking that women were being attacked in their own homes there. And Sid is really, really against anything that might hurt property values."

Josephine responded to the attention with an enormous yawn. Her lids drooped, and her head returned to her paws. Julie wished that she could rid herself of her own worries that easily.

"Property values are important." Mac's tone was dry.

"I thought you were supposed to be finding out who my husband bought the Viagra for." Julie deliberately tried for a lighter note. Having her stomach tie itself in knots was not a pleasant sensation, and she was getting tired of it.

Mac grinned, glancing at her, and the atmosphere did indeed lighten. "Hey, what can I say? I'm a full-service investigator."

Julie made a face at him, relieved that

the knot in her stomach was easing. "For your information, Mr. Full Service Investigator, Sid's going to Atlanta this afternoon. He'll be gone for three days. So what are you doing about it?"

"I know that. You think I don't know that? That's another reason I wanted to talk to you. Ordinarily, I'd follow him, because cheaters tend to hook up with their honeys on out-of-town trips. But under the circumstances I think it's better if I stay here. I don't like the idea of leaving you on your own." A serious note entered his voice as he said that last.

"You think the guy's coming back, don't you?" This time her spine was assaulted by an icy river instead of an icy drop. Julie shivered again, more violently this time.

"Slow down." He saw her shiver and shook his head. "I don't necessarily think he's coming back. What I think is, it pays to be careful. Whatever happens, I'll make sure you're safe until we get this all sorted out. Trust me."

Julie took a deep, steadying breath. "I do."

The smile he gave her then was slow and sweet, and sexy as hell. "That's my girl."

His girl. God, what she wouldn't give to be. Phase or no.

The Blazer stopped, and Julie realized that they were pulling onto the grass verge in front of the DeForests' big brick house, which was across the street and catty-corner to her own.

"What are you doing?"

"I told you, I want to search the house. Now's the best time, because none of your neighbors are home during the day, and Sid's headed out of town. What I'd like you to do is come in with me, show me around, maybe walk me through what happened Saturday night. Are you up to it?" He put the car in park and looked at her steadily. Julie's every instinct quailed at the prospect. She had not entered the house since Mac had carried her out of it; Sid had spent the last two nights in it alone. Left to her own devices, she was more likely to fly to the moon than walk inside that house again. Even thinking about it made her start to hyperventilate.

But if Mac thought this guy would be coming back . . .

She took a deep, calming breath, clenched her fists so that her nails dug into her palms, and nodded. Josephine, sensing her unease, looked up again.

"I'll be right with you every step of the way." A smile crinkled the corners of his eyes as he glanced down at Josephine, who was getting to her feet in Julie's lap and arching her back in a luxurious stretch like a cat. "And hey, you've even got a guard dog on duty. What could be safer than that?"

It was hard to picture Josephine as a guard dog, Julie reflected, but she smiled gamely nonetheless. And, paradoxically, smiling made her feel better. And braver.

She still had her *I'm so brave* smile firmly in place when she walked around the front of the Blazer, Josephine cradled in her arms, to discover Mac affixing a large, white, magnetic sign to the driver's door.

LAWN-PRO LAWN AND LANDSCAPING, it said, above a local telephone number. Reading it, Julie's eyes widened.

"I keep it in the back for occasions such as this," Mac explained, in response to Julie's look. "Nobody ever gives me a second glance with this thing on the door. You'd be surprised how many of these services operate in neighborhoods like this during the day."

Indeed, now that she thought about it, Julie could hear the muted roar of a lawn mower in the distance. A glance around showed her a man sitting atop an orange commercial mower several yards over, paying them not the least attention as he merrily did his thing. Ordinarily, she never would have noticed him.

"It's called hiding in plain sight," Mac said as if he could read her mind. Curling a hand around her upper arm, he practically towed her up her own driveway.

The contrast between the relentless sun and baking heat outside and the cool, dim hush of the house couldn't have been more unsettling as, using her key, Mac opened the front door and they stepped inside.

He closed the door behind them. Julie's heart raced as gloom enveloped them, and her stomach felt like it was playing Twister. Her breathing quickened; sure enough, she was going to hyperventilate.

Stop it, she ordered herself as she took several hesitant steps inside her own front hall. Carefully she regulated her breathing: in and out, slow and steady.

At least, she thought, there were no words of warning from her little voice. If she ever heard that puppy again, she was listening up big time.

Josephine, lying contentedly in her arms, was a godsend. The little dog gave her something to concentrate on besides her fear. She was no heavier than Kelly or Erin on the day they'd been born, and her woolly coat reminded Julie of a fleece the girls had slept on as babies. Holding the dog closer, she grew calm enough to look around. There was no visible reminder of her ordeal, she was relieved to see: no footprints, no drops of blood, nothing. The house was pristine, and smelled faintly of Murphy's Oil. Of course, the cleaning service came every Tuesday and Thursday morning; that also accounted for the fresh sheen on the marble floor and the gleam on the just-polished furniture. Strange that the house should be exactly as it had always been, unchanged by what had happened within its walls, while she felt as if the attack had altered her inner landscape forever. Fear was now part of her internal language, which it never had been before.

Her glance fell on the imposing staircase

with its wrought-iron railing, and her breathing quickened again as images of herself fleeing for her life down those steps scrolled unbidden through her mind. She could almost feel the hideous yank of a fist closing on her hair. . . .

"You okay?" Mac's hands dropped onto her shoulders, making her start. He was behind her, solid and strong and infinitely reliable, and it was this knowledge that calmed her down and enabled her to breathe normally again. She nodded, clutched Josephine closer, and, taking a tight mental grip on her courage, walked on toward the staircase, determined not to give in to the fear that threatened to engulf her.

Despite her determination, speaking was an effort; she swallowed, realizing her throat was dry.

"The cleaning people came today. If the police missed any kind of evidence, it's probably gone now."

Mac muttered something short and probably profane under his breath. Julie was almost at the foot of the stairs now, and he was a few paces behind her, looking around with weighing eyes. The marble floor, the crystal chandelier, the staircase that was designed to impress—the whole house that was designed to impress—would be new to him.

"I was in my bathroom . . ." Julie began, looking up the stairs. Then memory assailed her again, and she shivered and shook her head. "Mac, I don't think I can go up there."

"You don't have to do anything you're not ready for." He was right behind her again, and his hand just brushed over her bare arm in a comforting caress. "We'll stay downstairs, if you want." His eyes shifted past her to fix on the open door that led into the den. "Is that some sort of office?"

Julie followed his gaze, and nodded. "Sid's desk is in there, and his computer. He does quite a bit of work at home."

"Mind if I check it out?" he asked, already heading that way.

"Go ahead." She was talking to his back. Trailing him, she stood in the doorway of the den and watched as he conducted a quick search of the desk, opening the drawers and rifling through the contents, then turned on the computer.

"What are you looking for?" She was

feeling better. Steadier, less jumpy. Having her back to the staircase helped, she thought, but she also knew that one day— one day soon—she would be able to climb those stairs. The knowledge eased something that had been twisted tight inside her. Coming back inside her house had been a necessary step in reclaiming her life, she realized.

Mac shrugged noncommittally. "I don't suppose you know the password to any of these files, by any chance?" He was staring intently at the screen, typing as he spoke.

Julie shook her head. "No clue."

Mac grunted unsurprised acknowledgment as he continued to point and click, then peck away at the keyboard, apparently trying words at random.

"Ah," he said moments later with obvious satisfaction, watching as text popped into view.

Julie did a double-take. She was just about to ask how he'd done that—clearly he had either figured out the password to one of the files or somehow bypassed the system's security—when an unexpected sound from somewhere behind her made the hair on the back of her neck stand on end. She spun around. In her arms, Josephine stiffened. The little dog's eyes stared alertly toward the kitchen.

Because there was no possibility of mistake: someone was entering the house through the garage door.

18

TERRIFYING MEMORIES CAME BACK IN A RUSH, threatening to swamp every last vestige of calm that remained to her. Julie's pulse raced, and her breathing grew choppy. Cold sweat broke out on her forehead and her palms.

"I'm right here."

Mac had obviously heard the sounds too. He was behind her before she could break and run, his voice low, one hand wrapping around Josephine's muzzle. Even as he spoke he drew Julie back inside the den. A glance told Julie that the computer was now dark and still; Mac must have turned it off.

"Keep Josephine quiet," he breathed in her ear, closing her hand around the poodle's muzzle as he removed his own. Julie obediently held Josephine's mouth shut, but to the dog's credit she showed no inclination to bark. Still, she seemed almost as petrified as Julie felt, and Julie wondered with the part of her mind that was still capable of entertaining such speculations if the dog was somehow able to pick up on her emotions. Josephine's slight body was stiff in Julie's arms, and her eyes bugged out, as shiny and round as black marbles in a nest of white frizz. Like Julie, she was breathing fast, and her heart was thudding. Julie could feel it pounding in double-quick counterpart to her own.

"Shh." Mac's arm slid around Julie as they reached one of the two long windows overlooking the manicured back lawn and the pool. He pulled her with him behind the drapes that hung from ceiling to floor, letting the heavy taupe velvet and the whisper-soft sheer beneath wrap around them, hiding them from sight. Enveloped by the sickly-sweet aroma of the rose-scented air freshener that clung to the curtains, shrouded now in shadow, Julie discovered that she was trembling; fear washed over her in waves. Trying to keep her breathing under control, she leaned against Mac, her cheek resting against his chest, listening to the steady drum of his heart. Josephine remained stiffly alert in her arms. Julie prayed that the dog would remain silent and they would not be discovered. She didn't think she could live through another terrifying encounter, not even with Mac and Josephine the would-be guard dog for protection. Confronted, she would die of a heart attack on the spot.

Mac held her close, an arm hard around her waist. The sheer size of him was reassuring. She tended to forget what a big man he was until she was in his arms. A sideways glance told her that he had produced a gun from somewhere on his person, which he now held in his hand. It was the black, businesslike weapon she had seen before, when he had appeared like a guardian angel in her kitchen, when the monster had been hard on her heels and she'd been running for her life.

The world spun as she remembered, and for a hideous, horrible moment Julie feared she might faint. Mac's arm tightened as if he sensed her sudden weakness. She closed her eyes and rested heavily against him and counted to ten and forced the dizziness away by sheer force of will. Then Josephine whimpered, the slightest sound, and tried to pull away from Julie's hand. Julie realized that she was holding the dog's muzzle too tight even as the murmur of approaching voices made her shudder. Forcing herself to remain in the present, to remain focused, she loosened her grip on Josephine and apologetically cuddled her closer, drawn back from the precipice just in time. She could not, would not, let fear overwhelm her. If she succumbed to the mindless terror that hovered near, she might very well make some sound or do something that would reveal their presence, thereby endangering Mac and Josephine as well as herself.

But once she was in control enough to really listen, she realized that this was not the monster returned. At least one of the voices was all too familiar. This was—Sid. Sid and a woman.

Julie's spine stiffened. Her head rose like that of a doe's scenting danger.

"It's Sid," she whispered.

"Don't move, and don't make a sound." Mac's voice was scarcely louder than a breath. His arm around her hardened into an unbreakable band as though he feared she might pull away from him, might dart out and confront her husband there and then. Mac shifted position without loosening his hold on her, maneuvering so that her back was against the wall and he was in front of her, as if to both shield her and keep her in place. Julie once again got a good look at the gun in his hand. He had not lowered it, or relaxed in any way. His attention seemed to be divided equally between her and the newcomers who were now talking unconcernedly in the hall just a few yards away.

Julie realized that Mac considered *Sid's* presence a threat.

Before she could get all the implications of that sorted out in her head, her husband's voice came to her clearly.

". . . plenty of time," he said in a jocular tone.

"I guess I can tell her I had to run an errand, but I absolutely, positively have to be back by three." The woman's voice was young, giggly—and almost as familiar as Sid's. Julie froze, poleaxed.

"If you're in a hurry, we could always do it right here on the steps."

"Oh, Sid." A high-pitched giggle. Rapturous silence. Then, from a little bit farther away, as though they were climbing the stairs: "What time does your plane leave?"

"Four. God, you've got such a nice, tight little butt. . . ."

Even as Julie registered that bit of insult that had just been added to injury, the voices faded into indistinctness. Or, at least, Julie could no longer hear them distinctly, which worked just as well. There was another, muffled giggle, followed by distant footsteps and the sound of a door closing. She realized, with the kind of distant clarity that was a hallmark of certain dire situations, that Sid and another woman were in her bedroom. She felt as if, like Lot's wife, she'd witnessed something she wasn't supposed to witness and had been turned into a pillar of salt where she stood as a result.

She would never breathe, never move, never feel anything again.

"Come on, we're getting out of here."

Mac's voice was a growl in her ear. Pillar of salt or not, he was moving her, thrusting his gun down the back of his jeans and taking Josephine from her and wrapping his hand around her wrist and literally dragging her from their hiding place.

With no will to resist, Julie allowed herself to be dragged: through the hall, the dining room, the kitchen, the garage, while visions of what she was leaving behind swirled through her head. Sid's Mercedes was parked in the garage. The big, black Mercedes that he drove so proudly as a symbol of his success.

"Wait," she said hoarsely, and freed her wrist from Mac's hold with a sudden yank. Before he could stop her, she was back inside the house, in the cool hush of her own kitchen, quick and quiet as a cat as she snatched what she needed from the pantry cabinet. Mac was already coming across the kitchen after her as she brushed by him again on her way back down into the garage, illusive as a drop of mercury as he reached for her, silent and focused and totally intent on her task.

With a flip of her hand and two quick turns of her wrist, she had the Mercedes' gas cap off. Then she upended the five-pound bag of sugar she carried, and, carefully using one corner as a funnel, poured the contents down the tank.

"What the hell . . . ?" Encumbered by Josephine, Mac wasn't fast enough to stop her. He came to a halt a pace away, looking at her like she'd suddenly sprouted horns and a tail.

"Sid loves this car," Julie said with savage satisfaction, screwing the lid back on and closing the little door. Only a small amount of sugar had spilled on the floor. She kicked it under the car with her toe so that no telltale sign remained.

"Remind me never to tick you off." A quick smile just touched his mouth as Mac grabbed her wrist again and pulled her out of the garage. Julie crumpled the sugar bag into a tight little ball as she was hauled bodily down the driveway.

"Get in," Mac ordered when they reached the Blazer, jerking open the door. He took the sugar-bag ball from her and tossed it into the backseat. A quick glance back at her house told Julie that the curtains had been drawn across the master bedroom's windows. A stab of some fierce emotion—fury, she thought, more than pain—made her grit her teeth.

"That was Amber," she said through her teeth, looking at Mac. "The no-good dirty rotten bastard is doing Amber in my bedroom. *On my bed.*"

The thought made her so mad she wanted to spit.

"Get in," Mac said again, practically pushing her inside. This time she complied—she really had no choice—and he dumped Josephine in on top of her and closed her door. Seconds later he slid behind the wheel, tossing the white lawn-service sign into the backseat where the sugar bag and Josephine's rejected collar and leash and no telling what else already took up space.

Josephine stood on her lap, wagging her tail and staring up into Julie's face, her expression worried, as if she somehow sensed that a crisis was occurring around her. Mac leaned across, opened the glove compartment, extracted a doggy brownie from it, and tossed it into the backseat.

"Go get it," he said.

Josephine, way ahead of him, had looked around at the first stretch of his hand toward the glove compartment and was already springing like a mini-kangaroo over the seat as he spoke.

"So who's Amber?" With another quick, frowning glance at Julie, Mac got the car under way. Julie was barely aware of the changing scenery that meant they were moving. She felt numb, the kind of numb that signified deep psychic shock.

And why not? The life she had known for the last eight years had just been blasted into oblivion.

"She works for me. She and Meredith. At Carolina Belle. I don't believe this." Julie began to laugh, the sound high-pitched and unnatural to her own ears. "No wonder Sid needed Viagra—to keep up with her! She's only twenty—the same age I was when Sid met me. She's a brunette, like me. And last year she won Miss Angel of Beauty. He's replacing me with me."

"Men do that a lot." Mac's voice was even. The glance he sent her way was stark with concern. "There's a certain type they like, and they go back to it again and again."

"Oh, so now I'm a type." Julie bared her

teeth at him in a feral travesty of a smile. "Thanks a lot."

"Hey, it could be worse. At least you're a beautiful, sexy type."

This attempt to make her feel better, if that was what it was, failed miserably. Her fists clenched. "I hate him so much I want to kill him. I want to do him harm."

A flicker of a smile lightened his expression. "That sugar in the gas tank thing was a pretty good start. You know, that car cost about eighty grand."

"Yeah." There was a wealth of pleasure in Julie's voice. Then it faded. "Of course, insurance will cover it. He'll just get another one."

"Look, I know you're hurting, I know you're upset, but you need to focus on the big picture here. You got him right where you want him. He just handed you his head on a plate." Mac fished his cell phone out of the console and punched a button. "Hang on a minute. I want to make sure Sid's walk on the wild side gets recorded for posterity."

Before Julie could reply to that, someone on the other end of the phone answered.

The voice was distant and faintly muffled, but she could hear every word.

"Mac, man, where you at? Rawanda's been looking for you—seems Ed Barundi came stomping in, all hot because his girl-friend found out about the background check we ran on her and dumped him—and she said you're not answering your cell."

"Yeah, well, never mind that now." Mac frowned, and hung a left that had them heading back toward downtown. "You're working on the Laura Simmons thing, right?" There was an affirmative sound on the other end. "That puts you about five minutes from here. I need you to come on into Summerville as quick as you can and get as much audio and visual as possible on a couple shacked up in the upstairs front bedroom at 451 Magnolia in the Sutherland Estates subdivision. You got that?" He repeated the address.

"Who you got in there?" The voice sounded interested.

"Just do what I tell you," Mac growled. Then, before the sputter at the other end could resolve itself into words, he added: "Catch you later."

Then he disconnected.

Julie frowned at him. "Who was that?"

The phone rang shrilly before he could reply. He glanced at it, grimaced, apparently at the number that was displayed on the caller I.D. readout, hit the power off button, and dropped the phone back down into the console. "My partner. That was him calling back, too. Sometimes he wants more information than is good for him. Don't worry about it. We need proof that Sid's shacked up with your employee in the marital home so that it doesn't deteriorate into just a he-said, she-said kind of situation. Even if it's just the two of them leaving the house together. Whoever said a picture is worth a thousand words knew what he was talking about, at least in court."

"I'm going to have to fire Amber," Julie said numbly, losing focus as some of the ramifications of what she had just seen started to occur to her. "How does this sound? She walks in from her long lunch and I meet her at the door and say, *You're fired for screwing my husband.* She's worked for me for over a year. I liked her."

"Probably you shouldn't go back to work

right now. Give the worst of the shock time to wear off."

"Take two aspirin, and fire her in the morning?" Julie smiled without humor, then frowned, thinking back. As far as she'd known, Sid had only ever met Amber casually, on the very few occasions when he had stopped by the shop. If there had been signs of what was going on, she had missed them. "She's probably been sleeping with Sid for most of the time she's been working for me. I had no idea. I can't believe I had no idea."

"That's how it usually works." There was a certain rough sympathy in his voice.

"How it usually works *stinks.*"

"Yeah."

Julie was outraged; she was sick at her stomach; she was frightened and sad and angry and a thousand other emotions all at the same time. Then yet another unwanted ramification popped into her head.

"I'm going to have to tell my mother I'm getting a divorce." It was a groan.

Mac smiled faintly. "You say that like it's the worst thing in the world. What, do you have one of those mothers from hell?"

Julie tipped her head back against the

seat, closed her eyes and shook her head. "My mother is wonderful. She's super, fantastic, one of a kind. I love her. But—my being married to Sid means a lot to her. Sort of like I won the ultimate prize. When she finds out I'm getting a divorce, she's going to just die. She'll probably try to get us into counseling or something. And she'll definitely drag my sister into it. Then Kenny—my sister's husband; he works for Sid—will get dragged into it, too, and when I still insist on getting a divorce everybody will have to choose sides and Kenny'll lose his job and the girls—my nieces—will be destitute and . . ."

"Whoa," Mac said. "It won't be as bad as all that."

Julie straightened in the seat, clenched her fists and looked at him. "Yes, it will. It will be just that bad." A lump rose in her throat and she swallowed painfully. "How could Sid *do* this? When we got married, I thought we would be married forever. I was so *happy.*"

Her voice broke.

Mac's lips compressed. The glance he shot her was unreadable. "You'll be happy again. Think of this as a pothole in the road of life. You'll come out on the other side as good as new."

Julie made a disbelieving sound. "How do you know? Were you ever married?" A hideous thought occurred to her, and the lump was forgotten as her eyes widened. Another blow was more than she could bear. "You're not married now, are you?"

Mac shook his head, and Julie found that she could breathe again.

"Not now. For about nine months five years or so ago."

"You're divorced?"

Mac nodded.

"What happened?" Her voice was hushed, as if she was asking for the details of some dreadful accident.

Mac shrugged. "When I got fired from being a cop, my wife decided that she couldn't deal with a husband who was not only an embarrassment but couldn't pay the bills. She left me. Best thing that could have happened to me. Of course, I didn't think so at the time."

His insouciant attitude hid a world of remembered pain, Julie was sure. She reached out and laid a consoling hand on his jeans-clad thigh.

"She must have been insane."

Mac gave her another of those inscrutable looks, and covered her hand with his. His hand was far bigger than hers, long-fingered, broad through the palm, bronzed, utterly masculine. And warm. Very, very warm. Just like the muscled thigh beneath the jeans. Lately, it seemed, she had craved warm.

"Funny, I was just thinking the same thing about Sid."

It took a couple of seconds for that to sink in. When it did, Julie felt her heart skip a beat. She drew in a deep, cleansing breath.

There were two ways to look at what had just happened, she thought. One: Sid had betrayed her. Or, two: Sid had set her free.

It was Julie time, she told herself as she had once before. Only now, there was nothing and no one, not even her own conscience, to stand in the way of her going after what she wanted.

She looked at Mac.

"What are your plans for the afternoon? Do you have any, or are you free?" Her tone was politeness itself.

But something in her voice or expression

must have been off kilter, because he looked at her carefully.

"I'm as free as I want to be. Why?"

Julie smiled.

"Because I want you to take me somewhere where we can be alone and take off all my clothes and fuck me until I scream."

19

"WHAT?" MAC COULDN'T BELIEVE HIS EARS. He had a sudden mental vision of a small gray mouse with a head full of careful plans looking to the left, looking to the right, stepping cautiously into the road—and being flattened from behind by an eighteen-wheeler. His bodily response was so sudden and enthusiastic that it was painful. His mental response was less clear-cut. "Darlin', you want to be careful what you say. Somebody just might take you up on that kind of offer one of these days."

"I want you to take me up on it right now. I want you to take me somewhere we can be alone and take off my clothes and . . ."

"I heard you the first time," Mac interrupted hastily, not sure he could live through the exquisite agony of hearing it again.

Julie smiled, unfastened her seat belt, curled both long, slim, tanned and utterly bare legs beneath her on the black leather seat—did the woman never wear stockings? he wondered testily—and leaned forward to put a hand on his shoulder and her tongue in his ear.

"Jesus," Mac said, and drove off the road. Gravel from the shoulder flew every which way before he got the car straightened out and all four wheels once again on the pavement. By then Julie was back in her seat, her seat belt refastened, smiling at him like a cat with its eye on a nice, plump canary.

He had a feeling that he was earmarked for the role of canary.

"Don't you want to?" Julie asked, giving him a look that would have melted a glacier.

His instant, instinctive answer was, more than he had ever wanted anything in his life. He would gladly have surrendered one or more body parts for the privilege. But there were other important considerations to keep in mind, not the least of which was that his original objective here was not nailing Sid's wife, but nailing Sid. Sid was the key to finding Daniel. He was more sure of that with every passing day. He'd just had a major break: he'd managed to access All-American Builders' files from Sid's home computer.

Hard to believe Sid couldn't come up with a better password for his business files than Vader, as in Darth Vader of *Star Wars* fame. Sid used to use that name on a vanity plate on the front of his black Porsche when he was a teenager. The car, license plate and all, had made a big impression on the little kid Mac had been then. The moniker was still as appropriate as ever. In fact, more so. It fit Sid to a T, just as it always had. Like Vader, Sid was corrupt almost all the way through.

Of course, most people probably didn't know that once upon a time—Mac had no idea if he still was—Sid had been a big *Star Wars* fan. Daniel had been, too. Mac, as little brother, had soaked it all up.

And it had just paid off.

Thanks to the finger-sized memory chip

he carried on his key chain for just such emergencies, the contents of those files were dangling from the Blazer's ignition at that very moment. As soon as he'd accessed the information, he'd pulled the business end of the memory key from his ring, plugged it into an open USB port, and downloaded. The whole operation had taken perhaps a minute. When he got home, he would transfer what he'd captured to his own computer and examine it at his leisure. If what he hoped was on there somewhere actually turned up, all he would have to do was make a few calls to set in motion the ultimate payback.

Of course, sleeping with Sid's wife would be a pretty good advance payment on that payback. The trouble was, he didn't want to sleep with Sid's wife. He wanted to sleep with Julie. Beautiful, feisty, sexy Julie. Julie the temptress. Julie the enchantress. Julie the siren of his dreams.

Not Julie Carlson. Just Julie.

And that was a complication. A huge complication that he would never in a million years have foreseen.

For almost half his life, his goal had been to find out what had happened to his brother. He was as certain as it was possible to be without actually knowing it for a fact that Daniel was dead, and was almost certain that, whatever had happened, Sid was involved. If so, he meant to see that Sid got everything that was coming to him. The difference now was that he was equally determined to keep Julie safe while he did it. She was an innocent caught up in a dirty little war she didn't even know existed. She deserved better than to be a pawn in Sid's game.

Hell, she deserved better than to be a pawn in his game, too.

Looking at her, all big eyes and lush lips and sexy curves that hid an inner sweetness that was almost more attractive to him than her very attractive outer package, Mac could almost find it in himself to forget the past; he could almost walk away, taking Julie with him as payment, and call it even.

Almost.

He wanted her so much that under any other circumstances in the world he would have gladly jogged barefoot over hot coals to get to her. And here she was, his for the taking, begging him to carry her off to bed.

But no matter how much he wanted to, he discovered to his own disgust that he couldn't just turn his back on the past. Daniel's little brother was still bound by unbreakable ties of love and loyalty, even after all these years.

There was Julie to consider, too. To take her when she trusted him, when she thought he was no more than some stray PI who had stumbled into her life by accident then stayed to help her just because she needed help, would be wrong. In its own way, it would be a betrayal almost as bad as any of Sid's.

If there truly was such a thing as cosmic retribution, this time it seemed to be directed right at him. If he'd been in a laughing mood it would have been almost funny: after all, the cosmic joke was now on him. But he found that under the circumstances he couldn't summon even so much as an ironic smile.

He wanted Julie too much. And, in good conscience, he wasn't going to be able to take what he wanted.

"Hell-o-o."

Julie's tone brought Mac back to the present as suddenly as if she'd snapped his arm with a rubber band. He realized that he'd been lost for far too long in the labyrinthine corridors of his own private hell.

"Remember me?" She waggled her fingers at him in a smart-alecky little wave as he blinked at her. With her legs still tucked up under her and her truly inspiring body turned sideways to face him and her black hair flowing loose over her shoulders and her big brown eyes fixed on his face, she looked like the embodiment of every sexy dream he'd ever had. "I just asked you to sleep with me."

God give him strength. He was going to need it.

"I heard you," he said with commendable coolness. "You might want to slow down and think about what you're saying for a minute. What you're suggesting here is basically a revenge fuck. And believe me, darlin', if you go through with it you'll hate yourself in the morning."

"No, I won't," she said, those eyes going all heavy-lidded and sultry on him. If Mac hadn't been driving, he would have closed his own eyes to block out the sight. "I've got my life back, and from now on I'm going to do exactly what I want. And right now what I want to do is you."

Jesus H. Christ. If she made him any hotter he'd self-immolate right where he sat.

"You're a head case, you know that?" He shot her a grim look. If he slept with her, it would be even more of a revenge fuck than she knew, although it was growing harder with each passing second to keep that firmly fixed in his mind. "And you're turning me into one, too."

Julie stared at him for a moment without saying anything.

"You don't want to? Fine."

She uncoiled her legs, shifted position so that she was facing forward, crossed her arms over her chest and flopped her head back against the seat. Then she closed her eyes. Silence ensued. Finally able to focus on what he was doing, Mac took a deep breath, glanced around and realized that he had turned onto the expressway and gotten almost halfway back to Charleston with no awareness whatsoever of what he was doing. He was heading toward his house, he realized, and at the same time realized why.

Take me somewhere where we can be alone. . . .

Such was the power of suggestion—especially when he wanted what she was suggesting so much that he was going nuts trying not to think about it.

"Feel like going for a walk?" he asked, searching for an alternative—public—destination fast. "I think we need to walk. And talk. Yeah, some talking is definitely what we need to do here."

She opened her eyes and shot him a look. Forget sultry. Now she looked mad.

"I don't want to walk. Or talk. If you want to play psychiatrist, fine. Just not with me. Forget I said anything, okay? Just take me back to the shop."

Great. Now she sounded—and looked—downright militant. She'd done nothing but surprise him since she'd slammed into his car in the Pink Pussycat's parking lot. There was plenty of piss and vinegar mixed in with that innate sweetness, enough to keep any man hopping. He thought about the sugar down the gas tank, and succumbed to an involuntary inner smile even as he had the unsettling feeling that in her current state of upset she might be capable of any degree of mayhem. The best thing to do was give her time to cool off. No matter what she said, he was not letting her out of his sight. Not until he was sure she was not going to go off the deep end in some hideously self-destructive way.

Forget the gas tank. Uneasy visions of her finding somebody else to join her in her revenge fuck danced through his head.

"Did you hear me? I want to go back to the shop."

He'd just passed one of those clover-shaped exits where he could have done an easy one-eighty and headed back toward Summerville, and she had obviously noticed. Mac made a face at the windshield and kept on trucking down the expressway toward Charleston.

A more specific destination would no doubt occur to him when he got there. Maybe the beach. . . .

"Are you *ignoring* me?"

Now she was mad at *him.* Mac did a mental—at least he hoped it was mental, because if she saw such a thing he knew from experience that he was liable to get bopped upside the head—eye roll. God save him from women when they were being irrational.

God save him from women, period.

He tried a placating tone. "Julie . . ."

"Don't you *Julie* me. You take me back to my shop. Right now." She crossed her arms over her chest, and punctuated her words with a killing glare.

He strove for patience, and even tried to inject a note of humor into the situation. "You wouldn't want me to make a U-turn in the middle of the expressway, would you?"

"If that's what it takes."

Irrational didn't begin to cover it. Mac's patience was starting to fray around the edges.

"You got a death wish, that's your problem. Fortunately for us both, I don't."

"I want you to turn this car around right now."

Mac discovered that his teeth were clenched. He drew in air through them as he tried once again to think the situation through. The problem was, it was difficult to think clearly when his dick was roughly the size and shape of the Washington Monument.

Especially when his brain seemed to be in cahoots with his dick.

"Too bad," he said, perfectly pleasantly.

She stiffened like someone had just shoved a poker up her sweet little ass, and gave him the kind of glare that would have reduced a lesser man to blubbering idiocy on the spot.

"You know what?" She smiled at him. It didn't take more than the briefest of sideways glances to recognize it for the crocodile smile it was. "You don't get to make the decisions here. I do. Me, employer. You, employee."

Mac's patience snapped.

"No, it's more like, me, sane. You, temporarily nuts. Until that changes, you're not getting out of my sight. So live with it."

The exit he always took to get home was next, and Mac found himself pulling over into the appropriate lane automatically. Why not? he thought, and took it. There were many public places he could drive to from there. If not the beach, which was sure to be thick with tourists about now, then the Battery. . . .

"Don't you take that line with me, you—you *man*." Julie's fists were clenched and her eyes snapped. "Is that why you think you can tell me what to do? Because you're a man? Well, I've got news for you: So what? All that means is that your brains are zipped up inside your pants ninety percent of the time. Men make me sick. I *hate* men. All men. You included."

Mac had to admit, in all honesty and in light of his own situation, that there was at least a grain of truth in what she said. But in the interests of retaining what was left of his cool and keeping a lid on the situation, he didn't reply. Instead, he watched from the corner of his eye as Josephine, obviously having finished her dog biscuit, hopped up on the console from the backseat. Long strips of what looked like noodles hung from her mouth. White plastic noodles . . .

Mac's jaw dropped.

"She ate my sign!"

"Red light!" Julie yelled.

Glancing around, Mac saw that she was right and stood on the brake. The Blazer stopped with a lurch and a squeal of tires. Mac took a deep breath, looking at the rush of traffic charging past. During the day, this was one of the busiest intersections in Charleston—he knew, because his house and the office of McQuarry and Hinkle were approximately three blocks to the north and he had to fight through this mess every day—and, if it hadn't been for Julie, he would have plunged right into the middle of it.

The consequences wouldn't have been good.

Damn dog, he thought, giving Josephine an evil look. If he'd been into crediting animals with humanlike emotions, he would have sworn she smiled at him, plastic noodles and all.

Then his attention was abruptly, forcibly refocused. There, at the corner of a four-way intersection refereed by a posse of traffic lights, with cars lined up impatiently on two sides and rushing bumper to bumper across the middle in an impenetrable line, Julie simply opened the door and got out.

For a moment Mac couldn't believe it. One second she was making outraged noises in the seat beside him, and the next she was out the door, slamming it behind her so hard the car shook, then stalking with her back ramrod straight and her head held high between two idling cars as she headed toward the sidewalk.

"May God damn all female creatures to hell for all eternity," Mac said bitterly to Josephine, who didn't seem impressed. Then he shoved the car into park and got out.

Feeling like the biggest fool alive, furious enough to twist nails into pretzels with his bare hands if he'd been handed any, Mac went after her.

When he caught up to her, after making an end run around throngs of tourists and shoppers and what seemed to be a whole bus full of kids on a field trip, most of whom were armed with drippy ice-cream bars, she was still marching along at a pretty good clip.

"Just hold it right there," he said through his teeth, grabbing her arm.

She stopped dead, and whirled to face him.

Her whole body was quivering with temper. Her head was high. Her eyes were enormous and shooting sparks.

And tears were tracing bright paths down her cheeks.

"Fuck," Mac said, and meant it.

"Fuck *you,*" she snapped, trying without success to pull her arm from his grasp. She then ruined the whole touch-me-and-die thing she had going on by sniffling. He stared down at her, feeling as if he had just taken a punch to the stomach. She looked furious and pathetic and so gorgeous that she stole his breath, all at the same time. When he didn't say anything more, her eyes flashed dangerously, and she opened her mouth to yell at him—he could tell that was what she had in mind, her eyes telegraphed her intention and she was still bristling with rage—so he did the only thing any sane man faced with such circumstances could do.

He pulled her into his arms and kissed her.

And even as he did it he realized that he had just done a swan dive out of the frying pan straight into the sizzling heart of the fire.

20

THE SOUND OF BLARING HORNS penetrated Julie's consciousness slowly. Before she had quite registered exactly what she was hearing, Mac lifted his head and seemed much struck by the cacophonous sounds.

"Fuck," he said again, glancing around, then focused on her. Those beautiful blue eyes narrowed with some emotion she couldn't quite put a name to as they ran over her face. His mouth compressed into a thin hard line. She was in his arms, her body plastered to his, her hands locked behind his neck, her face tilted toward his, blinking up at him with some bemusement. The cause of her tears—indeed, the tears themselves—was forgotten for the moment. The sun reflected blindingly off the shopwindows and the roofs of cars cruising past, the smell of exhaust hung heavy in the muggy air, and Mac felt hard and strong and absolutely right against her.

Julie realized that once again she was just exactly where she wanted to be. Except, of course, for the blaring horns.

Mac had to raise his voice to be heard over them. "Look, I apologize, okay? Anything I said to upset you, I take it back." But, she thought, frowning, he didn't sound too happy about it. "Now, could we please get back in the car before the police show up?"

Comprehension caused Julie's eyes to widen. The honking, the shouts—Mac had abandoned the Blazer in the middle of the street. Before she had time to say anything, or even to fully surface from that soul-shaking kiss, he stepped back from the embrace, locked a hand around her wrist and strode back toward the car with her in tow, apparently taking her assent for granted.

Julie sniffed and wiped what was left of the moisture from her cheeks as she practically ran in her high-heeled sandals in his wake, not sure how she felt about being treated so cavalierly. The only thing she was sure of was, she wasn't ready to walk away from Mac again just yet.

This was getting interesting.

"Lady, do you need any help?" A paunchy man in a business suit turned to watch as she was hustled past. Julie realized that she and Mac were the cynosure of all eyes. Even preteens with their faces full of ice cream were staring with interest.

"I'm fine, thanks," she called back with a wave. Mac threw her an assessing glance over his shoulder as he pulled her after him into the street. The deafening honking had died down some. Julie realized that traffic on their side of the light was stopped again, and that at least one and possibly more traffic cycles had passed since she had gotten out of the Blazer. Cars were out of alignment in both lanes as those vehicles behind the Blazer that had tried to maneuver around it had been frozen in awkward place by the changing of the light.

Everybody inside every car that Julie

could see looked mad as hornets. She waved at them feebly. More horns blared.

For his part, Mac ignored them all, heading straight toward the marooned Blazer. Just as he reached it, a woman popped up on the driver's side. Obviously a tourist, in a neon-green floral blouse and a big straw hat, she waggled a finger at Mac across the hood.

"Don't you know better than to leave a dog in a car?" she said in a scolding tone. "Especially on a hot day like this?"

Mac groaned, jerked open Julie's door, thrust her inside, and said something like *give me a break* to the woman as he shut the door again. Julie, tenderly wiping the remnants of Mac's sign from Josephine's mouth as the poodle settled down in her lap, missed the rest of the conversation, but Mac looked thoroughly teed off as he slid behind the wheel.

The woman, mouth still working, bent down to look in Mac's window. He ignored her, except to shoot her a scowl as she tapped imperatively on it. The light changed. The Blazer moved into the intersection, where they took a left. As quick as that they were anonymous again, for which Julie was thankful.

"So, you want to tell me why you were crying?"

Julie's chin lifted defiantly. That she had succumbed to tears embarrassed her—but she hadn't expected him to see them, and, hey, she was having a really bad day.

"It's my divorce. I can cry if I want to."

"Good point."

"If we're playing twenty questions, why did you kiss me?"

"Because I'm as nuts as you are?"

Julie bristled anew. "I am not nuts."

Mac opened his mouth as if to reply, seemed to think better of what he'd been going to say, and shot her an exasperated look.

"Do me a favor: Just sit there and don't say or do anything until we get out of the car, okay?"

"Fine." Julie settled back in the seat, not too unhappily, content to wait on events. That searing kiss had said volumes, even if he was inexplicably grumpy now.

The Blazer turned down a residential street, then another. The houses in this neighborhood were nothing like her own,

Julie thought. These houses were older, small, with neat green postage-stamp yards punctuated by the occasional palmetto. Julie realized that this particular street was familiar just as Mac pulled to the curb and stopped.

She glanced around and began to smile. The last time she'd been here it had been the middle of the night, but she didn't think she was mistaken: Mac had brought her to his house.

Life was looking up.

Josephine apparently realized where she was, too, because she stood up in Julie's lap and yapped excitedly. Mac eyed the two of them with disfavor as he pulled the key from the ignition. When he opened his door, Josephine scrambled across his lap and hopped out.

"She doesn't have a collar on," Julie said, alarmed, grabbing for the dog and missing.

"Josephine has her faults, God knows she does, but she's not totally stupid. *She* knows enough not to go running off on her own."

There was so much not-so-hidden meaning in his tone that Julie stiffened. But he slid out of the car before she could reply. She opened her door and got out too, forestalling him in the act of coming around to fetch her.

"Was that some sort of dig at me?" Her tone was almost too polite as she walked around the hood of the Blazer toward him. He stopped where he was, on the curb, waiting, arms crossed over his chest, Oakleys once again in place. She couldn't see his eyes, but his stance and general attitude made it clear enough: he might have succumbed enough to bring her to his house, but he wasn't happy about it.

"You realize you just about caused a riot back there?" His usually drawling voice was clipped.

Julie stopped walking and glared at him, her fists on her hips. "Me? You're the one who abandoned the car in the middle of the street."

"Because you were childish enough to get out and take off. What did you think I was going to do, just drive away and let you go stomping off to God knows where all by yourself?"

"Believe it or not, I think I just about have sense enough to call a cab to take me where I want to go, which at the time was back to my shop."

"I *don't* believe it." Mac muttered this half under his breath, but Julie heard. She was just opening her mouth to verbally flatten him when a woman's voice called out.

"Mac! Mac! Have you seen Gus?"

Mac swung around in the direction of the voice. Shading her eyes, Julie discovered a wizened little woman in a faded floral housedress waving at them from a concrete stoop two houses down.

"No, I haven't, Miz Leiferman," Mac called back politely.

"Can you believe that man? I send him to take out the trash and he disappears. What do you bet he snuck around the block to have a smoke?"

"I wouldn't be a bit surprised." Mac cast a quick glance at Julie. Lips compressing, he caught her hand and started walking toward the house, pulling her behind him. "You take care, Miz Leiferman."

Mrs. Leiferman waved in answer, and turned to look searchingly up and down the street.

"She's a friend of my grandmother's, and the biggest gossip in Charleston," Mac said under his breath as he unlocked his door. "She probably came outside just to get a look at you. Next time I go see Grandma, I guarantee you I'll get the third degree."

He whistled for Josephine, who true to his prediction came trotting up, then herded Julie and Josephine inside. Mrs. Leiferman was still on her porch, Julie saw, and she was once again looking their way.

"The neighbors spy on you for your grandmother?" The notion was so irresistibly charming that Julie gave up on being annoyed at him and smiled.

"She used to live in this house, and they used to be *her* neighbors. I bought it from her five years ago when she decided to move in with her sister and I got divorced. I haven't done much to it, except get rid of some bric-brac. My grandfather's old '55 Chevy is still parked in the garage. Anyway, Aunt Rose sold her house just a few weeks ago—that's when I got custody of Josephine—and she and Grandma moved into a retirement home together, but she still keeps in touch with the neighbors."

"I think that's sweet."

The house was just as she remembered

it, Julie thought as she walked inside: cool and dark and pleasantly shabby. The curtains were drawn to keep out the worst of the afternoon sun. The couch and chair and TV were just where they had been before. The big difference was that newspapers and magazines no longer cluttered the floor by the chair. Looking closer, Julie discovered a pile of reading material stacked high on top of the TV, and her smile widened. Pet training seemed to be working: Josephine had obviously taught Mac to keep things off the floor.

"Yeah, well, you don't have to live with it." Sounding more disgruntled than ever, Mac closed the door behind them, shutting out Mrs. Leiferman and the street, then took off his sunglasses, placing them on a nearby end table. His gun, extracted from somewhere behind his back, followed the sunglasses. Meanwhile, Josephine looked up at Julie, wagged her tail as if in a doggy version of *excuse me,* and disappeared in the direction of the kitchen.

"By the way, you can forget about trying to pick a fight with me," Julie said to Mac over her shoulder. "It's not going to work."

"Darlin', I don't know what you're talking about."

Mac came up behind her. Julie was just opening her mouth to say something—she could never afterwards remember exactly what—when his arms slid around her waist from behind and his hands covered her breasts.

Sheer surprise caused her to stiffen and glance down even as the sight and feel of his hands flattening over her breasts sent fiery pinwheels of desire tumbling through her veins.

"Okay," he said, his breath stirring her hair, his body big and hard and swoon-making as it pressed against hers. "You got what you wanted. We're all alone. If you're still bound and determined on that revenge fuck, I'm your man."

Something about his tone—to say nothing of his approach—told her that he hoped to anger or shock her into declining. And, Julie reflected as she stood motionless for a moment while his hands tightened and squeezed provocatively, if she hadn't figured him out well enough by this time to realize exactly what he was doing, he might just have succeeded.

But she had.

She turned in his arms, slid her own arms around his neck, and took a moment to assess the situation. Her bare arms looked tanned and slender and graceful draped over the gaudy, parrot-filled palm trees growing up his rayon shirt. His tee looked very white indeed against the bronze of his throat. The breadth of his shoulders and the solid feel of his chest against her already sensitized breasts dazzled her. Even though she was wearing heels, the top of her head didn't quite reach his nose, and again she was reminded of the sheer size of him. He was frowning as he looked down at her, his brows drawn closer together than usual, his mouth still a little grim.

In Mac's case, Julie decided that grim was sexy. Actually, Mac was sexy, no matter what mode he was in. If grim was all she could get, she would take grim.

"So start taking off my clothes," she said, a tiny smile curving her mouth as her gaze locked with his. "And, later, don't forget the part about making me scream."

His eyes flared. Then his arms, which had been curved loosely around her, shifted so that his hands were gripping her hipbones. She got the sense that he was getting ready to put some space between them, and tightened her arms around his neck.

"Damn it, Julie," he began, his frown deepening so that his brows all but met over his nose.

"You're cute when you're grumpy," she said.

"Cute?" He sounded revolted, and she had to grin. Then she did her best to forestall further conversation by the simple act of going up on tiptoe and pressing her mouth to his. Kissing him like this just because she wanted to was such a luxury, she thought as her lips made the first butterfly contact with his. It signified that their relationship had taken a whole new turn. Above and beyond the blazing sexual attraction that was making her toes curl, there was an easy intimacy between them, a friendship, a caring, that she suddenly treasured. Being with Mac like this marked the beginning of a whole new chapter in her life, she realized with a feeling very close to wonder as her lips molded themselves coaxingly to the warm firmness of his and her tongue slid inside to beg his to come out and play. Even under the circumstances, doing this with just anybody wouldn't have been a possibility for her; he could call it a revenge fuck if he wanted to, but the truth was that the only man she wanted to sleep with was Mac.

Just like the only man she wanted to kiss was Mac, and kiss him she did. His tongue was soft and hot but resistant at first as she touched it with her own. Her tongue prodded his, stroked it, and finally managed to draw it into her mouth. She nibbled the tip, sucked on it, and suddenly his fingers dug into her hipbones so hard they hurt and his tongue woke up and filled her mouth, taking the play into her court with a vengeance. She'd meant the kiss to be brief, no more than the merest tease, but with his response a wildfire ignited between them and the kiss took on a life of its own.

When she finally pulled her lips from his because she absolutely had to breathe, she looked up at him to gauge the kiss's effect. There were unmistakable signs that it had been a rousing success: his jaw was set, a flush had risen to stain his cheekbones, and his eyes were smoldering as they met hers.

"Julie." His suddenly hoarse voice bore no relation to his usual drawl. His fingers still gripped her hipbones hard. "This is a mistake."

Not what she had expected. Julie narrowed her eyes at him.

"What are you, a reluctant virgin?" She gave him another of those tiny smiles, pressing closer against him so that her soft curves were flattened against the solid, tantalizing length of him, and threaded her fingers through the short crisp strands of hair that covered the back of his skull. She looked up at him through her lashes—being a former beauty queen had its practical uses, she actually knew how to do things like that—and fluttered them at him flirtatiously. "Don't worry, I'll be gentle."

"I'm serious here." He sounded grimmer than ever, but his voice was thick, and Julie realized that the war was won even as he fought conceding. For whatever murky reason—professional ethics? gentlemanly scruples? a truly commendable distaste for getting involved with a woman who wasn't yet divorced?—he was trying to resist what he badly wanted to do. Fortunately, from her point of view, he was failing. His gaze was hot as molten steel on her face as, belying his words, his hands abandoned the beach head of her hipbones to slide slowly around her waist. His arms tightened, pulling her so close that she could feel every hard contour of his body. Even through the layers of their clothes, the heat and brawny strength of him made her tingle.

To say nothing of the impossible-to-miss erection that prodded her abdomen just below her navel.

"I'm serious, too," she said softly, her parted lips reaching toward his again. "Make love to me, Mac."

His pupils dilated, turning his eyes almost black. He inhaled, then made a little hissing sound as he released air through his teeth. His face tightened, throwing the chiseled planes and angles into sharp relief. Then his head bent, moving so slowly that her parted lips trembled in anticipation. His warm breath feathered across her skin. Her breathing quickened. Her lids closed. Her heart gave a great, shuddering leap. She wanted him so much she felt woozy from just thinking about it, and, she realized, such intense wanting felt wonderful. It had been a long time since she had wanted anything this much—so long she couldn't remember when.

Then his lips found hers, and she quit thinking altogether as he kissed her.

Julie sighed into his mouth, tightening her arms around his neck, and kissed him back for all she was worth. He owned this kiss, controlled it, and she reveled in the hungry fierceness of it. His mouth slanted over hers, hard and hot and demanding, as his tongue claimed her mouth. One of his hands slid down her back, tracing the curve of her spine. Julie felt a tug, heard a faint but distinctive sound, and realized with the tiny part of her brain that was still capable of registering anything outside of that blistering kiss that he was lowering her zipper.

Her knees went weak.

Cool air touched the bare skin of her back in the wake of his hand, and she shivered. He must have felt the slight tremor. Even as his hand came to rest at the base of her zipper, flattening on the small of her back and pressing her closer yet to the urgent evidence of his desire, he lifted his head to look at her. His eyes were ablaze with passion, and his breathing was uneven. Her body was plastered to his, so close she could feel every long muscle and bone and sinew of his body—and every telltale thump of his heart. It was beating fast, like a runner's, and she realized that hers was racing, too. Straining against the unyielding wall of his chest, her breasts felt heavy and swollen; her nipples puckered against the suddenly too-confining fabric of her bra. A hot quickening in her loins seemed to spiral through her body, turning her blood to liquid fire as it spread.

He simply stared down at her for a moment without speaking, his eyes heavy-lidded and so hot they made her tremble as they moved over her face. She knew her skin was flushed, knew her eyes were wide and slumberous, knew her lips were parted and damp and clearly eager for more. There was no hiding how turned on she was, and anyway, she didn't want to hide it.

This was Julie time, she reminded herself. From now on, what Julie wanted, Julie was going to do her best to get. And what Julie wanted most in the whole wide world right now was—

"Mac." His name emerged scarcely louder than a breath.

"Last chance to change your mind." He sounded as if he was having to work to keep his voice steady. His hand was already sliding inside her open zipper. Her gaze fluttered over his lean jaw with its faint suggestion of bristle, touched on the sensuous curve of his mouth, admired the classic lines of his cheeks, the straight nose, the blue eyes, the blond hair.

"Not on your life." She shook her head, shivering as the pads of his fingers stroked warmly along her spine. Her knees had been weak before; now they were pure Jell-O.

Their eyes locked. His were hard and restless and nearly black with wanting her. One hand caressed her bare back possessively; the other still lay flat on the lilac linen at the base of her spine. She could feel it just above the flare of her bottom, pressing her close. Julie moved, tilting her pelvis against him instinctively, then caught her breath as his body responded with a sexy move that sent undulating waves of desire rippling down her thighs.

"Remember you said that." There was a warning note to his voice.

Then she completely lost the thread of the conversation as he dipped his head. His mouth was hot and wet as it found the sensitive skin of her shoulder, then moved lower and crawled across her collarbone, nudging aside the loosened bodice of her dress. Goose bumps sprang up in its wake, and she moved against him again. Without warning his head came up, and he reached up to grasp her wrists and pull her hands from around his neck. He kissed first one palm and then the other, his eyes gleaming at her over her hands, then let go of her wrists and reached for her. Julie held onto his waist for balance and watched his face as he slid her dress off her shoulders. His gaze had shifted to the skin he uncovered, and he looked intent as the handkerchief-fine cloth slid down her arms. Before he could bare more than her shoulders and the upper slopes of her breasts, though,

Julie stopped him by pressing one hand flat against the sliding front of her bodice.

"Wait." She shook her head at him.

He looked up then, meeting her gaze with a frown. She took a deep breath, martialed her wits and her knees, and stepped back out of his hold. He let her go without protest, although his mouth tightened as if to do so was an effort. His hands dropped to his sides, where they curled into fists as if he would prevent himself from reaching for her.

Julie smiled at him.

"Let me," she said.

At that his eyes flickered and flared and then seemed to ignite, but he didn't say anything. Taking silence for assent, she let go of the front of her dress and gave a provocative little shimmy. The fragile linen dropped with the faintest of rustling sounds to the floor. Then, still watching his face, she stepped out of the lilac puddle and nudged it aside with her foot.

For a moment she simply let him look, shaking the heavy black mane of her hair back from her face, keeping her back straight and her chin high. Her lips were parted as she breathed through them, and her hands rested lightly, sensuously on her bare thighs.

At least her husband-bait wasn't a dead loss, she reflected as his eyes seemed to scorch her. In fact, from the look on his face it had been worth every penny she had spent on it after all.

She knew how she must appear to him: slender and tanned and curved in all the right places, with a collar of creamy pearls around her throat and more pearls in her ears, her high full breasts with their puckered brown nipples swelling against the filmy, nearly translucent cups of her pale pink strapless bra and her stomach flat and smooth above tiny matching panties so sheer that the sable triangle of her sex was merely lightly veiled rather than concealed. She knew she had nice legs, long and elegant like the stems of hothouse roses, and she knew too that they should be looking extra enticing because her high-heeled sandals were designed for the sole purpose of emphasizing their loveliness.

In short, she knew she was nearly naked and looking hot. And just the idea that Mac was looking at her when she was nearly naked and looking hot made her want to jump his bones without further ado.

"Tell me something." Mac's eyes flickered up to meet hers, and his voice had a croaky quality to it that pleased her a lot. "Do you *own* any lingerie that isn't sexy as hell?"

Julie shook her head. "Do you mind?"

He gave a grunt of what might have been laughter. "It's a hard burden to bear, but I guess I can stand it."

Then his gaze dropped again. Julie's tongue came out to wet her lips because her mouth was suddenly dry. His eyes were all over her, hard and hot and hungry, sending delicious shivers of anticipation racing over her skin everywhere they touched. She watched his fists open, then clench, tighter than before, so tight his knuckles showed white, before opening again. Then he looked up, and his eyes met hers. The diamond-hard glint in his was enough to curl her toes.

"You are the most beautiful thing I have ever seen in my life, and I want you so much I am going out of my mind."

He moved even as he said it, so fast that she didn't even realize what he meant to do until he swept her off her feet and up into his arms and carried her off toward his bedroom, kissing her with a torrid eroticism that sent her senses spinning wildly out of control as he went.

21

LIKE THE REST OF THE HOUSE, the bedroom was dark, with the curtains drawn tightly over the windows, and faintly chilly from the air-conditioning. Mac carried her over to the bed, laid her down, and came down with her, his mouth moving from her mouth to her breast even as her back hit the mattress. The bed was unmade and smelled faintly of fabric softener, with what seemed to be a quilt and a single top sheet kicked to the bottom and spilling off one corner. The mattress was firm, and the sheet—she had some hazy awareness that it was dark blue—was cool and smooth against her back. But it was his mouth on her breast that riveted her attention.

Hot and wet and open, it rested against the tip of her breast, scalding her sensitive skin even through the barely-there layer of her bra. His tongue flicked over her nipple, causing it to instantly pucker into a tiny hard point that cried out for more attention. Then he did it again. Moaning, Julie dug her nails into his nape and arched her back.

"Mac . . ."

"Julie."

For the moment there seemed to be nothing more to say, for either of them. He shifted his attention to her other breast, kissing and licking her nipple until it, too, was hot and wet and throbbing. His jean-clad thigh slid between hers, pressing against the juncture of her legs, abrading the tender skin of her inner thighs and do-ing unbelievable things to the part of her that was already damp with readiness for him. The sheer pleasure generated by even that limited contact was unbelievable, and Julie tightened her thighs around his in in-stinctive response. He pressed harder into the center of her, and a mind-bending jolt of electricity shot through what was suddenly her body's focal point.

Julie gasped as a series of tiny, intense contractions followed, then went still in an effort to counteract the effect. It had been way too long since she had done this, she thought frantically as she relaxed her grip on his thigh and concentrated on drawing regular, steady breaths. He didn't even have her naked yet, and she was on the verge of coming like a house on fire.

Slow down, she told herself. She wanted to enjoy this. It had been so long—too long.

He lifted his head and flicked a glance at her. His thigh, solid and warm, shifted, rubbing against her sensuously as he moved. Julie felt her lips part, and, if the way she was feeling was any indication, her eyes glazed over. God, his leg moving against her there felt so-o good. . . .

"Let's see, what came next? Oh, yeah, you wanted me to take off all your clothes." A smile just touched one corner of his mouth; belying it, his voice was husky and his eyes were ablaze.

Julie took a deep breath, unable to do anything but curl her nails into his shoulders by way of a reply as he propped himself on an elbow and reached behind her. Deftly he unfastened her bra and pulled it off, tossing it to one side. He looked down at the breasts he'd bared while her gaze fastened on his face. His jaw was set and his eyes glittered like jewels.

He cupped her breast in his hand as if to gauge its size and shape, then ran his thumb over the nipple that was already distended and glistening wetly from his mouth.

"Oh, God, Mac." At the exquisite sensation she gritted her teeth and curled her toes and tried to remember to breathe.

"They're beautiful," he said, guttural now, meeting her gaze, then covered her breast with his hand and kissed her mouth.

Julie wrapped her arms around his neck and kissed him back as devouringly as he was kissing her, loving the musky taste of his mouth, the unmistakably masculine warmth of his hand caressing her breast, the hard pressure of his thigh pressing between hers, the weight and friction of his still-clothed body lying on top of her nearly naked one. She wanted him naked, wanted to be naked with him, more than she had ever wanted anything in her life. Her hands slid along his broad shoulders, over the slippery rayon covering his back until she reached his waist. Then she burrowed beneath the fabric to touch his skin. It was warm and faintly damp and smooth; the muscles beneath, she discovered as she slid her hands up his back, were tensile and resilient. He shuddered beneath her touch, and lifted his head.

"Take off your shirt," she said.

He met her gaze, then reached down to pull off both shirts in a single supple over-the-head move. Before the garments were even all the way off, Julie stared, entranced, at the magnificent flesh he'd bared. She had forgotten just how breathtaking his naked torso was. His shoulders were bronzed and broad and thickly muscled; his chest was wide and tapered and covered with a thick wedge of ash brown hair through which she could see his flat male nipples. His abdomen was the weight lifter's six-pack, ridged with muscle, looking impossibly hard and enticing above the waistband of his jeans. The jeans themselves rode low on his hipbones, revealing his navel and a tantalizing arrow of hair that disappeared beneath them.

Julie realized that she was looking at the human equivalent of Godiva chocolate, the thing she had always lusted after most in all the world.

Now, the thing she lusted after *second* most. Mac had just claimed a hard-won first place.

"God, you're gorgeous." She unconsciously put into words what she'd thought since she'd gotten her first look at him sans Debbie gear.

"I think that's my line," he said, and bent his head to kiss her. Even as she kissed him back she ran her hands over his chest, intoxicated by the feel of the crisp hair that covered all his muscles like a particularly erotic frosting. Her nails gently scored his nipples and he groaned and came down on top of her, stretching out at full length. He was heavy, but she barely noticed, and didn't care. Sliding her hands over his shoulders and around his neck, she absorbed the hard weight of his body pressing hers down into the mattress with a sensation bordering on delight. The feel of his hair-roughened chest, so warm and powerfully muscled, against her breasts was unbelievably erotic. She moved sensuously against him, enjoying the heat and pressure, the delicious friction, of his body on hers.

When he lifted his head again at last, breathing deeply and looking down into her eyes, she cradled his head in her hands and wordlessly guided his mouth to her nipple, arching her back as she offered herself up to him.

This time, when his mouth closed on her breast, there wasn't even a thin layer of cloth between them.

If she had died in that instant, she would have died happy, Julie thought, closing her eyes and shivering at the sheer pleasure of it. The feel of his hot mouth fastening on her nipple, suckling it, laving it with his tongue, was exquisite. She moaned and moved and pressed his head to her breasts with a complete abandonment of what few inhibitions she had left to her. Her hands were buried in his hair; her legs were wrapped around his like ribbons around a maypole. He was lying between her thighs now, and her knees came up instinctively to accommodate him. This shift in position brought his jean-clad pelvis hard against the part of her that ached and burned and wept for his possession. He rocked against her, the movement deliberate, and she cried out. No longer able to resist what she knew was coming, she began to surge upward in urgent answer to his rhythmic movements.

"Easy." His head lifted, and the mind-blowing pressure between her legs disappeared as he eased himself away from Ground Zero just that moment too soon, lifting himself deftly off her. Even as she reached for him, aghast at being abandoned at such a crucial juncture, he caught her hands and pinned them to the mattress beside her head, then knelt over her, his thighs on either side of her legs now, trapping them together.

"Mac." Julie wriggled in protest, which, given that he was now touching nothing vital, didn't do the slightest bit of good. She bit her lower lip in frustration, scowling up at him as he looked her over with obvious appreciation. What he'd just done gave a whole new meaning to the phrase *so near, and yet so far.*

"Let's take this slow."

"I don't want to take it slow."

"Yes, you do. You just don't know it."

Against logic like that, what could she say? Anyway, her heart was pounding so hard and she was breathing so fast that any kind of sustained, sensible talk—much less an argument on the merits of when to actually do the deed—was beyond her. He seemed maddeningly cool until she really looked at him. Then she realized that his eyes were heavy-lidded and burning hot and his lips were clamped into a thin line and his jaw was set as if he was having to work hard to maintain control. She watched him look at her, watched as the flush in his cheekbones spread to suffuse his whole face, and felt the worst of her frustration fade.

Then he appeased her even more by releasing her wrists to embark on a discovery mission, caressing each breast in turn, stroking over her stomach with an extra, comforting caress for the V-shaped bruise, dipping into her navel, trailing fire wherever he touched. His hands had a fine tremor to them now, she saw, and his muscled torso flexed with his every movement. Both circumstances were almost as potent an aphrodisiac as the way he was touching her.

"Pretty," he said softly, his fingers tracing the outline of her panties from hipbone to hipbone and over the filmy triangle between. Julie felt the tantalizing whisper-touch burn like a brand through the cloth to the soft nest of curls, then sucked in her breath as he hooked his fingers over the elastic and tugged her panties down her legs.

At last, she thought, and felt her body clench. He moved, kneeling beside her as he pulled her panties all the way down to her ankles. Watching dry-mouthed, feeling like her insides had suddenly been reduced to the quivery consistency of a jellyfish, Julie realized with a prickle of surprise that she was still wearing her shoes.

Mac picked up each foot and carefully eased her panties over the delicate high heels. Then he tossed the wisp of pink gauze in the same general direction as her bra.

Nails curling into the mattress from the sheer effort of maintaining some semblance of control, Julie looked down at herself, at the brown-tipped globes of her breasts still glistening from the attentions of his mouth, at the delicate curves of her waist and hips, at the satin-smooth plane of her stomach, at the sable triangle between her thighs. Her eyes slid down the long-limbed grace of her own legs, separated now to an indecent degree as he held a slender, daintily shod foot with one supremely masculine looking hand wrapped around her ankle.

The sight of herself, naked except for a high collar of pearls and strappy purple sandals with delicate high heels, spread out before Mac like a feast, was the most erotic thing she had ever seen in her life.

"Great shoes." He still held her right foot in his hand, and as he spoke he turned his head and pressed his open mouth to the delicate bone of her ankle, which was circled by a skinny purple strap. Heart pounding, Julie felt streamers of delight ripple up her leg from the place where his tongue caressed her skin; her breath caught as she watched his fingers working at the tiny buckle. "I especially like 'em when they're all you're wearing."

Even as he spoke, Mac got the buckle unfastened and slid the shoe from her foot.

He picked up the other one, and did the same thing.

Then he kissed that ankle, and suddenly his mouth was crawling up the inside of her leg.

As she realized where he was headed, Julie began to shake.

When he reached the velvety delta between her legs, she closed her eyes. He kissed her there, his mouth scalding. His tongue touched the tiny bud that quivered and ached for attention, and she cried out.

"You like that?" It was a rough whisper.

Julie nodded without opening her eyes.

"Thought you would."

Any other time, the smug masculine overtone of that might have caused her to bristle. But the pleasure she was experiencing was too exquisite to allow her to focus on anything else. She felt as if all her bones had turned to water and her insides to fire. Breathing in fast little pants now, clutching the sheet for dear life, she lay supine, her head thrown back, her body pulsing with tremors as he pressed his mouth to her needy flesh. His hands slid beneath her, closing on her firm round cheeks to lift her and hold her in place, and as his mouth worked its magic she thought she had died and gone to some place far more marvelous than heaven.

Her body burned and clutched and trembled; she bucked and squirmed under his ministrations like a worm on a hook. Her orgasm was there, right there, rising on the horizon like a blazing summer sun, blinding her with its promised brilliance, searing her with its building heat. . . .

And then he stopped what he was doing, stopped just like that, pulled his mouth back and heaved himself up and away from her and right off the bed.

"Mac!" Her eyes flew open. He was standing beside the bed, looking down at her, his eyes flaming, his hair mussed, shucking his jeans. She saw what he was doing, knew what was coming, but still felt indignant—and bereft. She lay there naked, watching him, trembling, weak with longing, so hot and hungry for him, her body so burning and empty and needy, that she couldn't even stay still. Her breasts rose and fell as she drew in quick panting breaths. Her legs and hips moved restlessly. Then his jeans dropped, and his shorts with them. She saw that he was enormous and *hung,* and she reached out for him because she just couldn't help herself.

He was already climbing back onto the bed when her hands found him. His shaft was burning hot velvet over steel and as her fingers closed around him he groaned and seemed at last to lose control. His eyes flashed at her, his jaw hardened, and every mouthwatering muscle she could see seemed to go taut as a bowstring. Then he was moving, pushing her down and coming on top of her, and she wrapped her legs around his waist and clung to his shoulders and arched up to meet him.

With one quick thrust he was inside her. He felt so unbelievably good, filling her to capacity and then some, that she cried out. Then he was taking her, hard and fast, plunging into her until Julie was so caught up in the pounding rhythm that she lost all sense of time and place in the fiery maelstrom of her response. Only dimly did she register that it was she who cried out again and again and again. When he kissed her, she tasted herself on his lips and shuddered. While she was shuddering he drove inside her with a shattering series of fierce, deep thrusts and she came, just like that, so violently that her body convulsed and she dug into his back with her nails and screamed his name, "Mac, Mac, Mac, Mac, *Mac!*"

"Julie," he groaned in answer, burying his mouth in the tender hollow between her neck and shoulder, and found his own release, grinding himself into her shaking body, then, finally, shuddering and going limp.

Afterward, she lay there, totally replete. Her eyes were closed and her body was motionless except for the random tremors that still racked it. Mac lay on top of her, sweaty, hot, his deadweight about as heavy as a truckload of wet cement. About as responsive, too. His face was buried in the curve of her neck, and his breathing was stertorous and growing louder.

She wondered if he had fallen asleep. From the feel of him, and the sound of his breathing, probably.

God, were all men alike that way?

For the first time since she had said *I do*, she had slept with a man besides Sid.

Could anybody say, adultery?

Julie opened her eyes. A wide bronzed

shoulder blocked her view of most of the room. When she shifted her gaze to the right, a fair-sized section of close-cropped blond hair, an ear, the hard curve of his jaw, part of his cheek, and a glimpse of his parted lips—if the breathing that fluttered them wasn't snoring, she didn't know what it was—came into view.

Looking the other way, she saw a single window with floor-length blue drapes closed over it, an unadorned white wall— and his hand still curved possessively around her breast.

Julie felt a stab of squirm-inducing guilt. What had she done?

Her marriage was over, she reminded herself, averting her eyes from the sight of those long bronzed fingers cupping her so intimately, in every way but the legal. She had nothing to feel guilty about. Indeed, she had done just what Oprah had said most women do on the demise of a mar- riage—fall into bed with the first presenta- ble guy who asks.

Only Mac hadn't exactly done the asking.

And he was a little bit more than present- able. All right, a lot more.

And she didn't regret it. Exactly.

How could she? The sex had been phenomenal. She'd definitely felt the earth move. She now *owned* the Big O.

But lying here with him like this, naked and sweaty and listening to him snore, felt—weird. Like she wasn't herself any longer. What she really wanted to do was get up and go home and take some time to just sort this whole thing out. But, she remembered forlornly, she had no home to go to. No home that felt like home, anyway. Not anymore.

First she'd been viciously attacked there. Then Sid had brought a woman—girl—child—*Amber*—into her house.

Julie realized that she was feeling sorry for herself, and took a deep breath. Instead of looking back with regret, she was going to look forward with anticipation. She was going to face her problems head-on, and deal with them one at a time. That's what she had always done, ever since she was a little girl. For too long now, her whole identity had been wrapped up in being Sid's wife. She was going to reclaim her life.

Phase One of her recovery was already over: she'd had down-and-dirty sex with a really hot guy.

Phase Two involved confronting Sid, firing Amber, contacting a lawyer, telling her mother, filing for divorce—in other words, blowing her life as she knew it off the map.

Okay, so the prospect was enough to give her hives. Get over it, she told herself. Phase One might have been more fun, but she was going to make it through Phase Two as well. The secret was, as she'd learned many times over, to just keeping trudging ahead one step at a time.

Her life might have been reduced to rubble, but she was going to survive. She was going to leave the shambles behind and move on.

And the first step in moving on was to get off this bed.

Some things—including the direction any future involvement with Mac might take—required perspective before any rational decision could be made, and in this particular case perspective required distance.

Stealthily, not wanting to wake him until she had come up with a mature and sophisticated response to the current situation, Julie pushed his hand off her breast. She would just wriggle out from beneath him and get dressed. . . .

He stirred, lifted his head, and looked at her. Julie felt her stomach clench as she met his eyes head on.

So much for distance.

Feeling trapped and a little panicky, Julie held his gaze. With his hair all tousled and his eyes sleepy-looking and a small smile curving his lips, he looked like a man who was content with the world. Which of course he should be. She had just given him her all.

At the thought, Julie winced.

He must have seen, because his smile vanished, to be replaced by a searching look, and then a touch of wryness around his mouth. The hand that curved around her rib cage—the one she had just pushed off her breast—tightened. Its warmth and size felt uncomfortably intimate against her skin.

Feeling more trapped than ever, Julie tensed.

"So, was it as good for you as it was for me?" There was a slightly ironic note to his voice that told her that he was aware that she was not exactly planning to wrap her arms around his neck and beg for more.

Thank God he wasn't going all kissy-face

on her, was Julie's predominant coherent thought as she registered his tone. She might be naked and he might be on top of her, but Mac was still being Mac, and she could deal with that. Kisses and cuddles she couldn't have faced. Not until she had her own feelings sorted out.

"It was good. Thank you very much. Now, would you please get off me?" Her tone was polite: the kind of tone she had used frequently in the past to thank the hostess of a dinner party for a well-prepared meal.

Apparently he didn't appreciate it. His eyes narrowed at her.

"So now we're on to the hating yourself in the morning part, are we? Jesus Christ, Julie, how predictable is that?"

22

MAC DIDN'T KNOW WHY he felt as if he'd just found the winning lottery ticket in a jumble of papers in his wallet only to discover minutes later that the damned thing had expired the previous week. He had a beautiful, naked girl in his bed. A beautiful, naked girl he'd just shown a hell of a good time. A beautiful, naked girl he'd had a hard-on for since he'd first laid eyes on her.

What was there to get bent out of shape about in that?

"I don't hate myself, it isn't morning, and I believe I asked you to get off me. Please."

If she used that ultra-polite tone on him much more, he was going to lose it, Mac thought, rolling onto his side but keeping his arm around her so that she couldn't just spring up and take off. A fleeting mental picture of her hightailing it naked down the street with him equally naked in hot pursuit had a certain appeal, but he didn't think there was much chance of that actually happening and, anyway, if it did Mrs. Leiferman would have a field day and he'd hear about it later in spades.

"You ever hear of pillow talk?" He didn't know why her clear desire to put the steamy little interlude they'd just shared behind her bugged him so: he would have bet dollars to doughnuts on her having just that reaction. Her skin was silky and supple beneath his hand, and he had to fight an urge to stroke it, which he had a feeling would not, just at present, be well received. Her entire right side was pressed up against him, soft and warm, and she smelled totally delectable. The elusive fragrance of the perfume she habitually wore, mixed with the scent of her skin and the unmistakable aroma of sex, was the most potent aphrodisiac ever to assault his nostrils. Probably the scent was what was playing games with his head. While he was inhaling it, he couldn't think straight. "Something on the order of, *Oh, Mac, that was just wonderful?*"

"What do you want, a blow-by-blow?"

It was her snippy attitude, he decided, that annoyed him so, as well as a few other things. Her hands were covering her breasts now, he noticed, as if to hide them from his view. The truly delectable leg closest to him was raised and bent at the knee and tilted inward over her body, which pretty much kept him from seeing any other salient body part, too. She seemed to be forgetting that he'd just done a whole hell of a lot more than look at just about every square millimeter of her. By default, his gaze returned to her face. Then he wished it hadn't. Her eyes were big and brown and shooting off sparks at him. Her cheeks were flushed a rosy pink. Her hair was a mass of shiny black waves spread out like a halo around her head. Mac frowned. Even with her lipstick all kissed off and her nose shiny and her expression peeved, she was so beautiful she grabbed at his heart.

Then she drew her lower lip into her

mouth and started to chew on it, and he felt himself start to get hard all over again.

Hell. What was happening to him here was not a good thing.

"Hey," he said. "Give the attitude a rest, okay? You had a good time. You came."

She quit chewing on her lower lip and glared at him.

"Let me up."

He lifted his arm obligingly, and was rewarded for good behavior by an excellent view of her shapely butt and legs as she scrambled off the bed and stood up with her back to him. Propping himself on his elbow, he rather grudgingly admired creamy shoulder blades and the delicate curve of her spine and a truly bodacious set of butt cheeks before she crouched down out of sight to retrieve the top sheet from the floor. He craned his neck instinctively, but it was no use: she was already wrapping herself in yards of dark blue cotton. As she straightened, pulling the cloth modestly around her legs and tucking one end in between her breasts, he happened to glance down at himself. What he saw sent him grabbing for the edge of the sheet—only the fitted bottom one was available, and persuading it to part company with the mattress required a vicious tug—which he dragged across his waist to hide the fact that he was now at full mast.

Once she was swathed from armpits to ankles in voluminous folds of cloth, she seemed to consider herself girded for battle. Shaking her hair back from her face, taking a deep breath, she glared at him.

"Could you get up and get dressed, please? I've got to get back to the shop. I've got an important client coming in at three."

Mac glanced at his watch and smiled at her. Admittedly, it was not a nice smile. More on the nasty side. But hey, sweetness and light was beyond him for the moment.

"I'd say you're shit out of luck, Miss America. It's four-fifteen. And I thought we agreed that you weren't going back to work today."

"Oh, no! It was Carlene Squabb." Her face was a study in consternation. Then her gaze fixed on him, and darkened stormily. "And if you want to talk about attitudes, *yours* could use some major work. I don't know what you're so grumpy about. You got what you wanted."

"*Me?*" Mac's gaze slid over her from the tip of her tousled black head to her delicate pink-painted toes, which he could just see peeking out from under the layers of sheet, and he felt his sense of disgruntlement increase right along with other sensitive meters of his state of mind. "I don't *think* so. It wasn't *me* who said"—here he assumed his Debbie falsetto—"*take me somewhere where we can be alone and take off all my clothes and fuck me until I scream.* All I did was oblige. And darlin', you did scream."

Julie's lips tightened and her eyes shot twin beams of pure fire at him. Then she seemed to make an effort to grab hold of her temper before she lost it entirely. Her fists clenched, her eyes closed—Mac imagined her mentally counting to ten—and she took a deep breath.

When she opened her eyes again the look she gave him was far cooler. Maddeningly so, Mac discovered. He'd rather by far fight with her than have her distance herself from him.

"Look, I'm not blaming you for this, okay? You're right, I wanted it, and nothing that happened here is your fault. I realize now that I'm in kind of an emotional state about ending my marriage, and having sex with you was a stage I had to go through to start really getting over it. If we could just put this whole thing behind us and forget it ever happened, that would be good."

A beat passed while that sank in. So he was a phase, was he? Mac found that he liked that less than anything that had come out of her mouth since she'd started talking—and that was saying a whole hell of a lot.

"Not a problem." Mac rolled off the other side of the bed and stood up, keeping a firm grip on the sheet as he went. No point in letting her in on the fact that he was ready, willing, and able to go on to Round Two. He watched her gather up her bra and panties and realized that he was really, truly, royally pissed off. Which was stupid, he told himself. She'd offered him every guy's wet dream on a platter—a mind-blowing sex session with a hot babe without any of the usual female icky-poo aftermath—and it was making him mad?

What the hell was the matter with him?

The obvious answer, of course, was that she was enough to try the patience of a saint, and he wasn't planning to put in for canonization any time soon.

"Do you mind if I take a shower?" She was back in polite mode, which, he supposed, was no more or less irritating than anything else she'd done since she'd gotten her rocks off. He was fifty kinds of a fool to let her attitude get under his skin.

But he couldn't seem to help it.

"Help yourself." He gestured toward the bathroom, as polite as she was now, and awarded himself mental kudos for the poker-worthy cool front he was maintaining. As she headed toward the bathroom, she flicked him a sideways glance and one of her little Mona Lisa smiles. Then he was left to stare at his own bathroom door as it was firmly closed in his face.

Shit, he thought. That was just what he felt like, too: shit. Never in his life would he have imagined he could feel so crummy after such truly great sex.

What had just happened here?

Mac was still trying to figure it out as he rounded up his clothes from the floor, pulled them on, ran his fingers through his hair and headed toward the kitchen. The phone began to ring, but he ignored it. He had a pretty good idea of who it was, but he wasn't in the mood to talk to Hinkle just yet. He'd grab a beer, then maybe, if Julie was still in the shower—in his experience, women could drag a shower that should take them five minutes out for days—take a minute or so to upload the contents of Sid's files into his computer. After all, that was what this was all about, really. Not doing Julie. Getting Sid.

The sound of the shower followed him into the kitchen. Not imagining Julie standing naked under the spray required more effort than he was capable of at the moment. The ringing had stopped, he realized as he grabbed a beer from the refrigerator and moodily unscrewed the cap. Taking a swig, he headed on into the living room, only to stop dead on the threshold.

Josephine had the telephone cord in her mouth. The instrument lay on the floor, on its side, the receiver belly-up like a dead goldfish.

"Damn it, Josephine!" he barked. The poodle, not being stupid, jumped to her feet and bolted for the bedroom, still clutching the cord in her mouth, the severed receiver bumping after her across the hardwood.

Mac said a whole string of cuss words as he picked up the decapitated phone. There was nothing to do, he acknowledged, turning what was left of it over in his hand, except toss it. The thing was definitely dead.

Fortunately the extension in the bedroom could take over until this one was replaced. He unplugged the corpse from the wall outlet, and placed it on the end table beside his gun to await a decent burial in the garbage.

Chalk the death of his phone up as just one more in a series of things, large and small, that had not gone his way today.

Mac yanked open the curtains, hoping that an infusion of sunshine would improve his mood. The room was immediately flooded with light, which made him blink and revealed his every housekeeping deficiency from the cobwebs in the corners to the dust on the coffee table. Great. He sank down on the couch, propped his stocking feet up on the coffee table, and took another swig of beer. His gaze fell on Julie's discarded dress, crumpled into a pale purple heap near the wall. If he was not a gentleman, he would just sit here and wait until she emerged from the bathroom to fetch it. If he was, he'd pick it up, shake it out, carry it back to the bathroom, knock on the door, and yell that he was leaving her dress on the doorknob for her when she was ready.

The decision wasn't hard. He stayed where he was, watching swirling dust motes joust in the sunlight and chugging his beer.

There was a knock at his front door. Mac frowned, and cast a glance over his shoulder out the front window. He and Julie had been inside for well over an hour. Mrs. Leiferman must be about to expire of curiosity by now. It wasn't her usual MO—his activities were usually only fair game when he was outside the house—but it was possible that the old lady couldn't take the suspense and had come up with the bright idea of coming over to borrow a cup of sugar or something of the sort.

But the tailored white pants leg he could see on his stoop did not belong to Mrs. Leiferman. It was definitely a male leg. It didn't take a genius to guess whose.

He got up and went to answer the door.

"What the fuck is the matter with you?" Hinkle demanded in a furious tone the moment he opened the door, pushing past him into the house before Mac could say a word. "You got a spark plug loose, gettin' mixed up with that shit again? You got your panties in a twist about Sid Carlson, that's your business. But I'm not getting involved, you hear? That dude is *bad,* and you know it."

"Hey to you too," Mac said mildly, closing the door. Natty as always in a white suit with a black shirt and tie, Hinkle stood in the middle of the living room, arms akimbo, glaring at him. Mac walked over, picked up his beer from the coffee table, drained the last mouthful, and gestured at Hinkle with the bottle. "Want a beer?"

"Hell, no, I don't want a beer. I want to know what the hell you think you're doing nosing around Carlson again. Soon as I figured out who I was taking pictures of, I about crapped my pants. I tried to call you, but you're not answering your damned cell phone—again!—and when you picked up here, you didn't say a damned word. So here I am, asking you to your face: What the fuck are you *doing?*"

Mac thought about explaining that it had been Josephine who picked up, not he, but it didn't seem worth the effort. Instead, he asked, "Did you get the pictures?"

"Did I get the—" Hinkle looked like he was about to blow a gasket. "It doesn't matter whether or not I got the pictures. We aren't going to use them. You hear me? Are N-O-T *not.* Remember the last time you tried taking him on? Remember that we were cops, back then? Remember things were going pretty good for both of us? And what did you do? You got a burr up your ass about Sid Carlson. You went after him, and he nailed your ass to the wall—and mine too. I'm not making that mistake twice, and neither are you, if I can help it. Face the facts, Mac: You aren't going to take Sid Carlson down. If you keep trying, he'll be the one taking you down, and this time I . . ."

He broke off, looking at something beyond Mac's shoulder, his eyes widening. Mac felt a premonition of disaster, and glanced around. Sure enough, there stood Julie, barefoot, his white bathrobe, so big on her that she looked like she was swimming in it, knotted around her waist. Her hair was twisted into a loose and fetching knot on the top of her head, her beautiful face was scrubbed clean, and her big brown eyes were questioning as they swung from him to Hinkle and back.

"Julie, meet my partner, George Hinkle." There didn't seem to be much else to do, under the circumstances, but make the necessary introductions. To a certain degree, anyway. No need to reveal Julie's full identity, because if Hinkle knew exactly who she was he would freak for sure. The urgent question was, how much had she heard? Mac looked at her hard, but couldn't tell.

"Julie—*Carlson?*" Hinkle choked, staring at her as if she'd been a six-foot-tall spitting cobra instead of a ravishing babe in a bathrobe.

So much for keeping her identity to himself, Mac thought, grimacing. He was surprised his partner had recognized her at all, much less so fast. But then, the light was good in the room now, and Hinkle had just been taking pictures of Sid, so he would naturally have Carlson on the brain. Plus, he'd been working security at her wedding, too, and a looker like Julie could be counted on to be remembered by any male between ten and ninety. And he could have seen her umpteen times since, for all Mac knew. After all, he also had a vested interest in keeping tabs on Sid, if for no other reason than to stay as far away from him as possible.

"Julie's a client," Mac said, which was perfectly true even if it was obvious to the most casual observer that Julie was far more than that. After all, how many clients came strolling into his living room clad in nothing but his bathrobe, obviously fresh from his shower? None that he could think of.

"Hello," Julie offered. She was unsmiling, but Mac still could not judge whether she'd heard more than she should.

"Shit," Hinkle said, turning incredulous eyes on him. Mac met that dumbstruck look impassively. Recollecting himself, Hinkle swung his gaze back to Julie. "Meaning no disrespect, ma'am."

Then his gaze moved to something on the floor, and his expression changed again. Following the direction of that appalled glance, Mac realized that his partner had just spotted Julie's dress. Julie apparently realized it, too, because she stepped forward and, with praiseworthy dignity, retrieved the garment, which she folded over her arm.

"You were at my house earlier, weren't you?" she asked Hinkle, her manner both direct and composed. Mac had to give her credit for not letting Hinkle—or him—see the embarrassment she had to be feeling. "I heard you talking to Mac over the phone. Did you—were you able to get pictures of my husband with his girlfriend?"

Hinkle gulped. "Uh—uh. . . ." His gaze shot to Mac. "Could I speak to you in private for just one minute?"

"He got them," Mac said to Julie, who met his gaze with absolutely nothing that he could decipher in her eyes.

"I'll just go get dressed." She turned to head back into the bedroom, then glanced over her shoulder. "Nice meeting you, Mr. Hinkle."

Hinkle gave her a sickly smile. "You, too, Mrs.—uh—Carlson."

Julie's very lack of expression made Mac apprehensive. Either she'd heard something she shouldn't, or she was still wallowing in her après-sex snit. Silence reigned in the living room until it was interrupted by the barely audible click of the bedroom door closing.

Then Hinkle, looking nearly apoplectic, turned on him with a vengeance.

"What the fuck are you *doing?*" he demanded in a fierce whisper. "You're fucking Sid Carlson's *wife,* you dumbass. Are you out of your tiny mind?"

Denying it would clearly be a waste of time. Mac put the beer bottle down on the coffee table, stuck his hands in the front pockets of his jeans, rocked back on his heels, and regarded Hinkle meditatively.

"Like I said, Julie's a client. She hired me—us—to find out if her husband's cheating on her. As you saw, he is."

"You're fucking sleeping with her." Hinkle did the best under-his-breath yell Mac had ever heard. It wasn't loud, but it was forceful. "And there's no *us* in this. Uh-uh. This is you on your damn fool own."

Mac pursed his lips. "Fine. I'll consider her a private client. That make you feel better?"

"No. No, it doesn't make me feel better. Who's going to *know* she's your private client, that's what I want to know? What are you gonna do, hang a sign around her neck? If Carlson gets wind that we're spying on him, we got a shitload of trouble. If he finds out you're also making it with his wife"—Hinkle visibly shuddered—"which he will do when lawyers get involved, you mark my words—he'll come after us—not you, *us*—with everything he's got." Hinkle shook his head. "Been there, done that. I don't know about you, but nothing in that experience made me want to go down that road again."

Mac said nothing for a moment. Everything Hinkle said was true. The last time he'd gone after Sid, Sid's retaliation had been stunning in its swiftness. Days after Mac had briefed his superiors on what he was doing and—he'd thought—set up a sting that would bring Sid crashing down, drugs missing from the evidence room had been found in Mac's locker. In the ensuing investigation, half a dozen witnesses had come forward willing to swear that Mac had sold them everything from coke to smack to LSD while on the job. The sting against Sid had come up empty—how ironic was that?—and in the end Mac, not Sid, had been the one to come crashing down. And Hinkle, who'd been tarred with the same brush just because he'd had the misfortune to be Mac's partner, had crashed with him. Mac had gone to Greg Rice, his captain and immediate superior as well as, he'd thought, a friend, in an attempt to at least save Hinkle's job, but Rice had said there was nothing he could do. The word had come down from on high: he and Hinkle were gone.

Mac's eyes had been opened by that fiasco: the tentacles of the beast he was hunting reached everywhere. Even his fellow cops had turned on him when the shit started hitting the fan, and he had never been sure just who had been motivated by genuine belief in his guilt and who Sid had gotten to.

In the end, it hadn't mattered. Although no criminal charges were ever officially filed, he and Hinkle had been fired from the department, and both their lives had pretty much gone to hell. Not much more than casual acquaintances when it had happened, they'd stuck together afterward— Hinkle had said it was because nobody else would have either of them—and built

McQuarry and Hinkle up over the interven-
ing years.

Looking at it that way, Mac could definitely see Hinkle's point: It had only been in
the last year or two that they'd actually
started making decent money, and now, by
going after Sid again, he was risking everything they'd built up.

"I can't just walk away," Mac said quietly.
"I'm too close to getting him this time. But
I'll keep you out of it from here on out. In
fact, if you want to buy me out, I'll understand. I'm pretty sure Don Hadley at the
bank will give you a loan. That would keep
you out of it as much as anything could."

"I don't want to buy you out." Hinkle
groaned. "Would you be smart for once in
your life and leave this alone?"

Mac started to say something, then
heard the bedroom door open again and
shook his head at Hinkle, warning him
without words to shut up.

Hinkle looked like someone had just
forced him to swallow a mouthful of vinegar, but he was silent as Julie appeared in
the doorway, looking so beautiful that Mac
was suddenly uncomfortable in a most
particular way, as if the front of his jeans

had all of a sudden grown too tight. It probably had something to do with the whisper-soft purple dress, he thought, or maybe the sexy shoes. He had a clear mental vision of how each garment had come off. . . .

"If you're busy"—Julie's gaze flicked to Hinkle, who offered her a nervous-looking smile—"I can call a taxi. I need to get back to work."

"I'm not busy." Mac picked up his gun and shoved it down inside the back of his waistband, then grabbed his sunglasses and his keys. His gaze slid to Hinkle. "I'll give you a buzz."

"Yeah," Hinkle said, looking as nervous as a beetle in an aviary, and headed for the door.

Josephine appeared—of course she did, she could see everybody was leaving, and she wanted to go too—and Julie glanced down at her.

"Do you want to take her, or . . . ?"

Mac gave Josephine a sour look. "Take her. There's less she can chew up in the car."

Julie was already gathering Josephine up.

"I'm going back to the office," Hinkle said

to him, holding the door for Julie. His gaze flicked to her. "Pleasure making your acquaintance, Mrs. Carlson."

"Good-bye, Mr. Hinkle." Julie was already walking down the steps toward the Blazer. With another speaking glance at Mac, Hinkle headed for his car. Mac followed Julie, glad to see that Mrs. Leiferman was nowhere in sight. Finally, at least one thing today was going his way. Maybe, if he was lucky, it would be the start of a trend.

Julie didn't say anything until he had the Blazer started and, hot air blasting, they were heading down the street. Then she fixed him with a gaze that made alarm bells go off in his head.

"So," she said. "Is there something I'm missing here?"

23

SITTING IN A PARKED CAR on a blazing hot day ranked right up there with hitting himself in the head with a hammer as one of his favorite things to do, Roger Basta reflected sourly. But the Big Boss had made it clear that he had just this one last chance to take care of Julie Carlson. If he failed, he wasn't likely to get another. People did not fail the boss. Not and live to tell the tale.

He'd been watching for her, waiting for her to come out of her dress store. When she did, he was going to get the business over with once and for all. No more elaborate schemes. No more worries about DNA or misdirecting the cops. "Keep it simple, stupid" was his new motto. Just do the deed and have done. With her out of the way, he could get back to his real life.

At least, until the Big Boss called again.

Maybe it was time he started thinking about retirement. He was fifty-five, not old really, but old for this business. He was getting tired. He was getting scared.

This hit on Julie Carlson was the first time he had ever failed. It was making him doubt his abilities. It was making the boss doubt his abilities.

If there was one thing he had learned over the course of his career, it was don't mess with the boss. People who did ended up dead.

For the first time ever, it occurred to him that he might not come out of this business with a nice little nest egg and a lot of years left to spend it. He might come out of this business dead. He knew where a hell of a lot of bodies were buried. Literally.

It might not pay for the boss to let him just retire and walk away.

Damn Julie Carlson anyway. He hadn't borne her any ill will at first; the hit on her had been just another job. Now it was more than that. Number one, she'd marked him. Very few of his victims had ever marked him, and those who had hadn't lived to tell the tale. Number two, she was making him look less than competent. Looking less than competent was bad for business. It was also dangerous.

As soon as she put in an appearance, he was going to kill her stone cold dead. Give him three minutes, and it would be all over.

It must have been well over a hundred degrees inside the car. He'd deliberately stolen one with tinted windows so no one could see him inside. If he ran the engine, and thus the air-conditioner, he might attract attention, and so he refrained. When one was sitting in a stolen car with murder on one's mind, attention was bad.

It was nearly five o'clock. The sun was dipping toward the horizon. Its rays poured through the windshield, both cooking and half blinding him. He was hungry, he had a headache from the sun, and he was all out of the Gatorade he'd been chugging to keep from sweating to death. To add insult to injury, his nose throbbed. He tried to assuage the pain with the melting ice pack he'd brought along, but all he really succeeded in doing was getting his shirt wet.

The nose made it personal. He was going to make her pay for that.

If she ever stepped outside. He'd watched her go into her store that morning, then scouted the area for the best place to wait and watch. He knew her work schedule: she closed up shop at five. He figured if he showed up at three, there would be no way he could miss her, even if she decided to leave early.

He couldn't afford to miss her again.

So he was prepared to sit out here and roast alive for as long as it took.

Then he was heading for Key West and a nice little vacation, before he returned to his regular job. He could retire from it, too, in a few years.

It was time he started making plans for his future. Serious plans.

24

"I THOUGHT WE AGREED that it would be best if you didn't go back to work." Mac stopped at the stop sign, then turned the corner as he spoke. "What with one thing and another, you've had an eventful day."

That was such an understatement that under other circumstances Julie would have snorted. But she didn't, because she was busy watching Mac's face. She'd come to know him well, she realized. The fact that he was avoiding her question spoke volumes.

"I have to go back to work. I called the shop from your bedroom to check on things, and Meredith—my other assistant—told me that my three o'clock is still there and things are not going well. Besides, I have to face Amber sometime. Better at the end of the day today than early in the morning tomorrow." Julie paused, her gaze keen on his face. "Now, do you want to tell me what was going on back there with your partner?"

Mac glanced at her, hesitated, then grimaced as if in resignation. "Remember I told you that there was a company policy against sleeping with clients? Hinkle was upset that I violated it."

Julie regarded him with a degree of suspicion. She hadn't been able to hear what was being said between the two men, but that Hinkle was extremely upset with Mac was obvious. Too upset for Mac's explanation to account for it?

"Is that the truth?"

His mouth twisted in a wry smile. "Absolutely." He glanced her way again. "What are your plans for the evening? After you fire your assistant, I mean."

"I guess I'll go to my mother's. I'm certainly not going back to my house." She shuddered at the thought.

"I could take you to dinner." It was said

casually, in almost throwaway fashion. They were on the expressway now, and traffic was heavy. That might account for his unusual attention to the road, but Julie didn't think so.

"Mac . . ." Julie hesitated. He was handsome, he was sexy, he was great in the sack. He was funny. He was dependable. He had an adorable dog. Just looking at him made her heart go pitter-pat; thinking about what they'd done in bed made her burn—with a certain degree of embarrassment when she mentally replayed all the details, and with a slowly building desire to do it all again. But she was particularly vulnerable right now, she knew, and she was growing dangerously used to relying on him for comfort and support. Add explosive sex to the mix, and the result could be bad. Her heart was bruised and battered enough from her marriage; a failed romance with Mac might break it entirely. "I'm not sure I'm ready for a relationship right now."

A beat passed.

"Darlin', who's talking about a relationship here? Not me. What I'm talking about is dinner—and lots of casual sex." He threw her a quick grin, and Julie, despite her mixed-up emotions, had to smile back. "Or not. That part's up to you. But I think you could still use a friend. And you have to eat."

Another beat as she mulled that over.

"Did you have any particular place in mind?" A smile played around Julie's lips as she looked at him. It was capitulation— to dinner only—and they both knew it. Suddenly the decision felt very right. Maybe getting involved with Mac right now was dangerous, but then, life was danger- ous. Josephine was lying contentedly across her thighs, and Julie stroked the poodle's springy coat. Being with Mac was like having Josephine in her lap: something that made her feel happy.

And from now on she was going to grab all the happiness she could with both hands.

"You choose. Any place you want."

Julie thought. "Considering that we have Josephine with us, how about O'Con- nell's?" O'Connell's was casual, with ex- pansive decks and patios that many of the patrons preferred to the large indoor din- ing room. Sid had never liked the simple dishes and breezy service; it was the kind of place she went to with Becky and her girls. Josephine would be fine at one of the patio tables.

"I can see you're going to be a cheap date." He smiled at her as he pulled off the expressway into Summerville. The sun was starting its downward trajectory, Julie noticed as they headed right toward it and the bright rays all but blinded her. It would be evening soon—and she would be having dinner with Mac.

Suddenly she was really, really glad about that. It was the proverbial spoonful of sugar in the bitter medicine that was currently her life.

"Mac," she said, "I'm sorry if I was a little—um, out of sorts earlier."

His expression told her that he knew what she meant: a little out of sorts after sex.

"That's okay," he said, his voice as grave as hers had been. Then he grinned at her. "You can be out of sorts with me any time—especially if it's from the same cause."

She laughed, and as she did felt a little more of the damage to her heart heal. It was going to take some time, she thought, but she was going to be okay.

He pulled into the Kroger lot and parked. It was nearly full at this time of day as people stopped by the grocery and the pharmacy and the other stores in the shopping center on their way home from work. The street in front of them was no less busy, with cars whizzing along it as their drivers hurried to beat the coming rush hour. Across the street, Carolina Belle's plate-glass windows were inpenetrable. All she could see in them was a reflection of the still-blazing sun.

Oh, God, now there was Amber to deal with, and Carlene. Back to real life.

"Want me to come in with you?" Mac had been watching her face. His eyes met hers; he was no longer smiling. She realized that he understood just how much she was having to steel herself to face what lay ahead, and thought, This is nice. She couldn't remember Sid ever particularly caring about what was going on in her mind—or her life—apart from him. "This could get unpleasant, you realize."

Simply knowing that Mac was on her side, that there was somebody else with her in this boat that she was pushing out into uncharted seas, strengthened her.

Julie shook her head. "No, thanks. I can do this. Then I'll close up and meet you back here at—six?"

"I'll wait for you. Come whenever you're ready. If you need me beforehand, call me." He tapped his cell phone.

"I will. But I shouldn't need you. Unless Amber decides to pull an Amy Fisher on me." Julie smiled to indicate that she was being facetious, lifted Josephine off her lap and slid out of the car, then glanced back in at Mac. "I won't be any longer than I can help."

"I'll be here."

Julie shut the Blazer's door and started walking, conscious of Mac's eyes on her back. Strictly for his benefit, she put a little extra sway in her walk and smiled to herself as she imagined what he thought of it. She hoped it turned him on.

To her surprise, pleasure, and slight dismay, she found that she was getting turned on thinking about him getting turned on.

Sex as an antidote to the divorce blues. She thought about that for a moment and concluded, works for me.

The heat hugged her like an overly effusive friend. People's voices, the rattle of shopping carts, and the whoosh of traffic speeding past on the street in front of her joined with the smell of melting asphalt and car exhaust to form a backdrop that was both exhausting and familiar. It was good to know that Mac would be waiting when she came out, she thought as she headed toward her shop.

It made her feel stronger, braver, safer. It made her feel as if her life wasn't ending, but beginning.

She stepped over the scraggly little bushes that separated the Kroger from the Taco Bell, feeling the tingle of pleasure she'd gotten from thinking of turning Mac on fade as she mentally rehearsed what she was going to say to Amber. *You're fired, bimbette* didn't seem to quite cut it, but she couldn't think of anything more dignified that conveyed her sentiments in quite the same way.

The shadow of the Taco Bell had just blocked out the worst of the sun when a green Lexus pulled up behind her and stopped. Julie glanced over her shoulder at it because its front bumper was close, but she kept walking, not paying any attention to it beyond that first instinctive glance. Vaguely she registered the sound of a car door opening and closing.

Seconds later a hard hand clamped around her arm. Julie was so startled that she jumped a foot straight up in the air. She whirled, heart pounding, to find herself face-to-face with Sid.

"What the hell did you do? Huh? What did you do?"

Dressed in a charcoal suit and crisp white shirt despite the heat, red-faced and scowling with his glasses slipping down his nose and his red silk tie askew, he looked furious. It was so unlike Sid to be anything less than completely dapper that she knew that he must be really enraged. His nostrils were distended, he was breathing hard, and his fingers were really hurting as they dug into her arm. For a moment, the briefest, flickering moment, she felt her stomach clench. She had always hated to make Sid mad, and the visceral reaction was still there—until she remembered all the reasons why she didn't have to put up with his temper anymore. The thought that had occurred to her earlier replayed in her head: He had set her free. He no longer had any claim on her. He had severed the tie that bound her to him by his own actions. From the time of their marriage she had been less a person to him than an accessory he used to flaunt his success, like his Italian leather shoes or his expensive silk tie. She realized that she'd been tired of being an accessory for a long time.

Their marriage had been over in all but name long before Amber had come on the scene.

Amber had simply awakened her to the truth.

Suddenly Julie realized that she was being given a second chance. She was Julie again, not Julie Carlson anymore but Julie her own true self. It was that Julie who reacted as Sid's good little wife never would have, that Julie who glared at Sid and jerked her arm from his hold.

"I don't know what you're talking about." Her voice was icy. "And keep your hands off me."

Surprise flickered in his eyes for the briefest of moments. Then his face darkened. He seemed to vibrate with temper as he took a step closer, looming over her almost threateningly, his eyes hard and angry as they bored into hers.

"You know what I'm talking about, all right. You were in the house, weren't you? Were you spying on me? You were, weren't you, you sneaky little . . . What the hell did you do to my car? I missed my plane! Do you know how important that meeting was? Because of you, I missed it!"

Despite her own rising fury, Julie was, for just a moment, rendered speechless. She could do nothing more than glare at him. The emotion that was uppermost in the maelstrom of her feelings, she decided, was total disbelief. Instead of apologizing, explaining, or even attempting to make some excuse for being caught red-handed in her house with her twenty-year-old employee, he was yelling at *her* for finding him out and damaging his car.

There was something wrong with this picture, but fortunately, Julie thought, she didn't have to stick around any longer to try to figure out exactly what it was.

"Hell-o-o? I found your Viagra. I saw you in my house with Amber. I know what you did. So you know what? I don't care if you missed your plane. I don't care if you missed your meeting. And I'll let you figure out what I did to your car. And just so you know, I think you're a total dickhead; a horse's ass; a mean, conceited, pompous, impotent bastard. Our marriage is over: I'm getting a divorce."

For a moment he simply stared at her, looking as stunned as if a kitten had suddenly morphed into a tiger and bitten him, while his face grew redder and redder until it was the approximate color of a tomato and his eyes bulged out at her.

"The hell you are." He grabbed her by the arm again and started dragging her toward the Lexus, his fingers digging hurtfully into the soft flesh above her elbow. He was breathing hard now, and his features were contorted in an ugly snarl. Julie dug her heels into the heat-softened pavement and resisted, and he turned on her ferociously. "You'll get a divorce when I say you can get a divorce and not before, you got that? You trashy little bitch, anybody would go looking for something with a little more class— and a little less ass—if they were married to you."

He gave a vicious yank, and despite her best efforts at resistance she stumbled forward. He was dragging her again, toward the Lexus, and she couldn't seem to get away. Julie felt a tiny spurt of fear mix with her rage. She had never, she realized, pushed Sid to the limit before. Always she had pretty much done whatever he wanted. Now that she was no longer his to command, how far would he go?

She discovered that she didn't want to find out.

"Let me go!"

This time his grip was unbreakable. She glanced wildly around even as she fought being pulled the last couple of feet toward the car. They were in the shadow of the Taco Bell still, back near the Dumpster, which of course happened to be the one fairly empty area in the whole vast asphalt sea. No one seemed to be paying the least attention to her and Sid; it was up to her to save herself.

She could scream, she realized. But the last small part of her that was still Sid Carlson's wife shuddered at the thought of creating such a scene.

On the other hand, she was damned if she'd let herself be manhandled into that Lexus by her furious soon-to-be ex-husband. Nothing good could come of that.

"Get your hands off her, Sid."

Mac's voice stopped Julie in the act of preparing to kick Sid as hard as she could in the shins. She glanced around again to see him looming behind her, reaching for her, his gaze fixed on Sid. Sid, for his part, stopped dead and stared at Mac as if he were seeing a ghost. His grip on her arm slackened from, she thought, sheer surprise. Mac caught her arm and pulled her away from Sid's hold. Freed, she moved instinctively to Mac's side. Standing in his protective shadow, she wrapped her arms over her chest and glared at Sid.

It would be a long time before she would forget or forgive that little pang of fear.

"Well, if it isn't Mac McQuarry." Sid's lips stretched into a mocking smile, but his eyes were suddenly alert and cold. He was no longer looking at her. His focus was all on Mac. "I thought you got run out of town a few years back. Something about being a dirty cop, wasn't it?"

Mac smiled, too, with as little humor as Sid, and their gazes clashed like rapiers. Julie could feel the enmity crackling between the two like an electrical charge. Her glance moved from one to the other: Sid shorter, leaner, older, looking like the successful businessman he was but still a little out of place on this blazing hot day in his expensive dark suit; Mac taller, broader, younger, handsomer, a blond surfer-god in his Hawaiian shirt and jeans and tennis shoes—and, surprisingly, with the grim set to his jaw and the hard glint in his eye, the more formidable looking of the two. It hit her with the force of a two-by-four over the head that there was some kind of history—unpleasant history—between the two.

Mac replied in a deadly voice that was like nothing Julie had ever heard come out of his mouth before: "Don't tell me you've forgotten the details. I haven't. For a long time now I've been meaning to drop by and congratulate you on doing such a good job."

"Is that supposed to be some kind of a threat?" Sid looked ready to explode. Then, suddenly, his expression changed, and he glanced at her and then back at Mac. "What the hell are you doing with my wife?"

"Looks to me like I'm keeping her safe from you, asshole."

Mac's snarling response reinforced what Julie had already sensed: the tension between the two was longstanding in nature. Mac had never mentioned that he knew Sid. . . .

"I hired him," she said, pushing her confusion to the back burner until Sid was dealt with. "He's a private investigator. He's got pictures of you with Amber. I'm going to fire her, by the way, just as soon as I see her. And, like I said, I'm going to divorce you."

Sid stared at her. Then he looked at Mac. Then, to Julie's complete and utter stupefaction, he began to laugh, jeering laughter that set her teeth on edge. Julie frowned at him. Of all the reactions she would have expected from Sid, this was not one. Beside her, she felt Mac stiffen. Glancing up at him, she saw that his face had gone utterly still, utterly blank.

"You stupid little bitch," Sid said, drawing her attention once more. "Don't you know when you're being used? He's been pumping you for all kinds of information about me, hasn't he? And you fed him everything you know."

Julie must have looked as shocked as she felt, because he shook his head contemptuously at her. "You didn't have a clue, did you? Sometimes I think your bra size is bigger than your IQ. This guy's been after me for years, and now he's using you to try to get to me. What did you tell him?"

Feeling suddenly cold despite the blazing heat, Julie ignored Sid to glance up at Mac. "Is that true?"

He looked down at her. His eyes as they met hers told her everything she needed to know: Sid was telling the truth.

"Julie . . ."

"It is true, isn't it?" There was a ringing in her ears as she faced the hideous knowledge that Mac had betrayed her, too.

"I can explain. . . ."

Sid cut him off with another of those jeering little laughs that brought Julie's gaze swiveling back around to him. "What did you do, go waltzing into his office and ask him to investigate me? He must have thought it was his lucky day. He didn't even tell you he knew me, did he?" Her face must have answered for her because he laughed again. "Like I said, he's been using you."

He moved, walking the few steps back to the Lexus and opening the passenger door, then jerked his head at her commandingly. "Now get in the car. We'll go someplace private and talk this through."

Julie's gaze locked with Mac's. She felt as if she'd just been punched in the stomach. She could hardly breathe. To her surprise, and burgeoning horror, this betrayal hurt far more than discovering Sid with Amber.

"Julie, listen. . . ." Mac focused on her now, ignoring Sid completely. His voice was low, his eyes pained. She cut him off with a curt shake of her head.

"It was a rotten thing to do." Her voice was scarcely louder than a whisper.

"Don't tell me you had something going on the side with him?"

Something in their attitude toward each other must have alerted Sid. He sounded so outraged that Julie almost wanted to laugh. Her gaze swung around to him.

"Actually, I slept with him this afternoon." Her voice was strong again, thank goodness. She swallowed, battling back the growing lump in her throat that she was afraid might, if she let it, turn into tears. "If you have anything to say to me after this, you can call my lawyer. I'll call the office tomorrow and leave his name and number with Heidi." As Sid sputtered furiously, she looked at Mac. "As for you, I never want to see you again as long as I live."

"Julie . . ." Mac said again, reaching for her, his voice hoarse, his eyes desperate. "Give me a chance to explain."

Julie eluded him with a deft sideways step.

"Go to hell," she said to him. His eyes darkened as if at a blow and his arms dropped to his sides. Her gaze swung back to Sid. "You go to hell, too."

Head high and back straight, she pivoted and started walking away.

"You cheating little slut, you get your ass back here," Sid roared. No sooner had the words left his mouth than Julie heard a flurry of movement, followed by the sharp crack of a blow. Glancing back, she saw Sid flying backward while Mac, fists still clenched, body poised for more, watched with a look of savage satisfaction. Julie saw that the scene was finally starting to attract onlookers, and kept walking. Behind her she heard rapid footsteps, and increased her own pace until she was nearly running. A hand grabbed her arm. She didn't even have to look back to know it belonged to Mac.

"Julie, please. I know it sounds bad, but . . ." He pulled her around to face him.

"Sounds bad? Is that what it does?" Hurt and anger and a sense of terrible betrayal made her voice unsteady. She jerked her arm from his hold and bared her teeth at him savagely. "Go away! Leave me alone! I don't want to listen to anything you have to say. Send me a bill and I'll pay it, and other than that stay the hell out of my life. Understand?"

It was only as she saw several passersby glance her way that she realized that she was yelling. From the corner of her eye, she saw that Sid, face red, fists clenched, was headed their way. A woman shopper complete with loaded grocery cart was punching numbers into her cell phone even as she kept looking at them, wide-eyed. Julie guessed that she was calling 911.

Julie could only pray that both men ended up in jail.

"You have to listen to me," Mac said.

"No, I don't," she bit out. Then, grabbing the shreds of her dignity with both hands, she turned her back on him and stalked toward the sidewalk. A movement across the street in front of Carolina Belle caught her eye. As she identified its source, her lips pursed. Carlene Squabb had emerged from the shop and was coming her way, obviously having spotted her through the glass, an annoyed expression that Julie knew all too well on her face. Julie almost turned on her heel and headed in the opposite direction. Of all the things she didn't need right now, listening to Carlene bitch about how Julie was neglecting her was right up there at the top of the list.

"Julie, please. Just give me a minute."

Mac caught her arm again, pulling her around to face him just as she reached the edge of the parking lot. Sid was closing fast, his nose bleeding, murder in his eye, but Mac didn't seem to notice, or care if he did. From the corner of her eye, Julie saw Carlene look both ways and step off the curb. It was only then that she realized that Carlene was wearing the pink sweater dress she herself had discarded earlier. Why on earth . . . ?

A sudden blur of movement on the street caught Julie's attention. Seemingly from out of nowhere a mid-size blue car hurtled toward Carlene. Carlene saw it coming: Julie could see horror in her widening eyes, her opening mouth.

Carlene tried to get out of the way, but there was no time. The car hit her with a sickening thump. She flew up in the air, twisting feet over head, limp as a rag doll as she seemed to cartwheel over the car.

Julie screamed, and, screaming, rushed toward where Carlene now lay limp and bleeding in the street.

25

CARLENE WAS DEAD. Julie could hardly believe it. Numb with shock, she walked out of the hospital at shortly after ten into the welcoming arms of the night. It was still hot, stickily humid, with a sprinkling of stars overhead and a beautiful crescent moon. Shivering at the cruel irony of such serene beauty on a night that had witnessed a terrible, brutal death, Julie was nevertheless grateful for the embracing heat. She was so cold that she felt as if she'd been turned to ice from the inside out; so cold that she felt like she would never be warm again.

Sitting there in that impersonal lounge

with Carlene's family as they waited for news had been one of the most wrenching experiences of her life.

Carlene had been the victim of a hit-and-run. The police were investigating, of course. They'd talked to Meredith and they'd talked to Julie, and they'd talked to scores of other people as well. There'd been dozens of witnesses, a few of whom had actually had the presence of mind to get at least part of the license-plate number. Neither the car nor the driver had yet been found, but the police seemed confident that they would be. Julie prayed it would be soon. She found the accident horrifying in more ways than one.

She could not get past the fact that Carlene had been wearing Julie's own discarded dress when she was hit. Julie pointed that out to the officer who had interviewed her, and he had dutifully written it down, but she had a feeling that the information had not made much of an impression and would wind up buried in a file somewhere.

The consensus was, Carlene had probably been the unfortunate victim of a driver who was drunk, or high, or elderly, or a kid, who had then panicked. The police were confident that both car and driver would be found, and then all questions would be answered.

When Julie had asked her, Meredith had said that Carlene, annoyed at being left to the tender mercies of a mere assistant, had been chain-smoking in the dressing room. She had dropped ashes on her own dress, which had burned a tiny hole in a particularly unfortunate spot on the bodice. Carlene had pitched a fit, blamed the whole fiasco on Meredith, and insisted that she could not possibly step outside the store in a dress with a hole in the tit. Meredith, not knowing what else to do, had invited her to take her pick from Carolina Belle's stock. Unfortunately, with her new implants, the only other garment in the store that would fit Carlene was Julie's stretchy sweater dress. So Meredith let her wear it.

And Carlene had died in it.

"You ever think that maybe walking alone through a parking lot at night might not be a good idea?"

The voice, coming from behind her as she headed toward her car, made Julie jump even as she recognized it. She was edgy, she realized, nervous, and didn't have to delve far to find the reason why: Carlene dying in her dress had scared the pants off her. She was just now fulling realizing it.

"Go away." She didn't even bother to glance over her shoulder. Maddeningly, just knowing that Mac was behind her and she was, therefore, physically safe made her nerves relax. It also made her heart ache, and her temper heat.

"I know you're mad. I'm even willing to admit that you have a right to be. But I can explain."

Having fished her keys out of her purse as she walked, Julie pressed the unlock button just as she reached the white Infiniti. Then she turned on him. Every muscle in her body hummed with tension; her eyes were blazing.

"Exactly what part of *go away* don't you understand?"

The moonlight turned his hair to molten silver. It was reflected in his eyes, turning them silvery, too. It cast deep shadows beneath his high cheekbones, his straight nose, his firm chin. He looked tall and broad and achingly handsome standing there regarding her so gravely, and Julie hated him.

It scared her to realize that she hated him. Hate was too strong an emotion to feel for this sexy near-stranger who had slept with and betrayed her. She didn't even hate Sid anymore. She'd gotten over hating him long since.

No matter what he had done, Mac was a tiny, unimportant chapter in her life. A phase. She should have been mad, but she shouldn't have been hating him.

Mac grimaced, and stuck his hands in the front pockets of his jeans. "Look, Sid and I go way back, okay? When I stumbled across you, I admit that my first thought was that I could maybe get some information from you about him. But . . ."

"Forget it," Julie said through her teeth. "You're wasting your breath. At this point, if you told me the sun rises in the east I'd get a second opinion. Now leave me alone."

She turned on her heel, presenting him with her back as she opened her car door.

"It ever occur to you that Sid might be trying to kill you?"

"What?" The question was so unexpected—and yet so in sync with her own uneasy feelings—that she stiffened and turned to face him again.

"Oh, not Sid himself. He's not the type to get his hands dirty. What he might do is hire somebody—a professional. A hit man. Think about it: The girl who got killed today—she was wearing your dress, wasn't she? And coming out of your shop? Maybe somebody thought she was you. Maybe the same somebody who attacked you in your house. And maybe he's still out there. You've escaped him twice now. Maybe he's going to try again."

Julie's heart leaped in her chest. Goose bumps prickled into life all over her skin. What he was suggesting was ridiculous, of course. Sid would never hire someone to kill her—would he? It was the stuff of bad movies.

She could barely keep herself from glancing all around, fearfully probing the shadows. If Mac hadn't been standing right in front of her, watching her narrowly to, she thought, judge her reaction, she would have done just that. But she refused to give him the satisfaction of knowing that he had succeeded in scaring her.

Even though he had.

"If you really believe that, you need to go to the police." Julie was proud of how cool her voice sounded. She slid into her car, and prepared to close the door. His hand closing on the top of the window frame prevented her.

"They don't listen to me anymore—especially when it comes to Sid. Remember I told you that I got fired because the guy I was investigating set me up? That would be Sid."

Julie's eyes widened. She stopped in the act of inserting her key into the ignition.

"You were investigating *Sid?*" Her throat felt suddenly dry. "Why?"

"Drugs." His eyes bored into hers. "At the time I thought he was running a drug operation, big time. Among other things."

For a moment Julie simply gaped at him. Then the sheer absurdity of the accusation hit her. Her brows snapped together, and she jerked the door away from him, closing and locking it before he could react. He stood there with his fists on his hips scowling at her through the glass. Julie started the car, then, unable to resist, rolled her window down the merest crack.

"You need professional help, you know that? If I were you, I'd run, not walk, to the nearest treatment facility. Now good-bye."

She rolled up the window and shifted into reverse at the same time, leaving him standing there in the shadowy parking lot glaring after her. Thank goodness he'd finally strayed into the realm of the ridiculous, Julie told herself as she drove away. For a minute there, he'd really had her going. But imagining Sid—meticulous, blue-blooded Sid with his golf games and his business meetings and his fussy insistence on order and punctuality—as a drug dealer was too much. Even in the throes of divorcing him, she couldn't go that far.

It was Mac's suggestion that someone was trying to kill her that had made her listen to him at all.

For some reason, his words had seemed to strike a chord. They took on a resonance inside her that would not be dismissed no matter how far-fetched the rest of his suggestions might be.

Julie realized that his warning echoed her own fears.

Turning off the main drag into the labyrinth of narrow dark streets that led to her mother's house—it would be a cold day in hell before she stepped foot inside her own again; she supposed she was going to have to hire movers to retrieve her things, and beg Becky to supervise—she became conscious of one particular set of headlights that stayed a consistent half a block back, making all the turns she made, slowing down when she slowed, speeding up when she hit the gas.

She was being followed. The knowledge broke over her like a cold wave. Julie's breathing quickened, and she reached in a panic for her cell phone.

Then she realized who it almost had to be: Mac.

Slowly she put her phone down. If she was wrong, if this really was a hit man on a mission, she was going to feel dumb as a rock before she died. But she didn't think she was wrong.

Just to be sure, she watched carefully in her rearview mirror as the black Blazer passed beneath the only streetlight on the route. And it *was* a black Blazer.

Mac was following her.

That infuriated her so much that she was parked in front of her mother's modest brick ranch house waiting when he got there. By the time he pulled up behind her, she was already out of her car and advancing on him, cell phone in hand.

He got out of the Blazer just as she reached it, shutting the door but leaving the motor running. For Josephine, Julie guessed in passing. She could see the poodle's fluffy white head peering at her through the window. The sight of Josephine cost her a pang. She realized that somehow, over the course of this nightmare, she had fallen in love—with Josephine.

Certainly not with the jackass leaning against the side of the Blazer with his arms crossed over his chest.

"If you don't leave me alone, I'm going to call the police," she threatened, waving her cell phone at him.

He ignored that. He was, Julie thought furiously, good at ignoring things.

"You remember I asked you about Sid's first wife? You said she was completely out of the picture before you came into it. That's more true than you know: after an evening spent at a party with Sid, she was never seen again. Just walked off the face of the earth. I've been searching for her for years without turning up so much as a trace. Her name was Kelly. She was only twenty-two."

"Are you trying to make me believe that Sid killed her?" Her voice quivered with outrage—and, if she was honest, just the tiniest, most infuriating smidgen of fear.

Mac shrugged. "I think it's more likely that he had her killed."

"You're insane." Julie took a deep breath. "If you really believe that, why don't you go to the police?"

"I *was* the police, remember? Once upon a time. I was a cop when I first noticed that Kelly Carlson was nowhere to be found, but the bottom line is, no witnesses, no bodies, no crime. The story was that the first Mrs. Carlson went home to her family in California. The powers that be at the department were fine with that—even though there was no family in California for her to go home to. Although she was from California originally, her parents had died before she married Sid. I can find no record of her anywhere on this planet after she left him. Now the department doesn't even want to talk to me. They might listen to you, if you went to them and told them that you think your husband's trying to kill you, but then again, they might not. There's no proof: not yet. And Sid and his family have some powerful friends."

"You're trying to scare me!" And he was succeeding too; put together the right way, everything that had happened could be interpreted in such a way that it was possible to conclude that Sid had hired someone to kill her. But how unlikely was that? Sid was many unpleasant things, but she couldn't picture him as a cold-blooded killer. It was far more likely that Mac was adding two and two and getting five—or lying again for some nefarious purpose of his own. Remembering how he had already lied to her infuriated her all over again. She turned on her heel, meaning to walk away.

"I'm trying to keep you alive." He came away from the Blazer then, catching her arm and pulling her around to face him. "I've been doing my homework lately, darlin', and I don't like what I'm learning. Did you know that Sweetwater's—remember Sweetwater's, Sid's after-hours hangout?—is owned by Rand Corporation, which also owns All-American Builders?

Yeah, Sid's company. Apparently Sweet-water's is a happening place: cash goes through there by the truckload. Word on the street is that it's used for money laundering by the mob. And Rand Corporation is owned by—want to guess who?—John Sidney Carlson the Third. In other words, Sid's dad. John Sidney Carlson the Second—Sid's grandfather—was chairman emeritus up until he died."

"You think Sid's father and grandfather are involved in money laundering? For the *mob?*" Julie stared up at him incredulously. Imagining Sid and his family as a southern-fried version of the Sopranos was mind-boggling. "That's ridiculous."

Mac shook his head. "No, it isn't. I don't have all the i's dotted and t's crossed yet. I haven't had time. But I think Rand Corporation and its offshoots—in other words, Sid and his father and grandfather, going back I don't know how many generations—are fronts for organized crime. I think they're into drug smuggling, gun running, gambling, protection rackets, money laundering, the whole bit. And I think anyone who gets in their way ends up dead."

"Are you saying that I'm in their way?"

"Did you know that there has never been a divorce in the Carlson family?"

Julie blinked at the non sequitur. "That's a sign of organized crime?"

"That's a sign of real bad luck for women who marry into the Carlson family. There's never been a divorce, but there've been lots of remarriages. The Carlsons' wives tend to die."

Julie gaped at him. Then, as she thought about it, her heart started to thud. The eerie truth of it hit her like a brick. John had been married twice before he'd apparently decided to limit himself to girlfriends. Sid had said his mother had been hit by a car when he was three; John's second wife had drowned.

Another equally scary idea flashed into her mind. Carlene had been hit by a car. Her own father had drowned. Julie's blood ran cold. It was a coincidence. It had to be. But—

"When I was a little girl, my father would sometimes do work for a company called Rand Corporation." Her voice was constricted.

Mac stared down at her with a slowly gathering frown. "He did? When?"

"I don't know—when I was seven or eight, maybe. He and my mother were divorced by then, but he would come by sometimes and give her his paycheck to pay for things for Becky and me. The checks were drawn on the Rand Corporation. I remember the name, because Becky and I were greedy to know everything we could about him. He didn't come around much."

She didn't think her tone revealed her pain, but something must have given her away, because his lips compressed. His eyes darkened on her face. He was holding both her arms now, and his grip tightened as if he would draw her closer.

"Julie . . ."

"Oh no you don't!" Julie remembered the old saying *Fool me once, shame on you, fool me twice, shame on me* with some force, and pulled out of his arms. Maybe his warning had merit and maybe it didn't, but she wasn't going to just take his word for anything anymore. "You've lied to me since I first met you. Why the hell should I start believing you now?"

He started to reply, but before he could say anything a light on the small porch of her mother's house blinked on. Her mother stepped out onto the porch.

"Julie! Julie, is that you?" She peered toward where Julie stood talking to Mac at the edge of the front yard just beyond the reach of the light. Her red hair was twisted onto pink foam curlers in preparation for bed, and she wore a knee-length flowered robe and slippers.

"Yes, Mama," she called. Her mother came to the edge of the porch, shading her eyes from the light with her hand.

"Are you all right?"

"I'm fine."

"Who's that with you?"

"Nobody, Mama." Then, to Mac, Julie said in a much quieter voice that was nevertheless strong with conviction, "I *don't* believe you. Not a single word. I don't know what you're up to, but whatever it is I don't want any part of it. Go away and leave me alone. I mean it."

"Julie, for God's sake . . ." Mac began, only to be drowned out by Dixie, who was coming down the steps.

"That is too somebody. Land sakes, Julie, it's not the man who punched Sid in the nose, is it?"

Julie almost groaned aloud. Trust the family's jungle drums. "Who told you that?"

Not waiting for an answer, she started walking quickly across the front yard toward her mother, and at the same time hissed at Mac over her shoulder. "Leave. Now."

"Becky told me. Kenny told her. Sid's secretary—Heidi whosit—told Kenny. She knew because she had to meet Sid at the airport with a fresh shirt because the one he was wearing had blood all over it and he told her that you had a lover who attacked him." Dixie's voice grew shrill with indignation on that last part. " 'Course, I didn't believe *that.*"

"Oh, did Sid go ahead and go to Atlanta after all?" Julie felt a degree of relief at the idea that at least one of her problems was out of the way for a few days.

"I guess he did, but that's not the point. The point is he's going around saying you have a *lover.*"

Dixie was quivering with indignation as they met at the foot of the steps. Putting an arm around her mother's shoulders, Julie determinedly steered her back up them. A quick glance back at Mac told her that he was still standing beside the Blazer watching them, making no attempt to go away. Gritting her teeth, she tried to push him and his crazy-making warnings from her mind.

"Mama, there's no easy way to say this." As they reached the level surface of the porch, she took a deep breath and decided to go for it. "I'm getting a divorce."

If she'd been looking for something to distract her mother from Mac's presence—and she had—she couldn't have found a better topic.

Her mother gave a little gasp. Both hands flew up to cover her mouth.

"Oh, my God, Julie! Why? *Why?*" There was the tiniest pause, while Dixie's eyes fixed on Julie's face with growing horror. "Was Sid telling the truth? I can't believe it! Never say you really do have a lover?"

"Have you ever thought that maybe she takes after you, Mama?" Becky opened the screen door to admit them, fixing their mother with a stern look. "How many lovers have you had? I bet you've lost count. Julie's allowed to have *one.*"

"Thanks, Beck," Julie said dispiritedly, realizing that her truly horrible day was about to keep on keeping on. She didn't know why she was surprised at Becky's presence—her mother was a great believer in double-teaming. If she'd been thinking straight, she would have *known* that Becky would be at her mother's house waiting for her. "Is Kenny watching the girls?"

"Yeah. He's pretty upset. Says this could cost him his job." Becky grinned teasingly at her. "Whoever would have thunk it—my perfect little sister with a lover. Way to go, Jules—you're making me look good."

"Shut up, Becky."

"Listen to me, Julie Ann." Dixie pulled her the rest of the way inside the house and shut the door. "Just because you have a lover doesn't mean you have to get a divorce. With a little work, I just know you and Sid can patch this up. . . ."

Julie sighed, allowed herself to be drawn into the kitchen where all their family pow-wows seemed to take place, and resigned herself: It was going to be a long night.

26

AFTER HOURS SPENT *NOT* SLEEPING in the increasingly cramped front seat of his SUV, Mac was beyond grumpy. All through the night, he'd kept watch over the house where Julie slept; via his cell phone, he'd sent Hinkle and Rawanda and Mother and just about everyone else he knew scurrying to round up information fast; and he'd done everything from taking Josephine on brisk walks around the property's perimeter to jumping jacks to remain alert. The night had passed undisturbed, except for the poodle's maddeningly frequent urge to pee and her determined destruction of a motley assortment of items he'd stored for possible later use in the backseat. What he needed most by dawn's early light was a shower and a cup of coffee, not necessarily in that order. What he got, instead, was the sight of Julie emerging from her mother's house, dressed in bicycle shorts and an oversized pink T-shirt with some kind of cartoon character on it, her hair in a ponytail and sneakers on her feet.

The mere sight of her made his heart speed up. And not just from the dazzling effect of her beauty on all his salient male parts, although that was there in the mix, too. What really got his heart going was pure, unadulterated fear.

She was, obviously, going for a run. Alone. From the spot behind the overgrown honeysuckle hedge where he had resituated the Blazer after she'd gone inside with her mother, Mac watched with utter disbelief as she ran down the steps and across the yard, then set off down the sidewalk at a brisk pace. Either the woman hadn't believed a single word he'd said, or she had a death wish.

Or both.

He said a few choice words under his breath as he sprang out of the Blazer, glanced at Josephine, who was stretched out sound asleep on her back, paws flapping in the air, amid the destruction in the backseat, obviously exhausted by her active night, and set off after Julie. The neighborhood was semi-rural, a quiet enclave of ranch-style homes on well-tended half-acre lots about five miles to the north of Summerville proper. He knew the area fairly well: it was a nice enough one, inhabited mostly by retirees and empty-nesters looking to downsize. A glance at his watch told him that it was twenty-six minutes after seven A.M. Most of these people—the intelligent ones, anyway—would still be in bed. One old lady came out on her porch to retrieve her newspaper as Mac jogged past. He waved at her. She scowled at him suspiciously.

He already knew that they didn't cotton much to strangers around these parts. He'd once done a background check on the daughter of a woman who lived in the area, and it had been like pulling hen's teeth to get the neighbors to talk to him.

It would be an ideal place for a hit. Few witnesses. Easy access to the expressway.

Just pull up beside her and *blam,* blow her away.

Mac's blood ran cold at the thought.

Up ahead, Julie turned the corner, still running at a steady pace and sticking to the sidewalk. He eyed her slender figure with growing wrath. She hadn't betrayed the least awareness of him, and as he got a good view of her profile—delicate features, swinging ponytail, bouncing breasts, long, limber legs—he saw why: She was wearing a Walkman.

An army division could have been running behind her in full combat gear and she wouldn't have heard. To a professional killer with a job to finish, taking her out would be a piece of cake.

Disgusted, he decided to show her just how vulnerable to a surprise attack she was. He increased his pace until he was right behind her and gave her ponytail a tug.

She spun, screeching, and thrust her hand in his direction as she danced backward. Before he realized what was happening, he found himself on the business end of a can of—was it Mace?

It was. Before he could react, the mist hit

his eyes like a flamethrower. The instant burning made him think of hellfire. He bellowed in surprise and pain, clawing at his face, his eyes, bending double, scrubbing at his face with the end of his shirt, all to no avail.

He was going to be burned, scarred, blinded for life. At least, that was how it felt. He knew, *knew,* that Mace hurt like hell but left no permanent aftereffects. There was faint comfort in the knowledge when his face felt like it was melting and his eyes felt like someone had stuck hot pokers deep in the sockets.

"Damn it, Julie!" It was a groan of agony.

"Mac! Oh, Mac! Oh, Mac!" Her hand was on his shoulder, the top of his head, his arm. He got the impression that she was bending over him, peering into his face, but he couldn't be sure because he couldn't see. "I'm so sorry! I thought you were the hit man."

Then the horror in her voice gave way to—was it a giggle? Yes, it was. A whole infuriating string of them. Seconds later she was talking through them to someone—he couldn't quite make out what was being said, or who the newcomer was, although the voice sounded male. Still bent almost double, staggering around like a blind, drunken hunchback, Mac felt stark fear override even the pain. She had rendered him—her supposed protector—all but helpless, and now, right at the worst possible moment, here came some unknown guy. Was it the hit man? Not likely. If it had been, she would have been dead by now, and so probably would he. Professional killers didn't usually hang about exchanging conversation with their giggling victims. Desperate to see who had accosted her, Mac scrubbed at his face with a different portion of his shirt, and managed to open his swollen, burning eyes a slit.

Just in time to get hit in the face with a burst of cold water so strong it could have been shot from a cannon. Julie had found a hose, complete with water and a little old man who had apparently brought it to her, and turned it on him.

"Oh, Jesus!" Stumbling backward, Mac tried to protect his face as the water caused the burning to intensify exponentially.

"Here, you do it," Julie said, thrusting the

hose into his hand. "I want to finish my run."

"You stay right here. Do you hear me?" It was a barked order, uttered as his fingers closed blindly around the pulsing rubber tube. He grabbed for her with his free hand, but couldn't find her. But at least she was nearby. He could hear her still chuckling at his plight. Did she have no clue as to how much danger she was in? Obviously not. If he could just get the stuff out of his eyes, he thought frantically, they'd be all right. Remembering his police training on Mace—no matter how much it hurt, water was the preferred vehicle for flushing it from the eyes—he tried angling the hose up so that the onslaught would not be as extreme and pulling his lids apart with his free hand at the same time so that the falling water could run into them, and groaned as he succeeded. Cold torrent or no, his eyes burned like be-damned.

"I saw how this fellow was chasing you before you squirted him. You want I should call the police?" The old guy was brandishing a cell phone and talking to Julie, and from his tone Mac supposed he should consider himself lucky the guy didn't have his own can of Mace.

Mac managed another look to find that the man, who appeared to be about as old as Methuselah, was wearing belted, baggy shorts that ended just above his knobby knees, a striped, tucked-in sport shirt, black socks, and dress shoes. He was standing shoulder to shoulder with Julie, phone at the ready. Both of them were watching Mac's suffering without a trace of sympathy that he could detect, although his vision was admittedly still pretty blurry.

"No. Oh, no." Julie laughed again—thus dispelling Mac's last hope that maybe there was some sympathy there he just was not picking up on—as Mac soaked the end of his shirt and scrubbed it one more time over his burning face. "I'm sure he's learned his lesson. Thanks for your help."

Then, to Mac's combined horror and disbelief, she turned on her heel and took off again, continuing her run with the same blithe disregard for her continued existence that had caused the whole fiasco in the first place.

"Damn it, Julie, come back here!" he yelled after her, blinking and squinting at her retreating figure, knowing that he was in no condition to follow. But, except for an airy wave that was scarcely more than a blur to his traumatized eyes, she paid no attention at all. Instead, she restored the headphones to their previous position over her ears and picked up the pace until she turned another corner and disappeared from sight.

"Damn it to *hell.*" But there was no help for it. He couldn't see well enough to go chasing after her. She was on her own.

By the time he made it back to the Blazer some fifteen minutes later, he was having waking nightmares about what might have befallen her. To add to the fun, his face and eyes felt like they'd been stung by about a thousand jellyfish, his clothes were dripping wet and icy cold, and he was being harangued from behind by Julie's would-be protector, who had followed him suspiciously all the way back to the car. As a consequence, he was mad as hell.

He was also just in time to watch Julie sprint up the steps of her mother's house and disappear safely inside. At that point, he didn't know whether to be glad or sorry. If the hit man had taken her out, at least he would have been saved the trouble of later wringing her neck.

The old man's cell phone started ringing, distracting him from his determined pursuit. Mac took advantage of the opportunity to jerk open the driver's door, meaning to collapse on the front seat and close and lock the door before the old guy could start in on him again. To his amazement, a snarling Josephine leaped past him like a fuzzy white missile and proceeded to commit felonious assault upon the now screaming old gentleman's bare, bony shin.

It cost him five hundred dollars, a look at Josephine's license—thank God the pink collar to which it was attached was still in the backseat—and a couple of Band-Aids from the glove compartment to make *that* go away.

Hanging grimly on to Josephine, wondering if she was (a) rabid despite having been vaccinated, or (b) just plain insane, Mac at last got rid of the now-raving old man and sank down in the Blazer's front seat for a badly needed period of R and R.

"What were you *thinking?*" This he addressed to Josephine, who was now sitting in the passenger seat beside him, once again daintily feminine in her favorite pink-and-rhinestone collar. She wagged her tail and looked innocent, clearly hoping to convince the unwary that she hadn't just tried to chew off a helpless old man's leg. Mac thanked God that she was a seven-pound poodle instead of a rottweiler, realized that he was talking to the dog as if she could understand him and, furthermore, reply, and dropped his head back against the seat in despair. He was the one who was losing his marbles, he decided. No, not losing. Had lost.

Out of the corner of his eye, Mac saw a white blur drive past. A horn honked. A hand waved.

Julie.

He sat up in time to watch the white Infiniti disappear around the corner.

Swearing a blue streak, he started the Blazer, did a one-eighty, and took off after her, despite a sudden, fleeting temptation just to leave her to the tender mercies of the hit man he was pretty damn sure was out there.

Not much to his surprise, she drove into Summerville and pulled up in the parking lot behind the strip mall that housed her shop. The one in which people who were not trying to keep their presence in her life a secret generally parked.

To hell with it. He figured that cat was out of the bag with a vengeance now anyway. As he slammed to a halt beside the Infiniti, he watched her walk across the parking lot toward one of the brown metal doors set into the back of the low brick building. She looked cool and beautiful—hell, when did she ever not?—in a snug black T-shirt and a teensy white skirt with her hair falling loose around her shoulders. There were a few other people in the lot—a man heading toward another of the metal doors, a woman carrying a garbage bag toward the Dumpster—but to all intents and purposes she was alone.

If he were a hit man, she'd be toast.

Fortunately for her, he was not. He grabbed Josephine—it was already too hot to leave her in the car with the motor turned off—tucked her football-style under his arm, and sprinted across the parking lot after Julie.

He reached her just as she was inserting her key into the lock of the metal door. The tension in her stance told him that she'd seen him coming. The tilt of her head told him that she didn't like it.

"What are you, a slow learner?" She gave him an evil look that was mitigated somewhat by the sheer beauty of those long-lashed Bambi eyes. "Leave me alone." Her gaze flicked down to the poodle, which was wriggling with pleasure at seeing her. "Hello, Josephine."

Josephine yapped excitedly and tried beating him to death with her tail.

"You two *should* be buddies," Mac said sourly. "You're both major pains in the ass. Now that you've had your fun for the morning, you feel like listening to my side of the story?"

"Take a hike." She got the door open, stepped inside, and tried closing it in his face. He snorted and strong-armed his way through.

"Okay, forget it. I lied to you and I used you. If that's going to be the bottom line for you, it's fine by me."

He was standing in an office, he discovered as he set Josephine down on the carpeted floor, that was dark and pleasant-smelling and approximately as cold as

Antartica in winter. Julie's face tightened as she looked at him, but she seemed to realize, rightly, that ordering him out would be a waste of breath because she closed and locked the door again, then turned to glare at him.

"Good. Then we're both happy. Or at least, I would be if you'd get the hell out of my shop."

"Not happening."

Mac walked a couple of paces into the room, casting wary looks around. Mirrors everywhere. A shiny black desk with nothing on it except a desk set and a telephone. A silver rack half-full of dresses. A gray flannel couch.

"It's freezing in here."

"If you're cold, it's probably because you're all wet." Her tone gave that a double meaning which she obviously relished.

He returned from a quick inspection of the bathroom that opened off the office to look at her.

"And I would be all wet because somebody Maced me."

Julie gave an unrepentant laugh as she crossed to her desk. "You shouldn't have scared me."

"Listen, Miss America, can you say hit man?" Her cavalier attitude was really beginning to irk him.

"No, but I can say bullshit." She straightened up from tucking her purse under the desk and gave him a great big go-to-hell smile. "And that's what I do say: bullshit, bullshit, bullshit."

"You willing to bet your life you're right?" Now that her office had been awarded the all-clear, Mac glanced around for the thermostat. If he didn't get that air-conditioner shut off soon, it was going to kill him. "Remember the guy who broke into your house? Remember the girl who got hit by a car while wearing *your* dress in front of *your* store last night? What are they, figments of my imagination?"

There was a pause. Julie stared at him without speaking. Then her lips pursed, and she glanced away.

Hah, Mac thought. He was finally getting through. He spotted the thermostat on the wall nearby and stepped over to it, turning the little knob until the blast of arctic air abruptly stopped.

"Leave the air-conditioning alone," Julie said, coming up behind him and smacking his hand away from the control, then turning the knob the other way again so that refrigerator-caliber air once again blasted from the vents. "I have clients coming. If you're cold, I have a simple remedy for you: leave."

"Keep sweet-talking me like that, and you may never get rid of me." He abandoned his surreptitious repeat attack on the knob to grab her around the waist and swing her back behind him when she would have walked out into the main area of the store. "Hold it right there."

"Let go of me! What do you think you're doing?" She glared at him as she whisked herself free of his hold.

"Besides forming icicles?" Drawing his gun from its berth in the small of his back—which was, thankfully, one of the few remaining dry areas on his body—he moved into the large, elegant room ahead of her, scanning it for any sign of disturbance or unauthorized occupancy, checking behind racks of dresses and a large potted palm and a pair of gray flannel chairs for an intruder. "Doing my best to keep you alive. Without any noticeable help from you, I might add. Is that front door locked?"

"Of course it's locked. I haven't opened up yet."

"Keep it that way. Only open it to people you know."

A beat passed during which she just looked at him.

"You're being ridiculous."

Without answering, he headed toward the back rooms—fitting rooms, he discovered, three of them, large and elegantly appointed and paneled in floor-to-ceiling mirrors. Julie, with Josephine at her heels, followed. Both watched his efforts with heads cocked in a way that was purely feminine.

"No hit man?" Julie's voice was sardonic as he emerged from the last of the fitting rooms.

"Not so far."

"I can't tell you how much that relieves my mind." She glared at him. "Now that you've made sure there's no bogeyman under the bed, you can get out of my shop. I have a business to run here, and you are in the way."

"What I can't understand," Mac said, ignoring that last speech entirely as he moved back into the main room where the blast from the air-conditioning was at least distributed over a larger area, somewhat lessening its effect, "is why you're here today at all. Shouldn't you close up shop for a while as a sign of respect to the dearly departed?"

Julie's brow wrinkled, and a flash of pain darkened her eyes. "I thought about closing, but I talked to the Miss Southern Beauty officials last night. The pageant will go ahead as scheduled. They mean to have a moment of silence during the opening ceremony tomorrow to honor Carlene, but otherwise there's no change. And I'm dressing seven other girls. Five of them are scheduled to come in for final wardrobe fittings today. If the pageant's on, I have no choice but to be here."

"I don't believe this." Trying not to shiver, Mac shook his head in complete and total frustration. "I'm talking about somebody trying to kill you here, and you're talking about a beauty pageant. Let's try to get a handle on our priorities, shall we? What we need to do is get you the hell out of Dodge. Lie low somewhere out of state, maybe, until we get some answers. Forget the damned beauty pageant."

"No," Julie said, fists on hips as she scowled at him. "I won't forget it. This is my business. And those girls are counting on me. Anyway, please explain to me exactly why I need you, because I don't have a clue. Let's just say, for a moment, that you're right about this hit-man thing. If I really thought I was in danger, I'd run to the police so fast you wouldn't see me for the blur."

"And they'd be real polite, and write up a nice little report, and that would be that." Mac's voice was flat. "Until you were dead. *Then* they might start an investigation. But, oopsy, too late for you."

Julie's eyes shot sparks at that. Mac supposed that his words hadn't been all that tactful, but he was tired and wet and cold and his eyes burned and her attitude was not only driving him totally around the bend, it was dangerous. For her.

And it bothered him a whole hell of a lot to realize that anything that was dangerous for her scared the socks off him.

"You know what?" she said with that little clenched-teeth smile he was beginning to know way better than he wanted to. "I'm prepared to take my chances. So you can just go away. You know, leave. Vamoose. Scram. Shoo. Whichever one of those works for you."

He returned her unflinching stare for unflinching stare, then took a calming minute to return his gun to its accustomed position inside his waistband. She could lose her temper all she wanted to, he told himself. He was going to keep his.

Then at least one of them would be operating with a full order of french fries. "Give it up, Julie," he said tiredly. "I'm not going anywhere. At least, not without you. You want to know why you need me? Because, whether you believe it or not, I'm pretty sure your life is in danger here. Which means you need somebody watching out for you, and from where I'm standing, darlin', it looks like I'm all you've got."

27

BY SEVEN P.M., JULIE WAS SO TIRED her eyes felt grainy. Tara Lumley was the last of her clients, and her handler had wanted some eleventh-hour beading added to her aqua evening gown. With Carlene out of the picture—a fact every single girl had bemoaned, right down to the shedding of tears, even while they schemed how best to take advantage of the loss of the widely acknowledged favorite—the pageant had been blown wide open. It was a free-for-all, and Tara wanted to do everything she could to catch the judges' eyes. They all did.

In consequence, Julie sewed and stuffed

and whittled and trimmed as she never had before in her life.

"You'll be there tomorrow night, won't you, Julie?" Tara asked anxiously as Julie let her and Linda Wheeler, her handler, out the front door, which, to pacify Mac, she'd kept locked at the cost of great inconvenience to clients and staff alike all day.

"I'll be there for the duration. Don't worry, you're going to do great." She hugged Tara, and Linda, then watched them walk out into the still-bright evening.

"Like hell you will," Mac said, appearing in the doorway between the showroom and the office, where he had spent most of the day alternately talking on the phone and using her computer, just as she walked past it. He was wearing a fresh pair of jeans and a plain black T-shirt that he'd had his assistant, Rawanda, bring him early that morning, and he looked so handsome that the girls had fluttered at the sight of him. Several had asked her covertly who he was when he had disappeared back into her office again after the cursory visual check he subjected all arrivals and departures to. Julie had told them that he was a visiting dress designer who went by the name of

Debbie, and had taken perverse satisfaction in watching their faces fall.

"What?" Julie stopped and glared at him. She was getting tired of this master-of-the-universe thing he'd had going on all day.

"I said, you're not going to that beauty pageant." Mac returned her glare with stony-eyed determination. His eyes were bloodshot, and there were lines she'd never noticed before around them and his mouth. In addition, his disposition had been deteriorating steadily all day. "Everybody and his mother expects you to be there. Let's try to at least make the guy who's trying to kill you work hard to earn his money, okay?"

Julie simmered. "I've got a news flash for you, bubba: You don't tell me what to do. Anyway, I've been thinking: Exactly *why* is Sid supposed to want to kill me? It can't be over money: I signed a prenup. It can't be because I made the colossal mistake of sleeping with you: He didn't know about that until just a couple of minutes before that car hit Carlene. Are you suggesting he wants to kill me just so he won't have to endure the trauma of divorce? Sorry, I don't buy it. So what's your rationale here?"

Mac's lips compressed. "I don't know exactly yet."

Julie made a derisive sound. "That's what I thought."

"Julie, what time do you want me in the morning?" Meredith emerged from the dressing room where she'd been tidying up. She couldn't have heard their conversation—it had been conducted in little more than hissed whispers—but she must have sensed the atmosphere between them, because she stopped in the doorway and looked self-consciously from Julie to Mac and back. "Oh, sorry, I didn't mean to interrupt."

"You're not interrupting," Julie said with a sigh, pointedly turning her back on Mac to smile at Meredith. Her head ached from doing so much close work with her needle—those bugle beads were tiny, and the design Tara had wanted had required hundreds—and she massaged the area just above her nose with a forefinger. "There are no appointments tomorrow, so why don't you just plan to meet me in the auditorium tomorrow night? Be a little early, in case any of the girls' gowns need work."

Meredith smiled. "I'm so excited. I've never been to the governor's mansion before."

"It should be fun."

Mac still stood in the doorway, silently smoldering, and Julie glared at him while Meredith went to retrieve her purse.

"I'm going now," Meredith said, returning with her purse tucked under her arm. Julie wasn't sure how much Meredith actually knew about what was going on, but obviously she knew that Amber was no longer there—Julie had left a message on Amber's answering machine firing her when she didn't come in again that morning—and something major was up. If nothing else, Sid had called twice and both times Julie had refused to take his calls, which she never did; and Mac's largely silent but impossible to overlook presence all day was a dead giveaway. But she hadn't asked any questions, and Julie appreciated that.

Now Meredith glanced from Julie to Mac and back, then seemed to hesitate. "Uh,

Julie—do you need me to stay? Are you going to be all right?"

"I'll be fine. You go on," Julie said, while Mac, obviously knowing when he was being insulted, however subtly, leaned one shoulder against the jamb, crossed his arms over his chest, and looked sardonic.

"See you tomorrow night, then," Meredith said.

"Thanks for all your hard work today." Julie walked her to the door and smiled at her as she left. She was glad to see that Meredith was looking slightly reassured as she set off down the sidewalk.

"You will not," Mac said, scowling, as Julie locked the door and turned back into the room, "see her tomorrow night."

"Want to bet?" Julie smiled sweetly as she walked toward him.

"Oh, yeah."

"Excuse me." The words were pointed, because he still blocked the doorway to her office as she reached it. He didn't move, and she had perforce to stop, glaring at him. He met her gaze with a meditative expression.

"Know what I've been doing today?"

"Besides being a total jackass and guzzling enough coffee to float the ark?" Julie asked. "No clue."

"I've been checking payroll records for Rand Corporation."

"What? How?"

Mac held up his hand. His key ring dangled from a finger.

"With this." He touched a black spark-plug-looking thing that hung on the ring with the keys. "I used it to download files off your computer yesterday. Sid's business records make interesting reading."

"Aren't you the sneaky one!" Julie marveled, punching him none-too-gently in the stomach and then, as he stepped back with an *ooph* and rubbed his belly in reaction, shoving past him into her office. "But I must say that it's a nice change to hear you actually *admitting* that you used me to get information on Sid."

"I am not admitting . . ."

Julie interrupted ruthlessly. "Know what? I don't care."

Silenced, Mac eyed her in exasperation as she retrieved her purse from under the desk. Josephine, who was stretched out beside Julie's purse, looked up and wagged her tail inquiringly. The poodle was once again wearing her sparkly pink collar, and looked adorable. Like Mac, she had been a big hit with the girls.

"Time to go home," Julie said to her, straightening, purse in hand.

"Your father received a steady paycheck from the Rand Corporation until fifteen years ago. Then it stopped. The same month as Kelly Carlson disappeared. The same month as . . ."

"Will you stop?" Julie headed for the door. "Enough with the conspiracy theories already. I'm tired, I'm hungry, and I've got a headache. For your information, I believe that Lee Harvey Oswald acted alone. I believe that Princess Diana's car crash was an accident. And I believe that you've gone totally out of your mind."

She jerked open the door and looked pointedly at him. "And now, would you please walk out this door so I can lock up?"

Mac gave her a narrow-eyed look, then snapped his fingers for Josephine. The poodle appeared, stretching and yawning luxuriously, and Mac scooped her up.

"Too bad you're not more like your dog," Julie said as Mac walked past her into the soft bright warmth of the summer evening. *"She's* a sweetheart. You're a sweetheart, Josephine."

Josephine wagged her tail.

"So what do you want for dinner?" Mac asked as she finished locking the door and turned to find him waiting.

"Are you suggesting that you and I might be going to have a mutual dinner? Not a chance." After taking a careful look around—not that she really, truly *believed* Mac's nonsense, mind you, but it had raised just enough doubt in her mind to make her slightly paranoid and, anyway, she couldn't get Carlene's awful fate out of her mind—Julie headed toward her car.

Mac and Josephine fell in beside her. "If you don't feel like eating, fine. You can watch me."

"I'm having dinner with my mother. She's cooking. She's still very upset because I'm getting a divorce. She needs to vent." Just the thought made Julie feel gloomy. She was going to hear about the folly of divorcing Sid for approximately the next hundred years.

"Call her and tell her you have other plans."

Mac obviously had never dealt with her mother.

"No." But the idea was tempting. Oh, so tempting. She was so not in the mood to be harangued.

Julie reached the protection of the Infiniti's back end and stopped between it and the Blazer. If there did happen to be more to Mac's hit-man theory than hot air, at least she wasn't going to get run over if she could help it.

The image of Carlene somersaulting over the roof of the car that killed her had replayed itself in her mind every time she had closed her eyes. As a result, she'd been awake most of the night. If Mac was right, that should have been her. The thought made her shiver. Maybe she *should* go to the police. Only Mac had said they wouldn't be able to keep her safe. . . .

"Okay, here's the . . ." *deal,* she started to say, but broke off as Mac handed her Josephine then dropped to his hands and knees on the pavement. While she watched, astonished, he peered underneath the Blazer.

"What are you doing?"

He took his sweet time looking, then rose

lithely to his feet, dusting off his hands and knees and retrieving Josephine from her. "Checking for bombs."

"Oh, my God." Julie rolled her eyes.

That was it. This was getting bizarre. And scary. She hated to admit it, but it was also getting very scary. She didn't know which part was scarier, though: the idea that Mac was insane, or the idea that he wasn't. In any case, she was going to the police—right after she had dinner with her mother.

"If you're planning to follow me out to my mother's again tonight, you can just forget it." Her voice was tart. She scowled at him.

"You don't have to worry. I'm not."

He opened the Blazer's back door and deposited Josephine inside. Closing that door, he opened the front passenger door and did something to the inner panel. Then he looked at her.

"Get in."

"*What?* No."

Julie turned to the Infiniti. Before she could punch the button that unlocked the door, he gave an unamused sounding laugh and scooped her up from behind.

"What are you doing? Put me down!"

She kicked wildly. She would have

punched him, but her arms were trapped by his.

Without replying, he stuffed her into the front seat of the Blazer with practiced efficiency and shut the door on her. As he walked around to the other side, Julie immediately tried to get out. The door wouldn't open. She realized with a burst of fury that he had depressed the tiny button on the inner panel of the door that activated the childproof locks.

"What the hell do you think you're doing?" Snarling, she turned on him with clenched fists as he slid inside. "You let me out!"

"Put your seat belt on," he said, and started the car, backing up in a smooth arc.

"I am not going anywhere with you! Nowhere, do you hear? I knew it all along: you're a dangerous lunatic! This is kidnapping, you no-good, lying . . ." Left groping for words bad enough to describe him, she grabbed for the keys, which were dangling from the ignition, instead.

"Oh no you don't." He caught her hand, slamming on the brake at the same time. The Blazer screeched to a halt in the middle of the parking lot. Removing her hand from the keys but keeping his hold on it, Mac turned on her. His expression was grim.

"Just so there's no mistake," he said in a lethal drawl that left her in no doubt that he teetered on the brink of losing his temper, too, "I think you should know that I'm having a bad day here. I didn't get any sleep last night. I got Maced this morning. I got soaked with a hose. I'm starving. I may be suffering from an overdose of caffeine. This damned case is a riddle, and I've got a pounding headache from trying to solve it. I think I'm catching a cold, thanks to your air-conditioning. I've spent the entire day in a dress shop listening to a gaggle of women think up ways to fool us poor men about the size of every female body part under the sun. And I've had to put up with your piss-poor attitude throughout. Tonight I have a ton of work I have to do, and I also need food and sleep. None of these things can happen while I'm chasing around the countryside after you. Which means that you're coming with me. And I don't want to hear another word about it. Am I making myself clear here?"

"If I don't show up for supper, my mother

will call the police," Julie said, snatching her hand from his.

"Told her about Sid's take on *till death do us part,* did you?"

He took his foot off the brake. The Blazer was moving once more.

"If by that you mean, did I tell her about your ridiculous idea that Sid's hired a hit man to kill me, no, I did not. I didn't want to worry her."

They were on the street now, moving toward the expressway. Glowering at Mac, Julie pulled on her seat belt. It would be stupid to die in an accident just to prove she could.

"Did you ever think that you might be endangering your family by being with them? Whoever our hit man is, he's obviously not all that careful about who he kills. If they're with you when he comes for you, he might get your mother or sister too—or instead."

The thought was so appalling that Julie was left with nothing to say.

"Give me your phone." Her voice was sulky.

He passed it to her. She shot him a look chock-full of loathing. Then she punched in the number.

"Mama? It's Julie. I'm not going to make it home for supper. I'll talk to you later. Love you. Bye." She punched the disconnect button and puffed out her cheeks in a relieved sigh. "I got the answering machine, thank goodness."

"Does your mother scare you that much?" Mac sounded amused.

"She'll scare you too," Julie said with relish. "She blames you for ruining my marriage, and nothing I say can convince her otherwise. She wants to meet you."

"She sounds about as amenable to reason as you."

Josephine chose that moment to climb into Julie's lap. Distracted, Julie scratched behind her ears, then stroked her coat as she settled down with obvious contentment. Thank God for Josephine. Josephine was better for the nerves than Valium.

"So, what do you want for dinner?" Mac asked with a half-smile after a moment.

Julie scowled at him. "My mother's tuna casserole."

"Great. I feel like pizza, too. That way I can eat while I work."

He picked up his cell phone and punched in some numbers.

"McQuarry and Hinkle." Julie had heard that voice before. She realized that it belonged to Rawanda, Mac's assistant.

"Order pizza. One with everything, and one with—" Mac glanced at Julie inquiringly.

"Vegetarian," she said, only because she was really hungry and feared what she would be forced to eat if she didn't. Pizza was way too fattening to be one of her diet staples. Pizza was also right up there with chocolate as one of her true loves.

"Veggies only," he repeated into the phone, and hung up.

They were on the expressway now, heading toward Charleston. Traffic was moderate. In the distance, a mountain of purple clouds rolling in over the bay promised rain later. Rain was a good thing, because it would usually cool things off for a few hours. It was also a bad thing, because after the initial relief the humidity would only get worse.

Julie said nothing for the duration of the drive, and Mac, after a glance at her face, didn't say anything either. When he finally parked, it was in an alley that ran through the middle of a block of small, not especially prosperous-looking office buildings.

"Now be nice," he said. "These people are putting themselves at risk to help keep you safe."

Julie glared at him. "I'm always nice. Unless I'm lied to. Or lied to and used. I have to admit, that tends to take away from my nice."

Mac laughed, and got out of the car.

When he came around to her side, Julie, holding Josephine, got out too. She didn't seem to have much choice.

"Let her down for a minute," he said, scrounging in the back and coming up with Josephine's leash, which he clipped to her collar. "It seemed like she had to go every five minutes last night, and I'd just as soon not have a repeat."

Julie obediently put Josephine on the ground. She held on to the leash and Mac held on to her with a hand wrapped around her wrist as if he was afraid she might take off running.

"Where are we going, anyway?"

"To my office. I've had people working on this since yesterday. I need to check in, see what they've found out."

Mac steered her back to the street, around a corner, and across a parking lot toward the third in a row of four nondescript buildings.

"Why didn't you just park in the lot?" Her high-heeled slides weren't meant for lengthy hikes.

"I thought you might feel like getting some exercise." He grinned at the look on her face. "Actually, I parked back there so that no one could tell we're inside from just driving by. Rest easy, though: By the time we're ready to leave, there will be a vehicle waiting for us right out front. Mother's dropping us off some new wheels. The Blazer's history for the duration."

"How convenient to know a car thief."

"It is, isn't it?"

Mac's office was on the second floor, behind a wooden door with a frosted-glass insert on which was painted in bold black script MCQUARRY AND HINKLE, PRIVATE INVESTIGATORS. The door opened as they reached it, and, glancing inside, Julie realized that its windows overlooked the parking lot and they must have been seen arriving.

"Did you time that right or what? Pizza just got here." Rawanda, looking plumply pretty in tight orange jeans and a purple T-shirt, greeted them at the door. "Whoa, boss, you lookin' rough. What you been doin' to him, honey?"

"For one thing, she kept me up all night," Mac replied as he ushered Julie inside, then grinned in response to Julie's outraged look. George Hinkle, neatly casual in a white polo shirt and dark slacks, looked up from where he was working at a computer on a desk near the door and nodded at her.

"Hey, Mac. Mrs. Carlson." There was a fair amount of reserve in his tone as he greeted her, and Julie remembered that he'd been upset about Mac's association with her. He didn't look any happier about it tonight. Which was fine with her. She wasn't sure how happy she was about it herself.

"Please call me Julie," she said, then made a wry face. "I'm about to lose the Carlson, anyway. I'm getting a divorce."

"We heard that," Rawanda said, shaking her head in commiseration. "Divorce is a bitch. I've done had two. Didn't make me a dime out of either one, either."

"You didn't tell me you'd had *two*."

Hinkle frowned at Rawanda, who looked self-conscious. Clearly there was a relationship between them—of which Mac, who was moving toward the pizza boxes a step ahead of Josephine, seemed to disapprove, if his expression was anything to go by.

"Uh, I might just have forgotten to mention one." Rawanda's gaze swung to Julie. "You want some pizza? No need to let the boss hog it all."

"Um, just one slice," Julie said, following Rawanda as the other woman headed toward where Mac was opening the pizza boxes. A heavenly smell reached Julie's nostrils, making her stomach growl. She realized that, between stress and the press of work, she hadn't eaten anything all day except a glass of orange juice at her mother's that morning and a pair of stray Hershey's Kisses found at the bottom of her work basket at the shop.

"Here." Mac put a slice of vegetarian pizza on a napkin and passed it to her. A six-pack of Coke had obviously come with the pizza, and he handed her a can. It wasn't diet, which was what she usually drank, but it would do. The whole supremely unhealthy meal would do. Oh, yes, she thought, biting off the tip of her slice and savoring the wonderful flavor, it would definitely do.

"You get that Simmons thing done?" Mac, sitting on a corner of the desk and biting into his own well-laden slice, asked his partner. Hinkle was on his feet now, helping himself to pizza.

"Yeah." He glanced at Julie, then back at Mac. "You want those pictures, they're on your desk."

Sinking down on the couch to savor her treat, Julie interpreted the glance that Hinkle had thrown her way to mean that the pictures were the ones he had taken of Sid and Amber.

The thought didn't even hurt.

Mac nodded. "Thanks." He took another bite. "So what have you got for me?"

Rawanda, her mouth full of pizza, shook her head and said, "Ooh, boy."

Hinkle took a bite out of his own pizza slice, then slid a sideways glance at Julie before replying. "The Rand Corporation is the parent company for all kinds of business enterprises. Some of them seem legitimate, or at least they perform real services, like All-American Builders or Sweet-water's. Others appear to be dummy companies used to move assets and money around, kind of like a shell game. Bottom line is, Rand Corporation is definitely mob-affiliated, if not mob-controlled. Julie's father, Mike Williams, drew a steady paycheck from the Rand Corporation for eleven years, ending in January 1987. He was listed as a transportation specialist, which I interpreted as a truck driver. Most of the personnel records have some sort of notation about the reason employment with the company ended—retirement, resignation, termination. His paychecks simply stopped being issued. No reason given."

"The same month Daniel and Kelly Carlson disappeared," Mac said. "All right, what's the connection?"

"That I don't know," Hinkle said. "At least, not yet."

Mac looked thoughtful. "Mike Williams stopped working for Rand Corporation in January 1987, but he was still alive. He was seen again after that date."

"He didn't die until 1992," Hinkle said, confirming Mac's words.

Mac's gaze moved to Julie. "Didn't you say that you saw your father off and on until you were fourteen, and then he dropped out of your life for a few years? When did you see him again?"

Julie took a swallow of Coke. Even after all these years, she didn't much like talking about the father who'd been pretty much a nonpresence in her life.

"I was nineteen. It was right before I won Miss South Carolina."

Mac got an arrested expression on his face. "Didn't you say you met Sid right after you won that?"

Julie nodded.

"I need you to tell me everything you can remember about your father, all the way up to your last meeting with him. Can you do that?"

28

JULIE JUST LOOKED AT MAC for a moment without replying. Suddenly the slice of pizza she had just polished off felt heavy as lead in her stomach. She wished, vainly, that she hadn't eaten it.

"I think Mr. Hinkle—"

"George," George interjected.

"George, then. I think George was right. I think my father was a truck driver. At least, there was a time when he was always saying he'd do this or that with us—Becky and me—when he got off the road. And he was on the road a lot." She paused, her eyes meeting Mac's as she took a deep, and, she hoped, unobtrusive breath. "I really don't know that much about him. He and my mother divorced when I was two. He was her second husband. She had four others after him. Men are—they used to be—kind of disposable for her. He never came around much, although Mama would call him sometimes—" Telling this was hard, she discovered, harder even than she had expected: it was way too personal; if Mac had not held her gaze, giving her a lifeline to grab on to, she would never have gotten so much out. "—when she needed money. When he had it, he would give it to her. I got the impression he didn't have it a lot."

"He dropped out of your life entirely when you were fourteen?"

Julie nodded, and swallowed. Mac got up from the desk and came to crouch in front of her, taking her hands. Julie's fingers tightened around his almost convulsively.

"Can you tell me about the last time you saw him? I think it might be important."

It was clear from his expression that he realized this was a difficult subject for her. His silent support strengthened her. She forgot that he had lied to her, had used her, and that there had been an ulterior motive to his friendship from the beginning. All she knew was that every time, when she had needed him, he'd been there for her—just as he was there for her now. She looked into his eyes, locked her gaze on his, and, reluctantly, cast her mind back ten years.

"Mama and Becky were both gone somewhere—I don't remember where now, but I do remember I was alone. It was just getting dark, and I was sitting in the living room of our trailer—we lived in a trailer, Mama and Becky and me—hemming a dress I meant to wear in the Miss South Carolina pageant and watching something on TV, and there was a knock on the door. I got up to answer it, and there stood Daddy, just as big as Ike. I hadn't seen him in about five years, and we just looked at each other for a minute, and then he said *howdy, Becky* and I kind of laughed and said *I'm Julie* and he said *oh, of course* and *how you doing* and that sort of thing. He came on in, but he seemed real uncomfortable—well, I was uncomfortable, too, because I didn't know him very well, even if he was my father, and he didn't even know me well enough to tell me apart from

Becky. Anyway, we visited for a little while—I can't really remember what we talked about, but nothing very much. Like I said, it was kind of awkward, and he seemed kind of on edge, like he was anxious to go."

Julie paused, and swallowed again, and her eyes dropped from Mac's eyes to his mouth. It was a truly beautiful mouth, even if it was a man's mouth and "beautiful" probably wasn't the right word for it. She stared at it and thought how beautiful it was because she didn't want to think about anything else.

"Julie?"

Unwillingly, her eyes met his again. God, she didn't want to go back there. These memories belonged to another lifetime— another Julie. A far too vulnerable Julie.

"Then he left. He walked out the door, and I walked to the door too, and watched him walk to his truck—it was a beat-up old truck—and then he turned around and looked right at me and I waved, and he said *I love you, Becky.*" Julie swallowed. "Then he got in the truck and drove away. I never saw him again until I went to his funeral. The whole time I was there at that funeral I just kept thinking, He was my daddy and he couldn't even get my name straight. How pathetic is that?"

All of a sudden she couldn't talk any more because her throat ached too much. She blinked because her eyes stung. She felt moisture spill over her lower lids and slide down her cheeks and realized she was crying. Embarrassed, she closed her eyes and pulled her hands free of Mac's and covered her face and willed the tears to stop.

"Julie," Mac said, and stood up and gathered her up in his arms and sat back down on the couch with her on his lap. Julie took a deep breath and lowered her hands and blinked at him, hoping the worst of her loss of control was over. After all, it was stupid—*stupid*—to cry over something that was so far in the past. Mac was all blurry, she discovered as she tried to focus him. The tears wouldn't stop no matter how she tried to hold them back, and as she took a deep, meant-to-be-calming breath, it turned without warning into a sob.

Mac's face tightened, and his arms tightened, and he said something that she didn't understand. Knowing that he cared made the tears flow faster despite her best efforts to contain them. She couldn't bear it, she thought, couldn't stand facing the fact that her father had never loved her enough to even make sure of her name, couldn't deal with the welling resurgence of the sense of loss and abandonment that had stayed with her all her life, and she closed her eyes, trying to block the world out along with the pain.

"Oh, God, I'm sorry." It was all she could do to choke the words out. "I'm making a total fool out of myself, I know."

"It's all right to cry." Mac's voice was very soft, and it was her final undoing. He felt so safe and solid and comforting, and she realized that she had needed safe and solid and comforting for years without even realizing it. The thought brought more tears with it, and she gave up the fight to contain them, melting bonelessly against him, wrapping her arms around his neck and burying her face on his shoulder and crying as if her heart would break.

There were vague sounds of movement in the room behind her, but Julie barely noticed. She clung to Mac like a fly to sticky paper and wept as if from a well of sorrow that would never go dry.

"We'll just go now," George said, presumably to Mac. "Call if you need anything."

"Yeah, we're gonna go," Rawanda echoed.

Julie had all but forgotten their presence until they spoke. It was as if she and Mac had been all alone in a bubble, and now, with the realization that others were present, the bubble had popped. She felt a fresh sting of embarrassment, and tried to at least stop the tears now and sit up and show them that, though she might have succumbed to temporary weakness, she had gotten it all out of her system now, and she was far from the crybaby they must think her.

But it was too late: she heard the sound of the door opening and closing and they were gone. Anyway, though she tried hard, really, really hard, she couldn't stop, she discovered to her horror. Now that the tap that led to her deepest, most long-buried emotions had been opened, she couldn't turn it off again any more than she could stop her heart from beating. It was as if she had to cry, just like she had to breathe, to live. The pain had been building up too long, and it had to get out. She hadn't cried, she realized, since her father's final visit, when she'd wept bitterly after he'd left because she'd been secretly wanting her father for years and when he had finally come he couldn't even tell her from her sister. She hadn't even cried at his funeral, and she hadn't cried—not one time—since.

It was almost funny that she was just at this moment realizing that. Was she in touch with her feelings, or what?

The thought brought a little giggle with it that came out sounding more like a gasping sob, and then Mac was kissing her cheek, her ear, her jaw—whatever he could reach—and rocking her back and forth in his arms as if she were a baby and murmuring soothing things to her, and she was acting like a baby and crying as though her heart would break.

Finally, when the tears ended and the sobs quieted into no more than an occasional long shivery sigh, she rested in his arms, spent. Her head was buried in the curve between his shoulder and neck, and she kept it there for a long time because lying against him like that was just exactly what she craved, and anyway she was too drained and too ashamed to look up.

Finally she did. She didn't sit up, but she lifted her head and looked at him. His blue eyes were grave and beautiful as they met hers, and his hand stroked her back through her thin cotton T-shirt almost absently. Her legs, bare to the tops of her thighs because her skirt was short anyway and had ridden up, were bent at the knees and curved around his torso. Her breasts were nestled against his chest and her arms were draped around his neck. He felt warm and firm and so good, so right, holding her that it scared her. She gritted her teeth and lifted her chin because she knew she'd made an absolute fool of herself, and then she gave him a wary frown capped by a prosaic little sniff.

He smiled at her, slowly, and his eyes turned tender.

"Hey," he said. "You're breaking my heart here, you know."

Then he slid his hand up her back to her nape and bent his head and kissed her.

At the touch of his mouth, Julie caught

fire. She was suddenly desperate for his warmth, for his tenderness, for the solid comfort of touching him. She pushed her tongue into his mouth, and at the touch of her tongue against his, Mac seemed to detonate. The kiss exploded. Suddenly they were both clinging together, desperate for each other, consumed with passion. His tongue was scalding hot as it thrust deep into her mouth. His mouth was hard and fierce, his arms around her as tight as steel bands. She was plastered so closely against him that she could feel the thud of his heart against her breasts. His hands, as they stroked down her back and pulled the hem of her T-shirt free of her skirt to slide, warm and faintly rough, up her rib cage, were shaking. Julie shivered in response, tightening her arms around her neck and kissing him as if she would die if she didn't. One hard warm hand found her breast, and she made a little sound deep in her throat and was lost, totally lost, to the licking flames of desire.

"Oh, God, Julie." The words were more growl than groan. Mac pressed her backward, and Julie felt the cool slide of leather against her back. Then he was looming over her, yanking her T-shirt over her head, unfastening her skirt and pulling it off, and she was helping him, pulling at his clothes too, until he was bare to the waist and she was tugging his jeans down his legs. He kicked off his sneakers, shucked his briefs, and then he was coming back down to her and she was spreading her knees for him and tugging at his shoulders to bring him closer. His thighs were hard and hot and rough with hair, and unbearably exciting against the silky smoothness of hers. His chest was wide and well muscled, with just the right amount of hair, and it made her mouth go dry just looking at it. His shoulders were broad and firm and slightly damp with sweat beneath her palms.

She wanted him with an intensity that made her dizzy.

But he paused, still keeping his weight from her with his knees and his hands, his gaze sweeping over her.

"Nice," he said, in apparent reference to the lacey white bra and panties she still wore but possibly also to what was inside them. His voice was thick and his eyes burned, and Julie moved sensuously beneath his searing regard. Her hand moved up to cup the back of his head, and she pulled his mouth down to hers. The kiss, which she had meant to be soft and leisurely, was fierce and deep and dazzling instead. When he lifted his head she murmured a protest, sliding her lips down his neck, her mouth open and shaking, as he pulled a little away.

With quick, deft movements he slid his hands behind her to unfasten her bra and pull it off, then bent his head to capture one of the full, creamy breasts he had exposed. Julie closed her eyes, moaning, and pressed his head closer as his mouth closed over her nipple. His mouth was hot and wet and unbelievably arousing as he suckled first one breast, then the other. Julie arched her back, offering him her breasts with abandon, clutching his head with both hands now as he kissed and sucked and played. She moved with mindless longing beneath him, stroking her hands down his back, over his buttocks, around the tops of his thighs.

He was hard and enormous, she discovered as her hands found him, and she wanted him so much she thought she would die if she had to wait another minute. He groaned as her hand closed around him, and lifted his head from her breasts to watch her face with glittering eyes. Breathless, aching for him, she guided him to her, only to come up against a barrier and be reminded at the last minute that she still wore her tiny lace panties.

She moaned in frustration as he pushed against the barrier of the fragile cloth, ready to rip the offending garment off with her bare hands if she had to to get what she wanted. But his hand was already between them, between her legs, touching her through her panties, rubbing her, making her gasp. Then his hand moved inside one leg opening to slide inside her, in and out, hard and fast, while at the same time he bent his head to kiss her breasts.

"Mac. Oh, Mac." Head flung back against the leather couch, hair spilling toward the floor, Julie reacted like a wild thing, squirming shamelessly beneath him, clutching his shoulders, lifting her hips in wordless supplication, feeling the heat and tension build inside her until she was shaking with it, until she was so hot she thought she would die if he didn't come into her right then.

"Love me, Mac," she whispered, her eyes opening. For a moment he loomed above her, looking down at her, his face hard and fierce, his eyes almost black with wanting her, his fingers still inside her.

"I do," he said then in a low, shaken voice. "God help me, Julie, I do."

Then he yanked her panties down her legs and kissed her and came inside her hard, all so fast that Julie could do nothing but cling and wrap her legs around his waist and cry out his name. He stretched her, filled her, bringing her to the brink of fulfillment just by that one single act of possession. Even as she cried out her pleasure and surged against him in response he moved again, withdrawing and then thrusting with the desperate urgency of a man now bent on his own release. She was with him with every movement, burning hotter and higher until she was consumed by the inferno, sobbing her ecstasy into his mouth, coming with a fierce frenzy that made her world explode into a million brightly colored starbursts of passion.

"Mac! Oh, Mac!"

Groaning in response, he found his own release, grinding himself deep into her shaking body and finally going still.

When Julie had spent sufficient time blissed out in sexual nirvana, she gradually started to become aware of her surroundings again. Her breathing was still faintly ragged but it was getting back to normal, she found, and her body was more or less functional. At least, she could wiggle her fingers and toes.

The rest of her was being crushed by a large, hot and sweaty male body.

At that moment Mac lifted his head and looked at her. Searchingly.

Julie met his gaze. "It was really, really good for me," she said gravely.

A smile stretched his mouth and eyes. "You're learning, Miss America. That's the kind of pillow talk I like to hear."

"You know, I kind of guessed that." Lying naked and sweaty on a leather couch was not nearly as erotic as it sounded, Julie discovered. It was like lying naked on a bed of tape: moving was all but impossible. Mac must have seen her discomfort in her eyes, because he shifted, rolling between her and the back of the couch, then pulling her over so that she lay on top of him.

For a minute she simply savored her new position. Then she folded her arms on his chest, rested her chin on her hands, and looked at him thoughtfully.

"Mac."

"Hmm?" His hands were shaping her bottom, and one particular part of him on which she was lying seemed to be recuperating from its recent exertions with amazing speed. She wriggled a little in instinctive response, and his hands tightened and squeezed.

"Did you say you loved me, just now?" Her voice was faintly breathless from his attentions.

He winced, and his hands stilled. "Paying attention, were you?"

"Yes."

He studied her face for a moment without speaking, then gave her a wry little smile.

"I'm so in love with you it scares me. Ever since I met you, it's like the sun has come out on my life. You walk into view, and I feel the earth move. You smile, and I go weak at the knees. You cry, and my heart breaks. Does that answer your question?"

Julie's eyes widened. "That's beautiful."

"I try."

"Is it true?" There was the tiniest note of suspicion in her voice.

He laughed. "Yeah."

Still sprawled naked on his chest, with her chin resting on her folded hands, she eyed him broodingly.

"Okay. You have one chance. Explain to me how you lied to me and used me to get information about Sid in a way that doesn't make me want to kill you."

He met her gaze, and sighed. "I bare my heart and soul to you—to say nothing of my body—and you still don't trust me? I'm wounded."

"You certainly could be if you don't start talking." The look she gave him was minatory.

He grinned. "Okay. Like I said before, originally Debbie had nothing to do with you. I . . ."

There was a knock at the door. Josephine erupted from under a desk, charging the door with a cacophony of shrill yaps. Mac and Julie exchanged glances. Frowning, Mac slid out from beneath her, getting to his feet and grabbing for his clothes. Julie scrambled to follow suit.

There was another knock, louder and more peremptory than before. Alarmed, Julie looked at Mac. Did hit men knock on doors? Surely not.

Mac was frowning. He had his jeans on, and was pulling on his shirt.

"Who is it?" he called, casting her a quick, assessing glance as he scooped up his gun from a table near the end of the couch; Julie hadn't seen him discard it, but she supposed he must have put it there when he was stripping off his clothes. She was on her feet, fastening her skirt—she already had on her bra and panties—as he moved toward the door, his arm stiff, his gun at his side and pointed down. Josephine was barking her head off; Julie realized that her own heart was racing.

"Open up! Police!"

Julie's eyes widened. That was a good thing, right? Maybe not, from the look on Mac's face. Hastily she pulled on her T-shirt, then looked around for her shoes.

"That you, Dorsey?"

"Yeah, it's me. Open up, McQuarry."

Mac looked around at her. She was dressed now, complete to her shoes, clutching her purse in one hand as she ran a quick brush through her hair.

After all, she didn't want to look like she'd just been engaged in what she'd been engaged in.

"It's okay. I know this guy. He's a prick, but he's an honest prick."

Julie nodded, breathing a little easier. Mac stuck his gun inside the back of his jeans, pulled his shirt down over it, and opened the door. Two uniformed cops stood there, looking stolid and unthreatening, their gazes touching on Mac, then moving past him to find Julie, who had just scooped Josephine up. Now that she was safe in someone's arms, Josephine was once again quiet.

"What can I do for you?" Mac didn't sound particularly friendly.

The beefier of the two cops grimaced.

"You're under arrest, McQuarry."

29

"YOU'VE GOT TO BE KIDDING ME."

Mac stared at Dorsey disbelievingly. The other man, a career patrol cop who'd been on the force when Mac was there, shook his head.

"Nope. You carrying? Sure you are. Want to make this easy, and give me your piece?" Dorsey stepped into the room and held out his hand. Behind him, the other cop drew his gun.

"You can't arrest me. For what?"

"Assault. We got a warrant. You . . ."

"What?"

". . . got the right to remain silent. If you . . ."

"I know my rights. Damn it, Dorsey, I'm on a job here. See that lady?" He jerked his head at Julie, who was watching the proceedings wide-eyed. "There's a hit out on her. Somebody's trying to kill her. I'm working as her bodyguard, and I'm all that's keeping her alive."

"Yeah, yeah." Dorsey drew out his cuffs, and locked one around Mac's wrist before Mac was more than peripherally aware of what was headed his way. The cold metal bracelet brought the reality of this preposterous situation home like nothing else could have. Dorsey was turning him around, reaching for his other hand, finishing off with his rights, and the other cop had him shoved up against a desk and was starting to pat him down.

"Don't hurt him." Julie took a step toward him, Josephine clutched close to her breast.

"Ma'am, we're not hurting him. Please stay out of this," said the other cop, the one Mac didn't know. Mac got a glimpse of Julie's whitening face even as he pulled his uncuffed hand out of Dorsey's hold.

"Damn it, McQuarry. . . ." Dorsey

grabbed his hand again as the other cop relieved him of his Glock.

"Mac, should I call somebody? Who should I call?" Julie sounded frightened now.

"Hinkle," he said, and told her the number, playing keep-away with his hand all the while.

"Can't you just make this easy on everybody, McQuarry?" Dorsey said with a sigh, then shoved his knee into the small of Mac's back, making him grunt with pain. While Mac was busy reacting, Dorsey grabbed his hand.

"You *are* hurting him!" Julie was standing by his desk now, her eyes huge and dark, her face pale. She held the telephone receiver to her ear. "Mac, he's not home. The answering machine picked up."

"Tell him what's happening. Tell him to haul ass down to the Seventy-third Precinct."

If he sounded desperate, it was because he was. Dorsey didn't have enough brain wattage to power a flashlight. It was going to be impossible to talk him out of this, and if he didn't talk him out of it, Julie was going to be left at the mercy of whoever was hunting her. Julie was still talking into the phone when, without warning, Dorsey jerked his arm up behind his back. The pain was sharp and intense. Mac made a sound, and twisted instinctively to ease it. The second bracelet clicked into place. His hands were cuffed behind his back.

Shit, this was going down. Right now.

They were already pushing him toward the door. "Julie, stay with me. Dorsey, you can take her down to the station with us, can't you?"

"No can do." His voice grew a tad more polite as he added, over his shoulder as they hustled Mac along the hall, "Sorry, ma'am."

"Julie."

"I'm here, Mac. Officers, you can't . . ."

One on either side, they shoved him into the elevator, and the closing door cut off her words. For a moment Mac stared at the dingy metal panels in stupefaction as the elevator lurched into motion.

"Julie!" he roared, only to be rewarded for his pains by Dorsey twisting his arms up behind his back again, both of them this time, and harder than before.

Mac groaned.

"You yell like that again and I'm gonna break your head for you."

His arms were released.

"Dorsey, you stupid shit. If anything happens to her, I'm going to take you apart limb from limb."

Mac was sweating buckets. The elevator clanked slowly down. Meanwhile, Julie was left behind on the second floor, alone except for Josephine.

"You hear that, Nichols? Sounds like terroristic threatening to me."

Mac took a deep breath. If he lost his cool, if he provoked Dorsey into doing something drastic, Julie would be left defenseless. If the hit man was in the vicinity, and Mac was growing more convinced with every passing second that he was—Dorsey was an honest if brutish cop, but this arrest coming when it had was too pat, somebody was behind it, and Mac's blood ran cold as he guessed who—Julie would die. At the thought, a burst of fear went through him like a wintry blast. He remembered the girl hit by the car in front of her store; he remembered the way Julie had been attacked before. Fear turned into stark terror. He had to force it back. Giving into it was the worst thing he could do.

He emptied his mind, channeling calm, readying himself, as the elevator finally, finally, reached the ground floor.

30

WITH JOSEPHINE TUCKED UNDER ONE ARM and her purse under the other, Julie was left gaping as the elevator doors closed in her face. Just like that, Mac was gone.

All she could see was herself, reflected in the dull silver surface. Staring blankly at her own image, she saw that her lips were slightly swollen from Mac's kisses, her cheeks were rosy with color, and her eyes shone. Even her hair seemed to have developed extra bounce.

She looked like—a woman in love.

Mac had said he was in love with her.

Despite the exigencies of her present situation, Julie was suddenly suffused with warmth. The corners of her mouth turned up in a little smile.

Get out of here.

The words in her head came out of nowhere, and the smile vanished from her face as if it had been drawn on a blackboard and then wiped clean in a single swipe.

Realizing that, Julie forgot about being a woman in love and went back to being a woman in fear for her life. The hair rose on the back of her neck; her pulse raced. She stood stock-still, electrified, her eyes darting fearfully around.

If she had learned nothing else in the course of this nightmare, she had learned that the little voice meant big trouble.

Hurry.

Oh, yeah. She was out of there. Like the wind.

The elevator was too slow. The stairs she and Mac had used earlier were to her left. Hanging on to Josephine for dear life—thank God for Josephine, Julie thought, she would have died of fright on the spot without her—she ran for the door, only to stop in her tracks as she heard—something. A sound just beyond it, in the stairwell.

It could be anything, she told herself as she strained to hear over the pounding of her own blood in her ears. A cat. A bum. A hit man.

Great going, Julie. Way to be calm.

All right, forget calm. Scared half to death would have to do. Her heart was thudding in her chest like a racehorse galloping toward the finish line. She was suddenly terrified to venture as much as one step farther—but she was equally terrified not to.

There were only two choices: the elevator or the stairs. And the elevator door remained stubbornly closed.

All she had to do was go down one measly flight of stairs, and she would be safe in the company of Mac and two burly cops.

Hide.

Even as she registered the word, the door opened. Just like that, with no more warning at all. Julie's blood ran cold. Icy dread froze her in place.

"Hello, Julie."

Julie's heart gave a great, panic-stricken leap in her chest.

She didn't know what terrified her more: the gun that was pointed at her, or the fact that it was being held by a man with a swollen, discolored nose.

They were armed, he was not. There were two of them to one of him. His hands were cuffed behind his back.

The only chance he had was to take them on in this confined space.

There was no talking sense to these guys. If he didn't win free, he was going to jail. And Julie would die.

The elevator stopped with a little ping, distracting their attention. The doors started to open. Mac called on every bit of training he had ever had as a SEAL, and pivoted on one leg, spinning like a top and slashing out with his raised leg with the force and fury of a tornado.

"Ahhhh!" Dorsey screamed as he went flying into Nichols, who smacked into the wall. Their guns somersaulted into the air, they went down in a heap, and Mac leaped on them ruthlessly, kicking Dorsey under the chin as he tried to rise, stomping on

Nichols' back. Dorsey crashed backward, his eyes rolling back in his head as he collapsed. Cursing, Nichols got his hands under him and tried to lever himself up, but Dorsey's legs were sprawled across his butt, slowing him just enough for Mac to kick him in the side of the jaw. Nichols collapsed like a house of cards. Then it was over. The whole thing had taken perhaps a minute. Both men were sprawled on the floor, unconscious and bleeding, but alive. His training had taught him to kill, but he'd tried his best to avoid that negative outcome. Even so, beating cops to a pulp was a major no-no, and Mac realized that he had bought himself a boatload of trouble. It was something to worry about later. Right now he had to get to Julie, and get both of them as far away as possible as fast as he could.

Moving quickly, he crouched and stepped through the loop formed by his cuffed hands. With his hands in front of him now, he grabbed his Glock from Nichols' belt, sticking it down inside the front of his jeans, then fished in Dorsey's pocket for the keys to the cuffs. Dorsey's breathing was shallow, and blood trickled from a corner of his mouth. Mac grimaced as his fingers closed around the keys. Sorry, asshole, he thought, and maneuvered the small silver key into the lock. It clicked open. He pulled the cuffs off, then checked the pulse of both men: strong and steady. They would live to make him rue the day. A quick glance around confirmed what he already knew: he was in what was essentially a metal box. There was nothing to cuff them to. Thinking fast, he snapped a cuff around one of Dorsey's wrists, knotted the chain around Nichols' ankle, then fastened the second cuff around Dorsey's other wrist.

That would slow them down.

Smiling faintly, he stepped out of the elevator, shoving Dorsey's legs in so that the door would close, then hit the button for the fourth and top floor.

The way that elevator worked, even if they were awake and aware, he would have just bought himself and Julie a good five minutes to get away.

Casting a quick glance around to make sure she wasn't somewhere behind him— no, she wasn't, and neither was anyone else; fortunately, the building pretty much emptied out at five—Mac drew his gun, turned, and sprinted for the stairs.

He went up them two at a time, practically running as he shoved through the heavy metal door that opened onto the second floor. The hall was deserted. She must have gone back to his office to wait.

Mac tried to ignore the little tendrils of fear that started to curl through his stomach as it occurred to him that Julie *should* have been on the first floor waiting for them to get off the elevator. She should have been on the stairs.

Returning to his office didn't seem like something she would do.

Reaching the door, he opened it and stepped inside, some instinct causing him to automatically assume combat stance.

"Julie," he called, doing a fast visual survey of the room. Everything was just as it had been left: lights on, computer on, pizza boxes still sitting atop Rawanda's desk.

But no Julie.

"Julie!"

His blood raced through his veins. His heart pounded like a trip-hammer. He did a quick search of the office, knowing already that she wasn't there.

In the few minutes that they'd been separated, Sid's hireling had gotten to her. He knew it in his gut.

"Oh, God, Julie."

The anguish in his own voice sobered him. Giving into emotion would get her killed faster than anything he could do. He had already made one mistake by bringing her to his office at all. He'd thought she'd be safe, with him right beside her, never letting her out of his sight.

He'd been wrong. He couldn't afford to be wrong again. His being wrong could very well get her killed.

He should have taken her and run while he had the chance. To hell with everything else: Julie was what mattered.

God help him, what was he going to do?

Her purse. Where was her purse? He looked around on the floor by the couch, where she had set it down. It wasn't there. It wasn't anywhere he could see.

She'd been carrying it as she'd followed him down the hall. He remembered now. Please God she was still hanging on to it. Please, please God.

He'd put a button-sized homing device in her purse that morning, just in case she got it into her head to try to elude him at some point during the day.

In his experience, women rarely went anywhere without their purses. That quirk of female nature might very well save her life.

He left his office, leaped down the stairs without sparing so much as a thought for the men he'd left in the elevator, and ran like a madman for the Blazer, cursing himself with each step for parking so far away. Finally reaching it, he jumped inside, and fished frantically around in the back for the global positioning unit the homing device worked with. Turning it on, he waited with bated breath for the screen to warm up.

Then—there it was. Or rather, there she was: a tiny green dot moving at a fast pace through the maze of streets laid out like a map on the dark screen. If she and her purse were still keeping company, that is. He wasn't ordinarily a religious man, but he was getting religion fast. He prayed that she was hanging on to that purse as he had never prayed for anything in his life.

Starting the Blazer, he stepped on the gas, meaning to peel rubber out of the lot. A small white shape bounding toward him through the darkness caught his eye. He stared, frowned, and stood on the brake, then swung open his door.

"Get in," he yelled at Josephine.

31

"HOW DOES IT FEEL to know that you're going to die tonight, Julie?" Sid's voice was eerily conversational. Julie felt her stomach cramp. She was so frightened that her body seemed to be drawing in on itself, with all her organs squeezing painfully together. He had been waiting for her in a dark-colored car that she had never seen before when the man with the bitten nose—Sid called him Basta—had brought her out of the building. He was driving now, heading north on a narrow, dark country road, with her sitting beside him and Basta—terrifying Basta, who smiled at her with the coldest eyes she'd ever seen—

silent in the backseat. Sid and his hit man: Mac had been right all along.

"You don't want to kill me, Sid. Remember how we loved each other? There's still something left of that."

Not screaming and clawing at the door in a frantic attempt to escape required almost Herculean control on her part. Any minute now she expected to feel Basta's hands slide around her neck, or his gun nudge the back of her head. Then he would squeeze, or pull the trigger—and she would be dead.

Oh, God, would it hurt?

Sid laughed. "I never loved you, you trashy little slut. I may have thought I did, once upon a time, but all I really wanted wanted was to fuck you, and now I don't even want to do that."

The words did not carry the sting he obviously intended them to have. The rose-colored lenses with which she had once regarded Sid had already been ripped from her eyes, and she was easily able to see him for the cruel, self-centered man he was. As much as she wanted to tell him so, though, now was definitely not the time. What she needed to do, what she had to do if she was to survive, was to reestablish their relationship, to somehow reconnect with him, at least in his mind.

It would be easier without Sid's hired killer watching her from the backseat like a vicious dog eyeing a rabbit. The knowledge that he was there made the hairs prickle on the back of her neck. She did her best to block him out, but it was hard: she could see his massive shadow from the corner of her eye, and she could hear his raspy breathing.

She could almost, even, smell onions. . . . But she wouldn't think of that. She wouldn't remember that night, not now. She would concentrate, focus, do what she had to do to save her own life.

"Do you remember when we first met? It was at the governor's reception just after I was crowned Miss South Carolina. Remember how much we talked that night? For hours. You wanted to know everything about me. I think I fell in love with you then."

Like Scheherazade, words were the only weapon she had. Julie folded a leg beneath her and turned sideways in the seat, doing her best to draw him into the memory. The darkness outside the windows seemed to close in on the car. Huge trees flashed past on either side of the road, illuminated only briefly by the slashing headlights. Sid was driving fast, much too fast for the twists and turns of the road. Wherever they were headed, it was somewhere far off the beaten path. The knowledge was like an icy finger running down her spine.

Forcing back the fear that would turn her into a gibbering idiot if she let it, she smiled at Sid.

"You still don't have any idea, do you?" Sid's laugh was contemptuous. "We didn't just happen to meet that night. You think I usually went to receptions for beauty-contest winners? Get real. I was there that night specifically looking for you. You want to know why? Because your father, who worked for us once upon a time, stole something that belonged to my father and me, to our company, and I was trying to get it back. I had information that you knew where it was, and the reason I wanted to know all about you that night was because I thought you might slip and tell me. You didn't, but I kept on seeing you, thinking you would tell me what you knew sooner or later."

"You dated me just to get back something my father stole?" Julie's mind flashed back over her practically nonexistent relationship with her father. If he *had* stolen something, she wouldn't have known anything about it. "What was it?"

Basta made a protesting sound, and Sid glanced at him through the rearview mirror.

"You don't need to know that." His voice was rough. "It was important enough for me to come sniffing after you to get it. You were a pretty thing then—that was about twenty pounds ago, wasn't it?—and I wanted to sleep with you. But you wouldn't sleep with me, remember? Not unless I married you. That was smart. I confused lust with love like many a man before me, and I married you. I hoped you would tell me what I wanted to know about the whereabouts of the company's stolen property once you were feeling real secure in our relationship, but you didn't, and I gradually figured out you weren't telling me anything because you didn't know anything. That's the story of your life, isn't it, Julie: You don't know anything. You don't know anything, and I don't want to sleep with you anymore: that makes you disposable. Just like the trash you are."

The truth of it hit her like a slap in the face. As his words swirled around her, painting various incidents in their past in a hideous new light, Julie felt dizzy. She realized that what he was telling her explained so much: the way, at the beginning, he'd always insisted on talking about her and never himself. His inordinate interest in her father. His contemptuous attitude, which had been growing stronger over the years.

She looked at him, realized with a terrible clarity that the whole last eight years of her life had been spent living with and loving a man who was capable of arranging to have her killed, and was finally, irrevocably, forever and ever, set free of any last vestigial ties of affection or loyalty that might have still existed somewhere deep inside her.

There was a smirk to his mouth that told her he was aware of the effect his words were having on her and reveled in it. It roused her from the shock of his revelation like a bucket of cold water. Grimly she reminded herself that what was important here was her survival: any lingering psychic pain she could deal with later.

"If you're nice, though, maybe I'll let you go down on your knees for me one last time before I turn you over to Basta." His tone was malicious, taunting. Julie realized that she had been wasting her breath, trying to rekindle their connection. There never had been a connection to rekindle. Sid had never loved her.

"Oh, do you have your Viagra with you?" The words were out before she could stop them. Julie was appalled—so much for trying to sweet-talk her way out of this—but not really all that sorry. She knew, deep in her heart of hearts, that she could talk for the rest of her life, and it wasn't going to change a thing: Sid meant to see her dead.

Time to move to Plan B. She wet her lips, casting a surreptitious look around the interior of the car. Time to move to Plan B— just as soon as she could come up with it.

Sid's face flushed. Even in the dim light reflected by the headlights, she could see it change color, see the self-conscious glance he cast in the mirror at Basta.

"You can just shut up about that. It was

for recreational use only, to give me a buzz."

"Yeah, right. I know you used it on Amber. Did you use it on the girls at Sweetwater's too?"

"Listen, bitch, I didn't go to Sweetwater's for the girls. Ever since we acquired it, I've been going there several nights a week to pick up the cash they take in. Did you know that we own Sweetwater's now, by the way? Of course you don't: I keep forgetting you don't know anything. The last couple of times I went there, though, it was basically for you: I was providing myself with an alibi so the big guy back there could break into our house and snuff you. Only he kept screwing it up, didn't you, Basta? You must have felt pretty stupid when she got away from you because she bit your nose. Then you ran over the wrong girl." He sent another of those quick glances into the backseat, shook his head, and laughed. "Well, never mind. You can pay her back tonight."

"Yeah, I felt pretty stupid." It was almost the first thing Basta had said since he'd shoved her in the car. Hearing his voice made Julie want to cringe. Along with the smell of onions, and the sight of his masked face staring back at her through her bathroom mirror, the memory of it had haunted her nightmares. Now she was hearing it again in reality, and the reality was far more terrifying than any nightmare could ever be. "About as stupid as I imagine you felt when you figured out she'd been cheating on you with Daniel's little brother."

Basta meant Mac, Julie realized. Frowning, she remembered Mac saying something about Daniel. It took a second, but she came up with the context. Daniel had disappeared at the same time as her father, and Sid's first wife. . . .

"Did you kill Kelly too?" she asked Sid fiercely.

There was a laugh from the backseat.

"No, I did," Basta said. "Just like I killed Daniel. And your father. And now I'm getting ready to kill you. Sid, you want to slow down. The road's up here on the left."

Julie felt her heart lurch. The journey was coming to an end, she knew. As Sid obediently slowed, then turned left onto a bumpy dirt road that was little more than a path, Julie suddenly had to work hard to breathe. It was difficult to draw air into her suddenly constricted lungs. Her hands automatically clenched into fists as her mind swooped around like a frightened bird, trying desperately to come up with anything that seemed remotely like a plan.

"The police will be looking for me. They were there—with Mac—they'll have missed me by now. They'll know you did this."

"Ya think?" That was Basta, sounding amused.

"You stupid little slut, I sent those cops to get your boyfriend out of the way. They don't just work for the city; they're on our payroll, too. In fact, I wouldn't be surprised if McQuarry didn't have an accident on the way downtown. Maybe shot while trying to escape, or something."

"There's your car, right there," Basta said. "Pull in behind it. Then you can leave."

As Sid pulled in beside what looked like the green Lexus he'd been driving the last time she'd seen him, terror rose like bile in Julie's throat. This was it—and she had no plan. Nothing. As the car rocked to a stop, she released her seat belt. Her fingers scrabbled for the door handle, closed over it, pulled . . .

"Childproof lock," Sid said mockingly, shifting into park, as the door failed to open.

Damn those things!

From the corner of her eye, she saw Basta move. Panting with terror, heart pounding, stomach churning, she turned fully to face him. His eyes met hers, glinting like jet in the darkness. She could only watch in horror as he lifted his gun. He was going to shoot her *now,* she realized, and realized too, with a terrible sense of fatalism, that there wasn't a thing she could do about it. Closing her eyes, backpedaling against the locked, immovable door, she said every prayer she had ever heard in her life.

She was still in the act of raising her hands to cover her face when the gun exploded like point-blank thunder.

32

THE MOON WAS RISING IN THE DISTANCE, yellow and round as a tennis ball. Mac got one look as the Blazer topped a rise, then lost all view of the sky—and all light—as the SUV dipped back beneath the overhanging canopy of trees. He was running without lights, following the green blip on the global positioning unit and the red glow of the taillights not too far ahead.

Julie was in that car.

Or at least, Julie's purse with the homing device in it was in that car.

Mac's blood ran cold as, not for the first time, it occurred to him that maybe, somehow, she had become separated from her purse.

At the thought that he might have gotten it wrong, icy terror ran through his veins. He knew as well as he knew anything that Julie had only this one chance.

The idea that, at this very moment, someone might be hurting her made him homicidal. If she were killed . . . If she were killed . . .

He couldn't even finish the thought.

Earlier, when she'd cried, he had gathered her up in his arms and faced the fact that he loved her. Now he was confronting the truth of how much.

If anything happened to her, he would rip Sid and all his cohorts, past or present, real or suspected, from limb to limb. He would go insane. He would howl at the moon.

For the rest of his life.

Oh, God, he prayed. Let her be all right. Let me be right. Let me be in time.

The forest was thick and dark. The road was curvy. Staying on it without any illumination beyond the occasional patch of moonlight required all his concentration. He dared not wreck. If he did, Julie was at far greater risk than he was himself.

It occurred to him that he might have to leave the Blazer at some point, and when he did he might not wish to be observed. Driving one-handed, he hefted his Glock and used the butt to sytematically smash all of the SUV's interior bulbs.

Up ahead, the taillights vanished. The green light on the screen made a right turn. The light didn't seem to be following a road any longer, and Mac wondered if it had left the pavement. The occasional glimpses of it that he managed as it had streaked through sections of moonlight ahead of him had revealed a midsize passenger car, not an SUV.

He needed backup, bad. Knowing that he was Julie's sole hope terrified him. His cell phone had been in the Blazer, and he'd tried calling Hinkle: answering machine. Twice. Who else could he trust? The answer was stark: no one. The reach of the mob was long, and their twin weapons of money and fear were powerful: no one was immune.

In the end, before the overhanging trees had taken the signal out, he'd done what he could: he'd called the cops. They would have found Dorsey and Nichols by now;

the entire police force of the state of South Carolina was undoubtedly looking for him. He wasn't their favorite person to begin with, and they sure weren't going to be liking him any better now that he had pulverized two of their own. Cops were clannish that way, as he knew from experience. By now, if they spotted him, they were likely to shoot first and ask questions later.

And a whole posse of them would be coming after him.

Among their ranks were sure to be some who had been corrupted by the mob. But only some; not all. Not even the majority. If he got enough of them together at one time, the public good would win out.

He hoped. No, he prayed.

He'd called his old captain, Greg Rice, putting the facts on the line and telling him what road he was on and which way he was headed. Then the trees had cut him off.

He trusted Greg more than most. If he was right, if Greg was solid, there were only two problems: Greg had made skeptical sounds as Mac had tersely laid the whole thing out. Mac wasn't sure Greg had believed a word he'd said. And the road he'd been on when the signal had cut out had been many twists and turns ago. He wasn't even headed in the same direction anymore.

For Julie's sake, he was willing to take his chances with his former comrades-in-arms. At this point, he didn't even care if they shot him on sight, as long as they rescued her first.

To his right, Mac caught just a glimpse of a pair of taillights disappearing through the trees. There was a dirt road cutting through the trees. He had almost passed it. Hanging a hard right, Mac turned off onto it. The Blazer hit the mother of all bumps, and Josephine, perched beside him, lost her balance, sliding off into the footwell.

"Sorry, Josephine."

The poodle scrambled back onto the seat, unhurt. She'd been riding with her paws on the dashboard, seeming to peer at the road in front of them with a concentration almost equal to his own, and Mac wondered just how much she understood.The green dot slowed dramatically, then stopped. Mac glanced down at the screen, registered that, then looked up again and stood on the brake. The Blazer was at the edge of a clearing. Up ahead, in the full glare of the moonlight, a dark-colored Ford Taurus pulled to stop beside a foreign luxury car—a Lexus, he thought, although he couldn't be positive because the Taurus was between him and it.

This was it. Zero hour. If Julie was in there, this was his chance. Shoving the transmission into park, he stepped out of the car, closing the door as quietly as he could, leaving Josephine, who was watching anxiously through the windshield, behind.

Crouched low, moving fast, gun drawn, he closed on the Taurus. There were three people inside. He could just barely make out the dark shapes of them. Julie was in the front passenger seat, pressed up tight against the window. He couldn't mistake her: her black hair gleamed in the moonlight.

Thank God, thank . . .

A gunshot, muffled but unmistakeable, exploded inside the car. Julie screamed and dropped from view. Gone, just like that. Mac's heart stopped, he almost pissed his pants, and he gave a great leap forward, grabbing for the door handle, staying low. He yanked the door open just as another gunshot shook his eardrums. Julie tumbled out, falling backward, eyes and mouth wide and screaming as she hit the grass.

For a split second Julie simply lay where she had fallen, stunned. When the second shot exploded almost in her ear, she'd been curled into as tiny a ball as she could make of herself, head down, arms around her legs, pressed as far back against the hard barrier of the door as she could get. With her eyes scrunched shut, she'd felt a warm liquid spatter her legs. She'd gone all light-headed and bells had rung and lights had flashed and she'd stopped breathing. Then she had felt herself tumbling backward, falling into nothingness, into empty, open air. The thought that had run through her mind was that she'd been killed and was being sucked straight down to—heaven?

She realized she was screaming only when Mac's face intruded between her and the sky. His hand wrapped around her wrist just as another gunshot exploded right over her head. Mac dropped her wrist and staggered back, cursing. Julie scrambled to her feet, crouching near the rear tire, ducking her head and covering it with her folded arms. Her heart was pounding so hard she had to be alive, she realized. She could feel her stomach churning, feel blood pumping through her veins. Oh, God, she was alive! She was alive!

"Run!" Mac screamed at her, or maybe it was the little voice again, because she didn't think she could hear anything outside her own head. Her ears were ringing so badly she might as well have been Quasimodo in the bell tower. But run was what she wanted to do anyway, and run was what she did. Mac grabbed her wrist again and took off, and she was with him every step of the way, abject fear giving wings to her feet. Mac kept turning around to snap off shots at Basta, who, she saw with a quick, terrified look over her shoulder, had emerged from the car now and was coming after them, crouched low like they were, shooting too.

Basta dodged and ducked when one of Mac's shots kicked up turf near his feet, giving them a few extra, precious seconds. Suddenly they were out of the moonlight, running like all the hounds of hell were after them into the concealing shadow of the trees, where the Blazer loomed like a solid black box in front of them.

Julie had never been so glad to see anything in her life.

Mac let go of her wrist.

"Get in!"

This time there was no doubt the voice belonged to Mac. Julie jerked the passenger door open and dived inside, nearly crushing Josephine, who leaped nimbly into the back in the nick of time. Mac's butt hit the driver's seat at the same moment. Julie huddled in the seat, feet on the edge, fists pressed to her face, shaking and gasping, as Mac wrenched at the gearshift. She looked up just in time to see Basta coming after them, his bulky body silhouetted for a moment against the backdrop of the moonlit clearing. She screamed, the Blazer careened backward, and she was almost toppled from her perch, catching herself with a hand on the dash. When she looked again Basta was nowhere to be seen; she asssumed that he was rushing toward them through the concealing darkness beneath the trees.

"He shot Sid!" It was a near-hysterical shriek. Her voice shook with horror. The first bullet, the one she'd thought was meant for her, had blown Sid's face off. Just like that, his features had been blown away and replaced with an oozing crimson pulp that made her want to heave when she remembered it. The smell of blood—she'd never realized blood smelled like bad meat—had filled the air. Then Basta had turned the gun on her. . . .

"Who? Who shot Sid?"

Julie screamed, ducking as bullets tore through the body of the Blazer with the fierce, sharp rat-a-tat of some kind of deadly popcorn. The windshield shattered; pellets of glass pelted them like storm-driven hail. Mac cursed and drove, turned halfway around with his arm slung over the back of his seat, looking over his shoulder as the Blazer bumped and rocked and skidded backward down the little dirt road. Panting with a combination of fear and shock, Julie turned and looked that way too.

"Who shot Sid?" It was a roar.

"Basta! The hit man! The one—I bit his nose!"

Another hail of bullets hit the Blazer. Julie dove screaming for the footwell. Then the gunfire stopped. Just like that. Nothing. The sudden silence was almost as terrifying as the thunder of bullets had been.

Cautiously she lifted her head. Either they were out of range or Basta couldn't see them, but Julie knew deep in every fiber of her being that he was still giving chase. As she crawled limply back into her seat, she realized that she was shaking like a leaf; adrenaline rushed through her veins, making her jump at every bump or sound.

"This Basta—is he the one shooting at us?"

"Yes!"

The dirt road being too narrow to permit them to turn around, they were still flying backward without lights; how Mac saw to drive Julie couldn't imagine. The stockade of giant trees she had seen on the way in was rushing past on both sides, now reduced to a featureless blur. The trees melded seamlessly with the road and the night itself to her eyes. If they wrecked, Basta would catch up to them; at the thought, Julie went all light-headed, and her heart threatened to thump clean out of her chest.

Oh, God, please, she didn't want to die like Sid.

"How did you get away from the cops?"

"I managed to persuade them to see reason."

"They were dirty: they were taking bribes from Sid."

"You know, I had begun to suspect that."

Miraculously, during the course of this conversation, they somehow managed to stay on the track. When the first glimmer of approaching headlights appeared through the woods Julie thought for an instant that Mac must have succumbed to human limitations and turned on the Blazer's lights.

No such luck.

"Shit," Mac said, and as Julie realized the truth she echoed the sentiment in her head. The headlights belonged to another vehicle, which was coming toward them from the direction of the road. The dirt track was too narrow to allow two vehicles to pass; trees formed a nearly impenetrable wall on both sides.

They were trapped.

"No," Julie moaned, hanging on to the

edge of her seat with both hands as she stared back at the oncoming vehicle.

"Hang on."

Julie nearly bit her tongue as the Blazer veered. Mac, whose eyes were apparently a lot better than hers, sent them haring off the track to the left, somehow managing to find a space between the trees.

The good news was, they were now going forward. The bad news was, they didn't get far.

No sooner had the headlights passed them, continuing on up the track toward the clearing without pausing, which made Julie think they hadn't been seen, than the Blazer plunged nose-first into some kind of hole or ditch.

"Yow!" Julie was thrown violently forward and smacked her forehead hard on the dash. It took a couple of seconds for the stars she saw to recede. By the time they did, Mac was at her door, flinging it open and dragging her from her seat.

"We're stuck. Come on." His voice was scarcely louder than a whisper. Head pounding, stomach churning, knees weak with fear, Julie nevertheless hit the ground running. Basta could be anywhere, near or far. He could be right behind the nearest tree. At any second he could open fire.

Against her will, Julie once again remembered Sid's destroyed face and had to fight back a wave of dizziness. Icy prickles of fear raced over her skin; gorge rose in her throat. Her hand welded to Mac's, she plunged through the forest like a frightened deer.

The next bullet might find her. Or Mac.

The realization kept her legs pumping as fast and furiously as her heart.

Seconds later Julie stepped on a rock, and nearly yelped in pain and surprise. Only the thought of Basta enabled her to bite back the sound and keep going with little more than a single, one-footed hop. It was only then that she realized she was barefoot: she had lost her shoes in the first wild rush toward the Blazer. The ground beneath her feet was slippery with leaves and sort of squishy, except for the occasional bruising rock. The humidity was thick as fog, and the smell of rotting vegetation hung heavy in the air. Under the trees, the night was so dark she could see Mac only as a dense shape plunging through the undergrowth just slightly ahead of her. All around, little glowing disks flickered on and off: fireflies. Mosquitoes were out, too. Julie could feel herself being bitten. She did not dare slap at them, for fear the sound of skin smacking skin would give them away. Although, unless Basta was right on their heels, he probably wouldn't hear. The night was alive with the whirr of insects, the eerie piping of tree frogs, the deep bass accompaniment of bullfrogs, the rustling of the forest itself. Nature's chorus was so loud that their own breathing and the soft thudding of their feet against the ground was barely audible even to herself.

As she listened, it suddenly occurred to Julie that Mac must not be in as good a shape as he looked to be, because his breathing was labored. Really labored.

In fact, he was rasping like a dying man.

"Mac . . ." Alarmed, she meant to ask him if he was all right.

At that moment he plunged forward with a splash and would have fallen on his face if Julie hadn't been slightly behind him, hanging on to his hand for dear life, her weight enough to counterbalance his forward impetus.

"Fuck," he said, just as she found it too, her foot plunging through liquid to sink ankle-deep into muddy ooze. This time it was he who kept her from going down face-first, grabbing her arm and helping her keep her balance.

Julie stopped from sheer necessity. Her feet felt like they were mired in wet concrete.

"We've got to go back," she whispered, clinging to his hand for balance and trying to turn around even as she spoke. The mud—she thought it was mud, it felt like mud, squishy, gooey mud—was reluctant to release its grip. The water that covered it was knee-deep and warm. Its smell was the rotting vegetation smell that had struck her earlier, only stronger. Julie realized that they'd stumbled into one of the swamps with which the area abounded. Rushes and foxtails grew all around them, brushing against her each time she moved, towering above her head. Tiny eyes stared at them from the trees. Raccoons? Possoms? Beyond that, Julie didn't want to speculate.

"We can't. Look."

Julie looked. Glowing disks about the size of softballs were bobbing behind them. Flashlights: she realized what they were as she saw a tree suddenly illuminated by a moving beam. They were just reaching the place where they had abandoned the Blazer, Julie calculated. . . .

"Josephine!" Horror struck through to her soul.

"She'll be all right. Nobody's after the dog. Come on, we've got to keep going. One good thing about this swamp: They won't come in here unless they have to."

Mac pulled her on, his feet making squelching noises with every step that Julie hoped, prayed, couldn't be heard much beyond their ears. She splashed after him, hanging on to his hand, moving carefully, both to minimize the sound and to keep from falling flat on her face.

By now she was way beyond terror. She was going on pure adrenaline, with Sid's fate for an impetus. If they were caught, that was what would happen to them. . . .

Without warning, Mac went down on one knee. Tethered to him by their clasped hands, Julie was nearly pulled over the top of him. He let go, and she pushed herself erect with one hand on his back, barely hearing the steady stream of under-his-breath curses that he was letting fly with.

She was too busy looking fearfully over her shoulder at the oncoming flashlights.

Until she registered that her hand on his back was covered with a warm, sticky liquid. Lifting her hand, turning it over, she saw that her palm, which should have been a pale blur, was not. It was black.

Horror struck at her heart like a blade.

"Oh, my God, Mac," she whispered. "You've been shot."

33

HIS FUTURE WAS ON THE LINE. Hell, his *life* was on the line. Basta knew it, and it was all he could do not to panic.

He had to get Julie Carlson back and send her off to join her husband. As for the man who had snatched her right out from under his nose for the second time, he was dog food. Basta knew who he was now—Daniel's little brother.

That made what was getting ready to happen almost poetic.

Sid's wife and Daniel's little brother, gone bye-bye together: talk about déjà vu all over again.

But he had other business he had to take care of first.

"How could you let this happen?" The Big Boss's face was etched with grief. Tears glinted in his eyes. He turned back from the Taurus, took a step, and had to support himself on the Lexus's trunk. He was dressed in a dark suit, and looked every inch the successful businessman he was. "My son. Oh, my son."

"He came out of nowhere, Mr. Carlson: Mac McQuarry. Dorsey and Nichols were supposed to take him out, but something must have gone wrong. Somehow he followed us out here. We never even saw him until he snatched the girl out of the car and shot your son, just like that. I got off some shots, but they escaped into the woods. They're in there somewhere. We'll get them back, I give you my word."

"Your word doesn't seem to be worth much these days. If you'd done your job properly, the little bitch would have been dead days ago and this would never have happened." John Carlson's eyes were as cold and distant as glaciers. Basta had seen that look in them before, although it had never been directed at him. The people it had been directed at were all dead.

Carlson turned to the flunky behind him. "Get some more men out here *now.* Tell them we need a heat-seeking device. Have some of them ring the perimeter of the area. I want these people found, and I don't want any more mistakes."

"Yes, sir." The flunky stepped a little apart from the group and whipped out a cell phone.

He'd made the right decision about his future, Basta thought. Before, he'd been a little unsure. If anything went wrong, his ass would be history. But that look told its own tale: He was history anyway unless he did something to save himself.

The Big Boss, the capo of capos, the mind behind the most efficient organized-crime operation on the East Coast, was done with him. And when the Big Boss turned his back, whoever he turned it on was toast.

Basta gnawed at a thumbnail, thinking.

"Excuse me, I gotta take a leak," he said to Carlson, and walked away into the dark. If he could have just kept on walking, that's what he would have done. But the Big

Boss was one of the few people who knew where to find him. He would never let Basta just walk away. Fair enough, Basta thought, emptying his bladder against a tree. Walking back toward where the boss waited near the cars, he pulled the small silver silencer from his pocket and screwed it onto the end of his pistol. Ordinarily, out here, he never bothered, because the area was remote enough that no one ever heard anything.

But tonight there would be people near enough to hear. Such as the boss's flunkies. If he screwed up again, it would be the last time, literally. He would be dead.

He'd taken out Sid on his own, as part of his plan to break free of this life once and for all. He'd meant to take out Julie, too, not because he was being paid to—he didn't care about that any longer—but because Julie could identify him and was, thus, a loose end. It never paid to leave loose ends. None of them would be here tonight if they had not left a loose end dangling fifteen years ago: Mike Williams. After Daniel's unfortunate demise, Williams had cut and run. Nobody had known then that he had taken the object of their frantic search with him—Williams had been little more than a flunky, after all—but still, the very fact that Williams had taken off should have set alarm bells ringing. Somebody should have followed up on it then, found Mike Williams and taken care of him, but no one had.

As a result of that screw-up, here they all were.

He rejoined the Big Boss, putting an arm around him and walking him across the grass, listening and nodding sympathetically as the man went on and on about his son. Something the boss had once said to him popped into his mind, and the sheer appropriateness of it made him smile inwardly: Keep your friends close, but keep your enemies even closer. To John Carlson, those had been words to live by, and undoubtedly still were.

Tonight the Big Boss was his enemy, and he was going to stick to him like a burr until the job was done. To survive, he was going to have to kill the man. He'd faced it earlier, known it was the only way out. Even before the debacle with McQuarry, he'd planned to hit them all tonight: Sid and

Julie, and then, on his way out of town, John Carlson.

He'd been going to make them all disappear. That was the only way to keep himself safe.

Sid had started fucking up the plan by calling him on his cell phone earlier in the day, raving mad because his wife was being unfaithful—with Daniel's little brother, yet—and insisting on being present when she bought the farm. The plan had been for Sid to be safely in Atlanta while Basta did the job, but Sid had screwed that up by coming home early, so crazy angry he wasn't thinking straight. That had actually worked out well, because Sid knew Basta's daytime identity, too—the Big Boss had been grooming Sid to take over one day, and Sid basically was in on everything—and was going to have to be taken out anyway. Basta had told him to come on, come join him, figuring on killing two birds with one stone even as he said it.

With Sid, the pissant little punk, in tow, he'd tracked Julie, even managed to get his hands on her despite complications. Then things had started going wrong. Daniel's little brother had rescued her seconds before she would have joined Sid in the great hereafter. And then, right on the heels of that disaster, the Big Boss had shown up out here without warning, complete with flunkies. According to one of the flunkies, speaking on the sly while the boss tearfully examined his son's remains, it seemed Sid had called him, apparently while Basta was in McQuarry's office building retrieving Julie, and had told him what was going down and where, and the boss had made the trip out here to make sure that this time the job he'd hired Basta to do got done. Basta suspected that his own demise was also on the agenda. This was the perfect spot, after all.

Actually, that was probably going to work out all right, too, Basta reflected, although it had been hairy there for a few minutes after the boss had arrived. Basta had been running down the dirt road in hot pursuit of his escaping prey when the boss's car had pulled up, catching him in its lights, and then he'd had to think fast.

What he'd come up with was that McQuarry had shot Sid while rescuing Julie.

Now the situation was dicey. But the

plan was still in effect. The key was to keep his head. The boss's men would be loyal unto death, just as he himself had been once, and all would be armed to the teeth.

If he wanted to survive and prosper, he had to take out the Big Boss, Mac McQuarry, and Julie Carlson.

Then he would vanish into the woodwork, and be home free.

34

"I'M ALL RIGHT," MAC SAID, but it was clear that he wasn't. He got up and kept going, but it was obvious that he was finding it harder with every passing minute. The mud sucked at their feet, making each step an effort. Breathing hard, Julie clung to his hand, for his support now rather than hers, and tried not to panic as she felt his fingers growing cold where earlier they had been reassuringly warm. She was afraid he must be losing a lot of blood; when she'd put her hand on his back, it had seemed like the entire back of his shirt was covered in stickiness. Suddenly she was terribly, horribly afraid that he might lose consciousness. She couldn't carry him—but she couldn't, wouldn't, leave him, either.

She prayed he was able to stay on his feet.

Behind them, the flashlights were drawing ever closer, sweeping the darkness in what looked like a systematic search effort. There were no voices, no sounds of pursuit, but only the slashing lights. On her own, or with Mac his usual hale and hearty self, Julie realized that she probably would have been hyperventilating with fear.

But Mac was depending on her now. She had to be strong for Mac. Sloshing through the marshy water, she held to that thought like a talisman.

Keep moving, she told herself as her heart pounded with fear and exertion, her legs trembled with effort, and her feet slipped and slid on the mud that squished up between her toes. She was wet to the waist, and had been bitten by so many mosquitoes she no longer even felt the welts. The swamp was alive with splashes and plops and things that seemed to slither past her legs. Tall cypresses grew all around, their rough bark a welcome resting place for her hand as she waded past, their sturdy trunks tiptoeing out of the water on roots that were like six-feet-tall high heels.

Mac was clinging heavily to her hand for support. Julie could hear the harsh sound of his breathing, see the slump of his spine. He stumbled from time to time, although he always regained his balance before he went down; but after each near fall his movements were more ragged than before.

They weren't going to make it. Not the way they were going. The knowledge grew steadily within her until it was a certainty.

Suddenly Julie realized that the swamp itself was their best, no, their only, hope.

"We need to hide," she whispered.

"Leave me." His words tacitly confirmed her judgment of his state.

"If you think I'm going to draw them off for you, you're wrong." She strove to lighten the moment. He made a sound that could have been a groan or a laugh.

"Julie . . ."

"Don't argue." Her voice was the merest breath. "There's no way I'm leaving you. Everything else aside, do you think I'd stand a chance out here on my own?"

He didn't reply, so he must have felt that there was some truth to that. A glance over her shoulder told Julie that the flashlights were gaining on them at a terrifying rate. The glowing disks were now the size of baseballs, where before they had been the size of quarters. As she watched them arc through the darkness, her heart started beating like a drummer in a heavy metal band. Her skin prickled. Her breathing grew ragged. She took a deep, calming breath, and prayed Mac was right: their pursuers would be reluctant to wade through the swamp.

"The cypressess. We could squeeze up under the roots." The idea came to her as she touched another one.

"Good plan." His voice was so faint now she could scarcely hear it.

They had to do it almost entirely by feel, but they managed to squeeze between the fingerlike roots. Inside was a hollow dome, affording them perhaps four feet of air above the surface of the water. Julie tried not to think about what might call the cave-like place home. Her hip bumped something, and she discovered that it was a gnarled knot of roots sticking up above the surface of the water. They were able to sit on it and rest against the curved inner trunk of the tree. Mac was crowded next to her, his breathing harsh in the confined space. The trunk was close and airless. The smell was mildew to the max. Julie could see nothing beyond their small shelter.

Which was almost more terrifying than anything else, she realized. It allowed her imagination free rein. Deliberately Julie blocked out images of Basta creeping up on them, slithering through the swamp like a poisonous snake. Unless he had wings, they would know he was coming. They might not be able to see, but they could hear.

Mac was shifting around uncomfortably next to her, and Julie could sense, from the tension in his body, from his breathing, from his restless movements, that he was in pain.

"How badly are you hurt?" It was a whisper; she was ever mindful of the butchers hunting them through the night. She turned toward him, reaching out to touch his arm, his shoulder. He was wet and muddy, like she was, but his skin was cool to the touch, whereas, in the clammy heat, she was sweating buckets she was so warm. Again she worried about blood loss.

"It hurts like hell, but I think I'm going to live." His rasping voice made the words less reassuring than they might have been.

"Are you bleeding a lot?" She touched his face.

"Some."

"Okay." She wet her lips, afraid he was grossly understating the case. Whether he was or not, the blood loss needed to be stopped. Julie pulled off her T-shirt—the only relatively dry article of clothing either of them possessed—and folded it into a tight little rectangle. "I've made my shirt into a pad. Show me where to press it."

"The right side of my back, just under my shoulderblade."

With some difficulty—the space was tight—Julie reached around him to find the spot. It was warm and sticky with blood, impossible to mistake. She pressed the makeshift bandage over the wound. She did not dare lift his shirt—she feared it might dislodge any clotting and increase the bleeding—but she pushed down firmly to try to stop the bleeding. Mac shuddered and made a slight sound.

"Am I hurting you?"

"No."

He was clearly trying to ease her fears about his condition. Determined to do what she could to keep him alive and conscious, Julie pressed harder.

"Ouch! Now you're hurting me."

"Sorry. I think it's probably really important that we get the bleeding to stop."

His reply was a grunt, which she took as acknowledgment that she was right. For a couple of moments after that they were both silent. Julie kept her hand tight over the pad, and listened for all she was worth to the sounds of the swamp. If Basta should come, or his friends with the flashlights, their only recourse would be to stay very still and quiet, like a mouse with a hawk flying overhead.

And pray they wouldn't be found.

The water lapped, warm and faintly slimy, around her legs. The tree creaked as the top of it swayed. There was a small plop nearby—a frog jumping in, she devoutly hoped—but nothing that sounded remotely human.

Julie realized her pulse was thundering, and her breathing was quick and shallow. To be able to do nothing but sit and listen for their pursuers was more nerve-racking than fleeing would have been.

"I'm so scared," she whispered, the words coming out before she could stop them. As soon as they left her mouth, she wished she could call them back. Saying it aloud didn't help; if anything, it made them both feel worse.

"We've made it this far. We'll make it the rest of the way."

He moved, and his lips brushed her mouth. The kiss was hot and sweet, and Julie closed her eyes and kissed him back and felt her fear recede a little as the familiar electricity coursed between them. Thank God for Mac, she thought. Without him, she would have been dead back there in the car with Sid. No, she would have been dead long before.

"You seem to be making a habit of saving my life."

"Maybe I think it's worth saving."

There was a loud splash out in the swamp. Julie tensed. Beside her she could feel Mac stiffen. But, though they listened intently, the sound was not repeated. Gradually they relaxed.

Mac said, "The police should be on their

way. I called my old captain while I was haring around after you. They're going to get here sooner or later."

It was meant to comfort her, Julie knew. But unspoken between them lay the truth: Basta might well find them first. And even if the police came in time, could they trust whoever showed up?

Julie shivered.

"How did you find me, anyway?" She'd wondered about that.

"I put a homing device in your purse this morning." He sounded as if he were smiling. "In case you tried to give me the slip."

If she'd heard that a couple of hours earlier she would have been mad. Now she was profoundly thankful.

"Mac," she whispered after a moment, desperate to get her mind off their plight. "Did you have a brother named Daniel?"

A beat passed.

"Yeah," he said. "Why?"

"In the car, Basta said he killed him. He said he killed Daniel and Kelly and my father, too."

Another beat.

"Ah." Mac sounded as if he were expelling a breath he'd been holding for a long time. "Did he say how? Why?"

Mac's voice was expressionless. Too expressionless. Julie realized that there was a lot of emotion connected with the death of his brother. "No. Sid said my father had stolen something from him and his father. He wouldn't say what. But I got the impression my father was killed because of it."

"What else did he say?"

"Sid?" Julie gave a bitter little laugh. "Nothing much. Only that he never loved me. That he basically just married me because he thought I knew where the thing my father stole was. That he was planning to have me killed one day from the time he married me."

There was the briefest of pauses. Then Mac snorted. "Sounds like Sid. He always was the biggest idiot I ever met."

Julie smiled a little in the darkness. "You really are a sweet man, you know that? Thank you for that."

"Hey, like I said before, sweet is my middle name."

A sudden roar from just beyond the stump was followed by a high-pitched cry and a sharp snap. Julie was so startled she almost fell into the water.

"Gator," Mac, sounding as if he was speaking through gritted teeth, answered her unspoken question. "Must've caught something. Don't worry, the roots are too narrow to let one get in here."

Great. Now she didn't only have to worry about ruthless murderers, she had to worry about alligators. Julie shuddered, then deliberately forced her mind on to other things.

"How do you know Sid, anyway?"

"Sid?" Mac shifted uncomfortably, and drew a deep breath. Julie had to move, too, to keep the pad pressed to the wound. "He was Daniel's best friend. Daniel was my big brother. Our dad was a cop who was killed by a prick trying to rob a convenience store of sixty bucks. That left my mom and Daniel and me. I was only five when it happened. Daniel was thirteen, and getting ready to go to high school. On behalf of the community, John Carlson—Sid's dad—funded a scholarship for Daniel to the same expensive private school Sid went to. Daniel was a player with the girls, a jock, a never-ending good time. Sid wanted some of Daniel's reflected glory, and they started hanging out. As a result of being pals with Richie Rich, Daniel began appreciating the finer things in life. The things Sid had and we couldn't afford. They stayed friends even after high school, and one thing led to another and Daniel ended up working for Sid. One night Daniel went to work and never came home. He was twenty-five." Mac took a deep breath, and Julie ached at the psychic pain she heard in the sound. Mac's next words were slightly uneven. "I think Daniel's disappearance killed my mom. She didn't live long after that." Another deep breath. "I always suspected—no, I always *knew*—Sid had something to do with Daniel's disappearance. With his *death.*"

Mac's voice was raw, and Julie cuddled closer in a silent gesture of comfort.

"You loved Daniel a lot, didn't you?" she asked softly.

She felt rather than saw him shrug. "He was my brother."

That stark statement made a lump form in her throat. She turned her head, meaning to kiss him consolingly. Her lips brushed his cheek before moving on in search of his mouth. His head turned and his lips found hers again, and suddenly he was kissing her as though he would die if he didn't. Julie kissed him back just as desperately. With the small part of her mind capable of focusing on anything beyond the kiss, she sensed his grief and anger for his brother as well as his fear and frustration at their current situation, and realized that those were fueling the kiss along with his elemental need for her. She felt a tremendous swelling of emotion, an almost primeval urge to give him comfort. Then she knew, and pulled her mouth from his.

"I love you, Mac," she whispered against his lips.

For a moment he didn't move. She could feel his breath on her lips.

"I love you too," he said after a moment, in a deep husky whisper drawl that made her heart start to slam in her breast. "More than anything or anyone in my life."

Then he kissed her again, a soul-shaking kiss that made her forget that she was supposed to be pressing a bandage to his back, made her forget that they were hiding in a swamp from a conscienceless killer who had already murdered who knew how many people, made her forget everything in the whole world but Mac.

She wrapped her arms around his neck and kissed him back.

He broke off the kiss abruptly, stiffening and lifting his head.

"Shh," he said. "Here they come."

Julie listened, and heard it: the faint squelch, squelch of somebody walking through the swamp. It was a rhythmic sound, far different from any they had heard before. Julie broke out in a cold sweat. Her stomach clenched. Her heart began to pound.

Then, beyond the encircling roots, she saw the slashing beam of a flashlight. Suddenly Julie realized that she was about as safe as a rabbit frozen in place while the hounds close in, and began to shake.

35

IN THE DISTANCE BASTA HEARD Julie scream-ing. His senses went on high alert. He was standing near the edge of the clearing looking out over the lake, in the high spot where they'd had to move so that the one remaining flunky who was playing body-guard to the boss could get his cell phone to work properly. It was a beautiful sight, with the moon shining on the surface of the water and tiny twinkling stars just begin-ning to put in an appearance. In fact, it was just about his favorite place in the world—or, at least, his favorite killing place.

"Sounds like they found them," he said to John Carlson, who stood beside him, his face etched in grief, tears glistening in his eyes. He almost would have felt sorry for the man, had he not been absolutely sure that the next item on the Big Boss's agenda, after Basta dispatched his pesky daughter-in-law and the supposed killer of his son for him, was Basta's own demise.

The rule was as old as the playground: first one to the finish line wins. He meant to abide by it.

He had hoped to get Carlson alone, but it looked like he was out of time. The flunkies who'd been searching the swamp had obviously struck pay dirt. They'd be turning up in a few minutes with the captives, like dogs bringing their master a bone. Basta knew how it worked. He'd been a dog with a master, too. But no more.

The dog was about to bite.

"Call the rest of them in," Carlson said, his back now to the lake as he stared vindictively toward the woods. A step or so beyond him, the flunky fumbled in his pocket for his cell phone, obviously meaning to pass on the boss's order. Basta realized that Julie wasn't screaming anymore. He didn't even waste his time wondering what they'd done to shut her up. He didn't care.

"Funny how things work out," he said to the boss, as though he was just making conversation. At the same time, he took a step back. Just as quick as that, he raised his gun, aimed it—the man was still looking toward the woods—and blew a hole through the Big Boss's head. The body dropped like a felled tree, dead before it hit the ground. The bodyguard dropped his cell phone like it was suddenly red-hot, going for his gun. Basta shot him in the head, too.

Nice and easy and quiet. Couldn't ask for a hit to go down better than that.

Humming softly under his breath, Basta scooped up the fallen cell phone, stuck it in his pocket—it would never do to leave evidence like that lying around for one of the flunkies to find and wonder about—grabbed the bodies by the ankles and dragged them the few feet to the dropoff over the lake, then rolled them off. The Big Boss was still twitching as he went over the side.

"This guy's fricking heavy," the thug carrying Mac's ankles grunted. "I don't know why we couldn't just kill him back there and leave him in the swamp, instead of lugging him all this way."

"You ought to be on this end." A second thug, the one with his hands locked under Mac's armpits, responded feelingly.

"Boss's orders." The third thug had his hand twisted in Julie's hair and his gun pressed to her neck. Walking easily over the uneven ground, he sounded unsympathetic to the others' plight. "He said bring 'em to him alive, so that's what we're gonna do."

"Quit your bitchin', Dye. We're almost there." The fourth thug was walking a few steps behind with his gun drawn and aimed at Mac, purely as a precaution, Julie thought.

Otherwise, there seemed to be no purpose in it. They'd beaten Mac unconscious. There was blood all over his face now, too. He lay limply between the two thugs, his head lolling against the one's chest, his middle sagging perilously close to the ground as they all, captives and captors, trudged across the moonlit field.

The killing field. As that thought took possession of her mind, Julie was suddenly so frightened that her legs would barely support her. She would have collapsed, she thought, except for the thug's hand twisted in her hair. She knew she was walking toward her own death, and she knew equally that there was nothing she could do to prevent it.

The instant, unwanted image of Sid's face being blown away made her queasy. Please God, she thought, please God don't let me die like that. Don't let Mac die like that. We've only just found each other. Please let us live. Please.

When the flashlight beam had hit them, shining directly through the roots of the sheltering cypress as if the thugs had known exactly where they were hiding, Mac had pushed Julie behind him and opened fire. To Julie's horror, his gun had made empty clicking sounds. Mac had said *Shit, it's wet* and stepped out with his hands up, dropping the gun on command. Then, as the two thugs had looked at Julie, squeezing out through the roots behind him, he'd launched himself at them like a missile.

Wounded and weak, he'd been beaten to a pulp.

So here they were, walking across the field, drawing closer to eternity with every step. She was wearing only her skirt and bra, with lots of bare skin on display, but she was covered with so much mud that she might as well have been fully clothed. The mud served another purpose, too: it seemed to keep the mosquitoes at bay. Not that she was going to have to worry about being bitten for very much longer.

The moonlight was beautiful, soft and white, painting the clearing with an other-worldly glow. It was a night for romance, Julie thought, for walks on the beach, for friends and laughter and love.

For Sid, and now for her and Mac, it was also a night for dying.

"Keep going."

The hand in her hair tightened painfully as she stumbled. Julie recovered, and they marched past the car where Sid's body lay. Julie averted her eyes. Her stomach churned. Gorge rose in her throat.

Sid had deserved a lot of bad things, but not to meet an end like that.

Several other cars were there, too. Julie did a double take at the big gray BMW parked beside the Lexus. That car was

John's. She would recognize it anywhere. For a moment hope did its eternal thing in her breast again as the thought that her father-in-law might help her popped into her head. Then she remembered that John was part of this, too.

Did he know Sid was dead? He would grieve.

It was hard to get her mind around the fact that she shouldn't care if Sid's father grieved. She felt as if her whole life had been turned inside out, and everything she had believed to be true suddenly—wasn't.

As they passed the cars, she saw something small and white slink out from their shadow and fall in behind them. Josephine, minus her usual happy prance. From her demeanor she was obviously aware something was amiss. Her head was down and her tail drooped. Julie felt a glimmer of joy as she spotted her, which was almost immediately superseded by fear. She would have shooed the little dog away, except she didn't want to call attention to her.

This murderous bunch might not bother with killing a dog, but she didn't want to take that chance. There was no reason for Josephine to die tonight, too.

The clearing ended in a grassy cliff overlooking a lake, Julie saw as they walked toward it. She was almost sure it was Lake Moultrie. It was north of the city, and she and Sid and Basta had been traveling in that direction.

Her father had drowned in that lake. The thought made her shiver. Until today, she'd thought it was accidental.

A man was watching them approach. The moon was big and bright behind him, making him no more than a dark shape. A bulky dark shape. A bulky dark shape with a gun in one hand.

But Julie didn't have to see his face to know who he was: Basta.

Her stomach tied itself into a pretzel. Her heart threatened to beat its way out of her chest.

"Where's the boss?" the thug bringing up the rear asked, glancing around.

"He had to take a leak," Basta said. He took a step closer, so that Julie could see his face now. The sight of that swollen, discolored nose struck terror into her soul. Her pulse began to race; her breathing quickened. She felt light-headed suddenly, and thought she might be going to hyperventilate. Deliberately she closed her mouth, forcing herself to breathe slowly and evenly through her nose. It was impossible to breathe too hard through her nose, she had found.

"Hello, Julie." Basta smiled at her, slowly and terribly. He glanced down at Mac, who now lay sprawled on the ground, then up at the thugs. "He dead?"

"Nah, but he won't be going anywhere any time soon. Dye here got to having too much fun back there, and clobbered him over the head a couple of times too many with his gun."

"Where's Stark?" The fourth thug was still looking around.

"With the boss. What, you think he went to take a leak by himself?" Basta's eyes narrowed slightly. Julie had seen that expression before, and it made her shiver.

Stall him.

Good thought.

Basta's gun hand, which had been hanging rather negligently by his side, started to move. The moonlight glinted off the metal barrel of his gun.

"I know where the thing my father stole is." Julie almost swallowed her tongue in her haste to get the words out.

Basta's gaze swung around to her. The gun stopped its intended trajectory, which seemed to be slightly to her left. Instead it rose to point directly at her.

"You don't even know what it is," he said.

36

"I MAY NOT KNOW WHAT IT IS, but I know where it is." Oh, God, here she was doing her Scheherazade thing again. She hoped it worked out better this time than last.

Basta looked at her for a moment. Then he glanced at the man holding her by the hair.

"You guys, you go wait for the boss by the cars. I need to have a little private conversation with the lady here."

Julie realized that her hands were shaking. She clasped them together in front of her. Her heart was racing almost as fast as her mind. The thug holding her let go of her hair.

"You. Sit down," Basta said to her.

Julie sat. Her knees had been about to give out anyway, so she practically dropped onto the prickly grass. She was close to Mac, so close she could have stretched out a hand to touch him. His face looked bad, with one eye all swollen shut and blood trickling across his forehead from a cut near his temple. But as she looked at him, she thought she saw his eyelids flicker.

Wake up, she willed him. Oh, please wake up. Although she didn't know what she thought he could do.

Josephine came up out of nowhere and crawled into her lap, distracting her. Julie hugged her close. Making Josephine go away was probably an impossibility, so she wasn't even going to try. Instead she was going to take what comfort she could get. She hugged the little dog close. Josephine licked her chin.

"I don't know," the fourth thug said uneasily.

"This is stuff the boss doesn't want you to know. If you hear it, he's probably going to have to have me kill you."

The thugs looked at each other uneasily. Obviously they knew what Basta was.

"Uh. Okay."

A quick glance over her shoulder told Julie that they were moving back toward the cars. If she ran that way—they would catch or shoot her in a heartbeat.

Basta looked at Julie again. His gaze flicked down to Josephine and his mouth quirked contemptuously.

"Where'd she come from?"

"She was in the jeep when we wrecked."

He grunted, dismissing the subject. "So where is it? The thing we were discussing."

"I'd have to show you."

Basta smiled, and moved his gun in a significant way. Julie's eyes widened.

She caught her breath.

"Really. It—it's in a place that's kind of hard to describe."

Basta pursed his lips. "Maybe you better try."

Uh-oh.

"If I tell you, will you let me go?" She knew better, but she wanted to keep him talking for as long as she could. Where, oh, where, were the police? Mac had said he'd called them. Of course, if they ever arrived, they'd probably be on the bad guys' side.

Her life seemed to be working like that lately.

Basta smiled. A scary smile. Just looking at him smiling at her like that made her blood run cold.

"Sure I will. Why not? You know, I never wanted you dead, not personally. Now that Sid's dead, there's no reason you have to die. No reason at all. Sid just picked this point in time to get rid of you because he was cheating with a girl you knew and he figured you'd find out and file for divorce. Divorce is a bad thing when you're in the mob. All those nasty lawyers looking into your finances. No telling what they might find. But with Sid gone now, that reason doesn't apply."

Julie drew a breath. She suddenly felt almost calm, probably because she'd now passed so far beyond fear that she was emotionally numb. A breeze blew in off the lake, making her shiver as if it was suddenly thirty degrees out instead of eighty. All right, she thought as the shiver intensified into a full-blown case of the shakes, so maybe she wasn't as calm as she'd thought.

"Is that why Kelly was killed? Because she was going to divorce Sid?"

Basta shook his head. "Kelly did a bad thing. She thought Sid was cheating on her, too. She left a voice-activated tape recorder in his office one day. She didn't catch Sid cheating, but she did catch me and Sid and Mr. Carlson discussing something she had no business knowing about."

Julie drew in her breath. "What?"

"A dead person." His eyes hardened on her face and the gun moved again threateningly. "Just like you're going to be a dead person if you don't tell me where the damned tape is. Right now."

"It's—it's . . ." Julie stuttered, unable to get the words out past her suddenly thickened tongue. Her muscles were tense and she felt light-headed. The wind off the lake was kicking up again and she was freezing, too, so cold her teeth chattered. Or, oh yeah, she'd decided that particular reaction was attributable to fear.

She'd never been so scared in her life.

"Where is the tape?" It was a deadly growl.

"If I tell you, you'll kill me," she whispered.

"Tell me." He pointed the gun at Mac. "If you don't, I'm going to shoot little brother here."

Julie's eyes widened with alarm. She glanced over at Mac, to find that he was watching her out of eyes that were open just the tiniest slit.

Oh, God, she couldn't let him shoot Mac. But if she told him anything, he would shoot her, too.

"Last chance," Basta said.

"I—I . . ."

Out of nowhere, a cell phone began to ring, interrupting. The sound was muffled but insistent. Basta, looking startled, reached into his pocket with the hand that was not holding the gun. In Julie's lap, Josephine stiffened and began to growl. As Julie glanced down at her in surprise, the poodle leaped from her lap like she'd been launched from a catapult and threw herself with all the fury of a rabid badger across three feet of space and onto Basta's leg.

"Aiiee!" Basta jumped and howled, performing a frantic one-legged jig in an effort to shake Josephine loose. "Damn dog! Damn dog! Get off me! Get off me, you!"

For a split second, Julie watched transfixed.

Run. It was a scream inside her head.

Oh, yeah. Good plan. She leaped to her feet, tugging on Mac's bloody shirt as she did.

"Mac!"

Mac looked up, and seemed to make a tremendous effort. He surged onto all fours, then onto his feet.

Julie grabbed his hand.

Into the lake.

Her little voice was, as usual, right on. Julie saw instantly that it was the only path of escape. She ran, and Mac ran with her, lurching and limping but nevertheless managing an amazing burst of speed considering the shape he was in.

"Bad dog!" Basta was still fighting Josephine as the land ran out beneath them. The dark waters of the lake sparkled in the moonlight what looked like a long way below. From the corner of her eye, Julie saw Basta spot them, then free himself from Josephine with a tremendous kick that sent the little dog twisting and yelping through the air. Basta turned, gun raised in a two-handed hold. . . .

And then she and Mac were leaping out into the darkness. She fell like a stone. As she did, sharp spears of sound whistled past her with a ferocity that seemed to punch holes in the air. She only realized that they were bullets when she saw them strike the water, sending up little white jets.

Mac gave a hoarse cry, and seemed to stiffen in the air. Oh, God, had he been hit? Then she struck the water and plunged beneath the surface. Mac went down beside her, and she was frantic until he grabbed her hand. At least he was alive, and conscious. . . .

When she would have surfaced, he began to swim underwater, pulling her along with him. They swam that way until they had to surface for air.

"Were you hit?" It was the first thing she asked him, voice frantic.

"Yeah. Don't worry, I'll be all right." She would have worried a lot less if his voice hadn't been tight with pain.

More bullets whistled around them. Julie's face was showered with spray. She gasped and dived, grabbing at Mac's arm as she went under. Mac was already with her, and they swam without surfacing for as long as they could. Julie hung on to his hand for dear life, terrified that he might lose consciousness. If he did, he might very well drown. She didn't know if she could keep him afloat. He was heavy, and she wasn't that strong a swimmer.

When they came up a second time, gasping, treading water, Mac was beside her and the cliff was a good distance away.

"You don't feel light-headed or anything, do you?" The darkness kept her from seeing much of his expression, so it was hard to judge the exact shape he was in. But he was breathing hard, panting really, and— was he lower in the water than he should have been?

"Don't worry, I won't faint." The faint dryness of that reassured her slightly.

"Where are you hit?"

"Left leg. Leave it till we get out of the water." He added this last and jerked the limb out of reach as she instinctively ran a hand down his leg.

They were well out from shore, probably, or so Julie hoped, beyond the reach of bullets. Plus, they had the darkness to protect them. Julie doubted that anyone could see them now from the shore. Anyway, the shooting seemed to have stopped. But their position had a major drawback: if Mac were to be incapacitated, Julie wasn't sure she could get him safely to land.

The water was cool, but not cold. Mac turned onto his back, floating, moving slowly toward the distant tree line of the eastern shore. Julie paddled anxiously beside him, listening to his breathing. It sounded labored, and his movements seemed frighteningly weak.

"I'm okay," Mac said, forcefully enough to reassure her to a certain extent. "Just stay beside me, and we'll get out of this yet."

Without warning, a helicopter swooped into view, its searchlight illuminating the lake, catching them in its beam. In the distance, from the direction of the clearing, Julie heard sirens and slamming doors and shouts of "Freeze! Police!"

"Police!" It was shouted over a bullhorn as the chopper came in low over the lake, its blades churning the water into froth, the searchlight never leaving them. Then, seconds later, still over the bullhorn, "This is Greg Rice. Mac, is that you down there?"

"About fricking time," Mac shouted back.

Then two life preservers hit the water. As Julie snagged one, she realized that they were, finally, safe.

37

BY THE TIME HE WAS IN THE AMBULANCE on his way to the hospital, Mac was feeling pretty rough until the pain medication kicked in. Then he felt more on the order of doped-up, which he didn't ordinarily like but, under these particular conditions, worked for him. They had hooked him up to an IV, which swayed precariously on its hook with every bump and sway of the shock-challenged vehicle. The siren blared importantly, practically deafening him.

There was, however, an upside to his present situation, he reflected. Actually, three upsides, or maybe one three-parted upside. Whatever.

The first upside was that Julie, wet and bedraggled but unharmed, dressed in a shirt loaned to her by one of the cops, was sitting beside him in the ambulance holding his hand. Josephine was huddled at her feet. How Julie had finagled that Mac couldn't even begin to guess, because animals normally were verboten in ambulances, but the dog was unharmed as well, and he supposed he now counted that as an upside, too.

Tonight Josephine had made up for all the bad things she had done since he had acquired her in spades. Never again would he think of doggy shelters in connection with her. She had earned herself a permanent place in his family.

Julie had, too. He just hadn't gotten around to mentioning it to her yet.

The second upside was that Greg Rice had told him that, thanks to his and Hinkle's work, the biggest organized-crime network in the Southeast had been cracked wide open. They could have their careers in police work back, if they wanted them—Mac was going to have to think about that; the private investigator thing had proven interesting, if nothing else—as well as apologies all around. In addition, no charges would be filed because he had beaten the bejesus out of two of the city's finest. Fortunately for him, Dorsey and Nichols were, indeed, dirty cops, and for that allowances would be made.

The third upside was that Roger Basta had been captured alive. He wasn't talking, but it was early days yet. When he saw the kind of charges he was facing, it was likely that he would sing like a bird.

Even though he now knew for certain that his brother was dead, Mac still wanted to find Daniel. Basta was the key to that. Basta knew where Daniel was. Refusing to dwell on the ache that always accompanied thoughts of his brother, Mac looked over at Julie and tightened his grip on her hand. There were lots of things he wanted to say to her, needed to say to her, but, conscious of the paramedic on his other side monitoring his vital signs on various beeping machines, he refrained.

What he said instead was, "That was good thinking, by the way, telling Basta that you knew where the tape he was looking for was hidden. Otherwise, I think he would have shot us right there on the spot. Wham, bam, thank you, ma'am."

Julie met his gaze. Her big brown eyes were tired and heavy-lidded and bloodshot, but they were still incomparably beautiful. *She* was incomparably beautiful.

"I do know where the tape's hidden. At least, I think I know. As soon as I knew it was a tape, I realized where it must be. When my father came to see me that last time, he gave me a teddy bear. It was the only present he ever gave me, and I've kept it all these years. He said it was for my birthday, and I should take real good care of it. He said he'd be back in a couple of weeks to make sure I was taking care of it. Of course, he never came back: he died before he could. But even at the time, I thought it was weird: he never visited us, but here he was, showing up on our doorstep and bringing a teddy bear as a birthday present to a grown girl. It's a soft, squishy teddy bear with a fat stomach. When I first got it, I used it as a pillow sometimes. I quit because there was something hard under all those layers of fluff. Hard and rectangular and about the size of a cassette tape, now that I think about it. At the time, I just thought it was part of the bear's innards. I'll bet anything the tape's in that teddy bear."

"Where's the teddy bear now?" Mac couldn't believe his ears. The key to this entire mess—and Julie had had it all along without knowing it? He stared at her incredulously.

"On the table beside my bed. I kept it all these years, but I never told anyone where I got it." Julie grimaced, making a face that was sad and rueful and a tad funny at the same time. "See, it was Becky's birthday, not mine. I was so jealous that he remembered her and not me that I never even told her about the bear. I just kept it for myself."

The look on her face smote him to the heart.

"Hey." Mac brought her hand to his mouth, paramedic or no paramedic, and kissed her palm. Then, because she still looked unhappy, he decided to hell with manly pride, and went for it. "Julie. I love you."

She smiled at him, a slow-dawning smile that was like the sun coming out. "I love you, too."

Ignoring the stone-faced paramedic,

Mac kissed each of the slender, rose-tipped fingers he held. Then curiosity overcame him, and he looked up.

"Didn't you ever tell Sid about the bear?" If she had, Sid would have immediately suspected what was in it and taken the thing apart.

She shook her head, and a sudden spark of amusement twinkled in her eyes. "He was so nasty about my family all the time. I couldn't tell him that my father couldn't even tell me apart from Becky."

Mac laughed. All the time, Julie had held the key to the puzzle, and Sid had never been able to worm it out of her because he was such a prick. Was that poetic justice, or what?

"We've got to tell Greg." As the thought hit him, Mac tried to sit up and found himself held back by the straps around his chest.

"I already did." Julie's hand on his chest and the paramedic's sharp admonition caused him to sink back. "He's sending somebody to get the bear. He said even if the tape's in there, he'll see I get it back once the tape's removed, good as new. I guess I'll have to tell Becky about it now."

"You're something, you know that?" Mac said to her tenderly.

She smiled at him, and suddenly he was flying higher than even the pain medication had taken him. He was high as a kite—on Julie.

Then they were at the hospital, and he was taken from the ambulance and wheeled into the emergency room, and there was no more opportunity to talk.

38

THREE WEEKS LATER, Mac was once again standing on the cliff overlooking Lake Moultrie. It was a hot day, with a sky so blue it would put sapphires to shame and bright sunshine pouring down: A happy kind of day, a day for hot dogs and kites and walks on the beach. For Mac, though, it was bittersweet. A crane was lifting a rusted-out Chevy Cougar from the water. He knew that car. Daniel had bought it two months before he disappeared.

Mac's heart ached almost unbearably as he watched it rise dripping into the cerulean sky.

Basta had told them where to look.

Basta, who, as it turned out, had another identity entirely: In his everyday life he was a high-level operative for the DEA. He'd worked for the agency for over thirty years, and was as dirty as they came. At first it had been garden-variety graft: He'd dealt drugs, taken bribes, fixed cases. By his own account, when he'd started busting dealers who worked for John Carlson, he'd gone over to the dark side for good. When Carlson had found out who he was and what he was up to, he had used that knowledge to get Basta under his thumb. In the end, John Carlson had owned Roger Basta. Among other things, Carlson made use of Basta's training and talents by employing him as his own private hit man, calling on his services whenever somebody got in the organization's way.

It both surprised Mac and made him proud to learn that Daniel had been a DEA agent, too. According to Basta, Daniel had been recruited right out of the military, where he'd been, like Mac, a Navy SEAL. As an old friend of Sid's, Daniel had long suspected that the Carlsons were involved in the drug trade. As a gung-ho young agent, he had gone to his boss with his suspicions. His boss had been Basta. Basta had had no choice but to let Daniel investigate; if he hadn't, he had feared that Daniel would become suspicious of him. From the moment he had started his undercover investigation of the Carlsons, Daniel had been marked for death.

Then Kelly Carlson had accidentally taped Basta, Sid, and John Carlson talking about a hit Basta had just made at their instigation. Listening to it and realizing what she was hearing, Kelly had grown frightened. She had run to Daniel, whom she had dated before she had married Sid, and told him about the tape. Daniel had told Basta. Basta, all ears, had instructed him to get the tape. Daniel had obediently gotten the tape from Kelly, and been on his way to give it to Basta when Kelly had called him, frantic. Something in the way Sid was acting toward her made her think he knew about the tape. So Daniel had hidden the tape and gone back for Kelly.

Daniel and Kelly had been killed that night.

Basta added that Mike Williams, who had also worked for the Carlsons as a gopher and nominal employee of Rand Corporation, had been instructed to follow Daniel wherever he went. Williams saw where Daniel hid the tape, retrieved it, and listened to it. Like Kelly, he got scared at what he was hearing. He knew he'd be killed if anyone found out that he knew what he knew. He ran—and took the tape with him.

But then he'd apparently gotten greedy. He had made the mistake of coming back five years later, trying to blackmail the Carlsons about the contents of the tape. For safekeeping he'd hidden it in a teddy bear, and given it to Julie. When they'd caught up with him and tried to beat the whereabouts of the tape out of him, he'd been vague, but he had told them just enough to make them suspect Julie knew where it was before he died prematurely during a further interrogation. Basta had made the death look like an accidental drowning. It had been anything but.

Then Sid had entered Julie's life in pursuit of the tape, and the rest was history.

The feds now had the tape, and it was as explosive as its billing. The hit had been on Henry Jacobs, a longtime federal judge. It was one of the most highly investigated crimes of the last two decades. It had never been solved—until the tape turned up. The recording clearly proved that Basta had done the hit, John Carlson had paid him to do it, and Sid had known everything.

When the police opened the trunk of the Cougar and found Daniel and Kelly, the story was finally ended. For Mac at least.

As the remains were lifted out and put into body bags, Mac realized that there were tears running down his cheeks, and he turned away. He leaned heavily on the crutches he was forced to use until his leg mended, and closed his eyes.

Ah, Daniel, he thought. I loved you, bro.

Seeing his distress, Julie stepped in front of him, slipped her arms around his waist, then rose up on tiptoe to kiss him. Her mouth was soft and sweet, like the rest of her, and he returned her kiss hungrily. He was surprised to find himself wanting her, even at a time like this when there were reminders of tragic death all around. It was, he supposed, an affirmation of life.

"I'm so sorry, Mac," she said softly, pulling her mouth from his at last, her eyes clouded with tears for him. He realized that he'd seen tears in her eyes too much lately:

at Sid's funeral, at John Carlson's, at Carlene Squabb's. He never wanted to see tears in her eyes again, he thought, unless they were tears of joy. He made a silent vow to do his best to make sure he wouldn't.

"It's okay," he said. "I've known inside for a long time that Daniel was dead. Finding him was the last thing I could do for him. I owed him that: He was my brother."

"I wish I could have known him."

Mac managed a smile. It felt slightly crooked, but it would serve. There was no sense in dwelling on the past. The living had to move on.

"He would have liked you. Hot chicks were his hobby."

That surprised a laugh out of Julie, and hearing her laugh eased some of the pain that all his sensible cliches could not quite pry out of his heart. He looked down at her, and realized that at least some good had come out of the tragedy: he'd found Julie, the love of his life. His gaze took in the glossy black hair curling softly around her shoulders, the beautiful face, the breathtaking body. She was dressed in a short, sleeveless dress in pale yellow, and looked as delicate and lovely as a sunbeam come to earth. Beneath the dress, her long tan legs were bare.

He loved the fact that her legs were bare. "Let's go home," he said.

They'd been living together in Mac's house, because Julie couldn't bear to so much as enter hers, and had put it up for sale. As soon as they walked through the door, Josephine greeted them with an excited yap and a wagging tail. Mac looked apprehensively around, but he couldn't see anything right off the bat that had been chewed to splinters. During a hospital visit in which Mac had made aggrieved mention of some of Josephine's less attractive traits, his grandma had looked guilty, confessed that she had totally forgotten about that, and stunned him by informing him that the dear little dog was driven into a frenzy by the sound of a ringing phone. When she had first become aware of this tendency in her beautiful Josephine she'd whisked her off to a doggy psychiatrist, who had come to the sad conclusion that, due to some unknowable trauma in Josephine's past, the dog saw the ringing phone as a threat and responded by attacking. His grandma had solved the problem by investing in a phone that, instead of ringing, played chimes.

Upon being released from the hospital, Mac had promptly done the same. He privately thought that such a simple solution was too good to be true, but Josephine, to his knowledge anyway, hadn't chewed anything since.

Relaxing as no immediate evidence of doggy mayhem met his gaze, he tossed Josephine one of the treats he'd brought in with him from the car, leaned his crutches against a wall, balanced himself carefully on his good leg, forgot about the dog, and pulled Julie into his arms.

She smiled up into his face, and lifted her lips for his kiss.

Instead he simply looked down at her. If he could only have one gift from fate for the entire rest of his life, this was the one he wanted: Julie.

"I love you," he said. "Marry me."

Her eyes widened on his face. For a moment, a heartstopping moment, he looked down into the big brown eyes that he knew would own him for the rest of his life no matter what she said, and waited for her answer.

She frowned, and looked thoughtful. "Is Josephine part of the deal? Bad habits, rhinestone collar and all?"

He smiled. "Absolutely."

"Then, yes. Yes, I will marry you."

Mac bent his head and kissed her. Then the earth spun on its axis, and the dust motes danced and sang, and the air around them was turned to steam heat by the blaze of their passion. He made love to her with a fierce intensity that expressed without words the way she made him feel. And when she was reduced to quivering, mindless jelly in his arms, he made love to her all over again.